"WOMAN, I NEED A SPELL . . ."

The woman sat cross-legged on a tiny rug, hands in her lap, head thrown back as if in a trance. She called herself Taragal, and she was very beautiful. Sir Guy supposed all witches were: selling one's soul must bring some boon.

The sorceress lowered her head and peered at him through hooded eyes. "What?" Her voice was a slow practiced contralto.

"I want something to consternate Robin Hood. Something to unman him, make him afraid of the night, strike God into his heart. What have you?"

The sorceress rose. Bones—finger bones? —and copper ornaments sewn about her clothes clattered. Something jumped underneath a table. It was a hare with two legs, one front and one back. Neat bandages covered the stumps of the other two. Guy tried to think what that meant.

She put a question to him. "Do you know the barrows of Sherwood?"

"Those piles of dirt? What about them?"

She laughed in her throat. A long fingernail snaked out to toy with his greasy locks. Guy caught the smell of her: spice and animal grease and woman in heat.

"Those piles of dirt hold the bodies of ancient ones. The people who were here in England first, who lived with the fays, who are all dead now." She tugged at the hair behind his ears. "Aye, we'll loose a terror . . ."

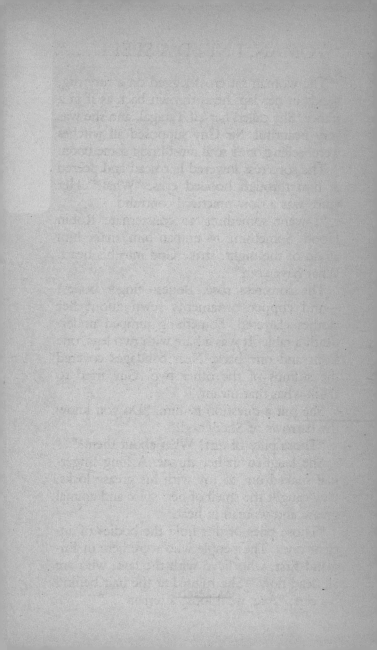

Tales of ROBIN HOOD

Clayton Emery

Acknowledgments

*Thanks to Al, Earl, Hunter,
Joanne, and the omniscient
ladies of the Nashua Public
Library Reference Department.*

TALES OF ROBIN HOOD

A Baen Books Original

Baen Publishing Enterprises
260 Fifth Avenue
New York, N.Y. 10001

First printing, April 1988

ISBN: 0-671-65397-0

Cover art by Larry Elmore

Printed in the United States of America

Distributed by
SIMON & SCHUSTER
1230 Avenue of the Americas
New York, N.Y. 10020

**Dedicated to Susan,
my witch, my tiger.**

The Tyger

Tyger! Tyger! burning bright
In the forests of the night,
What immortal hand or eye
Could frame thy fearful symmetry?

In what distant deeps or skies
Burnt the fire of thine eyes?
On what wings dare he aspire?
What the hand dare seize the fire?

And what shoulder, & what art,
Could twist the sinews of thy heart?
And when thy heart began to beat,
What dread hand? & what dread feet?

What the hammer? what the chain?
In what furnace was thy brain?
What the anvil? what dread grasp
Dare the deadly talons clasp?

When the stars threw down their spears,
And water'd heaven with their tears,
Did he smile his work to see?
Did he who made the Lamb make thee?

Tyger, Tyger! burning bright
In the forests of the night,
What immortal hand or eye,
Dare frame thy fearful symmetry?

William Blake
1757–1827

Chapter 1

Pain from its leg woke the boar, and the animal remembered its hatred of men.

The beast lifted its head and snuffled at the air. Birds in the bare branches made the woods ring with noise. It was dawn; time to hunt. It rose from its bed stiffly and shook off a coat of leaves. It banged its hide against an oak tree, scraping off the loose hair and popping the ticks. It slapped and ground its jaws, a gesture men called "nutcracking." It yawned.

The boar was round as a barrel, with a long conical head. Its coat was black. Long silver guard hairs stood out from its body to give it a frosted glow. The tail hung straight and undomesticated. As with Mars, an erect mane started between the leaf-shaped ears, travelled down across the shoulders and around to the chin. Nine-inch tusks dented the upper jaw to point forward past the snout. Six feet long and three feet high, the pig had wasted to five hundred pounds.

It would lose more poundage unless it found food. A harsh winter meant a lean spring. Last autumn's acorns and beechnuts were long eaten by the squirrels and deer that had survived the cold. Mushrooms were only spores. Frogs were still mushy eggs. Snakes had yet to crawl from their burrows. It would be weeks before fawns dropped, and mice and rabbits held their young until grass was

abundant. In all the forest, the boar would find only
scrawny deer, deep roots, and fledglings pushed out of the
nest.

The animal trotted out on its usual trail. Its nose sniffed
the wind continuously. It reached the border of its territory and started to turn. It stopped. A whiff of marsh gas
reached it. Curiousity and hunger stirred its brain. As
much as was possible, it thought.

This boar had a limp. Four years ago dogs and men had
cornered it with long spears and arrows. It had escaped by
tearing up three dogs and bowling past the men, but one
lone huntsman had held position long enough to slash a
rear tendon with a falchion. The boar had gotten away and
the leg had held together. But it festered and healed
improperly. As a consequence, the boar was no longer as
fast as its brothers. It must starve, or rely on another skill.
This one learned to think. The lame boar developed new
approaches: it took the sly route, became more alert for a
helpless cry, would lie waiting, trapped things. It survived.

Now habit weighed against dim reason. Habit pointed it
counterclockwise in its accustomed path while reason suggested a foray into unknown territory. The land before it
was an older part of the forest. At the center, tall trees
made a desert, for nothing could grow in their shade.
Stinking bogs held only the minutest life. The boar stood
and sniffed. What had stirred the marshes? It couldn't tell.
It clapped its jaws and acted. There might be no game in
there, but there was certainly none here. The animal
pressed off the path, cloven hooves chopping the bracken
in a single line.

Its stomach rolled and squeaked. The boar would kill
anything it met.

Chapter 2

"All right, lads and lasses, here's what we do. We fasten these ropes to the tops of these two trees. Then we stand back in there. When a party comes along, we swoop down on 'em like hawks on a chicken and knock them from the saddle. What do you think?"

After a long pause, Will Scarlett said, "Rob, what are yer, daft?" The rest of Robin Hood's band looked away.

The road was wide here, perhaps four paces, and sandy and dry. The tall and round oaks on both sides met overhead, but leaves were still a misty suggestion. The sky was clear and blue, if pale, and one could see a long ways down the tinted tunnel of road. The outlaws stood in a hollow at the side of the road where a tree had fallen. In honor of spring, this morning Robin had bade the outlaws change their winter brown to summer green. The Fox of Sherwood had with him the bulk of his yeomen: Marian and Little John; the Crusader Gilbert; Bold Jane Downey and a new woman, Grace; Black Bart and Red Tom; Will Scarlett; Ben Barrel and Arthur A'Bland; a new man, Brian; and the loyal Much the-Miller's Son. In tiny Lincoln green were the older children: Katie, Polly, Tam, and Tub. The forest bristled with arrows and smelt of mildew.

Robin Hood frowned at his cousin. "No, I'm not daft. No more than usual. What's daft about it? If there are six

of them and six of us and we swing out of the trees, we'll
bowl them over like ducks. There won't be one can get an
arrow off."

"No," Will agreed, "They'd be laughing themselves sick.
While you're hanging there like a sausage on a string, it'd
take 'em at least three or four seconds to loose."

"Before then you'd have knocked them over."

"With arrows in your bum."

Black Bart put in, "They'd see the ropes coming and'd
stop. The straight ropes stick right out."

Robin said, "I don't think so. People never look up
when they ride."

"But that's looking sideways," said Gilbert in his barbarous Scottish.

Robin cocked his head to interpret his words, then
replied, "I'd yell a signal, so we all got off at once."

Will countered, "If you're going to shout, then why
don't we just stand in the bushes and peg a few past 'em
and shout 'Stand and deliver!' That's always worked before."

"Give the man a chance," rumbled Little John.

Robin flailed his rope in the air. "Look. You always have
to be trying new things. If the sheriff and his lot get used
to what we do, they'll come up with something on their
own. And then we'll be in strife."

Bold Jane Downey said, "Couldn't we at least look for a
muddy spot like we usually do?"

"No, I want good footing for when we hit the ground."

"And break our ankles," finished Will.

Robin Hood glared at his cousin. Everyone was quiet.
Little John sighed, "It won't hurt to try. Let's have someone in the trees to tie off." The children clamored. Of the
volunteers, he tolled off the more agile ones. Bold Jane
Downey, Brian, Katie, Tam and Tub, and Red Tom shucked
their quivers, took the lengths that Robin cut with his
knife, then hopped and climbed through the great branches.
The idiot Much looked so woebegone that Little John gave
him a boost upwards, and Tom pulled him along.

Robin called, "While you're up there, keep a lookout for

robins. I'll give a gold crown to the first person to spot one."

Robin Hood then lined his followers up in the road. He made odd hand signals to his wife. Marian squatted so that Robin could shove his head between her knees and hoist her on his shoulders. He almost dropped her, but she clung to his hat, giggling. "Now. Marian is about the height of a man ahorseback. Let's get some more people in the air. John, put Polly on your shoulders. Ben, pick up Tub. And, uhh . . ." There was a squawk as Will Scarlett grabbed Grace by the wrist. She was almost as big as Will, but he got up her on his shoulders, weaving. The flushed woman covered her face in embarrassment. Black Bart, Arthur, and Ben walked alone. "We're ponies," said Bart. Will Scarlett and Ben Barrel waved to their sons in the trees.

"All right," Robin continued, calling. "String out in a line as if riding. I'll shout, 'Ro-bin Hood!' You lot in the trees swoop down, and I want a lot of screaming. Gil, watch for trouble." By now everyone was smiling. Robin, with Marian astride, started walking slowly. "All right, here we are, a party of fat barons, shuffling down the road, our horses so heavy with gold they can barely move. We're cranky and tired from too much ale the night before, and we're broody with sin. You got all that? C'mon, you slouch, you! Suddenly there's a blood-curdling cry, the most fearsome cry that a black-hearted tax-collecting bishop ever heard. 'Ro-bin Hooo-oooood!' "

With a crack of branches and cries like a fox in a henhouse, the outlaws left their perches. Much crashed full into a tree trunk. Brian's rope broke at the knot, and he travelled straight down. Red Tom left his branch carefully with his feet poised for the single men; he missed all three and disappeared into the branches on the opposite side of the road. Tam and Tub, each aiming for his father, leaped past one another and crossed ropes. They gyrated around each other for a few turns, tangled together, swore at one another in their father's choicest words, and landed in a heap. Katie slammed full into Robin and Marian and toppled them to the turf. Bold Jane Downey skinned over Little John's head, plucked off Polly's hat, poised on the upswing, and dropped, to land facing the highway with the hat in one hand and her dagger in the other.

By and by the bodies picked themselves up. These outlaws were all gristle and so mostly unharmed. Brian had a sprained finger and moss in his beard. Much was dizzy. Shamed-faced, people gathered around Robin Hood, but he clapped shoulders and announced, "A good first try, lads and lasses! A fine beginning! We can—" He stopped when Gilbert tapped him on the shoulder. The knight pointed north, up the road, away from Nottingham.

Beyond bowshot a party sat watching. There were a handful of men in red fur-trimmed cloaks and wide floppy hats. Their mules, more than ten, were tied nose to tail and stacked high with packs. As the outlaws turned, the distant men whipped their train around and galloped away.

Robin looked at Gilbert's grim face and raised his hands like a Frenchman. Then he started to laugh. At Gilbert's stoney expression, he punched him in the shoulder and laughed harder. Marian buried her face in her husband's shoulder and shook silently. The infection carried to the rest of the party, and soon everyone was laughing (except Gilbert). Will Scarlett laughed so hard he pushed his son over. Tam grappled onto his father's legs and the two wrestled in the road. Grace had to sit down or wet herself. Eventually Robin Hood wiped his eyes and pulled at his jaw and said, "Oh well, the next ones will be fatter. Jane, what say you get back up there and show us how you did that. Please?"

The next few days brought little traffic, but Shrove Tuesday was approaching and people would be on the move before Lent. Robin took all his available people to the road. Early in the year he liked all his fighters with him. The robber barons of England had all winter to imagine Robin Hood's army, and it grew in their minds through the dark days. The forest chieftain had no idea what arrangements the rich might make: how large a train they could gather, how many guards they might hire, and so on, but he liked to make a large showing. Often the intimidation of many drawn bows meant no fighting at all.

Now from the southern reach of road came the *chip-chip-chipchipchip* of a warbler. Ben, on scout, had some-one coming from Nottingham. A warbler's call meant a large group. Silently Robin Hood and six others slunk into the trees. On the same side of the road the rest of the outlaws crouched down with bows ready. Little John com-manded one end of the line and Marian the other. They got into position and sat still as snakes.

Robin Hood peered through wispy leaves at the advanc-ing chink and thud. Men laughed. Robin Hood smiled. It was the Sheriff of Nottingham himself with eighteen sol-diers. They were going north. Robin wondered where. Each soldier had a conical Norman helmet with nasal, armor of leather with iron plates sewn on, a longsword and poinard, and a shield with the sheriff's blazon of a chalice. Half of them had longbows sticking straight up in saddle rests. The others had crossbows across their laps, which meant they were cocked. The sheriff, Rowland of Notting-ham, Knight Templar, rode at the center of the party. He wore a velvet doublet brocaded with gold, a matching hat, and his old plain sword, but he resembled a stuffed owl that had fallen from the shelf and not been dusted off. Rowland had been a marked fighter in earlier years, but a king's posting had been his ruin. Unlike the earlier sheriff (whom Robin had killed), Rowland was not altogether a bad administrator. He had the foresight to see that a starving peasant could neither cast seed nor pay taxes. As such, he saw the people had food—when there was any— but no gold. He had a Norman hand, and he walked a weaving line among the graspers in London, the usurpers in Cornwall, the local barons, and his own greed. He ate well but slept poorly.

He was bad enough that Robin wanted to topple him from the saddle. The sheriff's horse walked into the clear.

With a joyous cry of "Ro-bin Hoooo-oooood!" the outlaw
chief launched himself from the tree.

His arboreal followers had expected some quiet signal to
get ready before the main attack, and thus they departed
their trees at different rates. While the sheriff's party froze
and cast about at ground level, Bold Jane Downey entered
the clearing first. With a jolt that made them both grunt,
she drove her heels into the shoulder of a man three times
her size and knocked him from the saddle. She then
twisted in the air and landed astride the saddle like a
goshawk on a glove. Soldiers around her threw up their
hands in the sign of the cross. Tam swung through the
packed crowd, missed every man in it, and missed again
on the backswing. Brian caught his foot and never left the
tree. But as a surprise, Robin's attack couldn't have worked
better. At that first weird cry, both men and animals
jumped. Horses bolted and riders yelled. Four soldiers at
the back hauled their mounts around and fled without
looking back. No one from Nottingham got off a shot. Red
Tom collided with a man who kept his seat as Tom
landed on his back with a *huff*! Katie bounced off a man
like a dandelion puff and kept swinging. Screaming like a
banshee, Will Scarlett latched onto a large man's head
while still holding the rope. The two of them fought for
control of the saddle while out-swearing one another. Will
gained an advantage by biting the man on the nose, but he
jerked on the reins so hard that rider, horse, and assailant
all crashed onto the road. All three lay stunned.

The Fox of Sherwood himself would have fared marvel-
lously if his battle-cry hadn't been so effective. Sir Rowland had nightmares about Robin Hood, and at that shouted
name his first reaction was to duck and cover his head.
Robin Hood sailed clean over the fat man and collided
with an oak tree. He lost his grip, fell from the branches,
and hit the turf like a crippled duck. He lay dazed. Despite the mad milling, five crossbowmen spotted the man
with the pheasant feather in his hat. (They'd heard enough
about him.) They thumbed safety latches and sighted on

the outlaw's back. But the party was suddenly surrounded by footmen in green with bows that seemed to reach to the sky. There sounded twin cries of "Loose!" and nine arrows crashed into the soldiers. Most had not toppled from their saddles before they were struck again. The rest of the sheriff's men gave up. They had been spooked, swooped upon, banged into, and now shot. They threw their arms aloft and shouted, "Mercy! For God's sake! We surrender!" When they looked for their leader, they saw him afoot behind his horse, empty-handed. Then the biggest man they had ever seen raised his hand and intoned, "Stand and deliver."

Robin Hood picked up his hat and dusted off his clothing. A scratch on the end of his nose dripped blood and he rubbed at it. He looked over the sheriff's mauled party. "See? That worked fairly well." Little John nodded solemnly. A man died crying in the road. A horse with an arrow in its back screamed and struggled to rise. Robin pointed Bart to the horse, then Gilbert and Marian to the wounded soldiers. He signalled the sheriff out from behind his mount.

Rowland was fragrant with winter grime and old wine. Robin doffed his cap. "Good day, Sir Rowland. And how did you winter?" He poked the prisoner in his stomach. "You've not been hibernating, I see, since you're yet to lose your winter fat. Hired any tall servants lately, or acquired any red cattle from wastrel sons?" While the red-faced sheriff remained silent, Robin went on. His people chuckled. "What hey, man? You're not one to be Silent Sol. Nothing to say to the man who keeps you in business? I'd invite you to sup, but your silver plate is all melted and given to the poor, and your cook's left us for greener pastures. Besides, we'll be eating horse tonight. We've feasted on venison until it's like ashes on our tongues."

The sheriff had come close to biting his own tongue off. Now he erupted, "Laugh while you may, jackal! I'll have you yet! I'll have your skull for a chamberpot!" Robin smiled. "I will get you! There are no end of loyal men who'll hunt you down! Before this summer is out I'll have made Robin Hood a subject for songs, dead as a rock and impotent as a breeze!" He went on and on.

Robin accepted his bow from Polly, leaned on the top of it and contemplated his old enemy. A soldier sent out a wail as Gilbert hammered an arrow through his shoulder. Black Bart and Little John gutted the dead horse. The sheriff ran out of breath as Robin Hood looked on blandly. "T'is a fine song, Rowland, but one we've heard before. Will you indeed hunt us down? Think now. With some of your and your predecessor's expeditions, we were hard-put to bury all the bodies. And what do we do here in the woods, after all, but follow God's plan? We eat, we sleep, we gather a harvest. We take no more than rabbits from a garden." He waved an arm around him. "We're a part of the forest. We'll always be here. So live and let live, Rowland. And loose no dogs who value their noses." Robin replaced his feathered hat and bowed in mockery.

The leader of Sherwood then spoke to the soldiers. "Stand away from your horses, you lot. Render your purses and belts and such wine and food as ye bear. Know you contribute to a good cause—our larder must be low indeed if we are reduced to soldiers' rations. And soldiers' mounts. We apologize for the inconvenience, and trust it will not happen again. Until the next time, anyway."

Robin himself took the sheriff's pouch and keys. Black Bart and Little John had quartered the fallen horse and lashed it over the back of a tall black, to that animal's dismay. With the skittish beast under tow, the outlaws of Sherwood smiled, backed away from the soldiery with their loot, and melted into the brush.

The sheriff cast about him. He had three dead, seven wounded, four gone, and all of them demoralized. He shook his fist at the greenery. "You bastard Saxon pig!" he shouted, "I'll get you!"

Robin's laugh floated back. "Not inside Sherwood, you won't."

The sheriff growled to himself, "Then we'll see you *out* of Sherwood."

Sir Guy of Gisborne cracked the suckling skull with the pommel of his dagger. He prised out the brains with his fingers, stuffed them in his mouth, then threw the rest to the dogs that skulked under the table. Guy's dogs were like the viscount himself: gaunt and murky of eye, with the skin stretched tight over their long skulls. The man's greasy hair swept straight back and down, and the tails twitched when he moved his head. Sir Guy ate with no relish whatsoever. As he supped he watched out his high window to where the serfs plowed the first furrows. There was frost yet under the dead grass, and the soil broke in blocks. The oxen and men found it tough going. Elsewhere people struggled with their heads down. Guy had had the trees near the castle removed so that nothing would obstruct the view of peasants slaving for him, but he got no joy from the sight.

At the next window stood a broad and brown man dressed all in leather, even to a cap that covered his hair. He wore a falchion on his hip. This was Guy's huntsman, called the Kite. He leant out the window to be as close to the outdoors as possible.

"Someone is coming."

A party of soldiers with wounded wended from the forest. Their livery marked them as the Sheriff of Nottingham and his men. The Kite snorted. Neither man moved. Sir Guy of Gisborne was a viscount, and the sheriff a mere knight. He would come to his superior.

It took some time for the sheriff to hobble up to the second floor of the keep. "It was damned Robin Hood, God rot his stinking soul! Guy, give us a drink, for God's sake."

Guy ignored him and kept eating. The Kite looked out the window. The sheriff helped himself from the silver ewer on the table. He drank long and banged down the cup. "Guy, I want you to kill Robin Hood. I'll give you whatever you need."

"What could you give me that I want?" Guy's voice was flat and lifeless. He scraped flesh from bone.

The sheriff's face was blotchy. "Kill him before Midsummer's Day, and I'll grant you his lands."

"What would I want them for? Rotting stones and overgrown fields."

"You can hunt on them. It's in the King's charter. It has running water. There was a mill. You know that. It abuts your land."

Guy drank wine.

"I can get you serfs to work the land. I could even clean the dungeons and give you slaves. You might mine the hills. But first you must find Robin Hood and slay him."

"Finding Locksley is not a problem."

"That's right. You'd only have to look. You could see their fires from a hill or tall tree."

Guy turned his cup over. "You're a fool, Rowland. You work harder than any serf. Saxons must go in and out of that camp all the time. Any one could tell you where he is. But come close and you'd collect a sheaf of arrows. He has more than forty men."

"I didn't see but ten just now, and some of them women."

"Whores, you mean."

The sheriff leaned across the table. "Guy—"

"*Sir* Guy."

"Sir Guy. Listen. We'll use guile. We can split them up. There must be times when Locksley is away. The stories are he's forever gallivanting in some simpleton's guise: a butcher or a beggar or a harlot. I can have another shooting match."

Guy curled a lip. "Yes, we know how well that worked. I'll warrant he stays back in the sticks and ruts with those whores, and has his minstrel concoct stories about him."

"And he has treasure. We could share that."

Guy was disdainful. "He has no treasure. Would a man with gold live in the woods?"

Rowland looked closer at his colleague. "You don't know him, Sir Guy."

"I know him." The viscount threw his silver platter to the floor. Instantly the hounds began to fight over the scraps. Guy raised his voice over the noise. "I would need help. I have two score men here. You'd have to lend me some of yours, say three score. An attack would have to be swift, else the curse'd Saxons would warn him." Guy got more nourishment from the hatred than the meal. He got up and paced. "Give me some time. I'll plan an attack and notify you when it's ready. You need not come personally. Just send your most ruthless men. And I need one more thing."

The sheriff prayed it was a cheap solution.

Guy pulled on his deerhide gloves, drawing them close about his long fingers. "You must have your abbot anul Locksley's marriage to Marian Fitzooth. I will have her to wife, soiled as she is."

The sheriff remembered now. "I know not an anulment. They've been married for at least—"

Sir Guy spun and slammed his palm onto the table so hard the tankards upset. "She's bedding with an outlaw in the *wilderness*! They were married under the *trees*! That's no marriage! A cleric can annul it! She was pledged to me by *both* our fathers, and she'll be *mine*, not that earl of nothing's! You *must* have Anselm arrange that! Or you can leave." A vein in his forehead pounded fit to burst.

The sheriff raised a hand. It was Guy the fool, he thought. A lord had his pick of women. Why fuss over one? "Aye, aye. Whatever you say. He owes me a favor. If you kill her husband it's a moot point anyway. Bring me Robin Hood's head and you can eat the wench for all I care."

Guy nodded. "See you arrange it. Now leave me."

"May I have assistance for my men? I have wounded."

"Take whatever you need, but keep your men away from mine. I don't want them associating with losers."

Shaking his head, Rowland of Nottingham hobbled away on gouty legs.

Guy spoke to his huntsman, who had not moved in the interval. "What's the name of that one in the kennels? The dark one?"

"Rodger."

"Fetch him."

The Kite left and returned in a few minutes with the kennel master. He brought with him an odor of dog shit. Rodger had recently been sent to Guy from an ally far to the west. The note that came with him related how the man had gotten into strife and needed to be relocated. He was too "obedient" to waste. Guy had set him up in the kennels, but reports were he was too rough with the dogs. You would never know by asking, thought Guy, the man hardly ever talked. He was tall and dark, with a handsome face. But his attention would wander, and he fixed on odd things around him.

"Rodger," said Guy, "I have a mission for you. If you do well, I will give you your own house, and your own animals to keep. Maybe a wife. If you fail, I shall hang you." Rodger showed no particular interest either way. He watched the dogs, who cowered under the table. Sir Guy took a casual turn around the room, picked up a riding crop, and wandered back. Abruptly he slashed the man across the face. Rodger staggered. "You are alive in there, eh? Eh?"

Rodger flinched. "Y-yes, milord."

"Good. Now listen well. Here's what you're going to do . . ."

Guy explained his plan, making Rodger repeat it several times. Guy finished, "Remember. You rob them, beat them, dally with the women if you like. But no killing, understand?"

"Rob them, beat them, dally them. I understand."

"You had better. Now go see the seamstress."

Rodger left, a red welt standing out across his face. Guy stood staring at the doorway the man had exited. "A strange one, that. It may work," he said to the Kite, "at least for a little while. On to other things." Sir Guy looked out the window at the sky and the sun. "Have my horse readied. Get one for yourself, and tell Delancey, Clement, and Charrette we ride."

The Kite left without a word. Sir Guy stared past his holdings at the forest.

"Sherwood won't be deep enough this time, Locksley."

Sir Guy and his retinue arrived at the tower as the sun went down. It had been a long toil up the ridge, for the trail was cut for men and not horses. The tower was at the very peak of the ridge, at the very end. It sat on a spit of sandstone that overhung a sheer slope. Down below stretched a broad valley, entirely forested. The tower was of dark grey cut stone. It was very old. Guy looked at the top as the wind whipped his ermine-trimmed cloak around him. They said the tower had been built by giants. They said the wind always blew here.

"You lot go back to the village." This was a rude hamlet at the bottom of the slope. At their approach, the peasants had fled to the woods or barred their doors. "Displace whomever's in the tightest house and get some food. We'll stay the night." His knights sneered at the thought of entering a peasant's hut, but they kept their mouths shut. They turned and picked their way down the hill. Sir Guy tied his horse securely to a rusted iron ring. His dogs shied away from the doorway, so he pressed alone against the dark.

The first floor was empty and small, the outer walls being so thick. There were only stone steps leading up. Bats fluttered close with their *wuffwuffwuff wuffwuffwuff*. Moss and guano made the steps slippery. Ammonia stank. Sir Guy lashed at cobwebs and climbed in blackness.

The top room was very dim with only three candles alight. There was neither starlight nor wind, for the windows had been closed up with stone. Dried plants and skins and whole carcasses —bats, a dog, a hawk—hung from the ceiling. Rotted stumps sprouting mushrooms covered a rough table. Fleshy, hairy roots were spread over a canted rack. A dead rat was pinned to a board, and silver squirmed among its ribs. Leaves and hair and dirt littered the floor, dark against the whitewash of old guano. Dusty cobwebs filled the corners. Incense smouldered in clay dishes, heating the odor of decay. The smoke moved around the room, coming towards him when he stirred.

The woman sat cross-legged on a tiny rug, hands in her lap, head thrown back as if in a trance. She called herself Taragal, and she was very beautiful. Guy supposed all witches were: selling one's soul must bring some boon. Her hair was like a cloud around her head. The color was uncertain, but it was shot with grey.

The lord waved a hand at the air before him. "Woman, I need a spell." He tossed gold coins on the floor. She accepted only gold, no silver. Convenient, he thought. The sorceress lowered her head and peered at him through hooded eyes. Guy had seen this before, and he thought it a trick to unnerve him. Probably she was near-sighted.

"What?" Her voice was a slow practiced contralto.

The knight waved again at the air and sat down on a wobbly bench. He shifted his sword to do so. "I want something to consternate Robin Hood. Something to unman him, make him afraid of the night, strike God into his heart. What have you?"

The sorceress rose without using her arms. Bones—finger bones?—and copper ornaments sewn about her clothes clattered. She wore the faded remnants of some lady's robes. Artful shreds hung from them. The most striking item was a thick gold circlet around her throat. It fit close with no visible seam. Guy wondered if Satan had put it there. She gave her robes a cat's shrug.

"Poison?" She took a step towards him.

"No, I want him alive."

"Sickness?"

Guy thought. "How would you introduce it?" The woman moved closer. He felt like standing up, but didn't.

"In their well."

Guy shook his head. Something jumped underneath a table. It was a hare with two legs, one front and one back. Neat bandages covered the stumps of the other two. Guy tried to think what that meant.

She put a question to him. "Do you know the barrows of Sherwood?"

"Those piles of dirt? What about them?"

She laughed in her throat. A long fingernail snaked out to toy with his greasy locks. Guy caught the smell of her: spice and animal grease and woman in heat.

"Those piles of dirt hold the bodies of ancient ones. The people who were here in England first, who lived with the fays, who are all dead now."

Guy brushed her hand away. "Men say giants built them."

She laughed again. The man found it an irritating sound. "Giants do not build things, no more than fairies." She tugged at the hair behind his ears. "Aye, we'll loose a terror. Your man the Kite shall fetch what I say. We'll lure some large animal onto a barrow. A wildcat perhaps, or a boar. Maybe even a wolf."

"There are no wolves in England."

She chuckled.

Guy hated this woman more every minute. "What must he fetch?"

The woman told him what he must fetch and where he must put it.

"Very well. He'll find one."

Scented smoke crept into Guy's nostrils. Taragal pressed her hips to his shoulder. She rubbed her crotch against him. Guy felt goosebumps on his arms: she was cold. Lazily she leant her head down and licked her tongue into his ear. He did nothing. She bit his ear, hard.

"God's teeth! Get away!" he roared, and he shoved at her. She laughed and returned to his side as he rubbed his bleeding ear. Guy shot erect and slapped her across the face with his gloved hand. "I said, *get away!*" He tried to shove her again, but coughed in the smoke.

The woman smiled and stroked her face. "Yes," she cooed, "you may hurt me. But not harm." She reached out a dirty fingernail and grazed his cheek. The slight scratch itched, then began to burn in earnest, but now he could not raise a hand to rub it. Taragal asked, "Do I get what I want?"

"Uhh . . . y-yes."

"Good. I need something else." She tugged at the laces along her shoulders, and the robes fell to the floor. In the dim light the man could see her heavy breasts undershot with grime. Her nipples were large and entirely smooth as if capped with copper. She had no body hair. Incense smoke wreathed her hair until it looked alive. She flattened against him, and her body was as cold as a marble statue. "You'll forget aught but to send me the Kite in the morning," she breathed in his ear.

"Yes."

He hooked his hands around her waist and pulled her close.

Chapter 3

The old crow ticked off the markers on the land below him: a pond, a split oak, a rill, another pond. The flock dipped and dropped, up over the tops of the trees and back down. It was spring and they were returning home. The birds hugged the terrain because it was a windy day. Only the youngest crows, showing off for the females, worked at their flying. They would tip a wing and invert themselves, fall upside down to touch a treetop, then flip over and shoot straight up. The birds played. They watched for inattention among their inferiors, and seeing it, dove like a spear to graze a head. The surprised bird would shear off and rejoin the flock higher up, now watchful for inattention in his or her inferiors. They flapped steadily along, never gliding for more than two or three seconds. At each new change in the topography the old crow would call out: scatter, reform, dive, bank.

The large and dusky crow was almost as old as an old man. He was blind in one eye. In his youth an owl had harried him one long winter's night. Instead of keeping his head under a wing, he had to watch with one eye, and it had frozen. But he survived. At ninety feet in the air and a swift pace, his good eye could still spot the tip of a chipmunk's tail as the animal foraged under oak leaves for acorns. He was still the strongest and bravest and wisest, still the unchallenged leader of twenty-two.

Now he called to skirt a meadow, a frequenting spot for sparrowhawks. They curved along the trees below the thrust of the wind. The land dipped. Ahead was a large swamp, a strange one, dead as a climax forest. In all his years the crow had never seen that swamp yield up the life it should. Usually where water and sun and grass and bole came together nature was richest. But this swamp was flat and stale and unmoving. It kept its life tucked close, and it let nothing escape.

A lieutenant to the right rasped, *Caw* (Be on your guard). He swooped lower and rasped, *ca* (Danger!). But the one-eyed leader had already seen. *Ca ca ca ca Caw*, he shrilled (Great danger! A man with a bow!). Down below, leaving the swamp, a man walked with arrow ready. He looked up. The congregation split left and right. The birds saw the man had a beard and a dark face, and that he wore all leather. His legs were wet to the thigh with mud. The crows knew him: he was a huntsman, a cruel man who savaged his dogs and prolonged a killing stroke. Where he walked he left death. The crows followed his back trail. The man watched them disappear.

At the middle of the swamp were brushy hummocks raised above the main and so usually dry. Small mounds ringed a larger one, and its top sported a blob of white writ with red. At the leader's command the flock dropped and touched down amid great scuffling and shoving. Then each crow folded his or her wings three times and preened them flat. The old leader walked in a circle to look around. The spot could not be better. The mound had only sparse grass. They had a clear view all around. Flies and midges swirled over the fresh meat. The crows milled around the food, nudging their inferiors, giving way to superiors, ignoring those too distant in the pecking order, jockeying for position. It was imperfect food, fresh and solid. Better it should have sat for a week in the sun, until it reached the consistency of a horse's eyeball or a clam. Yearling crows forgot and leaped forward to snatch a bite. They retreated under rapid pecks and curses. The upper-echelon crows picked first with their sharp beaks, plucking at the eyes, tugging at the open mouth. The easiest and quickest treat was the dried blood and ragged strips along the throat. The social shuffle went on. Mated birds continued their love games; they preened their lover's necks and fed each other like babies. Males stretched tall and thin to issue a challenge of aerial combat, or they squatted down bulky to hold their spot on the ground. Sentries watched in trees.

The sentry on the outskirts of the flock called once. The birds felt a drumming underfoot. A fast chafing shook the brush. Almost immediately there came another cry, then the sentry took to the air. The flock exploded off the mound as a great boar stampeded up the slope to steal their prize. Feathers fluttered like dirty snow. The boar caught no birds, and no sooner had it gained the top than it vanished. The earth gave way with a sigh, and the boar and dead baby disappeared into a hole.

The crows banked and hovered over the depression. The smell of sweet flesh was overpowered by disturbed earth. Light flowed into a chamber, more than half the barrow in size. Dust whirled. At the bottom of the chamber was a sepulchre of dry stone. Wide rotted boards had covered the top. These were now splinters covering the boar. The beast thrashed to his feet. He crushed mummy remains in dusty skins and stone jewelry. A flint-tipped spear snapped. A hoof pulped something soft. Realizing what it had, the boar stopped. The crows watched in dismay as the boar set to on the baby and the mummy. It chewed sweet and leathery flesh. It rasped fresh blood and ancient hair from the stone with its tongue.

There would be nothing left. The crows pulled up and away.

Chapter 4

"All right, lads and lasses, this spot will do." Robin Hood stopped walking. The children stopped trotting. The outlaw waited until they had caught their breath, then he pointed around with his bow. This was an open oak wood to the north of camp. They could see a long ways. "Now. Imagine you're here, after squirrels maybe. Suddenly you hear the signal from camp to disperse."

Allan asked, "What's 'disperse'?"

Robin smiled. "That means to run like the devil was after you." Tam laughed, but the other children crossed themselves. "And don't interrupt. Now, you know you're not supposed to return to camp when you hear that, so what do you do first?"

Robin Hood was a young man, tall and straight with corded arms. His brown face was seamed with lines of laughter. His brown hair was wavy and fell to just below his shoulders. His beard was light, and became lighter as the days lengthened. His hat was green, and it sported a pheasant feather given him by Marian. His tunic was the famous Lincoln green with layers of wool underneath, and since he worked in the forest and not the field, he wore trousers instead of hose. His boots were deerhide with the hair out. His broad belt had a silver buckle, and held a silver-wrought knife and a silver hunting horn. His deerhide quiver rattled with red-fletched arrows that had three red rings round the shafts. His bow reached over his head.

This morning Robin had with him the children of Sherwood. With their new green clothes and boots and their miniature bows and knives, they looked like a band of angels let out for a lark. There were nine: Allan and Elaine, the children of Allan A'Dale and Elaine; Tub and Glenyth, belonging to Ben Barrel; Katie, belonging to none; impish Tam, son of devilish Will Scarlett; Mary and Rachel, homely like their father Arthur A'Bland, plump like their mother Mary, and slow like both of them; and the quiet Polly, Red Tom's daughter. It was a question whether Katie, Rachel, and Polly were children or women, so to be sure they received the training of both. Today they would learn how to hide.

The Fox of Sherwood was their teacher. "I brought you here for a reason. What's the first thing anyone can tell me about this place?"

The children circled about to stare at the woods. Every parent had pressed his or her child to attend Robin. There would be questions later. They were also to be clever.

"There's no cover," said Katie.

"There's no trees as we could climb quickly," said Tam.

"You can see a long ways," said Allan.

"I'm hungry," said Glenyth.

"So am I," replied Robin. "Those are all good. Anything else? Polly?"

The silent girl screwed up her face and said, "We shouldn't be trying to hide here at all."

Robin Hood grinned. "That's probably the best. The first thing to remember when you're running is to run somewhere sensible. Don't just take off in a panic like a deer. A deer can move like the wind, and that's what saves him. Nothing can catch him. But people are *slow*. You have to think about not just what's on the horizon, but what's beyond it. *Think* where you're going, all the time. And it can be hard when the dogs are after you. But *think* where you're going. Repeat that, please."

"Think where you're going," chorused the children. Little Glenyth mumbled the rhythm.

Robin smiled. "Think where you're going. And if you remind me later, I'll tell you about the time I ran smack into a river. So we shouldn't have run here. We should have run to thickets, or to a lowland full of water, or up a stream. But right now we're here. Let's see what we can do." He strolled off with his flock behind him. "We can't go up, because the branches are too high. Besides, you better not get into a tree except as a last resort. Once you're in a tree, you're stuck. It's true a man tends to look ahead and not up—our necks aren't built for it, don't you see—but never mind. For now the lesson is: Stay out of trees. Repeat."

"Stay out of trees!" the children shouted.

"Good. Let's pretend we're badgers and look for hidey-holes."

So the lesson went. The children learned to look for a hollow under a bush, a hole where a windfall had its roots exposed, a runnel gouged by the rain where two slopes came together, a fracture along rock ledges, a large animal burrow, and other places. Robin showed how to flop in a depression and burrow under the leaves without exposing the moist darker undersides. He explained that they should fix the enemy's location in their minds, then keep their heads down, "lest the villain feel your eyes upon him." He drilled them how to put their ear to a rock to listen for a human tread, how to recite the rosary before looking ("But quietly. God will hear."), and how to peer from under a tent of leaves. He showed how to slip out of the hollow slowly, and how to decide which way to go next.

"Remember, if you have to make a noise, make it the way animals do. A squirrel or a rabbit—not that you find rabbits in these woods—will bolt from one place to another quickly, making a scurrying noise like this." He scrabbled his fingers across the leaves. "Then they stop and wait and look for danger. They'll stand there for maybe a minute or two, or longer if there's even a breath of anything on the wind. Then they'll pick their way carefully, or else bolt again. The only thing that walks through the woods like this," Robin picked his foot high and stomped it down, then crashed along with giant steps. The children giggled. "Yes, like this, try it." The children fell in line behind him, lifting their knees to their shoulders and stamping on all the twigs they could, giggling the while. Robin laughed. "Right. The only beings that walk like this are men, and horses, and cows. And we're smarter than cows, aren't we?"

Katie volunteered, "Tam's not."

Tam cried, "Am so!"

Robin laughed again. "That's true, Katie, Tam is smarter than a cow. But Tam has the disadvantage of bad blood. After all, it was his father who ran into an entire troop of the Sheriff's men, and he didn't have on a stitch of clothing at the time."

"He didn't?" the children breathed.

Robin squatted down on his haunches to look them in the eye. He nodded solemnly. "Not so much as a handkerchief. Didn't he ever tell you about that?" The children shook their heads, their mouths open. Tam squinted, not sure if he believed it or not. "Well, you just ask for it next time he starts a story. It's a good one." He addressed Tam, "And Will tells the best stories, don't he, Coz?"

Tam piped, "He sure does!" and he shook a fist at Katie. She extended her tongue, very lady-like.

"What had he done with his clothes?" asked Rachel.

"He'd given them to the poor," Robin replied with a straight face. The outlaw sat on his hams and arranged the trappings on his belt. The children knelt. "That's enough for today, I guess. Any road, I hope you all understand why we need to do this, learn to hide and all. Do you? It's because we're outlaws. If the King's foresters or any one of the Sheriff's men catch us, they can cut off our ears or fingers, or blind us or brand us, or hang us by the side of the road with our own bowstrings."

"They cut off David's ears," whispered Allan.

"That's right. And he was lucky. But Sherwood is large and gentle, and it holds us to its bosom like Abraham. The glens give us food in the form of deer, the streams give us water, the trees give us firewood. We eat the plants. We've even made peace with the fairies. Sherwood is one of the loveliest and most blest places on God's Earth, and we can live here as long as we treat it gently. But Sherwood and God can only protect us so far, so we have to know how to protect ourselves.

"But mostly we teach you these things because you're our children, and that makes you the most precious things in these woods. Do you understand that?"

They replied, "Yes, Robin," with bland faces and little embarrassment. They were used to hearing this. Robin pulled in and hugged the nearest child, five-year-old Glenyth. She squirmed.

"And will you remember what you learned today?"

"Yes, Robin."

Robin's eyes twinkled. "Let's see, then." He hopped to his feet and drew a bird arrow out of the quiver at his back. "I'll cover my eyes and sing a kyrie eleison. Then I'm going to come looking for children hidden in hollows. And any bottoms I see sticking up get a stripe of this." He swung the switch menacingly. "I'm starting—now!" Clutching their bows and knives, the children squealed and scattered. Robin Hood laid back on the leaves in a scent of moss and closed his eyes.

An hour later found them together again, each one except Tam spattered cap to toe in damp detritus.

"Good, good, good," Robin proclaimed, and he patted heads all around. "It's a good day when the only ones I can find are Glenyth and Tam." Glenyth held his hand and sucked her dirty thumb.

Will Scarlett's son rubbed his rump with both hands. "In another minute, I'd not have been found at all. I was almost there."

Robin shook his head and smiled. "You were no further up that oak than a boar with two broken legs. And there was no cover: I could see the topmost branches everywhere I stood. What did I tell you?"

"STAY AWAY FROM TREES!" shouted the chorus.

"Right," assented Robin.

Tam rubbed some more. "You'll not tell Da, will you?"

Katie barked, "I will!"

Tam balled a fist. "You do and—"

"Enough, enough," cooed Robin. "I'll not have the children telling tales to the adults. They've enough worries. We'll keep this to ourselves. You've all learned one lesson, and that's to follow orders. I thank you for your help, Master Tam." The boy grinned ruefully.

"Are we done?" asked Tub. His stomach had sounded a chime a while back.

"Done?" laughed the outlaw chief. "The day's just begun! The days are long now, Master Tub, and we've time for work and work and more work!" Tub grimaced. "Why, after dinner, you can all have sword practice with Gilbert and Will Stutly." Robin laughed again. "But there's no reason we can't have some fun too. Here. We'll fan out on the way back to camp. I'll give a silver penny to the one who pots something for supper." Instantly the children ran off, falling over themselves to nock their arrows. Robin held Glenyth back.

He cupped his hands and called, "But potting one another doesn't count!"

One hundred fifty years before, William the Conquerer had decreed half of England royal forest. No one could hunt or farm there without the king's permission. No fool, William had set aside land that no one wanted.

Sherwood was miles and miles of open glades and deep woods and low rolling hills. Sandstone and sand underlay a good part of it, although there were plenty of streams and rivers and swamps. The royal forest Sherwood merged with the free forest Barnsdale on the north and Charnwood on the south. Oaks and silver birches stood in untouched millions.

Robin Hood's current camp was in the depths of Sherwood where the land started to rise to the west. The camp was on a long, easy slope that had oaks above and birches, blackthorn, and ash below. Halfway down this slope was a bump two hundred feet across where stone projected through the thick green grass. Inside this lump was a cave too good to resist, and Robin's camp had grown in front of it, as if the outlaws were leaves pushed by the wind.

Masking the cave was a hall, called the great hall, although it was no more than forty feet wide and twenty deep. The hall was stone below and logs above. The roof was beams and planks with sod overgrowing the top. The lazy outlaws would sun there in summer. There was only one solid Dutch door in the front of the hall, and the only two windows flanked it. The windows were stained glass rich with blue, salvaged from Robin's ancestral home: at one side of the door Christ washed the feet of the apostles; on the other He drove the money-lenders from the temple with a whip of cords. The rainbow light illuminated the Spartan interior of the hall. Built for meetings and defense, it was undivided by walls or posts. Stone fireplaces made the two end walls. The back of the hall entered into the cave.

The cave entrance had been left unchanged since Robin Hood had found it in his youth, but the floor of the cave had been levelled and the stalactites—"stone spears" —removed. The inside was large enough for twice Robin's followers to dance. Dark and cool and dry, it was here that the outlaws kept stores and the little treasure they had. A tunnel at the back of the cave linked with a natural cut. This was the outlaws' bolthole for times of siege.

The cut and the cave had been made by a brook that ran down the slope. Long ago the boy Robin had diverted the water; it now flowed away from the cave to the east, where it continued down the slope, formed a pool behind a loose dam, then wended away into the woods. This brook was the eastern bound of Robin's camp, and only Black Bart's smithy was outside it.

The outlaws lived on what they called the common, a cleared area a hundred feet wide in front of the hall. Here were firepits, worktables, an eating table. The outlaws took their meals under the stars more often than under a roof. With the hill on the north and open sky to the south, the spot was like a scoop of sunlight, bright and sheltered in the winter, not too hot in the summer. Around the common was the oak forest, uncut since the dawn of man. Climaxed and uniform, the trees were thirteen feet thick at chest height. They towered into the sky like pre-dawn giants, so massive they scarcely moved in the wind. Crouched among the oaks like over-sized acorns were cottages.

There were eleven cottages around the common. The smaller ones were stone, the larger cruck cottages with their strong wishbone beams at each end. Roofs were thatched or shingled. Only two homes had glass windows, the others making do with vellum. The cottages were occupied by families of a sort, with one unused. The largest homes belonged to the biggest families, like those of Arthur A'Bland, Ben Barrel, and Allan A'Dale. Will Scarlett, otherwise called Gamwell, lived with his mother Old Bess, the midwife; his son Tam; old Will Stutly; and any number of arguments. David and Shonet, newlyweds, had a cottage that shone with whitewash, fresh thatch, and a sparkling window. Red Tom's home, occupied by a carpenter, sported an intricately carved door depicting the miracles of Christ. His daughter Polly was now the woman of the house, since Tom's wife had left "Sherwood and all its filth" in the winter past. That left the barracks for the unmarried men: Little John, Friar Tuck, Much the Miller's son, and the new man Brian. It was called the Bear's Den. Not far away—too close, some said—was the house of unmarried women: Bold Jane Downey, Grace, and Katie, now woman enough to be moved from the child's spot in Scarlett's home. This was the Nunnery.

The only other structures were Cedwyn's cottage and Black Bart's smithy. Cedwyn the witch liked her privacy, and people gave it to her. Her shack was far away at the bottom of the lower meadow. Gilbert lived with her "in sin." Crusty Black Bart had no home. He slept in his smithy when circumstances permitted, on a cot in the cave at other times. His smithy was removed far under the trees on the other side of the stream. That the water created a barrier against magic was left unsaid.

Below the common was the rambling lower meadow, kept a meadow by the presence of a great lime tree, the largest tree in Sherwood. It was this tree that had brought Robin here in the first place. A man would crane his head far back to look at the top, and still see only branches. The tree's girth was so great that it needed twelve men, or ten men and Little John, to encircle it by holding hands. It was more a mountain of wood than a tree, and a king could have built a fleet from it. Robin Hood was wont to say he wished the tree could talk: surely it could tell a man all he needed to know.

The meadow was good for animals, too. The open space let the sun bring forth grass and flowers. The grass grew thick and sweet. Bees came from miles to visit the flowers, and a swarm settled here on a late summer's day. Clover sprang up, and rabbits flocked to the white and purple tops. After the rabbits came foxes, owls, ferrets, weasels, wildcats, boars. Beetles and flies lived on the dung, mosquitoes and gnats on blood. Bats swooped low after the insects. Earthworms moved more easily through soil chopped by animals, and they laid many eggs. Moles and shrews fattened on the worms. Sparrows and robins and titmice and firetails scooped up insects, crows and ravens and jackdaws picked at the leavings. Turtles sought out the green banks of the pond to lay their eggs. Tadpoles and fingerlings ate them. Everyone came for the water, most especially the thirsty deer. The only ones missing were the wolves, who once had harried the deer and often had settled for mice. Life prospered in this glade, and the animals were as happy as animals can be.

Above, below, and apart from all this were the fairies.

It was spring in the year 1194, and like the squirrels and hawks and toads and flies who quickened with the sun, people started their seedtime chores, all the while yawning like bears or singing like meadowlarks.

Bart the blacksmith dragged down the bellows handle, pushed it back up, then dragged it down again. Left alone, the handle would ascend by itself, but Bart was not one to wait. At every compression the leather bellows roared at the fire until the coals were yellow on top and white at the center. Bart had three irons in the fire. Tub, the portly son of Ben Barrel, worked a file on an axe head.

"Less of an angle on that side, boy," Bart called as he drew an iron and attacked it with a hammer. "That—*thud*—side—*thud*—throws—*thang*—the—*tang*—chips—*crang*." Black Bart was a stocky grizzled man with a carbon-etched face. Sweat dripped from his nose and sizzled on the steel. Arrowheads dropped from his anvil like autumn leaves. He jammed an iron back in the forge, drew another, gave it five fast raps, did it again, and again. Tub depressed the angle of the file and Bart grunted assent. Tub could not understand how the smith could see behind him in this dark shop lit only by firelight, but he obviously could.

Bart yanked on the bellows, harder than before. Air gasped and gushed. Suddenly he called, "Whoops!" Then, "Out, boy! Run for it!" Bart was already clearing the door. Tub dropped his file and looked around. Elongated coals had spilled from the forge onto the dirt, but as Tub watched, they began to crawl along the floor.

Tub caught up with Bart on the dam. They trotted to the other side of the stream and stopped. The man and boy looked back at the smithy. There was no activity to be seen.

"What were those?" panted the boy.

"Salamanders, I think," puffed the smith. He snorted. "They'll cool down soon enough, and we can get back to work." Bart locked a nostril shut with his finger and blew snot, repeated the process with the other nostril, and wiped his fingers on his apron.

Tub's teeth were chattering. "Tam said you worship demons."

Bart jerked upright. "Worship 'em? Listen here, lad, I don't worship nothing. I don't have to. I'm a smith. Know this," and he jabbed a grimy finger into his palm, "fairies are afraid of iron, men are afraid of steel, and animals are afraid of fire. A smith is master of all three, and he don't give a damn what anyone does in the whole world. You understand that?"

The boy gulped, "Yessir."

"Don't sir me. Now, do you want to be a smith or don't you?"

"I don't know, sir."

"WHAT DO YOU MEAN YOU DON'T KNOW? WHAT'S WRONG WITH IT?"

In the Nunnery, Bold Jane Downey gathered her blankets and threw them outside on the grass. "Marian's sent word. She's determined to rid us of vermin if we have to burn and boil everything in camp." Jane was so small and slim she could be mistaken for a girl in a half-light. Perhaps because of this she was an absolute hellion. In a fight she wore a long sword on her back. She was never without a poinard. Her fair hair was hacked off just below the ears to keep down the lice and save her from "fussing."

Her housemate was a large ungainly-looking woman named Grace, whose parents had named her that in all hope. "What are we to wear while our clothes are boiling, then?" Grace was new to Sherwood. She had not wanted to marry, and the only outward act of her life had been to wield a tankard on her wedding night at the very last minute. After that she had run to the forest.

"Nothing, I expect." Jane pulled her ticking from the bed. Black dots scurried away from the light.

"Nothing?" squeaked Katie, a skinny girl with a snub nose. At thirteen, Katie had been proclaimed a woman and recently moved from Will Scarlett's home to the Nunnery. All three women—yeomen, Robin called them jokingly—were dressed like Marian, which is to say dressed like men.

"Nothing. We're to take baths. Every one of us."

Grace put her hands over her bosom even though fully dressed. "What, with the men around?"

Jane snorted. "No. She'll run them off into the woods. But I don't put it past them to sneak back here, the dirty hairy beasts."

Katie said, "I can stand watch with my bow."

Jane nodded. "Good enough. Let's hope they come creeping."

Allan A'Dale's family sat on wooden benches in the sun. Allan the Younger poked at a Bible with a slender forefinger. " '*Credo in unum Deum, Patrem omnipo-ten-tem, factorem coeli et terrae, vi-si-bil-i-um omnium et in-visibilium. Et in unum Dominum Jesum Christum, Filium Dei uni-gen-i-tum. Et ex Patre natum ante omina saecula. Deum de Deo, lu-men de lumine, Deum verum de Deo vero. Gen-Gen-Genitum, non factum, consubstant . . . consub . . . cobsub . . .*' "

" '*Consubstantialem Patri: per quem omnia facta sunt. Qui propter nos homines, et propter nostram salutem, descendit de coelis,*'(*)" said his father without looking. "You're doing very well." Allan A'Dale fashioned a toy cart for his youngest son.

(*)"I believe in one God, the Father Almighty, Maker of heaven and earth, and of all things visible and invisible. And in one Lord Jesus Christ, the Only-begotten Son of God. Born of the Father before all ages. God of God; Light of Light; true God of true God. Begotten, not made; of one being with the Father; by Whom all things are made. Who for us men, and for our salvation, came down from Heaven."

The oldest son sighed as only a child can. "Da! *Why* do I have to learn this?"

"Why learn this text, or why learn to read?" asked his father. Allan A'Dale's voice was always soft, as if a songbird were talking, and when he sang everyone listened. He was a handsome man, too thin, a tad too pale. His wife Elaine was as ephemeral as he, but their children, raised on venison and fish, were heartier versions of their parents, but still skinny. Their names were Allan, Elaine, and Dale. Their clothes were old and clean, trimmed with red and lace.

"Why must I learn to read? None of the other children do."

"To their sorrow. A man who can't read depends on others to learn about Our Lord. The works of Christ are all there, but what good are his teachings if no one could read them?"

The boy looked over the camp, where other children were bringing in faggots or fetching water. True, none of them were playing, but even working was better than this. "Tuck can read to us. We listen to him."

"And someone taught him as a child. I'll fancy Tam learns to read before long."

"Him? Never!"

Young Elaine attended the argument as she helped her mother card wool. She was thankful she was a girl and wouldn't have to read at all. The boy debated whether arguing with his father was better than reading. Both activities ate up his time when he could be playing. "But all this time I'm reading I could be learning to fight. A book isn't going to stop the Sheriff of Nottingham."

"You can read in that book what will happen to the Sheriff, not in this life but the next. A sword ends life, but a book can show you how to live forever." The children's requisite sword training was a sore point with Allan, who did not believe in fighting of any kind. Robin Hood demanded that everyone in Sherwood know how to fight and shoot. Reading was not required.

The awkward silence drew on, until Elaine put in a quiet, "Robin knows how to read."

Young Allan perked up. "He does?"

"Yes, he does. He learned as a lad. And he still found time to learn the bow and sword. And how to ride a horse, and do a hundred other things. Your father can read, but he can sing too, and he knows more than one hundred songs. God gives us enough time to learn all the things we need to know."

Allan A'Dale reached out a hand and closed the volume in front of his son. "But a boy needs to play, too. Run along, lad, and play until dinner." Allan the Younger lost no time in following that order. Elaine dismissed her daughter Elaine, and the girl vanished just as quickly.

The minstrel sighed. "It's a difficult course. Telling a boy not to fight rings flat."

Elaine sat beside him on the bench and took his hand. "Even if he must fight, it will never be for long. Man craves peace over war. Robin himself is that way. And I know Allan'll grow up just like his father. Wonderful."

Allan chuckled and drew his wife close.

Cedwyn ground the last of her herbs in a mortar. Spring was late. Gather what she may, the witch ran short every year: there was always the gap of weeks from when the shelves were bare until the dead earth replenished herself. As with food. And all their food needed gathering, for she and Marian could not keep a garden in the midst of all these animals. Cedwyn was short and thin, with a pretty-plain face and lank hair. She lacked an eye tooth. As a witch, she was never welcome except when needed. But she had a lover, and he was Apollo in armor. Pacing her cottage was Gilbert of Northumbria. Tall and stern, he had a face that was perfect except for a sword cleft on the jaw. His flowing hair was as yellow as an egg yolk. But to remind him of his mortal origin, Gilbert had a right hand that was a stick. The two first fingers were stumps, the others missing. The truncated thumb stuck up and could not move. All the hand and wrist was white with scar tissue. Whether this was wrought by fire or by God no one knew, for Gilbert could go a week on a handful of words. How a Welsh witch and a Scottish knight had come together was the largest mystery about them.

Love him as she did, though, Cedwyn's patience became as worn as the floor. "Gil, you're like a lion in a cage. Stop pacing and find something to do." She knew well enough he had nothing to do. Vowed to poverty, Gilbert owned nothing but his clothes, armor, a sword and shield. If he polished his sword any more it would disappear. Gilbert said nothing, just stepped outside. His shadow flickered across the door as he paced out there. Cedwyn put down her marble pestle. The work table was littered with more roots and twigs than leaves. "This wouldn't cure a chicken of the croup," she muttered to the air. She pulled a sack from under the table and stuck it in her belt, fetched down her bow and quiver and stalked outside.

"Come, Gil, we'll seek out a southern exposure. Maybe there's something up." Without a word the Crusader fell in behind her.

Shonet was again in bed. David of Doncaster fretted over her with a damp cloth. Newlyweds, Robin Hood allowed them leeway in their chores, but they were not after ecstasy. Shonet gave a twist on the bed and drew a sharp breath through her nostrils. The painted cross on the wall sparked fire in the bright sunlight. David held her hand as her fingernails dug deep. Then the pain was past, and she could smile at him. He mopped away sweat.

"Husband," she said, weakly. "I wish I could love you . . . What a lovely word, 'husband'."

"I could listen to it all day," he said. He kissed her lightly. Tears flowed down her face onto his lips, and she could not stop them.

"Oh, David, I wanted us so to be happy."

David was a handsome man with black hair kept long. He had lost his ears to foresters for poaching. His black hair mingled with Shonet's red-gold locks, her one vanity. "We'll be happy, darling. I'm happy now just being near you. And when you're well . . ." but she held his hand tight and started to cry again, and he had to hold her.

The rest of Robin Hood's outlaws were scattered around the camp and woods beyond. Ben Barrel and Arthur A'Bland dressed a deer. Their wives Clara and Mary diced the organs for sausage. Little John and Red Tom and Polly were abroad after cedar to split for shingles. Friar Tuck and his dogs rabbited. Will Scarlett and Tam were on watch, as were Brian and Much the Miller's Son. Old Bess mended girl's clothes, Will Stutly stitched men's boots. Children ran hither and thither fetching wood, sharp knives, water; shrieking to the sky; revelling in spring. Robin Hood wandered through it all, asking a question, paying a compliment, sharing a joke or snatch of song.

He found his wife pulling their bed apart. Robin and Marian's cottage was large enough to hold a bed, a fireplace, one chest, and two people, provided one of them was on the bed. The only decorations were Robin's baldric and shield, and a large cross. Marian wore a copy of her husband's clothes. A soft green cap decorated with a crow's feather spilled across her head. She hummed to herself. Without looking up Marian said, "Rob, dear, if you don't mind, I'd like to take a trip with Bess. She wants to visit her daughter."

Marian gasped as Robin grabbed her around the waist and spun her around. She squealed as he kissed her. Her body always reminded him of a deer after winter: she seemed too thin and tough. But she had a woman's curves for all that. Marian Locksley, once Fitzooth, had a long slender neck and slim face, with eyes brown like a doe's. Her hair was the color of the inside of a wine cask, a deep brown with glossy highlights that verged on purple. She half-struggled to free her arms as he kissed her along her white throat. "You, my little leman," he murmured between nips, "may do whatever you wish, and I will never say thee nay."

She giggled, "Oh? Whatever?"

"Whatever at all. I can deny you nothing. I am your slave." He kissed her some more. She squirmed as his beard tickled, but he would not let go. In fact, he kissed her all the more.

"Rob-in, stop—it!" she spun and pushed clear, backing out the door.

"I was just getting started," he said in a hurt voice. "You'll not deny my marital rights? It's your wifely duty. I'll have Tuck order you submit." He advanced with hands ready to grasp.

"And what need he do, show you with hands on?"

"I remember how."

"If I had a weapon you'd think twice," she warned with mockery. She had backed out of the cottage into the clear, and stood hunched, ready for flight.

"But you don't." Robin stopped. If she ran he'd never catch her. He took two steps backwards, and she followed.

"Anyway, may I go? Not that I really need my husband's permission," she added.

Robin put his hand to his chin to think. "Well . . ." As she relaxed he grabbed her by the wrist and pulled her to him. But he overcompensated. With a squawk she cannonned into his chest, the footboard caught him behind the knees, and the two of them crashed onto the naked bedframe. The boards gave way with a smash, followed by the collapse of the footboard and headboard. The last came down on top of them, cracking Marian on the back of the head.

"Oww!"

"Marian, I'm sorry! Are you all right?" asked her husband. He rubbed the back of her head, but he couldn't move to get up.

"I'm fine, dear." He could feel her giggles against his stomach. She made no move to disentangle them. "Anyway, I thought I'd go with Bess. None of us have been out all winter. We're all going mad here."

"Aye," said Robin in a muffled voice. It was dark under the headboard and Marian's hair. The crest of the Earl of Huntingdon pressed against the earl's head.

"I'll take Shonet too, perhaps. She's not looking well."

"And take Katie. She's like a March hare."

"I'm like a March hare myself," Marian giggled. She wriggled her hips against him.

Robin grunted. "Not that way. I mean she's stir crazy. I'll see about getting the rest of the lot out to do something. The road should be dry. How long will you be gone?"

Marian rubbed the back of her head. To do so she had to lean her weight on her husband's stomach, and he grunted again. "One day out, three there, one back. Five."

Her husband said, "I'll miss you."

She popped a kiss on his mouth. "You'd better. And while I'm gone . . ."

"Yes?"

"You can fix the bed."

"Yes, dear."

Robin Hood's table was almost thirty feet long and four feet wide. Robin had had this giant specially constructed, and Sherwood took every outside meal at it. There were two reasons for the enormity of the table. First was that no one had to sit at any but the head table. This lord had no favorites. The other reason was salt. Typically, a bowl of salt marked the division between upper class and lower at feasts, with the lower seated "below the salt." The Lord of Sherwood allowed no salt at his table, and even though people had to rise to fetch salt from the serving table for their meals, no one complained. (Most usually there was no salt to be had anyway. Then Robin always commented that God did not like to see His children separated.) At each end of the table, Robin Hood and Marian sat in chairs, the only chairs in Sherwood.

Supper was venison. Robin Hood and his followers were heartily sick of venison. Conversation was quiet because grousing was discouraged. People broke up the roast meat with their fingers and knives without hunting for the choice pieces. They champed their jaws and swallowed.

In the midst of the eating Robin Hood chuckled, then laughed to himself. "Funny the things God brings us. Here we choke down venison while anyone else in England would walk twenty miles in the rain for a mouthful of it. And during Lent no less. I can dip my hand into a coffer of gold, yet I'd give it all for a handful of prunes."

"Or leeks," called Tom down the table.

"Or a box of apples," muttered White Will Stutly.

"Or honey rolls," yelped Tam.

"Porridge with raspberries."

"Even a yellow onion."

"And some black bread, with *butter!*"

Robin stood up with his tankard.

"Let's take an oath! Tomorrow we'll sally afield and not return until we have some decent, er, different food. We'll buy from the poor or steal from the rich. And a gold crown for whoever brings back the best!"

The outlaws raised their jacks, shouted and drank. It was only water, but it tasted sweet.

"Allan," called Robin, "let's have a song!" Allan A'Dale smiled and went to fetch his lyre.

Will Scarlett rinsed his mouth and spit out the taste of deer. "It'll be good to get out, Rob. I wonder what we'll find."

Robin Hood laughed. "Something, Will. In Sherwood, you never know."

Moments later Allan struck his strings and they sang, the men and women alternating the parts.

"The keeper did a'hunting go,
And under his cloak he carried a bow,
All for to shoot at a merry little doe,
Among the leaves so green, O!

"Jackie boy? Master?
Sing ye well? Very well!

Hey down, ho down, derry derry down!
Among the leaves so green, O!
To me hey, down, down,
To me ho, down, down,
Hey down, ho down,
Derry, derry down,
Among the leaves so *green*, O!"

Chapter 5

"Halt in the name of Robin Hood!"

The arrested party consisted of two families. The first was that of Giles the Younger. With him was his wife Abbey; two young boys, Bodo and Aethelred; and Rose, twelve and coming into womanhood. The mother and boys were crowded into the back of Giles's tiny high-wheeled cart. Rose sat pressed against her father on the seat. Black and white-speckled chickens, strung up by their feet, flapped feebly around the outside of the cart. The second family was Robert and his wife Samantha together on a plowhorse. Robert's boy Rudolf walked with a pack stuffed full of wool cloth. The boys chattered with excitement at meeting Robin Hood. The adults were nervous. They had never seen Robin Hood before. They knew him to be a good man who protected the poor. But these four outlaws had the roughest clothes, hardly better than beggars. They wore long daggers and carried their bows nocked. The shine of steel seemed to be everywhere.

The clamor of birdsong made it noisy under the green-tinged branches, and a man had to raise his voice to be heard. Robert called, "Good day, Master Robin." He smiled nervously. "I'll warrant you need not stop us. The mud does that." The road here was actually not bad: crumbly sandstone came to the surface in so many places that one could steer a cart from high spot to high spot. It made for a bumpy ride but a quick one.

The tall man in Lincoln green laughed. "Very true, Master Traveller. On such a day, you could as easily have mud above as below." He lifted his boot to show how sticky was the soil, and laughed again. His men laughed with him. Then they stopped as the leader studied the party. "And where are you bound, good sirs and ladies?"

It was Giles who replied, "We journey to Nottingham for the fair, to sell these chickens and homespun. We may be home tomorrow night if the roads are clear all the way."

Robin Hood said nothing, but continued to scan the party, and then to stare at Rose. The girl blushed and lowered her face, peeping past the edge of her bonnet.

Giles did not like the probing stare. "Might we not go on, good master? We've nothing but our wares and a few coppers. I've heard Robin Hood and his men did not trouble honest souls." His wife nudged him, but he went on, "And I see no reason why your men should have their arrows bare."

Robin Hood caught the horse's bridle. The animal disliked the touch and tossed up her head. Hanging on, Robin of Sherwood turned slowly and addressed his men. "Get rid of those arrows, lads."

Abbey shrieked as the archers drew to full nock and took aim. The two men and the oldest boy had only time to grunt with surprise. The grunts exploded as the shafts were buried in their chests. The arrow that pierced Robert exited his back to prick his wife in the liver. Stitched together, husband and wife toppled from the dancing horse.

"Daggers on that lot, and quick!" shouted Robin, and the outlaws drew as they skipped forward. Abbey and the boys threw up their hands as the three outlaws set to. They stabbed down again and again as if killing mice in a flour bin. Their blades thudded against the bottom of the cart. Chickens squawked as they were crushed against the sides. Giles tugged at the arrow that was killing him. As

Robin Hood came close, Giles reached for his daughter, but the outlaw chief slid a sword through him. He toppled onto the cart tongue, then rolled off it to the ground. Robin Hood stepped past and hacked at the wife's head to end her screaming. Robert's horse ran away as the outlaws cut throats and blood spurted in the road.

Throughout the massacre the girl Rose had frozen and shrunk like a fawn under a bush. Robin Hood left his sword stuck in the mother and grabbed the girl by the neck of her chemise.

"Don't worry, lass," he hissed through clenched teeth. "We won't kill you." Tearing her clothes away, he wrenched her from the cart seat.

Chapter 6

Robin Hood and Little John crossed an invisible line. They had walked through climax forest with oak trees that were five or more feet thick. Suddenly before them were trees not a foot thick, and they stood amid brush and scrub. This dividing line was as sharp as if cut with a knife, and it followed the top of a slope.

"My father never let his serfs cut past this line. He left the big trees for me, because he knew how I loved them."

Little John nodded.

Robin led his friend to a sandy shelf where they could see. They overlooked a small valley. The new growth around them continued down the slope and across the bottom, then rose until it met the deeper woods on the far side. The road out of the intervale was just a slash in the timber. It looked impassable. At the head of the valley were the ruins of a hall.

The sun was warm on this southern face, so the two outlaws sat down with their backs against a bank. Birds flitted across the valley before them, and the smell of growing grass was strong and sweet. The two men had come north in search of food. They had managed to buy a small sack of rye and some dried apples. On the way back, Robin had chosen a path that led here, and Little John had followed.

Robin pointed, his thick finger one long callous along

the inside. "There was a mill over there, powered by a dam—that hump there. That paddock there was always boggy, so we left it for the cattle. We kept goats tethered on the slopes around, to keep the brush down, and let pigs loose in the woods. They'd grow big as horses on the acorns, and it was the devil's task to run them to ground."

Little John yawned, but Robin kept talking.

"My father disliked a moat. He said they bred mosquitoes. So we had a dry one. See the briars in a line? The sculleries set bread down there to rise. We had a drawbridge, but it was used so seldom the cranks got rusty and finally didn't work. In all the time Huntingdons lived here, there was never a siege."

Little John grunted.

"My father was a good man. He was a good lord to his people. There wasn't a harvest went by but the Earl of Huntingdon didn't cut wheat to save it from the rain. I learned the scythe before the sword. Other lords spent their time scheming to steal their neighbors' land and gold, but they went hungry in the spring. My father cared for the land and the people, and they rewarded him. That was before the crops failed, of course. My father was loved by the people. Not so good at collecting taxes maybe, but a good ruler. I remember sitting by his chair as he handed down judgements." Robin took on his father's voice. " 'No dowry, Master Ham? Well, we can't have Lucy lose her young man for lack of silver. How's this: after she's settled, Lucy delivers us enough of her Irish linen to make my wife a dress? That would make us quits, don't you think? Master Henry, Master Hugh—since you can reach no compromise, I grant the pig to Rupert and his family. They need it more than you two. They'll deliver you each a ham at Michaelmas. And I hope the taste washes the bitterness out of your mouths. What, sergeant?' (That was Will Stutly.) 'No arguments to settle today? All those people out there are content with their neighbors? Maybe I should raise taxes and create a little strife. Ha, ha, ha. Ah, well, I must take young Robin fishing, then. Maybe we can keep Will from falling in this time, eh, lad? Ha, ha, ha . . .' "

Robin Hood's laughter ran out. A growly murmur sounded at his side. "A good man, all right. Like his son. Worries o'ermuch, is all." Little John had sunk by inches until he was sprawled full length on the grass. His great quarter-staff leant against the bank. Robin reflected how like a lion was Little John: he could fall and nap, leap up and fight. He was even colored like a lion, his tawny hair drawn in a long braid down his back. John was a true child of nature, with a brown face and brown clothes, always calm, always content, never cold, never hot. He went bare-headed all year. And although Robin had been fed well as a child, and had grown tall and straight, he could barely touch the top of his friend's head.

Robin looked out over the valley. "It's a strange life we lead, John."

Little John chuckled. "It's an honest life and a full one. Where's the problem in that?"

Robin smiled at himself. "Nowhere, I suppose. Sometimes it just seems so detached from God's plan. We run around in the woods, we shoot at the Sheriff's men. We rob from merchants who wander through—and they'll be fewer of those if we get any better—but we accomplish no more than the deer."

" 'Be like unto the lilies of the field, they do not sow—'

"I know. But none of it is lasting. We've a permanent camp, collecting children and building homes, but we can't till the soil, nor do we build anything permanent. Where's the glorification of God?"

"We live as did Our Lord. Simply. We help as we can."

"I know. We rob from the rich and give to the poor, and the rich take it away again. And we're cut off. Most people are afraid of us because we live in the woods. If it weren't for Tuck we'd have no guidance at all. And what a flock! A grander bunch of misfits you never saw."

"Misfits?" With his hands folded over his breast, John looked like a giant's child dropped from the clouds.

Robin waved a hand. "Look at them! A mad Scotsman cohabiting with a Welsh witch. Look at your cousin Arthur there. He was a forester for the king. He might have been one of the men who cut off David's ears. One day he meets you, and *thump!* joins up, brings his whole family without a second thought. If they catch him, they'll hang him twice. Ben Barley came to Sherwood just to escape his debts. We've two women who are afraid of sex; foundlings; idiots; and who knows what. My cousin Will with his son coming up makes a pair of fools. And Bart! Bart! Just having him *around* invites the wrath of God."

John yawned cavernously. "That's all true. But it's neither here nor there. They're all loyal. They all love you. They'll follow you anywhere and fight when you need them."

"But why me?" Robin had his hands in the air again. "Why do they follow me? Every time there's a crisis, people turn to me as if I were Caesar himself. 'What shall we do, Robin?' Half the time I hardly know what to do myself. Why should anyone listen to me?"

"It's 'cause ye have vision. Most folks are empty vessels waiting to be filled. Like oxen at the yoke. Normally they look after themselves. They get food and they stay out of the rain, and they're safe enough. But comes trouble, they ask where to go and go where they're told. Face it, Rob, you're one of them what's got ambition and direction. You're the wind . . . and we're birds before it . . ." John's voice tapered off.

"I'm full of wind, all right, like a German eating beans. Sometimes I just wonder where—"

A loud snore cut him off. Robin Hood looked down at his friend.

"Well, they don't listen all the time, thank God," he muttered.

He stood and stretched. He watched the valley. Everything was still except for the snoring. Leaving Little John behind, Robin Hood picked up his bow and walked down the slope.

As a boy, Robin Locksley had spent almost all his time in the woods, sometimes with old Will Stutly, sometimes with Marian Fitzooth, but always larking under the leaves until sunset, returning tired and dirty with something shot from his bow, or some new scrape that needed mending. His mother would hug him, unmindful of the dirt and bloodstains, and his father would ask about each path taken, every animal sighted, every new hill and glade the boy had discovered. Now the boy, as a man called Robin Hood, returned home with none but field birds and butterflies to welcome him.

Robin Hood pressed through the brush of the moat. Dead leaves and briars crackled at every step. Clambering onto the tumbledown stone at the gate, he traced the line where the walls had stood. Ivy and honeysuckle covered the rubble. The tallest structure was a worn staircase that went only to the sky. Young trees stood where the main hall had been.

Robin stared at the trees. The sun disappeared overhead, and it got chillier. Vines clutched at his feet and mice scattered as Robin pushed to the biggest oak in the hall. It was nine inches through at chest height. It must be one hundred years old. Robin laid a hand on the bark. The tree was warm. He shoved at the trunk and found it solid.

"You wonder how it grew so soon."

Robin Hood jumped so suddenly he dropped his bow. He spun to face a man he had never seen before.

The man was very tall—almost as tall as Little John. He wore a tight doeskin shirt without sleeves and equally tight doeskin trousers. His belt was of twisted bark. Amidst thorns and bracken he wore no shoes. He carried no weapons. His face was broad and sun-brown but without lines; the face of an emperor. Brown shaggy hair was shoved back like a mane. When he moved, Robin sensed his whole person was alive with power, as if he took energy from the surroundings, and was ready to burst into life like a handful of black soil. The man's eyes were brighter than emeralds.

"Who the hell are you?" barked Robin.

There was a long pause as the man listened to the world around him.

Robin Hood picked up his bow. "I asked who you are! What are you doing here?"

After another long pause, the man spoke. "This is open forest."

"This is the land Huntingdon, where my father was earl. This land is mine." Robin was ashamed of the heat in his voice, but he was not over the fright of being surprised.

Again there came the pause. Robin could not get the man's full attention. In a voice like the sough of fire on a still night he intoned, "The Earl of Huntingdon is dead."

Robin wanted to curse but didn't. "The earl is alive, for I am he! Who are you to say me nay?"

"Huntingdon is dead." And when he said it, Robin believed him. Without the sun he was colder than ever. The green man continued. "Sherwood took the boy. The boy took Sherwood. Sherwood destroyed Huntingdon and his hall. She grew Robin Hood. Now thee own no land. The land Sherwood owns thou. Sherwood will have its protectors."

Robin Hood took a step towards the man but stopped himself. He held his bow upright before him and squeezed as if to strangle it. "But why? What had any of us done? We worked hard and worshipped well. What ever did my father or mother do to you or anyone? God, man, *why?*"

The stranger crooked a hand in a gesture Robin had never seen before. No, he thought, he'd never seen a man do it. The crooked hand was the cocked hoof of a deer ready to fly. The man said, "Know thee, Robin Hood, that as thee are with Sherwood, so Sherwood is with thou." Robin opened him mouth to speak, but no words came out. The brillant man turned, slowly, and walked away, stepping high, slipping through the brush without disturbing it. He moved onto a stone block, leapt light as a stag to the top of the wall, and sprang away, all unhurried. Robin Hood stood and watched the empty wall.

He was still watching when someone touched his shoulder.

"*Gaaahhh!*" His great bow went flying.

"You're touchy," said a growly voice.

"John!"

The giant blocked out the sky. He yawned. "Sorry, Rob. Couldn't keep me eyes open. This sun 'as bewitched me."

Robin Hood pointed at the wall. "John! I just met the Green Man! Hern!"

John peered. "Oh? What did he look like?"

Robin spread his hands. "He was dressed like a deer. Wrapped in buckskin. He had no shoes, here, in these briars. And he had the greenest eyes."

"No antlers?"

"Antlers?"

"Tha' say the Green Man has antlers." John rested his quarterstaff against his chest, put his thumbs to his temples and spread his fingers.

Robin shivered. "No, he didn't have antlers."

"What d'd he say?"

"He said . . . he said a lot . . . That I wasn't the Earl of Huntingdon any more. That Sherwood needed a protector, which I guess is me . . . There was more." Robin thought hard. "Ah! He said that—Sherwood was with me if I were with Sherwood."

"Oh. That's nice." Little John took his staff in both hands. "What say we get home."

Robin was in a fog. Why couldn't he remember? "Uh, yes. Let's." Robin Hood ascended the wall and looked around. He could see a fair distance, but only tall grass and Black-eyed Susans and insects moved. He hopped down the wall and through the moat, and without a backward glance at the ruined hall, entered Sherwood Forest.

"Let's have a story!" cried a child.

The girls abandoned their cat's cradle. "Yes, let's!"

"Who's to tell it?"

"Who?"

"Yes, who? Who?"

"You sound like a lot of owls," commented Old Bess.

The outlaws rested in the main hall. Evening tasks went on: fletching, filing, mending, dozing. Bess soaked her feet in a bucket. Will Stutly and Robin played chess. The flock of children swept from person to person, laying on grimy hands, imploring. The only one they didn't ask was Bart. Robin Hood was storied out. He was begging off when Will Scarlett walked in from the dark. "It's Will's turn!" he called.

Instantly the children circled Scarlett, shrieking. The man in red put his hands in the air. "I surrender, noble Sheriff! I confess! I took your gold! I had your daughter! Lock me away in your dungeon, where it's quiet!" Giggling, the wood elves dragged him to a bench and pushed him down. He waved them to settle down. "Sit, sit. You, too, Tam." His son was trying to push Tub aside on the bench. Will shot out his foot and Tam sat down hard. "Thank you. Now, are we all here? Where's Polly?" The girl was in her father's cabin. Rachel ran to fetch her while the children fidgetted.

From his settle by the fire, Friar Tuck muttered sleepily, "I hope this will not be another of your blasphemous tales. Or rude."

Robin inserted, "I'll put up with blasphemous and rude as long as it's exciting."

Rachel and Polly ran up breathless and sat down. Tub piped up, "Can you tell us about the time you were running starkers in Nottingham?"

Tam made a fist at the fat boy, but the others laughed. With a plain face, Will asked, "Who told you about that?"

"Robin did!" the children called. "Tell us, tell us!"

Bess peered at him across the room. "Yes, son," she said, "tell us. We'd all like to hear that one."

Will Scarlett grinned. "Let's see. One day around the Feast of—"

"We're only joking, Will!" cried Robin. But the children shouted even louder.

Scarlett waved a hand that cast a huge shadow in the firelight. "Naw, naw, never mind. It's not much of a story. And I'd have to leave out the best parts. Tell you what. I'll tell you a story about the gods. Ancient gods. They were like people, only funnier." Tuck jerked awake and started to object, but Will hurried on.

"This is the story of the strongest man that ever lived. He was stronger than Little John even."

"No!" gasped the children. Across the room, where he peeled small arrows, Little John chuckled.

"Yep! Now this feller—this god—his name was Hercules . . ."

Hercules was the son of a god (little gods, like angels) named Jove, and a woman from Earth. She was normal, like us, you see. Hercules's mother lived way to the south of here, past Canterbury, in a land called Spain, where it's so warm it never snows. Now this Jove came down one day, and he knew this woman. (It means he took her to bed. Now hush.) This little bugger Hercules was the result. Of course, he was born on the wrong side of the blanket, but then most nobles are.

Now when Hercules was a baby his mother used to take him down to the ocean every day. He was a heavy sod, and a messy eater, it was the easiest way to clean him off. She'd hold him by the heel and dunk him like you'd wash a pair of hose. And the patron saint of the sea, St. Paul, saw to it that the salt toughened the little titch up. In fact, one night when his mother was napping, the devil sent a sea serpent to eat the child. But the little baby thought the monster's nose was a plum hanging over him, and he bit it clean off. That's why sea serpents ain't got noses. (Which they ain't, right? What do you mean you don't know? Ask Robin, he'll tell you. There. See?)

Anyways, this Hercules was tough, but he was a stupid clot. One day when he was a little boy his mother sent him to milk the cow. Hercules didn't know how to do it, so he put his back under the cow's arse and lifted her up to get her udders over the milk pail. It was just a little cow at the time. Hercules held that cow in the air and squeezed her to get the milk out. Every day he did this. And every day, of course, that cow got a little bigger, and Hercules got a little stronger. By the time Hercules and the cow were grown, he was as strong as ten men, cause that's how many it takes to pick up a cow, which you would know if you've ever tried to get one over a fence in the middle of the night.

One day Hercules's mother sent him to pick some apples. As I said, Hercules was strong. He had muscles sticking out all over. But he was kinda thin between the ears. Standing under a tree, he found he couldn't reach the apples. So what does he do? (No, he doesn't shoot 'em with an arrow.) He just rips up the whole tree and brings it back to the house. Which worked out fine, because applewood is the best thing for fires. And shields. From then on, whenever his mother sent him out for walnuts or pears or anything, he just ripped up the trees and brought them back. But of course, trees started getting a little scarce in the neighborhood, so he had to go farther and farther to get food. One day he came upon this wall, and he looked through a crack, and saw a tree full of golden apples. So, he rips down the wall, pulls up the tree like you'd pick a flower, and brought it back to his mother (A boy's best friend is his mother), who was very surprised, because it's not every day you find golden apples on trees. (You ever see any?) So they used the gold to buy clothes and food and sack and such.

But it turned out that tree belonged to the King of Spain. The king had always been mad for gold, and he'd made a deal with the devil (You crosses *this* way, Glenyth.) that whatever he wanted would turn to gold with just a touch. He just stuck out a finger and *ping!*—gold. That's how he'd made the golden apples. In fact, his whole castle and everything in it was gold, including his teeth. (His chamberpot got frightful cold at night.) But for all that gold he had, he wanted more, which makes him like a certain sheriff we could name. And when he—the king—heard about his tree getting stole, he ordered his soldiers to bring Hercules in.

Ten of the ugliest soldiers in the land went to get this Hercules fella. Hercules was outside his mother's house, collecting water by squeezing rocks, and when he saw them coming, he picked up the jawbone of an ass to use as a club. The soldiers ran at him with their spears, and Hercules ran at them with his jawbone, but poor Herc never got in a single lick. For as soon as he raised his club, the stink from his armpits killed all ten men.

Now when the king heard that, he was mighty afraid. He figured he better invite this Hercules to his castle so they could talk. (No, that's not what I'd do either, Polly, but that's what he done.) So Hercules set off for the castle, after kissing his mother goodbye. As he was passing through France, a place *rotten* with thieves, he ran into some highwaymen. They wasn't the good kind like we are, but the bad kind what kills people for fun. But Hercules grabbed up those rogues and threw them away like you'd toss a stick, and the poor buggers came down in Arabia three days later.

Just before he got to the castle, by the way, Hercules had to cross a river, and when he did he lost one of his sandals. (That's a shoe with just a bottom . . . Oh, right, right.) Anyway. This was a great coincidence, because the King of Spain had had a dream that a man with one sandal would come to the castle and steal away his daughter, who was a beautiful woman (looked like Marian) named Cassandra. So when Hercules came into the castle, all wet and with only one sandal, the king almost watered his codpiece. He wanted to get Hercules out of there fast. So he said, "I want you, Hercules, to perform, uh, seven labors for me. If you don't do what I say, I'll have your mother imprisoned." So Hercules had to do what the king said. (*Because.* If Hercules just bashed the king on the head and went home, I wouldn't have no more story to tell. Now belt *up!*)

The king says, "The first thing I want you to do is to kill the Mycean Lion." That was a lion who was extra big and was always tearing up the flocks. So Hercules set out. After a time he finally caught up with the lion. He shot every arrow he had at it, but that only made the lion mad. Turns out nothing could penetrate his skin. It was hard, like iron, and arrows bounced off. As you might guess, Hercules was kinda surprised, and here came the lion. Herc threw down his bow and started running. He ran so fast, with that lion ready to bite his arse off, that he ran straight off a cliff. He and the lion hit the water, and that lion with his heavy skin sank like a rock. Hercules waited until it was drownded, then he dragged it ashore. He turned the lion inside out and peeled the skin off. And he wore that skin everywhere, because it was like a coat of mail. Besides, it stank so bad that on hot days no one could get within spitting distance without fainting.

Next the king sent Hercules out to kill the hygra. The hygra was a sort of a dragon with seven heads, and if you chopped one off, another would grow in its place right away. *Pop!* just like that. And the heads had fangs and teeth and poisoned stingers and big buggy eyes. Hercules found the thing living in this deep, black swamp, and sure enough, when he cut off one head another popped out quicker than a turtle's. Hercules didn't know what to do about that, and here it came, just like that damned lion. He caught one head in one hand, and another in the other, but there were still more heads going for him, and they was going to bite him where it hurt. Without thinking about it (or much else), he stuffed one head into another head's mouth. It worked so well that he did it again, and again. Finally, when he stuffed the last head into the last mouth (there were eight heads, then, I guess), the thing disappeared *pop!* like a bubble. And that was that. Hercules went back to the king.

The king wasn't pleased to see Hercules back, so he sent him out to challenge Achilles. Achilles was the biggest man on Earth, and it was his job to hold up the sky.

Hercules found him on top of a mountain, all stooped over and cranky. Achilles was having a terrible time keeping the sky in place, and you could hear him complain all the way to the walls of Jerusalem. Hercules didn't think the sky could weigh all that much—what is it but air and a few clouds, after all—and he said so. Achilles lost his temper at this little nubbin, and he said, "Oh, yeah? Let's see you hold up the sky!" and he tossed it to Hercules. Hercules caught the sky, but not before it dipped a little, so low that it broke off the top of the king's castle in London. But Hercules balanced the sky carefully, and he yelled, "There, see? One hand!" and he threw the sky back to Achilles. This time it dipped low enough that it knocked off the weathervane atop Nottingham castle. (You've noticed there wasn't one, haven't you?) Achilles propped up the sky on just his first finger and thumb, and said he'd like to see Hercules do *that*! And he threw it back, so low that some of the clouds spilled onto the ground, and that's why we have fog. (What? No, it hasn't been used up yet.) Hercules wasn't about to be beaten, so he caught the sky and held it with just his *little finger*. And Achilles got all red in the face and shouted, "I can hold up the sky with NO hands!" So Hercules tossed the sky back, and Achilles stuck out his head, and of course the sky crashed down on his brain pan and knocked him out. Hercules propped the giant there, with his back to the mountain and the sky resting on his stummick. He stole Achilles's red hose and took 'em with him to show the king he'd beaten him.

Now the king was in a panic, and he sent Hercules off to kill the minotaur, which was a beast what had the head of a bull and the body of a man. Oh! it was uglier than a bagful of assholes! It lived (What? I didn't say that. Hush.) it lived in a bunch of caves that were all twisty, so twisty that a person would get lost forever walking around in there. But Hercules met a friend who told him the secret, and that was to take a ball of yarn and unravel it as he walked. Hercules did that, and soon enough he found the minotaur, eating a whole bale of hay and waiting for someone he could tear up, just for fun. As soon as the beastie saw Hercules, he charged. Hercules screamed and covered up his head. But his shield was on his arm, and it was bronze, polished like a mirror, and the shine blinded the minotaur The thing couldn't see, and it smashed its head against the tunnel wall and got killed. So Hercules followed the trail of yarn and found his way out.

The king tried to think of other impossible things for Hercules to do, but none of them worked. He told him to bring a whale from the bottom of the sea, and Hercules caught one, and dragged it back across the land and stuffed it into the king's kitchen so that the serfs had to walk around on the thing's ribs and cut away steaks from the inside. The king sent him to catch Charon, the three-headed dog that guarded the gates of Hell, and Hercules brought the dog back alive so that it ate two or three soldiers a day.

The king was done. He didn't want to send Hercules out on another mission for fear he'd fulfill it. He just wanted to get rid of him. So he told Hercules to clean the stables for right now. These stables were immense, and they had been there a long time, and no one could keep up with the manure, so the horses were belly deep in the stuff. Hercules would have fainted for the smell if he hadn't smelt so bad himself. He stood there for a while, looking at the wrong end of a bunch of horses, and he thought he'd play a little joke on the king. So he picked up one end of the stable and shook it. Well, children, let me tell you, hundreds of hundredweights of horseshit came sliding out of that stable and crashed onto the castle and piled up until you couldn't see the highest gable. It took the king and his men a fortnight to dig their way out. The king looked around at his castle, and he had had enough, and he said that Hercules was out of debt, and would he please go home and stay there.

But by now Hercules had learned a thing or two, and he said that he liked it here, and could he stay and become one of the king's retainers? The king said no, and he offered anything, anything at all, if Hercules would just go away. So Hercules settled for marrying the king's daughter, taking half the king's gold (he could just make more, so what did he care?), and taking the land to the north of Spain for his home.

So Hercules settled in a fine castle, and married Cassandra, and got his mother to come live with him. And he had twenty-two children, because strong wasn't all he was. He lived to be one hundred and four, and do you know why? (No. No. No.) It was because he always ate the food that was put in front of him, and never, ever, *once* complained.

Will Scarlett leaned forward and lowered his voice so only the children could hear. The adults however, craned forward too, including Friar Tuck.

"Does anyone know the moral of that story?" he whispered.

"No," breathed the little faces.

"What's a moral?"

"Don't ask him," chimed Robin. "He has no morals."

"The moral of that story, children, is that sometimes being stupid is smart."

"Hunh?"

"Now off to bed!"

"*Awwwwww . . .*"

Chapter 7

The dog picked up his head. Something was coming.

This was the outermost farm of a belt around Nottingham. The dog's territory took in a little more than the farm. It extended along the edge of the woods, down the road to a ditch, back to a strip of winter rye, then to the woods. The dog marked it with urine and dung every morning. Today there had been the usual activity. A mole was swimming upwards through the earth, and would exit at the corner of the barn. The cow licked the walls of her byre. Tiny chickens poked at the manure pile after maggots. Mosquito eggs in the ditch continued to hatch: they would be painfully abundant by the day after tomorrow. But a party of swallows was working its way out from Nottingham and a bat family's young were about ready to fly, so perhaps the mosquitoes would not be so thick. Two horses had gone by on the road, and the dog had rapped at them all along his borders. Three territories over a ewe had lambed twins, and a fox had gotten the afterbirth. A man with cancer had minced past. A grey owl had hooted from the top of an ash tree but then flown on, deeper into the woods. The dog's master had this morning fed him porridge left by the baby, and the dog had snagged a mouse who had been too fascinated by the cat. He had licked the baby's bum when it was put outside. The dog watched it with half an eye to see it ate no plants at the edge of the yard. In the house, the woman prepared leek soup with lots of water. She was in heat, and if the man mounted her this night, would conceive. Likewise, a smallish bitch close to the town would come into her first heat in a few days. If the breeze held, it would rain over Nottingham by noon, but only a little water would fall here. There were minor tremors underfoot as the last frost seeped from the ground. The dog had tracked all these things, and more.

Now this something was coming from the woods. The dog, a large brindled mongrel, left his patch of sunlight and aimed his nose. The wind was behind him, the wrong direction, so he watched and waited. A tangle of blackberry leaned out too far. Whatever it was, it was tall, to a man's waist at least. A horse? A cow from the woods? A snatch of sound came: the chafing of brush against bony shanks. The dog felt and heard cloven hooves tread the earth. They were put down heavily. The stretch between them was long. A large pig, then. The dog considered for a moment, then gave his happy bark. That would bring the man without frightening the pig. He repeated it four times until he heard the man put down his manure fork in the barn. The pig stepped along the blackberry bushes. The dog could see where it poked its face against them to sniff. The man joined the dog, clutching a club and asking. The dog skipped in a circle and pointed to the woods, barking happily. If his master would fetch other men, they could surround the boar while he baited it. He had baited other pigs and only been lightly bitten, never slashed. The man peered at the woods.

Then the boar broke cover.

The man dropped his club and ran for the house. The dog stood frozen as the boar charged. This was not how a pig behaved. It should first circle and approach obliquely, advancing with teeth and tusks foremost, grunting and bluffing, looking for something to steal all the way. This boar came in a straight line. The dog curdled its nose and rapped an angry bark over and over. His ears laid back along his skull. He hunkered his head and thrust out his lower jaw. Hair along his shoulders erected to make him look bigger. He skidded his back feet against the soil for a better grip. The boar would stop short at fifteen feet, then the dog would lunge and drive him back. No pig had ever stood up to him. At the most he would have to snap at its snout or endanger the eyes to make it retreat. The door slammed behind him, and the bar shot home. The cow lowed in fright and chickens scattered. The boar came on.

As it approached, the dog's senses brought him strange information. The boar smelt and felt and sounded and looked all wrong. It came very fast and straight, as if ridden like a horse. It had a lame back leg, and the irregular drumming of that leg irritated the dog. The boar was huge, bigger than the dog had ever seen or imagined. As it got closer, the dog smelled all of it. There was day-old blood on the muzzle and in the shit along its shanks: blood of human babies and squirrels and other pigs and more. A dull gleam had the animal's eye. It grunted as the feet pounded, and the grunting had an alien sound like human language, like a chant. At the closest, the dog could read madness in its mind like brain worms: a smokey and ancient hatred for all things civilized. The knots of its face were runes of death, carved in wode and fiery snow. The sour blood in its veins drummed a charge. And still it came on.

The dog knew he had lost before they ever touched. Animals do not fight to kill, but to determine who is the stronger. An animal seeks to conserve energy and thus conserve its individual life and that of its species, so animal contests are loud and unharmful. They decide a victor—who should mate, who should stay celibate—without pain or injury or danger of infection. But this boar was playing by no rules. The dog spun and slunk low to the ground and ran.

The boar bowled him over with a smash of its shoulder. The dog scrabbled to his feet as the boar hit him again. The dog snapped in pure reaction. The boar never flinched.

It ground and champed its teeth. Great gobs of saliva broke from its mouth to clump on the ground and the dog's flanks. The dog hopped sideways and collided with the side of the barn. He hadn't even known they had come this far, and now the pig had him trapped. It opened its fetid mouth and clamped down on the dog's hind leg. The muscles along the groin parted one by one. The dog snapped again, but the boar's ribs were tough and tight. The animal loomed over the dog like a house. The pig bit again. In pain and terror, all training and learning left the dog and he reverted to a puppy's instinct. He flopped on his back and drew his legs aside, spilled a few drops of urine. This had been his first act for his mother, for her to lick him and keep the nest clean. It had been the act of his juvenile months, to submit to older dogs and know his place. Trapped between the rock walls of the barn and the warm earth and a mountain of meat, his senses jammed full of the stench of boar and blood and dung, the pounding of its heart and clashing of its teeth, the dog's mind fell away and he returned to the only behavior he knew.

The pig swung its head and bit and bit and bit.

Chapter 8

Marian, Bess, and Katie let the horses amble along the road, picking their way over rocks and ruts. It was early morning on the last day of March. Bird song and squirrel chat were loud. The road in this part of Sherwood was only five feet wide, but straight for the most part. Overhanging branches were fuzzy with tiny pale leaves: they were awash in a green fog. Marian rode with Katie behind. The two of them were in trousers and tunics like men, with sweaters on top. They wore none of the Lincoln green that marked Robin Hood's band. They'd removed their hats and let their hair loose. Tall arrows stuck up past their heads. Old Bess, in skirts and wimple, hung onto her horse's mane and let the reins lie. The horses were matched brown, rented from a friend at the edge of Sherwood on the condition the outlaws not eat them. The women had only blankets on the animal's backs, for the farmer had no saddles for his plowhorses. Though matched in color and yoked in a common harness, the beasts were different in temperament. Bess had the gentler mare. Marian's stallion required a firm hand and the weight of an extra rider to keep it from taking off. The horses clumped along, far enough apart so as not to lurch together, but close enough that the riders could talk.

"Aye," said Old Bess, "a cuter bugger I've yet to see. Spittin' image of his father."

"Does that make the old man any prettier?" Marian teased. They had to raise their voices above the forest song.

Bess made a wry face. "I suppose he must have somethin' about him to produce such a fair young'un. I never did think that boy would work out, but, Lord, I suppose."

The three returned from the distant town of Derby, west of Nottingham, where Bess's daughter and son-in-law had a farm. Gloria had been heavy with child in the fall, and Bess had worried about the issue all winter. Now there was a healthy boy named Will. They'd had an untroubled visit, but this fifth day away found them homesick for camp.

Bess's voice bobbed with the steps of the horse. "No, I'd have to say he's a good enough lad, all t'gether. He works from sun to sun and after, he don't drink ov'r much, and he don't beat 'er."

"He'd better not," Katie interjected from behind Marian.

Marian smiled. "Right there, lass, he'd better not."

They listened to the sweet cacophony of song for a while. "Lord," Bess remarked, "a body'd think every bird in Sherwood was on this road. What are they all about?"

Marian just murmured dreamily. Presently she said, "That man Bowen. He certainly took a fancy to you, didn't he, Bess?"

The old midwife laughed. "Oh, him. Just another old man with nothing to do. His son dotes on him. Won't even let him work the fields, he told me. Limits himself to cleaning skins and mending tools, telling the young'uns stories. And taking nips at the cider. Useless, like me." She laughed again.

"Oh?" said Marian innocently. "He seemed a hale and lusty man. He certainly didn't mind walking up to see you."

"Another fool with nothing better to do than chase women."

"Shame a man like that is widowed."

Bess started to laugh, but it came out a sigh. "Aye.

Probably drove his wives to an early grave. He had two, you know."

"Overworked them, I suppose." Marian said. The two women did not look at one another, but they both smiled.

"Aye, he kept his wives busy, or rather, they were always, uhh . . . busy."

Marian studied the sky, a rich, bright blue full of water and sunlight. The smell of growing leaves and turned earth was so heady she could have drunk it. The rain and now the sun would bring out the bugs in their millions any day now, but this day was perfect. She said, "It certainly was busy once we got there. All that talking and visiting and story telling. And there were some nights I swear the door opened of its own account. Someone downstairs there had to get up and close it a couple times a night. I thought that mighty queer."

Bess straightened her wimple. "Oh, that. Just that stupid hound. The daft bugger would push the bar loose with his nose. Then the door just hung open until someone closed it. Enough to give an old woman the pees getting her feet cold."

The two women laughed gaily. Katie was profoundly quiet.

Bess had to wipe her eyes from the laughing. "Speakin' o' the pees . . ." And she started to roll off her horse.

"Awps," said Marian. "Company."

Bess regained her seat as the women peered down the trail. The road ahead angled upwards, and walking down towards them through the green haze was a pair of piebald legs. The women waited on their horses. They were not worried. Marian and Katie had bows and poinards, and Bess had a heavy bone-handled knife in a sheath Will Stutly had cobbled together. They stood their ground here because the line of sight was clear. The horses reached out to crop tender young leaves.

"Shall I hop off into the woods?" asked Katie. "I can nock an arrow." Marian told her not to bother. The man approaching them looked harmless. His hose was ragged from heel to belt, his shirt the same way. He wore shoes that were only soles and a cape of shapeless wool. So gaunt and threadbare was he, thought Marian, he could only be a student. His satchel would contain books or leaves and nothing else. The man came closer, oblivious, then stopped suddenly. He put both fists in front of one eye to make a tiny aperture. With this makeshift telescope he studied the party. Then he came on.

"Good day to you!" he called when within hailing distance. He added "Ladies!" when he was closer.

"Good day to you, Aristotle!" answered Marian. "It's a fine day for walking, is it not?" The women did not dismount. Up close Marian could see the man had had, or had now, some pox.

"True, true." He set fists on his hips and his clothes flapped. "I fear the insects will be out before much longer, but that makes today without them even better. He peered at Marian and Katie. "I see you are armed, and glad I am to see it. What with the perils of the road, one cannot be too careful."

"Perils?" Marian laughed. "What perils are these? Nodding off and tumbling from one's horse?"

"No, milady. I worry most about this plaguey boar. He's not likely to listen to reason as might others."

"Boar? Pray tell."

The student was pleased to be delivering news. "There is a monster boar haunting these byways. It comes out of the forest by day and by night, and destroys wantonly. It's killed pigs and dogs and calves, and savaged at least three people who got in its way. It's huge, big in the body as a cow they say, and it must be mad with brain worms or salt-lack. People now work and travel in pairs all around Nottingham, and keep long spears handy. Though in truth the best advice is to run at the first sound. And as I said, this boar is more the scourge, because you can't cry poverty to him as you can to Robin Hood."

"Robin Hood!" The horses stirred at the women's surprise.

"Aye. I met him on the road today, and as God is my

judge I was never more terrified. I'd heard he'd took to killing indiscriminately. But he spared my poor life."

Marian's mouth hung open. "Sir, how do you speak? What have honest people to fear from *Robin Hood?*"

"Milady, he's taken to *killing.* Haven't you heard? Robin Hood's as mad as this pig. He ambushed the Sheriff's party and killed half a dozen men. That in itself will grieve no one, but then he attacked two families on the Great North Road. The only one to survive was a girl of twelve, and she'd been beaten and ravished most grievously. Used for *days.* And a party of nuns never arrived in town, yet people knew whence they departed and whither they were bound. *Ut potens cadeo.*(*) But he spared me. He jumped me, looked me over, asked me a few questions, and let me go. He even laughed some, and joked about my clothing. I'll tell you, everything I hold dear gets offered to Saint Isidore as soon as I may."

The three women sat stunned, spellbound. Finally Bess managed to say, "Marian, what can it mean?"

Robin Hood's wife was at a loss. "I know not. Some—"

But the student now stared like a chicken at a snake. His head jutted forward. His myopic eyes were wide. He said, "Marian? Marian!" Then suddenly he was off like a swallow out of a barn, past them and running down the road, shoes and cape flapping, mud flying out in clumps behind.

"By the Rood!" muttered Bess as they watched him go.

"Something's very wrong," said Marian. She yanked the horse's head around and kicked her heels. "Let's get along and see what's happening. Robin will know what to do about this."

The sun was approaching noon, but they delayed eating until they met up with Robin Hood. So far they had passed only one boy with some geese, and he had seen no one. Another two miles would bring them to the edge of

(*)"How the mighty are fallen."

the woods, in sight of Nottingham. This was the last brushy stretch of road, with high rocks to one side and a drop to the other. Marian mused that if Robin were anywhere, it would be—

"Stand, fair maidens!" came a hail touched with laughter. Four men stepped out of the brush, two with swords and two with bows at half-draw. Katie, afoot, hissed and nocked an arrow as smoothly as a blue jay preening a wing. Bess shifted in her seat and tossed the reins to the other side, away from the handle of her knife. Marian, ahorse, flexed her hand on her bow. What she saw rocked her brain like a blow. Two of them wore plain clothing. One man wore all red. The leader, with a sword, wore Lincoln green and a pheasant feather in his hat.

He walked up to her horse's head and took the bridle. "Nay, nay, fear not, ladies. We mean you no harm." He bunched the bridle in his fingers to hold the horse from bolting. The animal slammed the turf with heavy hooves. At the rear Katie backed away, swinging side to side as the men surrounded them. The leader grated, "Girl, drop that bow."

"Who are you?" demanded Marian.

He smiled like an angel. "We be the shades of Sherwood, milady, bold Rob—"

"Kill them!" Marian shouted, and she jabbed with her bow. A *twang* sounded behind her, and there came a grunt. Marian tried to hit the false Robin Hood in the face, but he deflected the blow with his arm while yanking wildly on the bridle. Marian made to jump off away from the leader, but misjudged and fell on her back. Arrows in her quiver snapped and fell out, but she held onto the bow. She scrambled to her feet like a cat. While the false Robin Hood was on the other side of the horse she looked to her charges. Threatened by the villain in red—who must claim to be Will Scarlett—Bess had fumbled out the carving knife and swiped at his head. The tip of the long blade nicked him on the ear before the knife clanged against his sword and spun away. Bess pulled frantically to wheel her panicked horse and crowd him. Katie's arrow had hit the first man high in the chest. He sat in the road looking down at it. The other archer loosed, as did Katie again. Both arrows whipped away into the green leaves of Sherwood. Marian pawed her long hair from her face. She had always worn it tied back if expecting trouble. Now she hoped it wouldn't adorn a corpse. She shuffled in the mud to keep the horse between her and the villain, and poked savagely at his legs under the horse's belly. In between maneuvers she watched Katie and Bess. The old woman and the false Scarlett went round and round, Bess's horse forcing him back, until the man stumbled in mud and fell. Katie and her foe nocked again, fast as drawing a breath. Fully aware of the danger at her back, Marian twisted and threw her bow. It struck the archer and made him loose the nock. Although the girl's breath whistled in her teeth, she had time to aim properly. Marian's own assailant roared and she spun. In Robin's green and Robin's pheasant feather, he got round the horse, brought up his sword, and came at her full tilt.

"WHORE!" he screamed, and drove straightarmed at the weaponless woman. Marian grabbed for her poinard, but it was gone. She sidestepped the lunge and reached for his arm as it went by. Marian heaved backwards to pull him off balance. He kept his feet. He tried to slam her with his body, but she held on. His eyes were mad with fury. He swung his sword arm high for a blow that would take her head off. Robin's voice rang in her ear, lecturing about hand-to-hand fighting: "Aim for the eyes or the throat. If a man can't see or breath, he's helpless as a babe." Marian Locksley's hands were as rough and calloused as a peasant's. She pulled at his arm and shoved with her legs, and her strong right hand hit the man's face like a spear. The index finger popped against his forehead as the middle and ring fingers rammed home in his eye socket. The false Robin Hood bellowed to shake the trees and wrenched himself loose of her fingers. Marian tasted a spurt of bile at the back of her throat. Backing away with giant steps, she stripped the ichor from her fingers, wiping them on her sweater again and again. Then she folded over and was sick in the road.

Above her own racking came other noise, but when she picked up her head the worst was over. Katie's foe had clapped a hand to his forehead and run for the brush. The man with the arrow through him lay on his back, twitching feebly. The thief in red was gone. The leader thrashed in the road, both hands pressed to his eye. He moaned and prayed and swore and screamed.

From atop her horse, Bess yanked Katie's hair to get her attention, but the girl was staring slack-armed. "Marian," Bess warbled, "we must away! That red devil lit for the bushes, but whether he's run away or gone for his bow I can't say! Hurry!"

Marian could not think clearly. She should dispatch the false Robin. And they should chase down the rest. But what if there were more of them? No, they would have been in on the initial attack. But two were unhurt. Bess was right: they had to flee now. And Marian had had enough fighting. Her knees and hands shook so badly she didn't know if she could climb a horse. With hysterical strength she shoved Katie up behind Bess and swatted at their horse. The beast started, then cantered away as Bess rammed in her heels. Marian looked for her own horse and saw trouble.

The beast was up against the rocks, ready to bolt after its mate. Stumbling in the mud, Marian spread her arms to block its path. Eyes rolling, the horse wheeled in a circle. Marian cooed and swore as the horse capered. It wanted away from the blood and the screaming, and it owed no loyalty to this frantic woman. Marian trapped it between herself and the downed man. The animal spun a half-circle, flattened its ears and prepared to kick. Marian was more frantic than ever. At any minute the red man or his partner might return. If that happened she would die. Another move forward and the horse would kick her brains out, or spin and get past her, leaving her stranded. "Easy,

easy," she cooed to its backside. The ears stayed flattened.
The beast watched from the back of its large eye, aiming.
She knew gentleness would work better than force here,
but there was no time! The horse whipped its tail in
warning. The hoof bobbed in the air, cocked. What would
Robin do? "Surprise him," his voice toned. She stepped
behind the horse into its blind spot, scooped a handful of
mud, and whipped it at the broad rump. Startled, the
horse jumped and tried to shove her away, but Marian was
past the feet. Slowed by the mud, she nonetheless snagged
the reins, grasped the base of the mane, and threw herself
across the horse's back like a child. The blanket slid off.
Marian had lost her bow and knife, but she couldn't stop
now. For a second she thought the horse would buck her
off, but she pointed him down the road and kicked. He
took off. Marian crouched low over his neck, expecting an
arrow in her back any second.

She caught up with the others a half mile ahead, and the
three kept going, casting behind them for pursuit. They
trotted almost two miles before they realized they had
missed the turnoff. Nottingham was ahead. They could not
enter the town together: Marian's face was too well known,
and she was in no mood to be clever. They halted the
horses and heard weeping. Katie clutched Bess around the
middle and blubbered unashamed. The old woman reached
a fat arm around to comfort her. "There, there, lass. It's all
right. You did fine. Wonderful, in fact." Katie's reply was
a series of gasps.

Marian pulled closer and rubbed the girl's back with her
left hand. Her sprained finger rang with pain. It had
swollen to twice its size and turned purple down to the
palm. "Aye, Katie," she quavered. She sucked a deep
breath. "You stopped two to our one. Wait'll they hear
that back in camp."

The girl cried more quietly. Bess asked, "What happened to the other one? He was pressin' his pate as he ran
away."

Katie huffed and sucked air. "I-I n-nicked 'im. Creased

him, 'cross—the brow. Oh, I'm a terrible shot!" she wailed. But the tears settled down to sniffles, and she rested her head against Bess's round back. She sighed. "Can we go home?"

Marian rubbed her finger and shook it. "Aye, let's."

Bess nodded back down the road. "What shall we do about them back there?"

Marian shook her head. "I don't know. We might have you or Katie tell the guards in Nottingham, but they'd probably hold you until they found the scoundrels." She fretted. "There's no one close by I can send to dispatch them, and that red one at least is unhurt."

"I nicked his ear," said Bess.

"Oh, good. Ummm . . . Best we get to Sherwood and tell Robin. He can set up a hunt for the lot. We'll skirt behind North's farm and be home before dark."

She clucked to her horse and they got moving. Bess handed Marian a water bottle. She uncorked it awkwardly with her left hand and rinsed her mouth. She was starving now. "We'll get some food there, too."

They came to the edge of the woods. Stone-walled fields, the earth fresh-broken and brown, lay before them, with cottages close to the road. Nottingham castle on its knoll could just be seen in the light haze. They cut along the edge of a field and slipped behind some spruce trees onto a deer trail. The sun was strong in this hollow corridor, and the warmth was flavored with evergreen resin. Bird song quieted as the sun topped the sky.

"Marian," said Bess suddenly, "did I hear right? Were those ruffians posing as Robin and Will and the rest of us?" She shook her head. "What will Robin say?"

Marian bit her lower lip. "I know what he'll say."

Chapter 9

The brown horse stumped along, his legs heavy. He would occasionally falter in his step. Horrid pictures flickered in the dim tunnel of his memory.

There had been green leaves and smell of foxglove. Sandstone had crunched under his hooves. They crossed a shelf of pebbles and heard birdcall. As always, the horse was thirsty for salt. A small stream scented with fern crossed the road. A small man approached, smelling of onions and fleas and sweat and sickness. He carried a bag of burlap that smelled of leather from a bull. Then the air was fresh again. Suddenly there were men whose pores stank of human blood and pain-giving. The horse shied. He had been nervous all day because the moisture in the air cut down his sense of smell. This giver of pain gripped the bridle of steel and beef leather around his teeth, and twisted to grind the bone in the upper jaw. The horse could not snort a warning. He tried to retreat, but the man held on. There were words around his head, but not for him. Then there was screaming and the smell of tears and a zipping of arrows made of goose feather and ash wood, and more human blood with its curdled smell of iron and fat. A howling like wolves raised the hair on his withers. Distorted people flashed by in the horse's rear view, and he spooked, mud gripping his feet and holding him down. Then his mate was smacked on the flank and she bolted, and he wanted to follow. The woman was in the way. A raving man with a pulped eye blocked flight in the other direction. The woman waved her arms. A bite would not suffice. The horse's thoughts stopped as automatic defenses took over. He spun and twisted his head to focus and presented feet that could stove a man's head in. If he could lash out properly he could get away. One hoof would be enough; two were not necessary. But the woman vanished. Then mud from somewhere struck him. A small boy used to throw rocks at him like that: for a moment the horse thought the boy had returned. He hopped sideways and the woman was alongside, smelling of straw and flowers and venison. The horse tried to shove her away with his ribs, but she was too nimble. She gained his back, but before he could buck she pointed him at the unobstructed road, and he picked up his feet and ran after his mate. They were running, then trotting, then halting. Then they walked, very slowly, where it was dry underfoot with evergreen needles. Here was the scent of spruce resin and starlings and field mice, hay far off, and cows and pigs eating last year's turnip greens. They followed a trail drummed by deer and frequented by foxes with kits. The rider was calm now, gripping the reins less tightly, giving no direction. Alongside the trail a rabbit thumped a warning and retreated down a hole.

The sun was warm on his flanks. Maybe there would be sorrel ahead. Maybe salt.

Chapter 10

Robin Hood strode through the drizzle with his people in tow. He had set twice a normal walking pace all this morning, and even his foresters, who could walk thirty miles in a day and dance that night, were hard put to keep up with him. Trailing the Fox of Sherwood were Arthur A'Bland, Shonet the Sower and her new husband David of Doncaster, Allan A'Dale, and Grace. There was no Will Scarlett or Bart with them to voice a complaint, so the party marched on sore legs while their leader blazed ahead like a forest fire.

Robin Hood paused when he got to the road. The party groaned as they sank down to rest, but the outlaw chief missed it. He studied tracks in the road under a trickling mist. "Let's go," he said, and he strode towards Nottingham. He had gone twenty paces before he realized he was alone. He stalked back to the party of outlaws.

"Get up, you lot!"

The party crouched on soggy ground amid wet bushes and avoided their leader's glare. No one individual could disobey Robin, but the group had reached an unspoken consensus. They were uneasy, but they stayed put. Robin showered them in silence harsher than words.

"Is this it?" he demanded. "Are we to sit here like toads while brigands and murderers besmirch our name? Shall we rest while they vanish like the night, so they might go elsewhere and ply their stinking trade?"

The only sound was the hiss of rain and the plink of drops falling around them. People flexed cold, pruney hands. Grace sighed, "I miss my loom," then clapped her mouth shut.

Shonet, who had been a prioress, spoke up softly. "Of course we want to find the brigands, Robin. We want them punished as much as you do. No one can sully the name of Robin Hood without answering to us all." Her bell-like voice was weak. She was white and pinch-lipped. "But we're tired. You've just walked us ten miles or more at a horse's gait. Can we not rest a moment?"

Robin huffed at the idea of rest and muttered under his breath. But he clipped out, "Very well," and leaned his back against a tree to stare at the road, as relaxed as a ballista cranked full.

David approached and said very low, "Robin, with your permission, I must take Shonet back to camp."

"Oh?" barked Robin. "Why?"

David avoided Shonet's pleading eyes. "She's not well."

Robin Hood turned and looked at the woman. "Oh," said he. "Yes, take her home. Of course. I'm sorry." Shonet did not protest any further as David led her away. Robin addressed the remainder of his party. "Take a rest, lads and lasses." But it was too cold and damp to stay immobile for long, and after a while someone let out a sigh and the party stood up. Robin Hood led them out onto the road at a milder pace.

They walked all that morning. They asked at farms and they asked the few travellers they met. Robin Hood talked very fast to people about the false brigands. Some people were convinced, and some were obviously not. All were cautious and afraid. Robin's mouth turned grimmer as the day passed. And they learned nothing about the masquerading knaves. They mustered their dinner in the rain: venison boiled for warm broth and two squirrels shot along the way. There was nothing else. After they had eaten, Arthur, a broad and slow-witted man, asked when they might return to camp. Robin Hood did not answer, for he did not know. Since Marian had come back with her tale, Robin Hoods's thoughts had dwelt entirely on how to punish the villains. It had never occurred to him that he might not catch them at all. There were two other parties along the roads looking, one under John and one under Gilbert. Someone would find them soon, but not, it seemed, Robin. Once he had digested this disappointment, he said, "I suppose we should start back soon. The days are longer, but not that much, and we're all wet and cold. The rogues are not in this end of the forest." He paused. "Although we've accomplished nothing, I thank you all for your aid."

The party muttered at that and found new energy in his words. They kicked apart their soggy fire and once more gained the road. But they had not marched long before Allan said, "Hush. What's that?"

Arthur the oldest and Grace of the town heard nothing, but Robin Hood did. It was the tack of many horses clinking, the sound carried on the mist. "Allan, go look," whispered Robin. He himself cast about, measuring the road with his eyes, gauging the cover, studying where to hide, and which escape routes to leave open. The minstrel trotted along the edge of the woods, hunkered down to peer through a stand of birch, then ran back silently.

"It's a party of monks," he explained in a whisper. "Perhaps forty, all ahorse. Mighty queer monks, though."

"How queer?" asked Robin.

Allan shrugged. "You'll see." The thud and plocking of shod hooves was clearer now. A crow left a branch with a *caw!*

Robin waggled his bow to the side of the road towards camp. Allan, Arthur, and Grace slipped behind the thickest scrub. Their green wool and brown leather made them invisible. Their leader however, stood in the middle of the road, and the outlaws wondered at that. Usually on a raid they all waited in hiding as Robin Hood gauged if the quarry were rich enough to bother. And never had four footloose outlaws tried to stop twenty men on horses.

The party that emerged around the bend was queer indeed; forty figures on many horses, all clad in black, all silent. Details resolved as they approached in the grey mist. Twenty monks rode in front. Their mounts were fine war horses, thick in the legs yet nimble. The men sat very tall and straight, and there wasn't one but had broad shoulders. Suspicious shapes were outlined by their robes. Behind the monks came the smaller figures of acolytes. They rode twenty hackneys and lead twenty more packed high. Half a dozen footsore dogs lagged at the rear. The forbidding troop rode up to the lone outlaw as if he did not exist.

The foremost rider stopped, and the others did likewise. This man, the tallest and straightest, on the finest horse, was presumably an abbot. No rod-shape showed under his kirtle, but a blockier shape that must have been fastened to his belt. The leader and his black party studied Robin where he stood with his bow stuck in the mud, his wrists draped across the top. The horses were nudged forward. A man to Robin's right said, "Move aside, lout!"

Robin Hood had felt reckless all morning, hoping for a confrontation with the felons he sought, or indeed anyone he might justifiably thrash. As this large and armed party had all but encircled him, he had second thoughts. But this slur was the last thing he needed. In one motion Robin Hood jerked up his bow, whirled it through an arc so fast it whistled, and laid it along the man's body with a resounding smack. The monk was tumbled from the saddle into the mud while his horse kept its place. Robin Hood scanned left and right, stuck his bow back down, then resettled his wrists across the top.

The fallen knight—as his mail skirt and scabbard revealed him to be—struggled upright and wrestled with his cassock to draw sword. Then he stopped. The large abbot had raised a hand. The bespattered knight quieted, then hoicked himself into the saddle to sit fuming at the outlaw.

The leader—presumably another knight, probably a noble—stared at the outlaw for a while. "It is Robin Hood?"

Robin started at the voice, deep and round and arresting. The abbot continued, "Yes, I know you, Robin Hood. They say you are a thief and a murderer."

The Fox of Sherwood narrowed his eyes and was a long time in responding. "Like all else you hear, that is half truth and half lie, although what *you* hear may be nine parts lie. There are brigands about this day who blacken my name, but I am a true and faithful outlaw, and king of Sherwood Forest."

"King," quoth the man.

The thudding of hooves shook the earth under Robin's feet. The animals blew steam out of their nostrils. A crow flew close, cawing, then faded away. In the bushes, Arthur and Allan and Grace looked at one another in bewilderment.

The abbot asked, "What would you have, O king, since we are at your mercy?"

Robin Hood's voice was cold. "T'is our custom to exact a toll of those who traverse our forest. We relieve greedy barons and bishops of their ill-gotten gold." He paused. "In the past, the poor got most of what we made. Of late the poor have gotten only half, while the rest went towards Richard's ransom."

"Indeed," said the tall man. "And has the king been ransomed?"

"Who knows?" retorted Robin Hood. "We collected money. Prince John collected the entire fee five times or more. Ours was sent away to Austria or some such place. That was the last we heard."

"Indeed," repeated the dark man. He reached behind him. "I have with me some forty pounds. Consider it yours." He unhooked a purse that fell heavily to the road. "My men have nothing."

Robin Hood examined the throng around him. The riders and their mounts swayed like trees in a quickening storm. The boys at the back whispered to one another. "There are forty pounds in the trappings of each man's horse alone. And probably that again in the swords under their cassocks. But I will accept the forty in hand." He walked to pick up the sack in the road. "Mayhaps the children hereabouts will be able to eat without their fathers resorting to poaching. It's been a long and lean winter, for Nottinghamshire and all of England."

The two men faced one another from their differing heights. The dark man loomed huge on his heavy horse. But Robin's followers, watching through the bushes, noted he did not seem at any disadvantage, and they wondered about the secret knowledge that protected him.

The abbot's voice rolled like approaching thunder. "We have heard Robin Hood drives his sheep to supper after he's shorn them."

Robin was taken aback for a moment. "Aye. Though feast we do not. These days we have a little venison and nothing else."

"King's venison?" queried the abbot. "How sweet it must taste. Let us to sup."

"Very well, your—" Robin Hood stopped himself. "Very well."

The outlaw chief pushed past a pair of horses. Once clear he swung his bow towards camp, a signal to his concealed people to run ahead. Then he turned to the somber party.

"Follow me."

The curious party arrived just as the sun was setting. Robin Hood walked at the head. He pointed the monks to the lower meadow: there the riders dismounted and hobbled and stretched their legs and relieved themselves. They stared and pointed at the great lime tree. Tuck's dogs growled at their rivals.

With their hands on their hips or their hilts, the Sherwood outlaws watched from the upper common. They had been told of the curious encounter by Allan and the other two who had run ahead. It was all as murky as the bottom of a bog. Marian wondered aloud why Robin brought guests: there was venison on the spit, but nothing else. As they watched the monks, Will Scarlett murmured to his son and the two of them laughed. The rest asked each other questions. They watched Robin where he spoke to the abbot. The outlaw chief stated some case with much waving of hands, and soon the black abbot gave orders. The acolytes attacked the bulging packs and loaded Robin with goods. They piled him with so much he had to call for John and Much to help him carry it all. Clutching the packets to his chest along with his bow, Robin Hood and his helpers walked past his people without a word. The parties of outlaws and monks stood and eyed each other like Saracens and Christians. Robin dumped the food on the serving table in the upper common. Marian and everyone else helped unwrap them. There were dried leeks and peas and apples, broad beans and prunes, loaves of brown and white bread, cabbages, pots of wild honey, dried salmon and herring, sausages and blood pudding.

Robin looked at the bounty before him. "Some good will come of this. We can stuff the young ones till they squeak. John, tell them we'll need more, and put it in my cottage."

Friar Tuck muttered, "T'will be a sin to eat all this during Lent." His mouth watered as he said it.

Marian asked the question they all hung on. "Rob, who *are* they?"

Robin Hood smiled. "What does Tuck say, 'All our sins come back to us'?" He laughed and kissed his wife. "Be patient and attend. We'll have more entertainment than a fair shortly." He walked off towards the lower meadow.

The "monks" and their assistants built fires in their temporary camp and drank perry from skins. They put out handfuls of oats for their horses and curried them. Robin's people helped prepare the food or stood around. It was after sundown before supper was ready and all were seated, the clerics on one side of the table and the outlaws on the other. As long as it was, Robin's table had not room enough for everyone to sit and sup, so some guests stood behind, as did the Sherwood wives and children. There was venison on wooden platters, rich hot soup, soft bread, spring water, slices of apple in honeyed sauce, flaked fish.

But the food was more hearty than the atmosphere, for there was not a word of conversation. Tuck led with a Grace to which all murmured "Amen" and crossed, but that was all. Robin refrained from a speech, omitted the call for a story from his guests, asked not after news. Except for the abbot, the spurious monks had thrown back their cowls and removed their helmets: they looked a dour lot, a scarred and grizzled assortment of men. The acolytes proved to be squires of varying ages. Robin Hood sat at one end of the table and the abbot at the other. Emnity floated down the table between them, and it clearly baffled the knights as much as the foresters.

The drizzling overcast had broken to reveal sharp-pointed stars. Anyone could see it was spring now, for the Plough was high in the northern sky and the Twins were halfway up in the east. An occasional spark wafted straight up as if to join its brothers. The firelight waved and dipped, catching highlights of the knights' armor, so they looked a part of the smoke and flame. The abbot wore a large gold thumb ring set with a sapphire that winked and sparkled. No one spoke. Even Will Scarlett opened his mouth only to fill it. Crickets chirped around them.

The knights ate venison and the foresters ate everything but. After a lot of chewing, the abbot called across thirty feet of table. "You set a good feast, Robin Hood. Fit for a king."

Robin called back, "Well it should be. T'is a feast of deer killed on the king's land, and water from the king's streams."

The knights at the table stirred. The abbot held his head very erect. Only the end of his nose showed from under the cowl. But the voice behind was rich: it was the voice of a bard, or an orator, or a lord. "You seem not to fear our king."

Robin Hood sounded nonchalant. "Should one fear a king, or should one love him? Either way, he is far away."

"A king's presence spreads far and wide, like the wings of God."

Robin pointed a spoon at Friar Tuck. "God is close, and we talk to him often. But the last we heard of the king he was in Jerusalem, fighting heathens. Better he should have stayed home to punish his lackeys, who pillage the lands worse than any Saracen horde."

There were continual stirrings along the table from the men in black. They stopped eating and wiped their hands on their hems. Will Scarlett wished for his sword. He tossed gristle to Tuck's dogs, and the knights's dogs growled. Robin Hood's cousin craned back to look down the table at Marian. He wondered why she sat at her place with her head down. She had never been slow to stop rude talk at the table.

The abbot called, "The king had done well, I thought, to appoint Hubert Walter as judiciar. Has he not guarded the realm well?"

"Aye," spoke Robin. He settled his belt so the hilt of his poinard was handy. "He keeps John Lackland on a short leash in the far counties. Blood spilt in the hills will never trickle as far as London. If one baron kills another, only the poor soldiers and serfs are inconvenienced. Walter keeps us well for a country that lacks a king." The abbot made to interrupt, but Robin bored on, "And lest you think otherwise, hereabouts people *love* the king. In this glade are his *staunchest* supporters. We work to preserve the name of the king, to keep it alive in the people's minds and hearts, to beat back the barons and bishops who rob at every hand and *claim* they do it for Richard. *We love* the king and we *await* his coming." He paused. "Mayhaps the king of England will return before the king of Heaven."

At Robin's left hand a knight shot to his feet, then another, then all of them, so quickly that the slowest were bowled backwards onto their fellows who stood. At Robin's right the outlaws were just as quick: children jumped as the bench toppled, and only Much and Cedwyn in her long skirts hit the turf. The parties glared at each other in the indistinct light. The only ones seated were the two leaders.

"Sire!" burst out a dark man. "Let me spit this bastard, this dog, this—this *outlaw* . . ."

"Try it!" shouted Will Scarlett. Little John, seated between Gilbert and Bart, grabbed each one to keep them from climbing over the table.

"Aye," yelled Red Tom. "We'll cleave your tongue from the hairline down."

"A knight does not brawl with a wolf's head!" spit a man. "He executes him!"

"Draw then! We'll feed your eyes to the crows, you bastards!"

"Crows and jackals make fair company!"

"Dast you call *me* a jackal?"

"Aye! And a pig while we're at it! Pigs are turned loose in the forest before they're hunted up!"

"Pigs have killed more than one forester!"

"Not a knight ahorse, they haven't!"

"What hey! Fetch us a knight then and remove this horse!"

"And horse's ass!"

There was much more, most incoherent. Marian pointed, and Allan and other parents moved the children back from the table. Gilbert tried to wrench loose of Little John's hand. It took three shouts before Robin quieted his troop. The abbot roared only once.

When it was quiet, Robin called down to the abbot, "There be wolves in your flock."

"And wild dogs in the woods."

"Dogs raised on venison are fit foes for wolves. Care to set your teeth against our claws?" His grin was like a fox's in the firelight.

That pricked the abbot's interest. *"En melee'?"*

Robin reached out to jostle Tam into Will Scarlett. The two were still making faces across the table. "No. Melee' brings more broken bones than a midwife can set in a night. Let us test man for man."

The abbot nodded. "Swords then."

"Blunt ones, so the loser can profit by the knowledge

gained. And a shoot with longbows, the weapon that keeps
England free."

A fiery knight raised his fists to heaven, but the abbot
nodded. "Very well. Pick your three best fighters."

Robin grinned again. "They are all my best." He turned
to his line of outlaws, each one champing at the bit.
"Gilbert. Scarlett." Robin paused long. Using Little John
was not fair. The third should be David of Doncaster, but
he was not here. Red Tom was a good fighter. Thin, he
had a sword like a wasp sting. Bart? No, they'd all get
hurt. He surveyed his eager followers. "And Jane," he
finished.

"*What?*" roared the far side of the table. "A woman?"
"Are you mad?" "Sire!" "*What?*" Of the entire mob under
the starlight, no one was more startled than Bold Jane
Downey.

The black abbot's face was invisible, his voice even.
"You would send a woman to fight a knight of the realm?
Have you no better man?"

Robin Hood was equally mild. "I must take what fighters I can get. Many people come here, but most cannot
live in the forest. The law of the land is so harsh I receive
supplicants without hands or eyes, or hamstrung so they
cannot walk. These I put up in a village, or on farms at the
edge of the forest. Bold Jane came to us when her husband granted her divorce. Seems he was tired of trying to
beat her and receiving better in kind. Cannot your knights
stand up to a woman?" The women of Sherwood laughed
merrily, and Katie made a rude sound with her tongue.

The abbot chuckled. He turned to the dark-faced fiery
lord, a captain perhaps. "Sir Colin. Pray select two fighters." He said to Robin Hood, "Gird thyselves." Then he
tossed his head and left the table. The monkish party
followed him to their fire in the lower meadow. There
they huddled and argued with much waving of arms.

Robin addressed his party. "Scarlett. Gilbert. Jane. Pray
fetch thine armament. Bart and Much, fetch practice
swords." Gilbert sent Tub for his shield: all the boys raced

for Cedwyn's hut at the dark end of the meadow. The other two repaired to their cottages, the women and girls with Jane, chattering like a flock of grackles.

Robin and Marian were temporarily alone. The lady of Sherwood stepped close to Robin but did not touch him.

"Robin, husband, I like none of this. You play a dangerous game."

"Leman," said her husband, "I but fence with monks found by the wayside. I've done it before. No one will be hurt." But seeing the concern on her face he added. "Or fear you it will extend further?"

"I fear you'll be hauled to London in chains and stuffed into a gibbet!"

Robin laughed. "But wouldn't there be a fine tussle before I were hauled away, eh?"

Marian had to smile. "Be careful how you tread, my love, and how you talk. That will be the death of you if anything is." Her husband merely chuckled and pulled her close. He squeezed her bottom while she shoved at his hands.

The outlaw contenders gathered in the common. The firelight lit and danced on armor and swords. Gilbert of Northumbria loomed silent in his battered Norman helmet with its frowning nasal. His coat of Damascan mail fit like a snake skin. Over that lay a weathered gypon of Lincoln green belted down. Strapped to his right arm was his kite-shaped shield with its red Crusader cross: the iron rim was notched in a thousand places. Will Scarlett looked like a clown. His red and fancy clothes were stuffed inside a studded leather coat borrowed from Friar Tuck. He wore a conical helmet that threatened to drop over his eyes, and he carried a round shield that lacked its boss. Bold Jane Downey wore a conglomeration of accoutrements: a child's leather helmet, her own leather jerkin, Grace's new shield. Her cheeks were flushed and her eyes bright. When asked, they all signalled they were ready.

The black abbot trotted out his knights. They had finally put aside their false cassocks. Each wore oiled chain mail, new bullhide baldrics, and tooled boots. Their wood and metal shields were shiny with fresh paint. Their swords were long and bright. To a man they wore common red gypons with an individual family crest: eagles and trees and crosses and badgers surged in the deeply-shadowed light. Along the hem of each coat were embroidered scallop shells, the mark of the Holy Land. The twenty attending squires wore clothes that matched their masters'. Only the abbot was without a squire.

Still with his hood up, the black abbot addressed the crowd. "Let the games begin. *Deus volt!*(*)" Sherwood and its guests formed a thin circle twenty feet across on the flattest part of the common. The large cooking fire was the only light. They did not mingle: where the half-circles of knights and foresters met, Little John guarded one end and Friar Tuck the other. People made sure there was room behind them for a retreat and that the children were not underfoot. Squires stood behind their masters with emblazoned shields upright. The six contestants stood in the dark beyond the ring and swung their practice swords. Gilbert muttered advice. Robin Hood stood just inside the circle. The abbot stood opposite. Eventually everyone stopped milling around.

The nobleman abbot adopted the role of host. "People of Sherwood, brother knights," his tones rolled out. In the pause could be heard the popping of the fire and the sigh in the leaves far overhead. "We gather for a contest of arms, that we might learn from it our weaknesses and our strengths, and by it be bettered for the battle against godlessness and anarchy. Good friar, give us a prayer."

Friar Tuck paused for only a moment, chewing the inside of his fat cheek and fingering the buttons that ran from his neck to his foot. Then with head lowered he boomed, "Lord God, fairest in the firmament, pray look down upon us here and bless this flock, that we might please You in Your sight. All that we do and all that we say

(*)"God wills it!"

is done in Thy name, as we strive to achieve the *humility* and *innocence* that is ever our goal. Amen." Tuck fixed his eye on the abbot in black. Everyone on the circle crossed his or her chest except the witch Cedwyn.

The abbot got to work. "First in arms, we present Sir Carfew of Suffolk, our best." A burly dark man with a crescent moon and star on his chest stepped into the ring.

Robin hooked his thumbs into his wide belt with its big silver buckle. The fingertips of his right hand rested on his silver horn. The outlaw chief said quietly, "Sir Gilbert Whitehand of Northumbria, Defender of Christendom in the Holy Land, Lion of Judea, Scourge of the Saracen." The Apollo in armor entered the ring and stalked to the center. His blue eyes were hidden under the jutting brow of the helmet. Along the circle, Cedwyn put her fingers behind her back and crossed them. Sir Carfew frowned at Gilbert's left-handed grip. The knights whispered as they realized for the first time who this was: the mad Scot of Acre who fought left-handed and had always been carried from the field. A man who fought left-handed was dangerous—the wounds he inflicted on a man's unprotected right side were terrible. Further, he had the advantage that he was fully accustomed to fighting right-handed knights, but they were unaccustomed to left-handed opponents. The two contestants met at a sword's span. Black Bart and an older knight came forward. Each checked that the edges of both swords were blunt. Then they retreated.

The black abbot let the silence drag until everyone had turned to look at him. Finally he said, "Let the first blow fall at the command 'Begin'. The first man to hit the turf or call 'Enough' loses the bout. No killing blows and no thrusts. This is sport."

The two gladiators shuffled their feet and glared at one another, shoulders hunched, swords half raised. The abbot paused dramatically, then shouted, "Be—"

A Celtic shriek rent the air. Like a tiger Gilbert leapt forward, his borrowed sword droning. A wide sweep smashed across Carfew's wrist and bicep. As Carfew cried

out, the Scotsman slammed his shield into his opponent's
and his fist shot out so the sword pommel cracked the dark
man's cheek. Gilbert gave a savage shove with both sword
hilt and shield, and Carfew flopped backwards to lie stunned.

The three blows happened so quickly there was a blank
pause from the crowd. Then Scarlett whooped, Cedwyn
squealed, and Tuck raised a hallelujah along with the rest
of Sherwood. But the knights grumbled, especially when
they picked up Carfew and found he had a cracked wrist
and loose teeth. "Foul blow!" they muttered, "Knavery! A
lucky stroke!" Robin Hood only beamed. Gilbert stood
ready, his chest heaving.

Although his face was invisible, the black abbot had the
stance of one appalled, and his words ground out. "I
would see, Master Woodsman, if your man can repeat
that." A chorus of "Ayes" came from his retainers. Sherwood sounded jeers.

Robin Hood waved a benign hand. "Gilbert takes not
well to games, your—abbothood," he smirked, "but send
another lamb for our lion."

All of the abbot's men vied for a chance, and irritably
the black abbot signalled another to him. The tallest of the
knights stepped to his master. They consulted in whispers.
Then the man moved to the center. He had a thin beard
and a sly sneer. A black linden tree was painted on his
chest. Gilbert watched the man move as the weapon edges
were tested.

The abbot held his hand in the air as he talked. "I
present my man Sir Crampton, the first into Acre. He is a
man always—ready. Begin!" And the hand slashed down.
Crampton had been inching his arm back all the while.
Now the sword shot forward, straight at Gilbert's guts. But
there was a flick of light and a clack of steel, and the blow
swept out and away. At the same time Gilbert hooked the
edge of Crampton's shield and jerked it aside, skipped
forward, cracked his knee into the man's balls, skipped
back as the man doubled, and smashed his sword onto his
helmet so hard the metal split. Then Crampton was down,
coiled so tightly into a ball he retched onto his knees.

Gilbert watched to make sure the man was helpless, then looked up at the circle of knights. "Next?"

Sherwood hooted and burst into laughter. Ben Barrel slapped Arthur's shoulder so hard he fell over. Cedwyn clapped and hopped and hugged herself. Scarlett beat his shield with the sword. "Nay! Nay! Save some for us, you greedy pig!"

Robin walked up and placed his hand on Gilbert's granite shoulder. He addressed the abbot. "In as much as Gil won, we'll not tally that blow as rule-breaking—it's already cost your man his supper. In truth, t'were my fault. Gilbert was four years in the Holy Land with our king, battering Saracens into—if not believers, then at least sympathizers. Perhaps it's not fair to send out this warhorse. Bring up the next and we'll loose Scarlett. I can vouch for my cousin: he's only a terror to the ladies." The foresters laughed anew, and Will Scarlett capered a little circle with his hands up like a jester.

"Montague," barked the abbot.

This was a broad curly-bearded man with a badger and hill for a crest. There was no assessing his strength or weakness by his walk: he was older and had learned to hide his light. He circled Scarlett like a farrier judging a horse. The knights behind him called out deadly instructions.

"Good e'en to you, sir," said Will gaily and he bowed. Montague nodded and put up his sword.

"Begin," called the abbot.

Montague shuffled into a wide and sure fighting stance. Will Scarlett, unable to stand still for even a moment, began to shimmy around him. He searched for an opening and found none. The man's defense was as impregnable as a mountain. Without warning, Will let out a banshee wail and charged with sword and shield straight out before him. Montague parried both and swung at the ribs behind, but Will had already danced away. Montague of the badger continued forward, testing, testing, feinting now and then, watching. Scarlett, like a clown in his oversized

helmet and baggy armor, backed away or charged, carol-
ling like an idiot all the time. Sherwood shouted along
with him. Robin Hood shook his head distastefully and
saw Little John do the same. Before Will knew it he had
been backed into the circle, which did not fall away quick
enough. In the moment's distraction Montague swung.
The flat of the blade smacked into Will's thigh. Scarlett
howled and tried to cover with his shield. Montague rapped
the top of the shield so it struck Will in the forehead. He
dropped. A cheer rang out from the knights.

Robin Hood ran to investigate. Will Scarlett sat on his
bottom and fended off his son and mother. "Naw, I'm all
right." He rubbed his forehead fiercely. "May the Lord
damn me for a week!" To the looming knight he said, "I
thank you for the provident blow, good sir. You could
have done me a great injury."

Montague pointed his sword like a finger. "If you're
going to fight, learn how to fight." And he walked off
towards his brother knights. They clapped him on the
back and wrung his arm as he took his place in the line.

Now the women of Sherwood gathered around Bold
Jane Downey, each whispering last minute instructions. In
her leather jerkin and short blonde hair she looked like a
child play-acting. Robin walked up and took her by the
shoulder. "When you're out there, lass, *watch* the other
man and shut the rest out." Jane gulped an assent and
entered the circle. Chivalry demanded she be given an
opponent that was her equal. The abbot pondered for a
while with hand to lip, then called up a young man named
Ewan. This was one of the squires: evidently the abbot
had no knights of moderate ability. Bold Jane Downey
kept a long sword span away. The knights along the circle
grumbled.

The black abbot set his arms akimbo.

"Are you sure, Robin O' Hood, you want a woman out
there?"

"Aye."

A huff or a sigh. "Then begin."

Everyone shouted, but the contestants stood still. Eventually the boy began to shuffle, testing. Jane only turned. Bold Jane Downey was reckless and riotous in everything she did, but a real armed combat before an audience was new to her. She would let the fight come to her. The boy advanced, and she retreated, setting one foot firmly before lifting the other. Heartened, he took a casual swipe. Jane caught it on her shield. The boy repeated, and the same thing happened.

"If you intend to fight," he muttered so only she could hear, "let's get this over with." Jane remained silent, unsure of her voice, but she did assay a blow on his shield. The iron-strapped wood didn't budge a hair. Women groaned. The boy swore and fell back on his training. He laid into Jane with steady practiced blows. She took one on her shield, then another and another as the pace increased. He pressed, pushing her backward. The Sherwood women wrung their hands, cried advice, and shouted encouragement. The knights were loud but inarticulate: they were unsure what to say to their comrade, and hesitant to deride the woman's ability. The banging of sword on wooden shield rang through the night woods, a steady noise like a blacksmith's hammer. The ring of people broke and moved aside: Bold Jane Downey was pushed dozens of feet beyond into the lower meadow. She was not making any swings now. Then her foot slipped on the dew-speckled grass and she fell. Her opponent stopped immediately. Ewan wiped his forehead and blew out his cheeks, as glad to be done as Jane. People pelted down the meadowside. The knights had won, but it was Sherwood that cheered the louder. Ewan was swept aside as two dozen people grabbed at Bold Jane Downey. She was blind from tears of shame and embarrassment, but before she knew it the sword and shield were gone and she was hoisted into the air and atop shoulders, and carried back towards the fire.

"Give 'er three cheers!" shouted Will Scarlett, and the foresters rocked the night.

"And three for Robin Hood!" shouted Little John, and it echoed off the hill and the trees. The family that was Sherwood surrounded its defenders. Grim Gilbert, dizzy Scarlett and teary Jane Downey were prodded and poked and hugged and kissed, and laughter was the foremost conversation.

Forgotten at the edge of the firelight, the black abbot muttered in his beard. "Damned if they don't cheer Robin Hood too, and he didn't do a thing!"

Marian poked her husband with her left hand and gestured towards the black abbot. Robin walked to the man's side with an eye on the sullen knights. They had fetched up and broached a small cask of ale. They passed around a pair of cups while the squires watched. Carfew of the splinted wrist and Crampton of the ruptured balls were plied the heaviest. For a moment Robin and the abbot were alone.

"Your men fight well, sire," said the chief of the outlaws.

"They damn well better. But so do your men, and women," replied the man in black. "A goodly wench, that Jane. Comely. Since we needs stay the night, we would—"

Robin broke in, "I'm sorry, sire, but she's married."

The abbot's chin snapped up at the interruption. "Indeed? To whom?"

Robin cast his eye at his people yonder. "The lean fellow with the carrot hair. Red Tom, we call him. A fair devil with a sword."

"Indeed. What about that biggish wench? With the full hips."

"Grace. She too is married."

"The girl with the long braid?"

Robin Hood searched among his people. "Polly?" he asked. "She's not twelve!"

"And so unmarried. They are never too young to learn."

Robin clamped his teeth together. "Unmarried, yes, for she has the pox, contracted from her parents. Marian tells me she's a constant discharge, stinking—"

The abbot held up a hand like an axe blade. "Enough, enough. There is no lack of women in your court, but all married or untouchable. Having picked them from the gutter, why need you keep them to yourself?"

"You have that amiss, sire." Robin's voice was even. "We are a Christian community. We live as we are taught, that women are made in the image of the Virgin. They are protected by the law of God and the law of the land."

The two men glared at one another in the darkness.

The abbot said, "We could loose our knights and take what we want."

"That you could," retorted Robin. "But no man who truly loves the king would do so, for Richard was ever a man of honor."

The abbot's voice seethed. "Never mind. We'll pass on the contest between man and maid. Like as not they *all* have the pox. Prepare you the archery shoot. The night wears on."

Robin Hood nodded and moved away quickly. "Arthur, Much, fetch torches! John and Will, cut us wands! The rest of you fetch your quivers!"

The archery shoot was to be held in the lower meadow. With no moon, the sky was jet black, sprinkled with a million stars. Torches had been set at the end of the meadow to bracket the wands. These were peeled willow branches three fingers wide and six feet long. At thirty paces, they were luminous stripes against the black trees.

The black abbot led his men in procession to the shooting line where a spinney of upright bows and bowmen awaited them, their backs to the great lime tree. Not all were present: Elaine and Clara had retired with the smallest children. Hobbled horses were shoved out of the way.

The abbot resumed his role as host. He pronounced, "We have heard, again and again, all over England, of Robin Hood and his Merry Men, and how well they shoot. Every man, they say, can put out a wren's eye in a forest at one hundred paces." Robin's people did not respond.

"Now we would see how they fare against *our* archers, the best in the King's army."

The abbot faced the outlaw chief. "Our score stands at two victories for us, one for you. How—"

"How count you three victories from four contests?" Robin interrupted. Behind him the folk of Sherwood rumbled.

The abbot's voice was icy. "We defeated the clown and the woman. Your Crusader won one bout."

"*Two* bouts!" yelled Bart. "He folded up *two* of your men without drawing breath."

The abbot replied, "The first bout did not count. Upon that we agreed. The contest was started over, and your man won. Take that small victory to your heart, and *bide your tongue.*"

Bart muttered an obscenity and spat into the grass. Tam charged, "He *cheats!*" but Will put a hand over the boy's mouth.

Robin Hood tugged his beard for a moment, then laughed. "Carry on. How shall we shoot?"

The laughter made the abbot fair shake with rage, but he and Robin talked. They discussed the matter for some time, and it was finally decided that five pairs of archers would shoot six arrows each. A pair would shoot three and three, so the first two shots could serve for ranging. All hits would count as a point. The side with the higher score won.

"And the winner of each round administers a buffet to the loser," added the abbot.

Robin laughed again. "We'll sear our fists rapping your chain mail. But we agree."

The abbot added in a slow, cool tone, "You and I shall shoot at the last."

Robin nodded. "Agreed."

The first to shoot were Arthur A'Bland and a short man named Herwyck. Arthur was a slow man, steady in his habits, but the crowd's scrutiny unnerved him. Plus, the night shooting meant he could not see the ranging marks on the belly of his bow. He snapped his hand on the release, and his first shot did not even land in the firelight. The knights hooted, and even some on Robin's side snickered. Sir Herwyck's shaft fell short of the wand by five feet, but in line. Arthur drew his bow again and took closer aim. At this range an archer shot blind. The thin wand was obscured by the arrowhead, so the archer had to sight the target, project it in his mind, line up the arrowhead, and fire at the projection. Still, most men in England could split such a wand two out of three times at one hundred feet. But the firelight made the distant circle wobble like a wheel out of kilter, and Arthur missed his second shot, as did Herwyck. These shots were closer, and on the third shot both cleft their wands. Thus no one received a buffet.

The wands were replaced. The abbot called up a young man named Suffolk, and Robin Katie. No one commented on a woman this time. At the draw, Katie held her breath so long folks thought she'd pass out. The archers shot quickly, and after three shots the girl had scored twice, the man once. The knight put hands on his hips and a smirk on his face to receive the buffet. Katie was nervous as a cat but determined to uphold Sherwood's honor. She wound up for the punch and let fly. It barely rocked the knight, and she hurt her hand. But Sherwood cheered anyway. The knight Suffolk received little cheer from his side; for he had lost to a woman, and a girl at that. At the back of the crowd, money moved from a knight's hand to a forester's.

It was Robin's turn to call up an archer. He called Little John. The foresters buzzed. The giant was only a middling shooter. A standing joke in Sherwood was that John should always throw his bow to knock down a deer. The black abbot pondered with his hands behind him, then called forward a stout fellow with barrel-like legs and a beard that spilled down his chest. For all that the man had nimble fingers, and he nocked an arrow entirely by feel. Little John took his time. He toed an imaginary line. His left foot pointed along it at the target and the right just crossed it. He turned his head fully sideways to face the target, then drew his oversized bow until it creaked. Robin sighed. Even Robin Hood's tutelage could not stop Little John bringing his cheek to the hand and not the other way around. When he loosed the string gave a resonant *brong*. The tall man and the fat one shot three arrows apiece. The wands were undisturbed.

"But I think John's last grazed the base," called Tub. Two from Sherwood and two from the road took torches to inspect the wands, and Little John's was indeed barked.

"I win, then," he stated. The stout man looked unhappy. He set his arms akimbo and cringed.

"Not too hard, John," called Robin.

"Naw." The giant slid up his sleeve and spat on his fist. He set his left forefinger against the man's breastbone to take aim, for it would be unfair to hit the man below the ribs. Then he lilted back his fist and swung. The impact sounded like an axe hitting a knot. The knight sailed more than his length backwards and bounced on the turf. Sherwood cheered, but Robin worried that his friend had gone too far—that blow must have caved in the man's breastbone. But after much wheezing and hauling up on his belt by his fellows, the knight could sit up. He did not rise.

Both groups were then quiet as Ben Barrel and a knight shot, both scoring once. The knights chafed for a chance to get in their blow.

Robin Hood lingered long over his next choice, tabulating his people and rubbing his beard. Bart? he thought. No, too hotheaded: he'd get in a fight if he won or lost. Scarlett? Worse. Red Tom was a swordsman and no archer. Why was it a man was one or the other, but never both? He scanned the group again and again, when Marian said, "I'll shoot, Rob."

Robin hesitated. Even with a sprained finger she was a dead shot. But what if she had to take a buffet? Katie had been in no danger from that slim youth, but these knights would probably leap to thump Robin Hood's wife. But before he could voice anything his wife was on the line with her slim bow. As all the knights watched, the black abbot called to him a handsome man with a forked black beard like a Saracen's. The man smirked and swung his bow with casual ease. The abbot conferred with him in whispers, then sent him to the line.

Marian took her time. Wisps of dark hair traced her jaw, and her full mouth was set in a luscious frown as she concentrated. Her first shot barked off the wand. Robin Hood barely saw it for watching his wife: she looked so beautiful in the firelight, stolid yet ethereal, like a spirit of smoke. Some knight made a lewd comment at the back. Robin Hood flushed with anger and the Sherwooders near him stirred.

The dark man scored first time—his wand splintered under the shaft's impact. The pair waited while new wands were shoved into the ground. Marian tossed a smile at her husband, and he smiled back. Marian's second shot zipped through the top of the wand so it oscillated wildly. The Moor's hit along one side. Then the foresters gasped as Marian's third shot lost itself in the woods. The man hit solidly.

Marian huffed at the distant target, or herself, then calmly turned and handed her bow to Katie. She set her fists on her hips and addressed her dark opponent. "Make it a good one," she said, and she stuck up her chin.

The knight grinned widely, very ready to deliver a blow. Some of the knights called advice in glee. "Put in a twist at the end!" "Follow through!" Other knights were silent, and four turned their backs with their squires. Sherwood held a collective breath. The only sound came from Little John, a rumbled "Mind . . ." Robin could say nothing. The Moor smacked his fist into his palm twice, then whipped it far back and forward. The man's horny fist crashed into Marian, not into her breastbone, but into her breadbasket. The air exploded out of her body. Helpless, Marian folded around the man's fist. He shoved her away roughly and grinned over at Robin Hood.

Robin Hood leaped forward to kill the man, but stopped after travelling six inches. Little John had grabbed him fast by the shoulder. For the first time in their lives Robin came close to striking his friend, but the big man just held on and pointed.

"Bastard!" shouted Will Scarlett, and he lunged for the man with the forked beard. The villain grabbed his sword's pommel, but not fast enough, for Will got him by the collar and pulled him over, driving the man's head into an upcoming knee. Two knights shoved Will back with gloved fists and fell on him swinging. The other foresters were close behind. Bart charged a dozen knights with nothing but murder in his eye. Bold Jane Downey came behind but was arrested by Friar Tuck. Tuck's dogs took off for the monks' six. Sherwood was a breaking wave as Gilbert slashed his sword into the air, the polished steel flashing like fire in the night. The rattle of knights' swords and foresters' bows was deafening, when all was cut short by twin cries of "HOLD!"

Robin and the black abbot stood back to back, facing their troops with hands upraised. "We'll stop this now!" cried the outlaw, and the cleric shouted, "Put up thine swords!" It grew relatively quiet. People kicked the dogs apart. The major sound was cursing as Tam pounded the backs of the men atop his father. Little John picked up the boy in one hand and a knight in the other and tossed them in opposite directions. Bart was face down in the turf and pinned, and Robin left it at that. He stared down Gilbert until the sword returned home, as did the ones behind him. Other foresters unnocked their arrows. Only then could Robin see to Marian. She leant upon Mary and Grace and whooped for breath, then gave her husband a game smile. Robin Hood nodded thanks to Little John, glared at his followers, then spun and addressed the black abbot.

"Our games are done," stated the outlaw chief. "Your men may camp here in the lower meadow and leave in the morn."

Robin could sense frost in the man's voice. "We go where we wist. And you agreed to a contest betwixt us. On your word, you must keep it."

Robin Hood snorted and barked to his party. "You lot, stand back! *Stand back!* Brother Black and I will have it out."

"We needs replace the wands."

"The one will suffice," said Robin, and without a backward look he stepped to the line and fired an arrow. The shaft left the bow like a hawk and buried itself in the ground fifteen feet from Marian's chipped wand. Men and horses muttered in the dark. Robin waited without a word for the abbot's shot.

Brother Abbot had a borrowed bow, and he took a long time in the shooting. He was hampered by the hood, and looked again and again before finally shooting. Although the arrow's flight wobbled, the shot whisked alongside the intact wand. As soon as the arrow landed Robin shot. His arrow plunged into the darkness, not even passing through the distant firelight. The abbot's next shot again grazed the wand. All saw it tremble. Robin Hood did not even look. His arrow whistled away, lost. The black abbot took his time, as before, but missed clean.

"But I have won," he exclaimed, too intent to have watched Robin Hood. Everyone in the glade knew what had happened except he. "You shall stand for your buffet!" he crowed. His knights smirked.

Robin Hood tossed his bow to Little John rather than set it on the dewey ground. He waited, hands on hips, without cringing. The brother drew back his sleeve, revealing a long sleeve of mail, and delivered a thunderous blow at the base of Robin's sternum. The outlaw chief grunted sharply, staggered, and sat down. The abbot rubbed his fist and laughed. Marian hobbled to her husband. Friar Tuck and Will Stutly growled, and Sherwood stayed where they were, seething.

The black abbot turned at a tap on his shoulder. Little John loomed like a tree. "Perhaps friend abbot would buffet with *me*."

The abbot stepped back. Before he could answer, there came a grunt from the trampled grass. "Nay, John, you mustn't." It was Robin, struggling to arise. Little John helped him.

"T'was a low blow, Robin. This abbot—"

"No," gasped his chief. "He is no cleric."

Scarlett called out, "What is he, then?" Sherwood took up the cry, and the knights shushed them. "None of your damned business." "A greater man than your outlaw rogue." Ugly words were tossed back and forth, but the two leaders stopped it with cuts in the air.

It grew quiet. The abbot commanded, "Tell them, Locksley. Tell them who we are."

"Not an abbot," Robin repeated, rubbing his breast. "You travel the king's realm in disguise, though why I cannot guess." Everyone strained to hear his hoarse voice.

"To see how people feel about their king, is why we travel thus. We have learned much this night."

"And how shall you relate it to our king?" asked Robin. Heat gathered in his voice. Marian touched his arm. "The king is far away, held for ransom in Austria."

"Little do you know, locked away in the woods," sneered the other.

Robin replied, "Aye. Little enough. Here we only gather gold and do without to make the ransom, which was five times what London could expect to gather in a year."

"And was it not worth it, this king's ransom?"

"It would be if our king took his place on the throne and tended the country!" Both men now shouted.

"A king has more responsibilities than a bumpkin can dream of!"

Robin cried, "There must be plenty, that every baron in every castle can bleed the people white and the king not care!"

"The king cares for his subjects! But the royal house must be put in order!" The Sherwooders looked at one another in confusion, while the knights clasped and unclasped their hilts.

Robin's face was red in the firelight. "The royal house? Does that extend to the walls of Acre?"

"Aye! To Jerusalem and many other places—"

"When there are heathens more bloody in Cornwall!"

"—fighting to free the Holy Land from the filthy feet of the infidels!"

"Infidels! Aye, I've met a few on the road to London!"

"Better would the king's campaign have gone, but his holy crusade was *deserted*—"

"—how holy a crusade that sees three thousand helpless men beheaded—"

"—deserted by the Earl of Locksley!"

"—who returned home to find his castle razed, his serfs dead or scattered, and his monies and lands confiscated, all by men making free in the *king's absence!*"

"THE KING HAS RETURNED!"

With a snarl the abbot ripped open his cassock. On his breast gleamed a rampant lion on a field of red, and above that the leonine head of Richard I, Lionheart, reigning sovereign of the House of Plantagenet, King of England and France.

"The king!" breathed the crowd on both sides, and the entire multitude, knights and squires included, dropped to their knees without a thought.

Robin Hood stared at the man before him. Richard had all the markings of a king: he was handsome, tall, strong, with a rich voice brimming with power. At his waist hung the famed Danish axe that had felled so many men in the service of God. The gold lion burned in the firelight, ready to rend. Robin did not know what to do. He alone still stood. Even Marian was on her knees beside him. Finally centuries of breeding and training took over, and he dropped to his knees before his lord.

"Sire."

Richard glared around at the multitude, his hands still locked in the rent material. The sight of so many bowed heads calmed him. Slowly he tugged off the black cassock and let it fall. He frowned, then set his hand lightly upon Robin's head.

"You have our forgiveness, Robin O' the Hood. Rise. Rise, all." A rustle shivered through the glade. The king took a deep breath, breathing in the worship. "We have learned much this night. T'would seem there be one corner of England that harbors hearts that are loyal, if somewhat independent." Richard shook back his golden hair and smoothed his beard. People bowed their heads when the king looked their way.

"You have indeed doughty attendants, Locksley. We know of your work, and we do appreciate the sacrifices you made to bring us safely home. And there are indeed enemies abroad in this land. We need fighters in our court."

Beside Robin Marian bit her knuckle, for she knew what was next. Her husband waited with a man's slow lack of understanding.

The king raised his chin. "Robin Hood, and the rest of you. We are prepared to grant you all a full pardon for your crimes. You will be free to return to your homes without persecution." A buzz rose among the foresters: some relieved, some only confused. "After," continued Richard, "after you have served in my court for a year. Or more. T'will take some doing to bring peace to England and France."

Now there was confusion everywhere. Robin could only stutter a reply. "Pardon? You would have us—leave Sherwood, sire? But we—how could—we must serve—in London?" Marian squeezed his hand and blinked back tears.

"Aye, forester, t'is true. You have performed well in these dreary woods. Now you may serve us directly. Bring your people to London as soon as possible. Bring them all." He laughed. "There's room. We will find enough work to keep you occupied for at least a year. And you shall all, *all*, draw the wages of full knights!"

Robin Hood was thunderstruck, unable to speak while the king waited. Finally it was Marian who replied. "Sire, your majesty, we thank you. We'll gladly serve in whatever capacity you see fit. But we need some time to prepare. May we have some pause, say, say, until May Day? We'll be prepared by then, ready for court, and better able to serve."

Richard nodded his magnificent head. "Aye, good sense. We may not have returned to London by then ourselves. May Day it is." He nodded sharply, and the audience was done. He called to his men to pick up their accoutrements and lay out a camp in the lower meadow. With a final squeeze of Robin's shoulder he strode away. Robin Hood watched him go.

Beside him was his wife. He stared at her blankly. "Marian. Marian . . ."

The Lady of Sherwood pressed her fingers against his lips. Then she pulled him close and held him. Tears ran onto his breast, but it was Robin who shook.

Chapter 11

The young buck sniffed the doe's vagina and licked at her urine. Audible only to her, he clapped his tongue against his palette. She quivered down the lengths of her slender legs. She was ready, and so was he.

This herd would disband soon. The velvet buds of the males were beginning to branch. Dark winter coats paled to a mellow golden brown. The paired fawns in the does' wombs would not wait much longer. Soon the females would seek sheltered coves, while the males departed for the solitary life of summer when their antlers would grow and harden. These were roe deer, delicate creatures of the woods and open glades, and it was time to leave. The closed deer yard they occupied had been foraged clean. Hard round droppings were everywhere. The shallow beds reeked from countless sheddings of urine. Birch bark was stripped to the height of the tallest hart. Oyster mushrooms were chewed away. Oncoming clouds of flies would soon drive the animals to the north, up the low slopes of sandstone to green grass—not too far, just far enough. The deer were intent on foraging, building up their starved bodies after the long winter. They wandered from the confines of the yard to nose through the leaves and sniff out lichens. They grasped spring grass with their nimble lips and tore it loose, coughed up vinegary stomach contents and chewed and chewed with their pointed back teeth. They kept their faces in the wind, and swivelled their ears constantly.

Lately however, the sap had risen in the male's testicles, and he and the doe had been circling one another for days. Normally one would not approach a doe in spring, but this maid was barren. The teats near her groin were drawn flat, never to be used. The buck lusted to test his new strength on her. But his first chance came elsewhere.

The oldest buck in the herd, a thick-necked, grizzled male, had finally decided to contest the young buck's advances on the doe. The old stag's eyes were grey with cataracts, but his fuzzy brow promised the twelve tines of a royal buck, the size of the antlers alone determining his mastery in the herd. He snorted at the buck and pawed the ground before him, and the young male did the same while the doe watched, immobile. They rapped their soft spikes against brush, although it hurt to do so. The old buck pawed and waited a long time for a sign of submission, to see the young one turn and flee. When it was not forthcoming, he charged. Usually one good butt did it. But the young buck stood his ground. He sensed a mate in the barren doe, and he wanted her. He met the charge of the stag in mid-air, leaping upwards as if from a springboard, forehead foremost. The two deer bashed their heads, and both recoiled from the pain on the tender buds. Blood trickled along their white brows. Even before the old buck landed he had had enough. Without looking back, he turned and trotted away. He was more interested in eating anyway.

The young buck returned to the female. She trembled all over now, as did he. He licked her rump and nuzzled the soft pink lips under the tail. Then he hoisted himself onto her back and, after some fumbled lunges, slid inside her.

There came a rustle from downwind, and the deer snapped their heads up. They snorted, stamped their hooves, then as one bounded up and away. They crashed over and through the brush and vanished.

Lost in rut, the young buck sensed the alert too late. A man-smelling shaft with oiled steel and resined feather lanced into his side and through his heart. His vision went dark. His lungs filled with blood and he fell. The barren doe pulled her loins loose and shot away into the brush.

The young buck thudded to the ground.

Chapter 12

Little John dropped the noose over the deer's head, tossed the rope over a branch, hoisted the carcass into the air, and tied the end to the tree. The rope bit deep into the powerful neck until the head stuck upwards at a strange angle. The hind feet were just clear of the ground and stuck straight out.

Little John and Marian worked under the trees near the pool where it was cool. The camp was quiet: people were quiet on this bright morning. Marian had brought several large wooden bowls. She stropped a flensing knife on a steel, rubbed it on her sleeve, and handed it to the giant. Little John set his hand against the deer, drove in the point, then cut from the ribcage almost to the tail. He sliced carefully through the lining of the abdomen. Guts and organs slid down to protrude outside.

"Did he run far?" asked Marian. She stropped a short knife with a rounded point and handed him that.

Little John thanked her. He cut around the anus and testicles to loosen them, then slid his hand down into the body to draw them up inside. "Naw. Got him through the lungs. Dropped like a stone. We got most two cups of blood apiece. We were lucky to find him. Deer are getting scarce."

"Strange, what with the bounty of birch seedlings popping up."

109

"Aye. Maybe it's that damned boar scaring 'em away."
Little John continued to snip. He sliced through the dia-
phragm, then reached high up inside, severing the wind
pipe and esophagus, careful of his fingers. "Who's out after
the rogues?"

Marian accepted a pair of lungs and put them in the
bowl. "Gilbert. Scarlett. Brian. Tam, of course."

Little John reached behind the spine, and with one
small push the barrel of guts rolled onto the greensward.
He picked up the liver and sliced it open. Slimy flat
worms writhed inside.

"Full of leeches."

Marian took a look. "But not a lot of holes. It'll be all
right once it's cooked." She set it in a bowl.

"Do we want the stomach?"

"No. We've enough with this. Give it to the dogs. Just
throw it wide." There was no need to whistle: Tuck's
Samson and Deborah were just out of arm's reach, licking
their chops and whining. John threw the stomach with its
stinking contents far away. The dogs spun and leaped after
it. He tossed intestines and chunks of gristle after them.

Little John continued. "Do you think we'll find them
after all this time? They've had days to get clear of the
forest." He prised the carcass open so it could cool. With a
pointed knife he trimmed out the ragged areas where the
arrow had entered and exited. Then he picked up an axe.

Marian nodded. "I don't think so. Where could they
hide? Our friends would have told us about them." She
paused. "Maybe not right now, with this false Robin Hood
story going 'round. But I guess they've fled the forest or
crawled under some bush and died. That fellow I put the
eye out of could not have gotten far." She said it quickly
and shivered. "For their sake, and ours, I hope they're
dead and gone."

"Aye. Rob's been like a man possessed since you came
with that bit o' news. He won't rest till he's found them or
made sure they're gone." He hacked at the ribs, then
chopped through the pelvis with three sharp blows as the

branch above quivered. He wedged sticks in the cavity to keep it open. "It's tough on Rob, being in charge. He's been skittish as a new bride lately, between these murderers and rumors of this boar. And meeting the Green Man. If he did meet him."

The knife and steel stopped in Marian's hands. "What? What do you mean, John? Rob did meet him."

"Aye, he thinks so . . ." The giant rubbed a finger across his chin and left a smear of blood. When he moved his head, Marian saw the tip of his braid was red too. "But sometimes, I wonder if what we see before us is what's really happening. I mean, think of it. If what we see before us isn't real, how would we know?" He peered inside the empty carcass. He ripped up a handful of grass and wiped the inside clean.

"You think Rob didn't meet Hern?"

John had his head in the deer. His voice sounded hollow. "Ah didn't say that. He met someone. But you know how it is with fairies. And everything else. You just never know."

Marian said, "Yes. Rob's so honest, he takes everything at face value."

"So he thinks he met Hern, and he told him that Sherwood would always be with him, or some such fairy blather. It made Rob feel good, but I'll believe what I see." Little John tossed the grass away and dusted his hands.

"And now there's this foolishness with the king."

It was said. They sighed in concert and were silent. Little John incised the deer's skin around the neck just under the noose, then around the arms, then around the back legs above the hocks. He snipped the hide down the throat and peeled it back like opening a collar. The under-layer of fat let go with a ripping noise as the giant jerked it downwards.

Marian said quietly, "You did well in restraining Robin in that final meleé. I thank you."

Little John shrugged. "Ah, well. If they'd have killed anyone it would have been Rob. T'wouldn't be no skin off

Richard's nose if he were dead." The giant laid the skin on the ground with the hair down. They had decided to pin the hide to a wall so it might dry into rawhide. No one wanted to brew the mix of deer's brains and human urine that would tan the hide into soft leather. Little John stepped back and stared at the skin. "To think I almost struck the *king*. Ah'll never understand how Robin can address a royal like that. It's not right. It's unseemly."

Marian was startled by this condemnation. How many had joked that Robin Hood would never need a dog while he had Little John? She said, "You know him. He gets very passionate about justice and . . . individual responsibility. Having the king's ear sent him over the hedge, is all. He thinks Richard shouldn't leave England in the lurch while he's off widening his borders. And Rob's always been disappointed in Richard about Acre. You were there. You recall the massacre."

Little John used a light saw to cut off the feet. "Aye. That was a nasty piece of business. But folks said we couldn't let the garrison go. They'd just cross over the line and come at us again."

"So Richard had three thousand men beheaded."

John sighed and knit his brows. "Aye, that he did, and it bothered Rob sore. But when I think of Richard, I remember him in battle. He was always at the front, swinging that bloody great axe of his and breaking the Saracen lines. We were hard put to keep up with 'im. He walked up and down that coast like he owned it, and he almost got to Jerusalem. I alw'ys reckoned that's what being a king is all about."

Marian brushed back her hair with the crook of her wrist. In the pond, a fish *clooped* after water beetles. "You're right. That is important. But Rob just thinks there's more. He thinks a king should work for peace, so people can live properly, the way God intended. He says Richard crusades for personal glory, not the glorification of God, and that's wrong. He'll take all of Christendom and say it's for Christ."

Little John stared at the naked white beast which hung before him. The dark eyes in the furred brown head stared back, as if surprised to be attached to such a body. Flies came to settle. Little John poked at the carcass with a shorn foot, and it swung heavily on the rope. He threw the foot to the dogs. "And we're to go with him, off to London."

Marian's laugh surprised him. "Oh no, we won't, John. We'll stay right here in Sherwood."

"But Richard's commanded us go."

Marian shook her hair back and gazed out over the meadow. New grass was brilliant green under the morning sun, but there were rainclouds in the south. "But we won't. I don't know how, but we'll stay here. We'll always be here. We don't belong anywhere else. Can you see Scarlett loose in London with Tam? Or Gilbert? Or Bart? Look at you, John. If we took you to London, you'd be forever banging your head on the lintels." They both laughed. "We'll get out of this. Rob'll surprise us with something. He's always surprising us. And himself."

Little John chuckled. "You really think we can stay?"

Marian stood up straight and drew a deep breath. "Yes, John, I do. Don't you fret. We're for the forest and that's all there is to it. They can't displace us any more than the deer. And speaking of deer, let's get this one on a spit."

Little John nodded, and they started in.

"Down that way," remarked Will Scarlett. He pointed down the thinnest of paths. "There's a cottage with a couple of oldsters. I forget their names. Robin keeps an eye on 'em."

The search party stood in a light drizzle that dripped from the new leaves. Gilbert the Crusader was in command, although with Will Scarlett along the leadership was sometimes in doubt. With them was a new man, Brian, and Will's tiny son Tam. Brian had been a tiler looking for work when Robin Hood met him on the road.

He had thin brown hair and a thin beard, and no great
span between the eyes.

"Why do they live in the forest?" he asked.

"Daft," replied Will. "They're fools. Only fools live in
the woods."

Tam Gamwell was Will Scarlett in miniature. "Da," he
said, "we live in the woods."

"We're different. Different sorts of fools, that is."

Gilbert led down the track, shield foremost. The others
had their bows and knives, Gilbert only his sword. Because of his hand, he could not use a bow. Wet bushes
slapped at them from both sides. The party had tramped
the old stone road all day, asking at every farm about
outlaws posing as Robin Hood and his band. Everyone
they met was terrified by the name Robin Hood. They
knew of outlaws, yes, Robin Hood's people. Once they
stopped shaking, they said two parties of travellers had
disappeared: one a group of nuns, and the other a pair of
families on their way to market. Neither group had arrived
home. Because of that, the sheriff's men were also out
asking after the outlaws. The soldiers related many versions of the same stories with additions—that Robin Hood
had gone mad and now slaughtered innocents. The fear in
people's eyes made the party cold and bitter.

Brian spoke up. "How long do we look for these villains?"

Before Gil could answer, Scarlett piped up, "Until Rob
calls it off. He's like that. When he sets out to do a thing,
it gets done. And there's always somethin'. Rob's full of
ideas. Maybe we'll track this boar next. Or maybe we'll go
after Guy of Gisborne."

"Who's that?" Brian asked.

"*Sir* Guy is a prick of a lord who fucks dogs and eats
babies." (Brian crossed his chest twice.) "He's slimy and
yellow. He looks like he's been dead a week. He and Rob
have hated each other since they were boys. Guy was
betrothed to Marian, but Robin stole her clean away. See,
he was a thief before he even knew it. Anyway, Guy has a
castle—two, I think—up near Barnsdale. He's a real

hellion. He kills someone every once in a while just to show he's lord. And every once in a while he tries to stick Robin with some filthy plot. He's been pretty quiet all winter, though. Maybe he choked on his own bile. We should go up there some time and piss in his shoes."

Brian said, "But we have to go to London."

Will hawked and spat into the bushes. "So what if we do? It'll be fun! And we won't be gone long. We'll come back and pick up where we left off."

"Before we go, we needs bring these fell murderers to justice," Gilbert droned in his guttural accent. Rain sprinkled along his coat of oily mail made him look like a fresh-caught pike. "We owe it to Robin."

Brian whispered to Tam, "What'd he say?" Tam shrugged and twirled a finger at his temple.

Scarlett said, "We'll either find 'em or we won't, and probably it'll be won't. I'd like to have the bastard who posed in red, though. I'd see if he dances as well as me. You think they scotched both those parties: the nuns and the serfs and all?"

"Scotched?" growled the Northumbrian.

"Kilt 'em."

They broke out into a clearing. There was a house with a tiny garden and three goats. The house was badly off: most of the mud had fallen from the wattle, and the thatch was gray with age. It probably leaked. There was no one in sight. A tiny plume of smoke crawled out of the chimney and spilled down along the roof. They hung back in the bushes.

"Seems quiet enough," said Brian.

Gilbert growled, "Aye. Your bowstring ready?"

"Yes, sir. Fresh waxed, and my bow's oiled. Goose grease on me feathers."

Gilbert nodded and studied the setting with a soldier's eye. Scarlett joined him. "What?" he asked.

"We dinna ken how many are inside, if they're here. We'd no want them to harm the hooseholders."

Scarlett grunted. "Let's send Tam to the door. He can

say he's looking for a pig. A boy would get the door open quicker than a man."

Gilbert thought. "Awright. Go, laddie. See who's inside, but don't do anything daft like your da."

Tam handed over his bow and quiver and baldric and ran for the cabin. The goats bleated at the stranger. The three men watched as the boy pounded on the door. It opened a hair. Tam talked animatedly. Then he lost his balance, fell against the door and tumbled inside. The door slammed shut.

Gilbert snapped out a curse as the three men broke for the house. Before they got there the door opened again and Tam waved them on. They trotted up and pushed inside.

The interior of the house was damp despite the fire. The roof leaked in many places, turning the rushy floor to mud. An old man and woman in rags, both bent almost double with age, were inside with two others. A bedraggled man in red cringed in the corner. A bow and arrow were on the floor before him. On a pallet near the fire lay a man in dirty green smallclothes. His head was turbanned in a bandage that covered half his face. He looked pale and sick.

"Once I knew they were here," Tam chattered, "I pretended to stumble inside. The red one there drew his bow, and I told him if he dast shoot the nine of us would carve him like a pheasant. So he threw his bow down." Gilbert appealed to heaven with his eyes, but Scarlett tousled the boy's head until he almost fell.

But Will's face frosted over as he regarded the red-clad bandit. "You, you bastard. Gambolling through these woods posing as *me*." Suddenly Will had a knife out. He advanced on the terrified thief, but Gilbert snagged his shoulder with a hand like a vise.

"Leave that," said the Crusader. "We'll take th'm to Robin. He'll want to ask them questions before he hangs th'm." The bogus Will Scarlett whimpered. "You," Gilbert demanded, "Whar's t'other with the cleft pate?"

"I dunno. I dunno," was all the man could manage.

Scarlett snarled, "Let me tickle him with this. He'll talk," said Scarlett, but Gilbert shook his head. Tam watched his father with unbelieving eyes.

Of the wife Gilbert asked, "Tha' other. Can he walk?"

The woman started to speak when her resolve broke. She quailed, "We didn't know who they was! They forced their way in here! We didn't know they'd done anything wrong! We would have told you! They wouldn't let us leave! Don't harm us, for God's pity!"

Gilbert's voice stopped her. "Don't fret yerself, woman." He walked to the pallet where lay the man in green. Water dripped from Gilbert's mail and scabbard, and his eyes were unseeable under the frowning Norman helmet. His knotty left hand was clenched in a fist. The disabled man on the pallet looked up, sullen and unafraid.

"Get up," spoke the knight.

Slowly, painfully, the villain rolled over on the sickbed, got to his hands and knees, and rose. Gilbert scooped up the green cloak from the floor and threw it to him, and the man stumbled against a post. Will flicked his knife at the man in red, and the two villains crept out the door. Brian kept an arrow loosely nocked, as did Tam.

Gilbert clumsily fished some gold florins from a pouch and held them out to the couple. "From Robin Hood." The old man shook his head, but the wife snatched them up. Gilbert left the two of them to argue it out.

The party disappeared into the wet brush and rain.

Robin Hood sat in a tree facing west. This watchstation was a small roofed platform two miles from camp—a half-hour walk, or a fifteen-minute run. He was alone in a quiet leafy bower. It was April. He could see the forest coming back to life. The rain did not bother him. Rather it sparkled on the leaves like quicksilver to create a thousand hues of green before his tired eyes. The sonorous patter made its own music. The wooden boards under him smelled of oak sap with a hint like wine. Robin usually found this

duty a welcome bout of solitude and peace, and today the
forest called to him as never before. If not for the concerns
of men, this would be Paradise. But his mind rattled with
problems, the foremost of which was: Must he leave Sherwood? His brow ached from hearing that question toll
again and again.

"*Tan, tan, ha-roo, ha-roo, ha-roo! Tan, tan, haroo! Tan, tan,
ha-roo, ha-roo! Tan, tan, haroo!*"

The outlaw turned on the platform. It was Robin Hood's
own call coming on the breeze, blown on a cow's horn by
Allan A'Dale. What now? Could it be anything but that
Gilbert's party had found the impostors? Robin Hood came
alive, so much so he almost banged his brains out on the
platform roof. "Please, God," he prayed aloud, "make this
it. Let me come to grips with something I understand."
He hopped from the platform clear to the ground and
broke into a trot for camp.

Halfway back he passed Will Scarlett on his way to
replace him. "We found 'em, all right. They ain't much to
look at." Robin Hood ran.

He found every man, woman, child, and dog in the
lower common with Gilbert's party and two prisoners.
Everyone was talking.

"I dunno," said Little John. "I'd hate to torture them."

"I don't see what's the problem at all," said Red Tom.
"When a man's a killer, you hang him. This buzzard's
probably got stretch marks on his neck already."

"We don't know what they've done just yet," stated
Marian. "We must find out everything they've done so we
can make amends to the survivors."

"Heat some iron," said Black Bart, "and put it where it
hurts. They'll talk then."

"Robin won't see them tortured," said Allan A'Dale.
"And neither will I."

"You've neither suffered fra th'm nor captured th'm,"
Gilbert told Allan.

"They're getting mighty hungry," said Old Bess. "Wave
some meat under their noses."

"I'll side with Bart," said Friar Tuck. "Visit some heat on them. They'll be *bathed* in fire before very long."

The crowd parted to let Robin Hood through, and he got his first look at the marauders of the King's road. Robin Hood glared at his doppelganger. The man hunched on the wet ground, barely able to sit up. He wore green from Lincoln, and under the turban bandage, had brown hair and a brown beard. That was the only resemblance. *Wear green and say you're Robin Hood,* thought the outlaw chief, *and who'll know?* Beside the false Robin cowered a man with red clothes and a white face.

Robin asked Gilbert. "Where's the other one, that Katie creased?"

"No sign."

Robin shot a query at his double, but got back only an insolent glare from the bloodshot eye. "Bold one, aren't you?" demanded Robin. The Sherwoders moved back at the tone in his voice. "How many parties did you waylay and bury under the leaves? We know about the farmer families and the nuns. Who else was there? And where have you put them?"

The man glared up in silence.

Robin Hood erupted with such fury that the doughty fighters of Sherwood jumped. The outlaw chief ducked and grabbed the bandit by the front of his jerkin and lifted him clean off the ground. He half-dragged, half-carried the man twenty feet and slammed him against a birch trunk. "Answer me, you dog!" He slammed him again. "Who have you murdered while wearing my name? Talk, or I'll take the words out of you with a knife!" The battered face against Robin's exuded pus and hatred, but not a word passed the man's lips. Slowly Robin ground his fists into the man's throat, cutting off his wind. Seconds dragged, the fetid breath of the bandit mixing with the forester's. Then the outlaw chief took hold of himself. He dropped the villain to the turf and worked his fists. He started at someone behind him. It was Little John.

"Rob, Gil has an idea."

Robin Hood glared at the prisoner, then turned and stalked back to his people.

Gilbert spoke low. "The red one'll talk 'f ye get him awa' from his sergeant."

Robin pulled at his beard and thought. Finally he nodded. "Bart, fetch manacles." The red prisoner was plumped down near the green one. When the smith and his apprentice had returned, Robin addressed the prisoners as Sherwood listened. "You two are alive to answer questions, and ye'll be married to trees until you confess. You'll have water to wet your tongues but no food. When we get the same story from both of you, you'll get your punishment. I intend to hang the two of you from Nottingham tower, so all the world can see how you've polluted the name of Robin Hood." Robin's followers nodded grimly: the Sheriff of Nottingham had two hundred soldiers and Robin Hood twenty, but if Robin said he'd engineer a spectacle in the center of Nottingham, he'd do it. He went on in the silence. "Even if we do have to leave the forest, we'll have cleared our name. And *that* will put an end to *that!*"

He pointed to his evil mirror. "Bart, fit manacles to his feet and batter them shut. John, pick this one up."

The red-clad brigand flinched as Little John pulled him upright. Fear had cut new lines into his forehead. He flicked his eyes at his leader but received no response. The one-eyed rogue was inhumanly impassive. Robin wondered if the man were all there. Tub fumbled a hinged cuff around the one-eyed prisoner's ankle and slipped in a pin of soft steel. The boy held a hammer as a brace. Black Bart stretched his arm and delivered a ringing blow that peaned over the pin. The smiths trailed the chain around the birch. Bart pushed the man into place and fitted the other cuff so the prisoner had to sit facing the tree. Bart set the other pin, and when he was done a team of oxen could not have dislodged that chain.

Robin waved his hand in dismissal. The giant trotted the red man away north with long steps. Bart and Tub followed with another set of manacles. Some of the foresters followed towards the upper common. The rest dispersed to their chores.

Robin Hood was left alone with his doppelganger. The brigand gazed up at the Sherwood leader from his prison on the ground. The man could hardly see: his face was so swollen it looked about to burst. His skin was as yellow as old pus. He was so transported by pain he might have been somewhere else entirely.

"Heal quickly," Robin grated. "I'll scrape my knuckles raw beating you." The man said nothing. Robin Hood turned and walked away.

He stamped up the trail alongside the mound, and then higher. The slope was noisy with talk, all coming from the false Will Scarlett. The foresters had sat him near an isolated oak not far from where the brook bent away. A hammer battered steel.

". . . I don't know where he's from. I don't even know what his real name is, I swear by the Holy Mother's grave I don't. He's queer. When he talks you'd swear it's all lies. It can't be true what he says most of the time. We had to call him Robin Hood. He hired me in Nottingham. I had no work—I have a bad leg, see, here?—and he asked me if I wanted some easy coin. He said we'd make a lot of money, that now with spring and all there'd be people all up and down the road, coming out of Nottingham, heading south for London and them places like that. There was another man, a man all in leather, brought Knut and Bally from the west, and that was all of us. This one, he said all's we had to was pretend we was—was Robin 'Ood and his men and people would be scared and hand over their gold. But then they just killed them people. Knut and Bally did that. And this one. He went mad when he had someone helpless. He'd play with 'em, like a cat with a mouse. He'd make 'em scream. We tried to stop 'em, I *swear* we did, but it weren't no good. You wouldn't believe him when he's angry. He's like the devil. After we killed the first lot, I din't want no part of it, but they said I was in it, and they'd—"

He stopped. The faces of the foresters around him were grim, but Robin Hood's face was like red iron. The outlaw chief ground out his words. "How many did you kill?"

"Not many." The man shrieked and put up his hands at Robin's advance. "Some. Just a few! Ah, a party of farmers. There was a girl—I didn't *touch* her, I swear—and a young boy, and, and a farmer on a mule and his wife behind, and another couple like that, on a horse. Then there were the nuns. Four of them. If I'd known we'd ever raise our *hands* to nuns, I *swear* I'd have died first. My *sister* is a nun." The man blubbered so he could barely speak.

"Who else?" came a demand like a whipcrack.

"Two merchants, travelling together with a lot of gold. A beggar. He said we had to kill him, because he knew we weren't Robin Hood and his men. A milkmaid. But we let lots go. A student who couldn't see. Soldiers. Uh, uh, a boy with geese and another with a pig. A lot of people, we let a lot go by. They didn't see us. We didn't hurt lots of folks . . ." He held his face and sobbed. "I wanted to leave so bad, but he said what we were doing was . . . was . . . the same as what Robin Hood did—"

Robin Hood's face had gone white from this litany of death. At this last he leapt like a lion and struck the man full in the face. "*Bastard!*" he screamed. He brushed aside the man's clumsy defense and slapped him again and again, as hard and painfully as he could. The prisoner coiled into a ball, and the outlaw punched him in the ribs, then kicked him savagely in the back, grunting with each kick the same as the victim. His shouted curses gave way to animal growls, and still he pounded the villain. Bart sent Tub away with a cuff on the ear. The others tried not to watch. Finally Robin stopped, exhausted. His throat was hoarse and spittle dripped from his chin. The prisoner was lumpy and bloody.

Robin Hood finally swayed upright as if drunk. "*You!*" He spit out. "God *damn* you! He will take you—in His hand—just long enough to hurl you into the deepest pit in

HELL!" At this final blow the prisoner howled loudest of all and sank into bitter weeping, his face pressed against the wet rotted leaves on the forest floor.

Little John stepped forward and touched his friend's shoulder. Robin Hood made to shake off the hand, but the giant held on. He dragged his friend around and led him away. "Rob," he crooned as they stumbled down the slope, "it ain't your fault. We was penned up here most of the winter. It ain't our fault. You know that. They're evil men, Rob, but we've stopped them."

Robin Hood nodded his head to all of it. He wiped tears from his face. "But this is *my* forest," he croaked. "I'm supposed to watch over it. I'm supposed to—protect the people in it."

Little John retained his grip until he found Marian. Without a word the giant handed Robin over to his wife. She led him into their cottage and closed the door.

Robin Hood ran through the woods as hoofbeats drummed behind him. His breath rasped in his lungs, sweat soaked his clothes, bracken stung him. Suddenly he was ringed by deer walking upright like men, with their cloven hooves outstretched to cut and stamp a man flat. Each stag had green eyes rimmed with red. They closed in. Robin screamed and he was back in camp. It was deserted. Shouting filled the night. A conch shell trumpeted. A cave yawned open and disgorged naked men painted blue. They hurled flint spears and screeched in an unknown tongue. Robin Hood ran for the hall. The door crumbled under his hand and he fell inside. His followers were there. They cowered and called to God. A giant boar with green eyes erupted from the cave and burst amidst his people. Marian was trampled underfoot as she dove to rescue a child; Robin could hear her bones breaking under the black hooves. Blood spotted with silver splashed everywhere to drip from naked branches. Robin Hood was caught in the open, away from the trees. The wind roared and picked him up. People fell away. Their dead white faces glistened in the dark as he was lifted higher. The wind tossed him like a leaf. Then Jesus appeared before him, a hundred feet tall with clouds around his shoulders. But His crown of thorns spread into antlers that sprouted from His head. Finger bones rattled at His throat. His robes were skins. Robin covered his eyes. God abandoned him and he fell screaming.

He jerked awake. Wind shook the treetops with rushy sadness. Marian woke beside him. He gasped and reached for her and hugged her tight. His sweat dripped onto her black hair.

"What's the matter, Rob?"

Robin pawed sweat from his brow and threw back the blanket. He flopped back to stare at the ceiling. "Maybe we should leave the forest," he croaked.

Marian's voice was gentle. "Why, Rob?"

"Because we don't belong here?" He tossed his head, felt the solid stone wall beside him. The wind sucked at the door frame and rattled in the chimney. "It's not natural to live in the woods."

"Hugh of Lincoln lives in the woods."

"He's a holy man. He's building a church."

"We could build a church."

"Not in Sherwood. Tuck says it's a wild place, too far from God and Rome."

"Allan says it's a sacred place, the way Eden was before the fall, when Man was innocent."

Robin gulped. "Cedwyn says it's sacred too, because it's full of magic. That druids practiced here, and older people before them. God knows what they did."

Marian stroked his head. "The boy Robin I knew said it was the most wonderful place in the world."

"That was a child speaking. As adults we see." He ran his tongue around his mouth. "Our very presence in these woods changes them. We cut the trees and turn the soil and piss in the streams. What would—Hern think of that?"

"Hern? He would think you take what you need, as he

does himself, and as the deer and squirrels do. 'As long as we care for the forest, it will care for us.' "

Robin craned back to look at his wife. "What?"

Marian propped up on one elbow to look at him closely. She was still dressed. It was only afternoon. "Rob, you say that all the time."

Robin Hood breathed deep. The smell of the deep woods, carried by the wind, was sweet. "But we have to go to London. I gave my word."

"We won't go. Something will turn up."

"What?"

"Something. Have faith in God, and in yourself. With your heart, and these stalwarts beside you, you've nothing to fear."

Robin Hood lay back and sighed.

"Listen to that wind!"

Chapter 13

The tiny bird hopped along the edge of the nest and craned his neck in every direction. A storm was coming. He could feel the wet quiver along his wingtips. He surveyed the camp, looking for food and danger.

This was a sparrow, the most English of birds, sturdy and steadfast, strong in adversity. He had a stocky body striped in brown and white, with a black mask and bib and a rusty hood. His beak was thick, made for cracking seeds. At four years old he was in his prime, master of the brush around the camp in Sherwood. His weapons were to snap his wings, to dance, to sing, and to dive. Aggressive and fast, he could defend his home against anything twice his size.

He came out to get food for himself and his mate. The winter molt was over, the swollen sex organs had reduced, the rush of hormones was gone, the hours of *chip, chip, chip* were behind him. He'd found a nesting site and fought for it, and found a mate to go in it. The female was there now. The nest was a bulky bundle of grass and deer hair. It was deep among the spruce boughs and close to the ground. She would sit there day after day, moving only to turn the five eggs and regulate the heat.

The male saw pictures of food in his mind. To build up their bodies, the two birds needed more than seeds. They needed insects, and the male sparrow knew where to get them—at the deerhide nailed to the humans' building. He leapt into flight. He skittered through the air and landed on the packed ground. The hide was warm on the building's side, but the insects were gone. The dogs had craned on their hind legs and licked and licked until the deerhide was clean. The sparrow hopped into the air and made three smart circles. He would look elsewhere. Perhaps the waterbugs were active on the pool.

Tiny, glittering colors in the open field caught his eye. He heard the buzz of wings. Children pelted through the grass, chasing one another with curved sticks in their hands; clouds of insects—juicy grasshoppers, crunchy crickets, and bitter butterflies—rose before them. The bird flew out from under the branches. On the wing, the sparrow rolled in mid-air to scan the sky for the hated shape, but the tarnished vault was clear. He spun along the air currents into the meadow. Like ripples on a pond, bugs shot aloft and rained down around the children, and the sparrow zoomed among them. He filled his beak with the ones he wanted, mashing sweet bugs on his tongue, transported by the glory and lust of life and flight.

A dim shadow suddenly rippled along the ground below him. The bird dropped the load in his beak even as he twisted in evasion. The spot in the sky was *the* shape: short, broad, with back-hooking wings and a long forked tail. It was the female sparrowhawk who lived in an oak tree on the slope. A rustle shook his spine as he banked. A large face shot by. It had a brown hood with perfectly circular eyes. The hawk banked too and came after him. Red-brown bars on a white breast filled the sky. The sparrow dove and turned and listened to the wind shriek through the hawk's wings. He was tugged backwards by the cuts the predator made in the air. A child cried out. The sparrow fled for the bush, but he could already feel the outthrust talons that would smash into him and hook and tear his body. The sparrow's heart fluttered faster than his thoughts.

Then a short arrow zipped just past his head. He heard

the *thunk* it made in the hawk's breast, the shearing sound as bone and muscle parted, the gurgle as the heart ran dry. The children whooped as the hawk struck the tall grass with a clatter.

The male sparrow gained his bush, dipped low past the spruce needles, then swept up into his nest. He clutched a solid twig and rocked to a halt. He panted. The female looked at him concernedly. Although still hungry, the sparrow decided to stay here a while and rest.

There was definitely a storm coming.

Chapter 14

After the afternoon meal it started to get dark. Little John wandered over to Gilbert on the common. The Crusader sat cross-legged on a stone and, as he often did, stared into the fire. There was no one else around.

"Rob must still be asleep," John said.

Gilbert said nothing. His blond hair whispered around his cheeks and nose. The fire heeled over almost flat.

"Guess I'm in charge," said John.

Gilbert nodded and watched the fire.

"Looks like rain. "

Gilbert craned his neck back. The clouds were stacked just beyond hand's reach. "Aye. "

Little John twirled his quarterstaff between his hands, drilling a hole in the ground. He too stared at the fire. It had no color in the rising wind. It looked like a swirl of water on the charred logs.

"I'll have Allan blow in the scouts."

Gilbert nodded, and Little John walked away. The fire whooped as its ashes blew off.

"Looks like rain," John called. Allan A'Dale stood in the door of his cottage and frowned up at the sky. "Call in the scouts, will you?"

Allan nodded. "Of course." He left the children, who marvelled at a hawk they'd killed, then hurried across the common. He clambered up the grassy slope that covered

most of the hall. The wind riffled his fine hair, plucked at
his fine-woven garments. The only man-made objects atop
the hillock were a forked bipod and a long horn. Robin
Hood had found this horn one midsummer's eve as a glint
caught his eye. It had been lodged in the crotch of a tree
high above the ground. It was longer than a man's leg, and
the brass was etched deep with runes that no one among
them could read; not Tuck with his Latin nor Cedwyn
with her Welsh. They left it out in all weather atop the
mound because they did not want to bring it indoors.
Allan A'Dale was very careful with it. He lifted the horn
from the grass and rested it on the bipod. He rubbed his
hands along it to warm it lest it crack, but this was only
habit. The horn always felt slightly oily, as if just polished,
and always slightly warm. The bard pursed his lips and
blew the long four-beat note that signalled return. After a
count of five he blew again. Will Scarlett reported that he
had once heard that noise in Nottingham, fifteen miles
away.

Will Scarlett was at the moment up a tree to the west.
When he heard the signal, he hooked his bow on a lower
branch, swung his legs over the edge of the platform, and
leaped ten feet to the ground. His cousin had warned him
a thousand times that someday he'd break a leg that way,
which gave Will all the more pleasure to do it. If Will had
his way, he'd jump ten feet up, too.

" 'Bout time," he commented to himself. "No one'd try
to invade us this night. A man'd be daft to be out in this
weather." He began to walk back to camp, then picked up
a trot as the light failed. It was dark near the ground. The
wind blew so strong it moved the tops of even these
giants. This was climax forest. The trees were massive and
tall, impossible to climb without aid. There were few small
ones. Their thrashing made one feel all at sea. There were
clicks and clatterings, and the wind stirred the leaf mold to
make a graveyard smell. Occasionally there came a sharp

crack, followed by a thud. Each time the forester instinctively threw his arm over his head to fend off a widowmaker.

Will Scarlett smiled as he trotted along. A night like this would not find people in their cabins. Everyone would gather in the main lodge near two roaring fires, to roast venison and tell stories. If Tuck would allow, maybe they could dance. He'd like to get his hands on Bold Jane Downey and dance her head against the ceiling. Or toss his mother around. And what about Cedwyn? Could she dance, and would Gilbert let her? It might be fun to see.

There was another sharp crack and he flinched before he realized it came from behind. Scarlett whirled to see what was coming in the semi-darkness. Racing across the forest floor, smashing aside broken branches, came a boar, straight at him. It looked as big as a house, with white tusks like swords.

Resisting a scream, Scarlett ran between the trunks. He never looked behind, he just bolted pell-mell. As he pounded along, arms and legs pumping, his brain screamed panic. He knew a boar could outrun a man—anything can. The contest could be very short and very painful. But ahead there should be, yes! a twisted oak with low branches. It was in a tiny clearing underlaid by rock. Will Scarlett tossed his bow and flew into the branches like a Barbary ape. A grunt from the ground showed it was none too soon. He clawed for height. A sprig slapped across his eye but he pushed upwards anyway. He shoved through the thick-packed lower branches, aiming for the trunk. His mouth and lungs burned for air. He jammed his foot in a crotch and stepped up, pulled with his arms and back. He wanted to get as high as he could. After he caught his breath he could retrieve his bow (if it had hung up in the branches) and pot the brute. Failing that, he could blow his signal to camp. But what a big pig, and what a bastard!

There was a crash as the pig slammed into the trunk. Will was almost shaken loose; only a wild grab and a quantity of swearing held him in place. He scissor-locked his legs around a bole—and there came another smashing blow. "This is insane!" he yelled to the night. Animals didn't hurl themselves against trees. "Get away with ya!" It must be possessed, he thought, and his hackles rose. A branch pricked his neck. He debated climbing higher. He swore.

The monster below whomped the trunk again, and there came the fatal crack of heartwood. It couldn't be, Will thought, this tree was more than a foot thick! Sweat broke out on his forehead so fast he was chilled. His perch revolved, and not just from the see-saw of the wind. The tree's back was broken. Will Scarlett stood to ride it out. Even if the tree hit hard, he thought, the branches should hold it up off the ground. But if the boar below could knock over a tree, it could reduce lesser branches to splinters in no time. This tree was too far from its neighbors to gain another, and he couldn't see in the blackness anyway. With a crack the trunk let go and Will's sanctuary slumped to the ground. Scarlett caught a whiff of dung, worse than human, and he retched. He prayed. He fumbled for his horn. The cord snagged in the branches, but by wrenching he got it to his lips. Even a confused bugle would bring help.

He lost the horn as teeth closed on his right leg. He screamed. Leather and clothing parted. The boar's teeth were bigger than acorns and sharp as knives, and they had him. His right leg was being pulled straight down by five hundred pounds. The monster yanked, throwing its weight on its jaws. It grunted with exertion. White haze sprang up before Scarlett's eyes. He couldn't move. His left leg was immobile, caught in a fork below. The branch beneath him groaned and bent. Soon either his right leg would be torn off, or his left leg would break as he was dragged over the bole like a string. Scarlett's ear thrummed with a rapid pulse. The bole threatened to split his crotch. He pressed with both hands against it, but his arms were buckling. He gathered his breath and screamed as loud as he could.

His leg was disintegrating. He heard ripping sounds from all around and inside him. Then he blacked out.

*   *   *

"Alive! Alive, there!" Allan A'Dale slid on his butt down the mound. "Help! I heard a call from the west for help!"

Robin Hood stuck his hatless head out of his cabin. A bow was in his hand. It was very black outside. The clouds seemed to hang among the treetops. Marian joined him in the narrow doorway.

"That's Scarlett!" rasped Will Stutly from the main hall entrance. The wind whipped his words away.

People spilled past the old man out the door. Robin Hood did not even note who was armed. "*A moi!*" he cried, and he took off for the western point. Little John pelted after him with his great staff. Allan A'Dale snatched up a torch, Black Bart and Bold Jane Downey came right behind with swords. Much made to follow, and Grace, but Marian waved them back.

The five made for the dark woods. Robin Hood dashed from tree trunk to trunk, pushing himself off them into the wind. He knew all the trees on the three paths to the outposts. He knew he couldn't get lost, but the thrashing of treetops overhead was distracting. Everything in sight, even these trees, like pillars of the gods, seemed to sway. Allan shielded the torch with his body as they pressed along.

Not far from camp, Robin Hood felt a thrumming under his feet. "What's—?" Suddenly he was jerked backwards. His feet left the ground as a section of earth reared up at him. A mouth snatched at his foot. Teeth clashed. He smelled pig shit. Then he landed on his backside in the leaves and John was in the lead. Little John had seen the giant animal and pulled Robin aside. With his free hand he whirled the staff by one end and slammed it—on the turf. The beast was gone.

Robin struggled to rise. Allan crowded him on one side and Jane on the other. "What is it?" Jane cried.

"Must be the boar!" roared John.

"Here it is!" shouted Bart at the back of the party. "Harrr!!!" Everyone yelled at once. The blackness around them was impossible to fathom. It heaved and twisted and growled and sucked up the meager torchlight. Leaves and branches chittered overhead like goblins. "The bugger's right here!" "There!" "Look out!" Black Bart shrieked again and slashed down his sword. He stepped back into the light and held it up. There was a glint along the edge of the blade "It bleeds!" he said. "We can kill it!" Allan and Jane let out a prayer.

Robin Hood had gotten to his feet. "Form a circle with swords out. We have to get to Scarlett."

"We don't know where he is!"

Robin shouted against the wind and his own fear. "He's got to be between here and the post. Now leave off the damned boar and follow me."

Placing each foot carefully, hugging close, the five people crept along the forest floor like a caterpillar. Allan's torch was their only light. The circle defense kept the beast at bay, but it never strayed far. It disappeared into the black, only to return behind them a second later. It leapt and snapped and threatened to charge again and again. But Bart's sword had taught it a lesson, or else it had as much difficulty in the Stygian night as they. Inch by inch, with countless jolts to the heart and nerves, they negotiated their way through the howling, tortured wood until they found Scarlett, draped in a broken tree like a dead fledgling. His red-black clothes were awry, and patches of white skin glowed ghostly. A dark pool under him sparkled in the wild light.

Robin thrust his hand into his cousin's shirt. "Alive," he shouted over the rush, "for now. Pry those branches back. Allan, hold the torch there. John, catch him. Easy, onto the ground."

"Get your fingers into his crotch," yelled Jane. But Robin Hood had already rammed his fingers into thigh muscle for the large artery. It pulsed only weakly, almost dry. Robin unbuckled his broad belt and gave it to Little John who cinched it around the leg so it bit deeply. Robin shucked his hat and quiver and leather jerkin and sweater and drew his cloth shirt over his head. He used it to wrap the leg. Muscle hung in ropy strands. Allan caught the sparks that fell from the torch in his bare hand.

"*Harrh!*" came a cry from the dark. It was Black Bart. "Get back there! you black bastard!" Steel clacked on bone. "Take that, you rotten fucker! Nobody—"

"Bart! Let's get out of here!" called Robin. The night ground away at their courage. Panic was close by. Robin Hood loaded his unconscious cousin into Little John's arms. The giant wrapped a hand around the victim's head to shelter it. "Form a circle." From behind them Bart shouted again, his voice cracked. He rejoined the party.

"I'm losing this torch," called Allan. The torch was made of folded birch bark wedged into the slot of a hardwood handle. It flickered to a glimmer.

"Never mind," Robin replied. "Let's get back, and pray while we're doing it." The five stepped slowly up the trail. Allan led with the light. Jane crowded him with her sword. Robin Hood walked by Little John, knowing he was not needed. He was inhibited by his bow and John's quarterstaff. Black Bart walked backwards, often on Little John's heels, his wicked sword pointed back the way they had come.

They had not gone far when Jane Downey, not quite so bold, called. Robin couldn't hear her, so she shouted louder. "It's here! Ahead of us!"

"Damn it to *Hell!*" Robin cursed. They were a mile and a half from the camp. Their path followed the edge of the hill. Smaller trees clung to the slope here, larger ones to their right. The boar flickered like a devil among the largest trees. Robin Hood rushed forward. "Stand away!" He shoved Jane back and threw away Little John's staff. He reached over his shoulder, drew an arrow, and nocked it within a heartbeat. "Whip up that torch!" he cried. "Set some leaves alight! I want to see the bastard! There!" And he loosed. "Take that, agent of Satan!" He shot again. All around him people touched the torch to the ground, crossed

their chests, called out as they spotted the monster. Again
and again Robin shot, dragging his powerful bow into a U
and loosing his clothyard shafts. They left the bow so fast
they seemed to vanish. The light did not improve. The
leaves refused to ignite, and after a time the birch in the
torch was gone. When they could see the boar now, it
carried with it spikes like a hedgehog. It continued to
circle, but stayed behind tree trunks.

"What does it take to kill it?" quailed Jane.

Robin held two arrows in his hand. "More than we have
with us, God knows. But it's back there now. Come,
quickly." And he set off at a trot. Their retreat turned into
a rout as their speed increased, but the boar did not rush
them again. After an eternity they left the woods and
entered the clearing. The wind was stronger here. They
had to crouch to fight it. Robin Hood sent his people past.
Little John ran with Scarlett in his arms and never jostled
him once. He was not even out of breath. Bart stayed with
Robin despite his protests.

"Rouse the camp!" he called after the others. "Bring
everyone in! We'll peg it here!" The night rushed around
their legs like flood water and threatened to pull them
down. Black Bart cursed fully and steadily. The Fox of
Sherwood and the smith watched the woods for sign of the
boar.

"Do you think it's dead?" Robin panted.

"Naw."

A shout came from the doorway of the hall. It was Jane,
silhouetted against the light, the only light for miles around.
"All are inside!"

Marian pushed past her. She looked around wildly for
Robin Hood and called, "Not David!" But here the man
came out of the dark, a ghost with a ghostly burden. David
staggered with Shonet in his arms, asleep or unconscious.

Robin and Bart cast a last look at the woods and ran for
the hall. On the way they helped Shonet's husband. "What's
wrong with *her*?" demanded Bart, but David did not
reply.

"Guard the door!" Robin called as he ducked inside.

There was tumult around Will Scarlett. Old Bess burst out crying to see her son's leg split like a fish. Will Stutly dragged her away. Gilbert and Cedwyn yelled to boil water. Red Tom swept an arm down a table to clear it, knocking bowls, crockery, and candles to the rush floor. Tam clutched at his father's head and sobbed until Allan picked him up. Mary and Clara shrilled and swatted children. Finally Marian shoved people aside and took over. "Put him down," she said to John. "Make room for Gilbert and Cedwyn."

Glum Gilbert, destroyer of men, had learned healing from the Arabs in the Holy Land. Cedwyn, the witch from Wales, had nursed countless animals back to life. Marian had her common sense and her herbs. Together the three set to work. Gilbert pulled off his helmet and pointed with his useless right hand. "Cut his breeches off. John, lie acrost his chest. Shut that bairn up, some'on. Cedwyn, is it broke? Dig there. Good a'nough. Cut off that bit there, and that, he don't need it. Here, let me!" They learned Will Scarlett had revived. He bucked upright so hard Little John twitched. A scream ripped out. Mary ran up with the birthing tongue, a triple layer of leather, and Marian fixed it firmly between Will's teeth. With a rope wrapped in cloth, Red Tom tied the man's good leg to the table planks. Allan A'Dale held Tam where he could watch but not interfere. Clara stropped meat-cutting knives.

"Get more water!" Marian called.

"We can't!" shouted Jane. "The curse'd boar is outside!"

"We *need* water!"

"Bart!" snapped Robin. "Take Arthur, Grace, Ben, and Much, and fetch water! All you can carry!" Black Bart called assent and commanded the others to snatch up swords and buckets. They shuffled off into the night.

Everyone left clustered around Robin Hood. The children covered their ears to Will's screams. The surgery took place by fireplace light in the hall proper, the wood and stone part built onto the front of the cave. Robin Hood ordered Brian and Jane to guard the door, then led the rest of Sherwood into the cave, five paces deep into the hill. The cave was twenty paces wide and thirty deep, with a smooth sand floor, crannied walls, and an irregular ceiling. This cavity was mead hall, dance floor, winter storage, and refuge in siege and storm. A single torch in a sconce lit the eerie space. Forgotten, David tended Shonet on a straw pallet. Robin frowned and shook his head. He turned and addressed the timorous crowd, singled out old Will Stutly. "Will, you're in charge. See that all the war arrows are pulled apart and checked for splits. Tub, Katie, flatten that bump. While we're at it, count the gold and tally it. And, uhh, move those barrels over to there. Scour them with sand first. Hop to, now! Don't stand around! Will, you know what to do. Tuck, Tuck! Help!"

Robin ran back to check the defense at the door. "Have you seen the boar?"

"I don't know!" said Brian. "It's too dark." Just then Bart's party boiled in the door. They'd taken eight buckets. They now returned with three half full. Every one of them was soaked. Black Bart was last, and he threw his weight against the door.

"Here it comes!"

The door bucked. A snout the size of a wine cask, full of teeth like knives, jammed through the doorway and snapped shut. Bart slashed at it and the blow bounced off. Robin Hood could see shorn arrows like quills in its head. It took him and two other men to slam the door. They could not shoot the bar because the boar pressed so hard.

Robin Hood shouted for men to fetch the siege panel from the cave. Black Bart croaked, "Get some silver, damn it all!"

"Silver?" asked Robin.

Bart didn't answer until Robin asked again. "There were silver in the blood under Scarlett. His purse must have rent. But a' course there were steel there too. His knife."

"That's why the boar didn't finish him off?" whispered Robin.

"I don't know. I don't know nothing about this."

The men pushed with their might against the door, which groaned inward slowly but surely. A cloven hoof like a war hammer clomped on the threshhold. Ben Barrel fanned a torch bright. Robin Hood grabbed it and poked it through the slit of doorway. The door snapped back into place.

A blast of wind shook the building. Above them in the darkness, trees groaned and lost limbs that crashed down. Bart pointed with his thumb at the stained glass windows that flanked the doors. "They'll be next!"

Robin Hood looked at the depictions of his Lord. The polished leading reflected the light until Jesus seemed suspended in some parti-colored spider's web. "No," he gasped, "Black magic can't breach those portals. Besides, they're too small."

As they leaned on the door, the noise inside grew as loud as the wind without. It was Gilbert shouting. "Ah *said*, God rot it, it comes *off*!"

"*No*, you're *wrong*! It *stays*!" Bess screamed, her warbling tones rough with stress.

Gilbert waved hands that were shiny red and dripping. Marian and Cedwyn wept as they worked. Little John watched the argument with his head turned to the side where he lay across Will's chest. Red Tom was hard put to keep Will's roped leg pressed flat, the man kicked so hard. Robin Hood ran over. He could just see Will's white face. The cords in his neck stood out as he bit the leather brace. His eyes started from his head, boring into the ceiling, seeing nothing but pain.

"I'll nae hear nae more!" Gilbert roared. His thick accent was almost incomprehensible. "This leg is nobbut bone and skin, and if we dinna cut it off, it'll rot and take 'im with it! Tom, fetch yer tools!"

"Nooooo!" Old Bess cried.

Everyone froze as a howl set their hair on end. It was

the squeal of the giant boar. It sounded tortured, wracked. It rang on and on, then stopped, and the silent pause that followed was just as terrible. Then the wind banged against the hall anew. "That ain't no normal wind," muttered Little John.

Robin Hood trotted back to the door and pressed his hand against the oak. With each gust of wind it seemed to bend inward. He looked for the progress of the siege panel and found Allan A'Dale by his side. He'd handed Tam to Elaine, her with a baby at her breast and two children at her skirts.

"Rob. Those brigands. They're out there in the wind. They'll die."

Robin Hood had forgotten about them. He glanced at the back of the door. "So would anyone else who went for them."

"I'll go."

Robin pondered. "No."

"Rob—"

But his chief just repeated, "No." The door creaked in the frame. The entire front of the hall, stone and all, groaned as the wind and boar struck yet again. The very air vibrated.

"Allan, help them with the siege panel, and quickly! Get—"

With a whoop like a giant bullfrog's, the chimney fires at both ends of the hall snuffed out. Sparks and hot ash billowed into the hall to blanket Will Scarlett and his attendants. The men at the door were choked by the smoke. Robin Hood could smell his beard burning. He cried for light and people fell over one another to bring torches from the cavern. The chimney mouths gurgled and slobbered like gargoyles. The boar banged outside the door, grazed the wood with long keening gashes. The Fox of Sherwood grabbed a torch from someone's outstretched hand and pushed people aside. "Marian, get Will in the back room! Just pick up the table and carry it! Tuck, here!" Ben Barrel and Arthur and others dragged a solid oak panel, six inches thick, eight feet wide, and seven feet high. Robin Hood and Red Tom the carpenter had devised this to withstand a siege. The panel fit into sockets in the floor and ceiling, and had brackets of iron at the sides. Once in place, it covered the door and both windows. An invader would need a pair of axemen or a ram to get through it. There were no other windows in the hall, and the only other exit was the secret passage at the back of the cave. Now the men wrestled it into place as the infernal knocking continued outside. Hot pitch fell on Robin's hand, but he didn't even notice. Bart stepped between the door and the panel to pick up a sword. "Not there, Bart!" called Robin. But his premonition came too late. The wind outside snapped like a whip, and Jesus washing the feet of apostles disappeared under a hammer blow. The barbed end of a four-foot branch rammed Bart in the thigh. He fell against the panel and went down like a tree himself. People scampered for the back room even as Much dragged Bart backwards to safety.

"Get back here!" Robin Hood commanded. He dropped his torch, snatched up the branch and tried to stuff it back through the sundered window, but something flashed in the dark before him—tusks snatching at his hand. The forester jumped back. The night sucked at the jagged edges of twisted lead with a vampire's bite. The new hole brought inside the roar of noise. They could hear trees cracking and branches thumping as the gusts increased in fury. This was no English storm: this was like the cyclones sailors talked of in the south; storms that could pull the breath from a man and leave him empty as a fruit rind. Robin felt dizzy. He swayed on his feet. Was this the beginning of the cursed dream he'd had—God—only this afternoon? The boar had broken in and killed Marian. God had abandoned him. Someone grabbed his arm and pulled. Robin Hood realized he had been standing in front of the hole hypnotized. He shook his head violently. "Never mind," he called, and his voice was a croak. "Get this panel in place." With their leader out of the way, the

foresters slammed the panel into place despite the press of
the wind. They shot the triple bars in their iron brackets
and hammered the pins home into floor and ceiling. Robin
drew his knife and cut a cross into each timber that made
up the panel. As if cheated of a prize, a tremendous
drumming started on the roof. There were ripping sounds
as long-seated turf peeled away. A kick shook the ground
under them—it could only be rocks from the hillside bound-
ing down.

Robin Hood waved everyone back into the cave. "Tuck!"
he called, "a prayer, and a quick one!"

The fat friar had been readying last rites for Will Scarlett.
Now he hurried over. Illuminated by a torch held aloft by
Jane Downey, he shoved back his sleeves as he always did
before singing. Then his cleric's voice, high and clear as a
boy's, pierced the dim light. "*Libera nos, quaesumus,
Domine, ab omnibus malis, praeteritis, praesentibus, et
futuris: et intercedente beate et gloriosa semper Virgine
Dei Genitrice Maria, cum beatis Apostolis tuis Petro et
Paulo, atque Andrea, et omnibus Sanctis . . .*([1])" Every
man, woman, and child joined in with single-minded fer-
vor, the only exception being Cedwyn, who listened and
marvelled at the wind.

Robin's arm was grabbed yet again, this time by Old
Bess. "Rob, ye're his cousin. Don't let 'em cut off his leg.
For the love of God, Rob!" The Sherwood leader stepped
into the cave and looked at the leg.

Marian put in quietly, "He'll die if we try to keep it,
Rob."

Everyone watched as Robin demurred. Always deci-
sions, he thought, and never easy. He looked again at his
cousin's face. Already the man looked like a skeleton. He'd
die by morning—Robin had seen it too many times. He

([1]) "Deliver us, we beseech You, O Lord, from all evils, past, present, and to
come; and by intercession of the Blessed and glorious Mary, ever Virgin,
Mother of God, together with Your Blessed Apostles Peter and Paul, and
Andrew, and all the saints . . ."

stepped forward and tried to take Bess in his arms, but the woman pushed him away and demanded his decision. "No," he finally said, "wrap it and leave it. Will Scarlett without a leg is no man. We'll let God decide."

Gilbert threw up his hands. "A' right, a' right. H'a these rags been boiled? Did you say a Station of the Cross? A' right, gi'e 'em here!"

"*Gloria in excelsis Deo. Et in terra pax hominibus bonae voluntatis. Laudamus te. Benedicimus te. Adoramus te. Glorificamus te. Gratias agimus tibi propter magnam gloriam tuam. Domine Deus . . .*(²)"

Everyone jumped at a crack like a mountain splitting. In the silence that followed, Cedwyn intoned, "That was the birch we chained the outlaw to." People stared at the witch, then turned away.

No sooner was the explosion over, than the wind began to taper off. The storm did not stalk away, it just stopped. The building took a few smaller blows, but nothing that compared with what had gone before. As the noise retreated, the forest seemed to sigh.

Then it rained. There were spatterings, then a rush, then a roar. A torrent fell upon the camp, coming straight down like a waterfall, but somehow the outlaws knew it was real rain, honest rain to wash away the stink of evil. People clutched their families close and breathed freely again.

"There. That's done," said Robin Hood, and he crossed his chest. "Marian, how's Will?"

"Out cold," answered his wife. "We've given him mandrake root. He'll live." Robin Hood thought otherwise, but he kept it to himself.

The leader of Sherwood stood in the cave and looked out into the hall with his torch. Water dripped onto the floor. The wind had damaged the roof so much rain found

---

(²) "Glory to God in the highest. And on earth peace to men of good will. We praise You. We bless You. We adore You. We glorify you. We give You thanks for Your great glory. O Lord God . . ."

its way inside for the first time since the hall had been completed. No one had relit the fires in the twin chimneys. It had been such a happy place, he thought, now it was cold and dank. Robin reached out and put his arm around Marian.

In the cave, Sherwood sat on blankets on the sandy floor. Torches scented the air with birch tonic. Bart lay on his back, his head on Jane Downey's thigh, rubbing his leg, cursing. Clara and Mary and Elaine held their children. Will Scarlett was wrapped in blankets, still as a corpse. Tam sat alongside his unconcious father, just touching the man's cold hand, as David held the deathly Shonet's.

Robin Hood asked the husband, "What's wrong with her?" Her skin was waxy, her lips drawn in, wrinkled and old-looking.

"She's sick. Has been for days. Weeks."

"Why did you not tell us?"

"She wouldn't let me. She says it's God's way of visiting sin on her." David started to cry. "The sweetest, most loving woman on Earth. She never once raised her voice to anyone. God wouldn't harm her, would He?" Friar Tuck came over to him and got to work. He put his hammy arm around David's shoulder, fingered his beads, and they prayed.

Much had built a fire on the dirt floor, and the smoke found its way out the back tunnel. The outlaws sat around small and withdrawn, like children lost in the woods. They looked to their leader as he sat down. He looked back. Outside the rain drummed down, but they could hear only a whisper in here.

"Rob," said Marian when she sat at his side. "Tell us a story, please."

Cedwyn spoke up, "Aye, Rob. Tell us about you and Gil in the Holy Land."

"Where it never rains," added Katie.

Robin Hood leaned back, but there was no support. The fire warmed his face. He shook his head wearily. "You've all heard that story a thousand—" But he was cut off by a chorus of demands, just once more, please, for the children. It was easier to give in than to fight.

"Gil should really tell the story, now that he's here, but you're not the talking kind, are you, Gil? Ah, well, let's see. I was a true knight, wrapped in armor and boiled like an egg, serving the king's cause . . ."

Chapter 15

The female squirrel huddled in the nest and pulled her young ones tight. It was a wicked wind, worse than any she had seen in her three years.

Their tree was strong, a fragrant birch with a sturdy squat bole and well-shaped radial limbs. Their nest was at the base of the largest limb, large because it stuck way out past the forest's edge. Men had removed the smaller trees around, but had not touched this branch high above their heads. Unrestrained, it reached out far for the sunlight. Unshaded, it grew leaves large and glossy. Unprotected, it swayed in every breeze. The storm now took this branch and worked it. The first gusts made the branch bob. The next ones shook it. The peak winds pulled it far, then dragged it past the recovery point. The squirrels hunkered low. The limb popped and splintered, then tore from the trunk. With it went the squirrels' home.

The nest was peeled apart by the wind. Layers of nut hulls, acorns, feathers, fur, and bones were plucked open, and the wind carried it all away higgledy-piggledy. With alarms of motherhood jangling in her tiny head, the squirrel snatched up a blind baby in her teeth and leapt clear to the grass. The gale tumbled her end over end. Unable to see, she sniffed and crawled until she smelled the remains of a robin's egg. This was in a depression she knew, under a yew bush. She deposited her baby in the depression and went back for the others. Her tail was her biggest ally. That wonderful organ was an umbrella, a blanket, a stabilizer, and a parachute. It gave her lift when she leaped. It kept the wind from her ears. It lofted her when she dropped and steered her on her way. In its animation, the tail might have been working the squirrel. Frantically she hunted along the wreckage of the nest as the wind tugged her. A feeble squeaking brought her to the second baby. It clung to the bark with needle claws. She scooped up the loose skin in her teeth and carried it to the grass nest. Then she went for the other two. The third crawled aimlessly, mewling among whirling leaves. She retrieved that one, but could not find the fourth. Panicked, her heart fit to explode within her, she quartered the tree trunk, the sundered nest and its leavings, the heaving ground around it. Nothing. An eddy of wind carried a snatch of mewing to her ears. She ran back to her nestlings. They had crawled into the wind after her. She nestled deep in the depression and huddled the children to her teats. She wrapped them in her tail. They nuzzled and slept.

She had three. For a short time she thought about the fourth, then she forgot. She dozed and waited for the storm to stop.

Chapter 16

Robin Locksley stood atop the bulwark and peered out over the Christian army besieging Acre. It was one vast hot hellish stew.

Acre was a crumbly rock against the sea, a sagging sandcastle about to be washed away. Men in pointed helmets and red crescent flags decorated the top. The fortified city was filled with three thousand Moslem soldiers and at least as many civilians. They looked down from the sheer stone walls onto the Christian army, surrounding the city in a U from the northern shoreline to the southern shoreline. Surrounding the Christian army was the rest of Saladin's army. The Moslems on the outside could wave to their brothers in the castle, and often did. That was all they could do, because a flotilla of European ships cut the city off by sea as the Christian army did by land. The Moslems inside Acre were trapped, and Saladin on the outside was stuck. He could not help the people of Acre, but neither could he depart and leave the Christians free to roam the countryside. Not that they would. One hundred thousand zealous Europeans had been here for two years, and they meant to take the city of Acre.

This gathering was the combined armies of Philip Augustus, King of France; Richard the Lionheart, King of England and France; and the followers of Barbarossa, the dead Emperor of Germany. Each Crusader considered himself sworn to a king or lord, not a country, but there were men here from Denmark, Frisia, Pisa, Genoa, Venice, Champagne, Northern Italy, Germany, France, Scandinavia, and England. Salted into the mix were Venetian merchants, crossbowmen, pilgrims, Moslem mercenaries, peasants, wives, children, holy men, students, pilgrims, artisans, servants, and prostitutes both repentant and active. The land these people jammed was a maze of trenches, bulwarks, redoubts, shanties, privies, tents, picket lines, field chapels and gaming dens. The only trees were catapults, trebuchets, ballistas, siege towers, and the first windmill ever seen in the Near East. There were dogs, cats, rats, hawks, horses, and flies, flies, flies. There was typhus, scurvy, and dysentery. Supplies, more than ten armies could use, were stacked everywhere. Where both ends of the Christians' ground met the sea, ships were jammed so tightly they could scarcely maneuver. To and from these ships moved a constant flow of weaponry, wounded, horses, firewood, barrels of fresh water, gold, but never enough food. Between the twin battle fronts, people made love, loaded siege weapons, bartered supplies, diced, played chess, repaired weapons, and prayed. Under the molten sun, people argued in twenty languages.

"Zee anything?" asked Siegfried.

Robin stood above a redoubt, a fortified sandbox near the outer ring of Moslems. His garb was like that of other Crusaders. Over a linen shift he wore a thick felt gambeson: a smock with padding quilted inside. Over the gambeson he wore a habergeon: a coat of heavy leather from knee to neck to wrist with iron plates sewn on it. The plates overlapped, and *skreeked* at every move. Over this was his green linen surcoat with the Huntingdon coat of arms, a hunting horn over a sheaf of wheat. A leather baldric held his sword and dagger. A kite-shaped shield of linden wood and leather, painted with the family crest, stood upright in the sand. Robin's great bow, crazed from the heat, rested alongside a quiver of arrows. On his head he wore a padded cap, a separate hood of mail, and a conical helmet with the Norman nasal. He wore horsehide gloves to protect his hands from the metal he wore, and high boots that failed to keep out the sand. He wore the golden spurs of a knight. The last layer he wore was black crawling flies.

Robin shook his head to the question. Sweat trickled through his beard to drip off the end of his chin. It painted a rusty triangle down his chest. He called down, "No. Maybe they're moving around more. Might be preparing for a fight. Or maybe they're taking a nap. I could do that." Both men had spent the morning feeding rocks to *Male Voisine*(*), King Phillip's huge mangonel.

Siegfried spat in the sand beside him. Even that tiny movement made him slide downwards. Siegfried was a shortish man with a round face and bright blue eyes. He wore an outfit similar to Robin's, with dark colors and a molded breastplate. His helmet had gold filigree along the brow and a sculpted dragon crest.

Siegfried said, "No, dey will attack. Dey haf the advantage ofer us. Dey are usted to de sun, not like us Nor'teners." He squinted up at the sun, so yellow it was white. He continued to wrap rawhide. The major crisis in his life was a broken axe handle. "Don't know if I trust dis wood. It break too easy. Not like goot Nor'ten wood. Going to get me killed, I think."

"Don't say that. It's jinxy." Robin watched the Moslem line. Heat waves distorted the air so much he could barely see the turbaned helmets and pennanted spears of the enemy. The shimmer made his eyes water. They could have elephants over there for all he knew. The air carried the smells of sickness, sewage, horses, and sweat. He said, "I wish we had the castle. Then we could set up flies like they have and sit in the shade and watch the Moslems roast below."

Siegfried chuckled, "But dey got no food."

(*) Bad Neighbor

"We don't have any either."

"And if ve had der castle dey would siege us. Better to be camped in der middle like dis. Den we haf a choice of which vay to attack. I tolt der commanders dat ve should attack to der west in der morning, and to der east in the evening. Den der sun is not in our eyes. But no vun listens." The creak and slap of catapults sounded all around them.

Robin worked his fingers in his gloves. They were sloppy wet and pruney inside. A flea hopped away before he could kill it. "That's the truth. No one listens and everyone argues. You can't get a draught of water around here without an argument. Even the Moslems would rather argue than fight."

The German wrapped, unwrapped, and rewrapped the axe haft with his leather thong. It was green rawhide stripped from a dead horse. "Dem buggers talk your ears off. I'd rather be tortured."

Robin squinted around his helmet's nasal at the city. The walls were a tumbledown mess. As he watched, another stone struck and bounced away. Christian sappers behind shields mined their way under the great walls: walls so wide, it was said, that along the top two chariots could easily pass. The sappers had reported that underground they could hear Moslems digging a countermine. A Moslem soldier who saw Robin standing raised his bow and shot. Robin watched the arrow wing down and bury itself in the sand twenty feet away. He waved. "We'll have the castle soon enough. Now that Richard's here the negotiating will go hot and heavy."

"Negochiating? Is dat how your king vins vars? I like it ven he charges along like a battering ram, chopping everybody in his way. *Chop, chop*! Dot's my idea of negochiating."

Robin sat down beside the German and sighed. "Richard is an well-rounded king. If a situation calls for a battle, he battles. If it calls for a poisoning, he poisons. We can hurl stones all day, but he'll win by promising somebody something. Being so sick might have slowed him down, though. What are you going to do with that tail?"

Siegfried had two feet of rawhide left at the end of the axe handle. "Dis vill be for tying. Hadn't you better watch der lines?"

"We'll feel them underfoot if they charge." There was no shade to be had in the trench. He picked up some sand and let it trickle between his fingers. Flies covered the two men from heel to helm. They didn't even brush them off their faces. "Did you know we're losing two men to sickness for every one that falls in battle? People have something that makes their skin fall off. They don't even have a name for it. Who would have thought our biggest enemy would be plague?"

The German asked for a nail, but Robin didn't have any. "Vat you expect? With dis many peoples piled up like hogs? Rotten food or no food and shit everywhere, and dead horses and bodies. Ve should set peoples to vork digging middens and graves, but nobody vants any muck in their area. 'Get away from dere!' dey yell at you. 'Dis is our area!' Dis is not a battlefield. Dis is a mess!"

People came and went all the time they sat there. Their trench might have been the main path to a town well. Another knight came up on a chestnut horse, riding not walking, heedless of enemy arrows. He gave not a single nod to either man, but fastened his horse to the picket line beyond, then came and sat down. Robin knew this man by sight, but not his name. He had a handsome angular face, long golden hair and blond beard. He fought left handed because his right hand was a club of scar tissue and missing fingers. Fire, Robin guessed. He had seen this man once or twice before. He was in the forefront of every charge, and was always carried back on his shield. He fought like three madmen. The grim knight settled to the ground and polished his sword, which already gleamed like a mirror. When the knight made no move to introduce himself, Robin said, "Good day. I am Robert Locksley,

Earl of Huntingdon, sometimes Robin Hood. From Sherwood Forest and environs. This is Siegfried, of . . ."

"Hohenstaufen."

The man said, "Gil-berrrrt." The accent was from Scotland or Northumbria, barely understandable. He had no coat of arms, so he wore the red cross of the Crusaders on coat and shield. A poor knight, Robin thought, who had made no formal vows, and had received the accolade in the field. Yet his coat was fitted chain mail, which took a craftsman a year to make. Few men in the Holy Land wore such expensive armor. As Robin pondered, he recalled that even the Moslems spoke of a man named Gilbert. They called him the Lion of Judah. Robin wondered why he had come to this spot in the line. Had he had a falling out with his comrades? Or did he expect the fighting to be hottest here soon?

Robin shrugged. "Welcome to our castle." The Scotsman made no reply.

Sweat ran out of Robin's moustache onto his chapped lips, and he blew it away. "Is it always this hot?"

"Hot? Ha! Vait until summer!"

A waterboy limped along the trench, and each man got a dipperful of water. Siegfried gasped. "I vish we could get good water. Dis stuff gives you the shits."

"In Sherwood it rains when you need it. There are pools of clear water everywhere, and streams that trickle over the rocks. On hot days we would strip off our clothes and just lay on the bottom. Or we'd sleep on beds of cool moss. When I get back I'm going to soak in those pools like a frog till I'm wrinkled all over."

The German snorted. "Me, I could use some *biere bitter*. Or some *sauerkraut*. Dat's good in der heat."

"What is it?"

Siegfried waved one hand. "What you call . . . Food."

"Oh."

"Ve're better off den der Saracens, though. Dey can't drink no spirits. Dat shows you vat kind of religion dey

haf. Dere won't be many converts from der Chermans."
He snorted again.

Nearby an onager groaned as knights cranked the rope
spring to the full. With a *whomp* the arm snapped forward
to bash into the padded frame. The onager crew together
said, "Oops!"

Robin watched Siegfried. "You're not really going to tie
that to your wrist, are you?"

The German nodded.

"You shouldn't tie it to your wrist. Someone'll grab it.
Wrap the ends *around* your hand and hold it in place
against the haft. Then if someone grabs it, or it sticks, you
can let go."

The German appeared not to hear. "Dat, and dey cut
away the end of your prick if you become a Moslem."

The man Gilbert snorted and entered the conversation
for the first time. "They don't cut off tha end. Just tha
loose skin."

"How do you know?"

"Ah just know."

"Unt how do you know?"

Gilbert snorted again. "Ah've done it meself, to laddies.
Little bairns." The Englishman and the German looked at
one another.

Robin asked, "What do they do with the skin?"

"Make a saddle."

Siegfried and Robin both said, "What?"

"Tha's a joke. Y' make a wallet with tha leftover."

Siegfried waved his knife just past Robin's nose. "But
vat's dat got to do with religion, I ask you? Vat's wrong
with the vay God made pricks? Dot's for Jews." He bit
down on the leather. "Ya. I am decided. I tie it around my
wrist. Den if I fall off my horse I won't lose it."

"Ye'll fall off because someone'll pull y'off," commented
Gilbert.

"How many times haff you dropped your sword from
the back of a horse?"

"Never."

Robin took out his own sword to work on it. "You know, that's the queer thing about this Crusade. Our religions. We're here to free the Holy Land from the heathens. But do you know what the heathens call us?"

No one answered as a whore passed by in the trench. Sweat made her green-trimmed clothes cling to her body. She dragged a dirty child who rubbed its eyes with both hands. The three men watched her go. After the whore hobbled an old man. Robin recognized this man: he'd walked on crippled feet all the way from England to fight Saracens. The old man sat down with a groan.

"There you go, lads," he wheezed. He had no teeth. "Meat on the hoof."

"The Bishop of Longfort must have been wrong," said Robin. "He said we were suffering an acute lack of women."

Siegfried spit on his axe handle. "A bishop vould know."

The old man said, "Poxed. You can tell."

Robin mused, "I've heard there were women disguised as men in this campaign, fighting ahorse."

"Thar's three," supplied Gilbert.

Siegfried said, "I hear der Moslem women pluck out der private hairs."

"They don't."

"I didn't believe it anyway."

The old man coughed into his hand, a long, dry cough. "There's some cleric who has a remedy for pox. He makes you fast for seven days, then he baptizes you naked in salt water."

"I'd rather have der pox."

"Anyway," Robin continued, "do you know what the Saracens call us?"

Siegfried said, "I don't like the vay they keep changing things. Now everyone is vearing der helmets that is closed, so you can't see who dey are. Haf you tried looking out of vun of dose? It's like sticking your head in a wine barrel." He huffed.

"I can't afford a helmet, and no one will give me one," lamented the old man.

"They call us infidels," said Robin. "But do you know what they mean?"

"Unbelievers," supplied Gilbert.

The German said, "I'm hungry. Vonder if the last ship brought any fresh meat."

"No."

"Unbelievers, yes. But that means heathens. You see? We call *them* heathens, and we feel that we have to drive the heathens from the Holy Land. Except they call *us* infidels, which means heathens, and *they* feel they should drive *us* out. D'ya see?"

Siegfried asked, "Vere's dot big friend of yours, der big, big vun?"

Robin nodded towards the sea. "What I mean is that we're all just people here. Look at the other night, when we pitted our children against the Saracens'. They had as much pride in their sons as we do."

"What?"

"The other night. It got on towards supper—what there was—so we stopped fighting. Somebody started an argument, a Christian. 'You lot ever think of quitting? Just giving up and letting us have the Holy Land?' And a Moslem says, no, they'll never give up till they've driven us out. 'But what about your children? Are they going to fight, too?' And the Moslems said, yes, they would, for as long as necessary. So they got into an argument about whose children were the better fighters. Finally someone proposed a contest. The Moslems brought up their children, and our side brought up ours, and they had them wrestle Cumberland-style. Whichever child won got to ransom his captive for a florin. Some of those little beggars made a fistful of money. That's the sort of thing that makes me think they're just people."

"Ve haff to fight dem anyway," said Siegfried.

"Aye."

The old man said, "Remember when Richard was sick? Saladin sent him chickens and fruited snow. And when his horse was killed, Saladin sent him one of his own."

"I could use some snow, ja. And some *biere*."

"Nobles are of one blood, no matter their color," Gilbert growled.

The oldster said, "Richard even tried to marry his sister to Saladin's brother."

"She said no."

Robin said, "Yes, but that's my point."

"Vat is your point?"

"That . . ." Robin stopped. "Well, I've forgotten now. But this whole fete of arms is so . . ."

Siegfried asked, "I know vat it vas. Vat happened to your big friend?"

Robin shook his head. "He's unloading ships. Because he's big they think he's stupid, and they use him like an ox."

"Dere's no horse could hold him anyway. But if dey didn't bring meat, vat did they bring?" Siegfried had tied the axe handle on, and stood to take practice swings. Sweat flew off his hands as he parried and slashed.

"More rocks, probably. Richard's 'pebbles from Messina to kill Saracens'."

"More recruits for the fever," said the old man. "No women."

"No food."

Robin said, "They should have brought meat. Richard owns all of Cyprus now. He could send down a hundred beeves a day."

Siegfried asked, "Richard owns Cyprus? Der whole island? Vhen did he take dat?"

"On his way here." Robin stopped his sharpening and stared up at a sky devoid of clouds or birds. "He's supposed to be freeing Jerusalem. But on the way he stopped and took Cyprus because it was unguarded. He's been hawking it to every ruler with money. Anyone here can become King of Cyprus if he can pay the price."

Siegfried stood up. "Barbarossa refused to take Constantinople. Mit fifty thousand men, it could have been his for der asking. But ve rode right past, bound for der Holy Land." The German sighed.

Robin said, "What happened to him? I heard he had a stroke bathing in a river."

Siegfried shook his axe. "It was no bath! He fell off der horse and got tangled in der trappinks! He vas the greatest king der ever vas! If Babarossa were here now—"

The ground beneath them trembled. Down the line a drum tattooed. "Ahorse!" came a far cry, "To arms!" A horn sounded.

Robin and Siegfried grabbed their shields and scrambled along the trench to their horses. Mindful of archers, they kept their heads down. On the way Gilbert's horse shot past them. The blonde man was wedded to the brown body. They heard the horse grunt as he dug in his heels, and the fierce energy in Gilbert lifted the animal over the breastwork like an eagle.

Clambering ahorse and bunching the reins in his left hand, Siegfried growled to no one in particular, "Now ve see who loses vat."

With a cross upright before them, drums rolling and pennants flying, the Crusaders marshalled their forces and thundered out of the camp. They crossed the narrow sand bridge over the gully that separated the lines. Below them gleamed the bones of ten thousand footmen who had mutinied and thrown themselves against Saracen lines without cavalry support. They had lain in the pit until their bodies rotted to skeletons. On the grassy plain beyond waited Saladin's lines. It might have been Saladin himself who scampered on a belled horse between the two armies with only a pair of retainers, ignoring the rain of arrows as he exhorted his troops.

The Crusaders' charge soon disintegrated into the same old pattern. The Saracens—as all Moslem soldiers were called—wore very light, very flexible scale armor, almost like heavy cloth. They had light helms and greaves, and their mounts were unprotected. The Franks—all Crusaders, no matter their origin—wore full armor, sometimes fifty pounds of it, and their horses almost as much. The Saracens rode forward and peppered the enemy with arrows. Then they turned and fled. The Franks pursued like a tidal wave, swearing and charging about and catching nothing but arrows in their hides. In any battle where the Saracens held a line, the Franks smashed it down without missing a step. In open territory, the Saracens skittered about like leaves, giving the knights plenty of room and plenty of feathers. It was common to see a Crusader with twenty arrows stuck in his armor and shield, unharmed, charging blindly after a laughing Saracen. This warfare was, as one Crusader put it, "like fighting a swarm of bees with a club."

A corps of fast Saracens materialized upon the left flank, and they caught the eye of Gilbert Whitehand. A man screaming that loudly and that well was followed automatically, and thirty-odd knights split off the main line, determined to run the Saracens to ground in the small defile they could see beyond. Robin realized it was an ideal spot for an ambush just as the trap closed. Howling "Allah! Bismallah!" three score heathens descended from both sides of the draw. Their murderous short bows—all horn and wood and wire—sent arrow after arrow into Christian mail. Arabian horses danced up and down the sides of the defile where the Franks could not go. The Saracens picked up momentum coming down one slope, ripped through the slow-turning Franks with lance and scimitar, then vanished up the opposite slope. Robin wheeled his horse in circles, trying to close with someone, anyone he could stab, but a horseman would be gone before he could see it, and two more would pink him from behind. Dizzying scenes flashed by as he lunged and swore: Gilbert dismounted and slashing, Siegfried yanked off his horse, a nobleman gripping a scimitar lodged in his breastbone, a Moslem with a knout—

Something smashed into the back of Robin's helmet. His nose hammered into his horse's mane. The blow drove

out the light of day. He slid, unable to catch himself, and
the ground came up at him . . .

Robin Locksley was bathed in fire. Fire licked around
the base of his skull, scorched his eyelids, and trickled
down his throat. He heard a splash, and water hissed on
the fire, putting it out. He must be camped in Sherwood,
and had rolled too close to the pit, but now the rain had
saved him. More water slid across his face. Someone touched
his arm. Marian? He opened his eyes to look directly into
the face of a Moslem.

With one hand pinning Robin's, the man took Robin's
chin and gently rolled it. The movement called up pain
from the back of his head. He massaged Robin's neck. The
man murmured a question in Arabic, which Robin did not
understand. An echo in a voice from Northumbria said,
"He asks if tha' feels better."

"Yes, thank you," Robin replied in English. "Tell him
he is gentler than any Christian leech." Gilbert told him,
and the doctor smiled. He was young, with a black forked
beard and a brilliant white turban. Robin noticed he smelt
very clean. The man tugged Robin onto his side, gently
prodded the bump on his head, then applied a pad and
wrapped gauze around his skull. Holding a candle aloft,
the doctor looked deep into Robin's eyes, moving his own
head to see better. Finally he grunted something and gave
Robin's cheek a pat. He dropped his washcloth into a
silver bowl, rolled up a small packet of tools, and left.

Robin and Gilbert lay on the floor of a tent on thick
parti-colored rugs. Their trappings, weapons, and helmets
were gone. Gilbert had a bruise on his cheek, a scrape on
the back of his head, and more tatters. Past the mouth of
the tent they could see many Moslems around the distant
fire, eating and talking, joking. The tent city they were
part of seemed very large.

Robin made to sit up and retched. Once upright however, he felt stronger, if dizzy. "What happened?" he
asked.

"We lost."

Robin took a moment to thank God for his life, then ask Him why, of all people, he must be imprisoned with a dour Scot. "Were we all captured? The whole party?"

"Aye."

"Where are the rest?"

"Split up. Sent to another camp."

"What about Siegfried?"

"Dead."

Robin rubbed his temples. It hurt, but this pain was a different variety, so it was almost no pain at all. "Oh, well, his heart wasn't in this anyway. I wonder, should I light a candle in his memory or get drunk?"

A Moslem approached his tent. He was tall and very dark, with gold in his smile. He wore a flaxen shirt, baggy green pantaloons, and yellow boots with pointed toes. His turban had a jewel on the brow. He said something in very good French, but Robin Locksley had no more use for French than any other Saxon. "What does he want?" he asked of Gilbert. The Scotsman addressed the Moslem in his own tongue.

The man answered. Gilbert relayed, "He asks if we would care for supper. They have fresh lamb and cheese." Robin's stomach answered: dinner had been scant and far away. As he stood the night became temporarily blacker, but he managed to walk. He had never realized before what a great feat walking really was.

Soon Robin and Gilbert were seated on a rug in a ring of rugs. They accepted cubes of lamb, duck and crane, olives, fresh figs (which tasted like plums to Robin), white butter on flat bread, raisin wine, and delicious oranges that Robin could not get enough of. They were offered grasshoppers in wild honey, but declined. The night was deliciously cool after the blazing day, and they could smell the ocean. They might have been at sea, for the desert sky was all around them rather than simply above, and stars were scattered everywhere. There were many men around the fire, their faces so dark only their teeth and eyes shone in the firelight. They wore fine clothing embroidered with silver and gold threads. The air was scented with cinnamon and cloves and other scents he did not recognize. Their language was a murmurous chuckle. Robin Locksley of Sherwood was newly arrived in the Holy Land, but if not for the presence of the blonde Scotsman beside him, he might have forgotten who he was and where he came from.

The Moor who had fetched them turned out to be the lord: a "sultan," as Gilbert explained. He was very gracious and solicitous during the meal. He asked them many questions about their home and their families. The questions took a long route, since Robin needed Gilbert to translate, and getting a full account was like pulling teeth. The Moslem plied the two Christians with food until they had to refuse. As the plates were taken away, and everyone washed in bowls of water scented with rose attar and flower petals, the sultan settled back onto cushions with an air that suggested he would be there for some time. He made a long speech.

Gilbert told Robin, "It's verra flowery, but he asks if he can offer ye the milk and honey o' Paradise."

Gilbert waited for a response. As always, Robin reflected, men looked to him to run things: why he never understood. Robin was not about to be out-honored, but neither was he prepared for a battle of wits. His head sang from the recent blow, he was sleepy from all the food and wine, and he did not feel entirely attached to the earth underneath him. Yet he told Gilbert, "Ask him—very civil, mind you—why he offers this boon to his enemies?"

The sultan's eyes lit up as he spoke. The strange phrases sounded stranger still when converted to English by a Scotsman. "It is the duty of every Moslem to seek converts. Our cause is just, and our religion the only sure way to Heaven. We would rather have friends beside us in the mosques than enemies under the ground. If you like, we could convert you to the side of the light."

Robin's first thought went not to his Christian soul but

to the end of his penis. But the idea of converting was absurd, and he said, "I can understand the gift you think this to be, and can appreciate it. However, we do not abandon our religion or our cause so lightly. The quest for the cross has made thousands of us leave our homes and brave many dangers in uncharted regions, all for the love of our God. Our reward will be not only milk and honey, but the chance to sit at the right hand of God. I do not think you'll find many Christians who will throw that away."

"Ah. But in our Heaven there are always sheep dripping with fat, and many young boys, and women with breasts like ripe melons."

"Our Heaven is peaceful and full of beautiful things, and we shall consort with angels and the Virgin Mary herself. They both sound grand. Perhaps we'll see you there."

The sultan laughed, as did Robin, but Gilbert had nothing to add except a sulky silence. Then the sultan suddenly clapped his hands and made an announcement. Robin had to poke Gilbert. It was, "Enough debate. I can see you are both dedicated men, and it would be a sin for you to spend the night arguing with an uneducated blasphemer like myself. I only wish I had a holy man here to make you see the true light. Not five minutes would you wallow in the dark pit when thrown the rope of true wisdom." He called out orders to his followers, and eight of them strode off towards the center of the tent city.

"I will show you something, something that few of your people have ever seen. Something that will show you Allah favors this land above all other lands." The retainers staggered up with poles that supported a large box under a speckled carpet. The sultan reached out gingerly to pick up the corner of the rug.

"Sirs, behold!" And he whisked the rug away.

There was a snarling explosion like thunder, and the Christians exclaimed "God's blood!" as one.

The box was a large cage, and inside was a cat as big as a horse. Its taut body was a gleaming orange with black stripes that flowed up and down. The firelight shimmered across its coat. The underbelly was whiter than the stars overhead. The face was a riot of orange and white and black stripes and long animated whiskers. Amid the face, like emeralds in a pot of gold, great round eyes shone first green, then red, then green again. The cat spat like a furnace and slashed at the air and lunged, rocking the cage and churning the sand underneath. Its growls rang like a storm felt through the ground.

"God's blood!" Robin breathed again. "What is it?"

The sultan's voice was full of pride as he talked. "It is called a tiger," Gilbert said in a reverent tone.

The Moslem retainers had backed away from the cage, and framed against the night, with nothing to compare it to, the beast loomed larger and larger until it filled Robin's sight. It really was as big as a horse, only lower to the ground. Rampant, it would stand taller than a man. The beast paced in the confines of the cage, back and forth, turning always in the same direction, its vision tracking them. Its movement was hypnotic. The soundless footsteps, the rhythm of its legs, the suppleness as it turned in its short walk held them rooted. Back and forth went the beast, its whiskers brushing the bars with each turn. It lulled them with its movements like the rush of the surf or the glitter of a fire: a vibrant display of a power denied to men.

After a long time Robin asked, "A tiger? But where does it come from? Is it kin to a lion?"

The Moslem's voice came from the dark itself. Robin had to prod Gilbert to get a response. "Somewha'. It comes from the East. Its stripes hide it in the grass, so it can sneak up on deer. God, look at it! It's . . . God's greatest work." Robin knew the sultan had not said the last part. Gilbert stared at the beast, and the beast stared back at Gilbert. Studying the two profiles, Robin reflected they had much in common. Both had feral eyes under shaggy brows. Both were fearsome in battle: too fearsome to face. And both beings were fierce energy trapped in metal wrappings.

The sultan talked at length, but the Scotsman had stopped translating. After a time, long into the night, the Christians were led away under guard to their tent. Gilbert curled up instantly, to growl and grind his teeth in his sleep. Robin laid awake for a long time. When he nodded off, in his dreams he ran through Sherwood as a tiger.

Thunder drummed against Robin's head where it touched the ground. He was up in an instant. "An attack!" he cried, but Gilbert was already at the tent flap.

It was indeed an attack. Armored Saracens on buff horses swept through the camp with fire and sword. Robin flopped down beside Gilbert. "They'd not destroy their comrades-in-arms, would they?" he asked. Gilbert said nothing. He set his feet under him, waited for a cadre of men to pass, then bolted out the tent. Robin cast a look around for his non-existent weapons, then ran outside after him.

The raiders descended with the wrath of the holy. Robin never did learn if the two Moslem factions had argued over religion, position, hostages, or spoils, but there was hatred on both sides that burned brighter than the fires springing up everywhere. All the raiders were ahorse, and they pointed long lances that shivered in the wind. There were more than sixty raiders in three groups. The first wave rode abreast and aimed their lances at the backs of the men afoot. The second wave charged among the tents, whirling torches through the air and hurling them onto canvas and straw. The third wave swung sabers to cut down men who ran or raised weapons. The defenders of the camp were veterans, but they had been unprepared for a night attack from their own countrymen. The raiders knew their trade. As Robin watched, the first phalanx drummed by, horses in step, and pinned men through the chest. They slipped the lances from the bodies and rode on, and Robin saw more than one man broken under hooves. "Allah! Bismallah!" was shrieked out on both sides.

Billowing fireballs of light shone against the speckled sky
as tents burned at every hand. Long twisted shadows
writhed everywhere. Robin saw fire reflected on armor,
horse sweat, and gouts of blood until the whole world
seemed aflame. But nowhere could he see Gilbert. He
shouted and could barely hear his own voice. Horsemen
swooped by as he clung to the shadows. Robin had his
armor, though not his helmet, and he pulled the chain
mail hood up around his bandaged head. He and Gilbert
had to get away. The horsemen would go afoot to cut the
life from the wounded. Where could Gilbert be? Had he
fled into the night? That did not seem like the man. Then
he had a thought. Robin pitched between the burning
tents and made for the sultan's grounds.

There was Gilbert, pounding on the tiger's cage. It was
such an eerie sight Robin stopped in his tracks. The Scottish
knight stood wrapped in shining chain and the white smock
with the red cross. He was also without his helm. Golden
hair flew all about his head. Before him in the cage crouched
the tiger, a fiend carved of fluid gold and marble and the
black fabric of the night. The furious creature spat and
growled and roared at the shouting and flames and smell
of horses. Between them stood the rigid iron bars. And
the knight ripped at the lock and chain as if to break them
with main strength.

Robin looked for the destroying engine of the raiders. A
contingent of cavalry pirouetted a bow shot away and came
to a rest, ready to sweep through the camp again. Robin
reckoned they had less than a minute before the party
would ride upon them. He rushed to the knight and
grabbed his scaled arm.

"Gilbert!" Robin hissed. "We must away! We've no
weapons!"

The knight fretted with the lock. Robin saw now that he
had a poker he had snatched up somewhere. He did not
seem to hear. The hoofbeats picked up in the distance.
The knight was getting nowhere. Almost in their faces the
tiger sprang upwards in a frenzy. The cage bucked as its

back connected with the top. Gilbert swore as he gashed his hand. Far away in the leaping firelight Robin saw a battery of sweat-shiny faces fix on him. Below the faces were champing horses with white eyes. Their nostrils shied from the bloody lances held just past their heads. On the ground in the alley between them Robin could see only dying men. The raiders thumped their knees to impart a new charge to their mounts. The forest of lances wavered and steadied. Gilbert was fixed only on the tiger, and the tiger on him. Part of Robin's mind informed him he could slip away in a trice. But another part was yanking on the taut chain around the bars.

A hammer, he thought. A club. A rock. A lever. A bar!

Robin raced to the nearest tent and batted aside the burning billowing cloth. His hands found what he needed, and he dragged the hot tent pole away to the cage. He forced himself to ignore the charging Moslems. He could feel pounding under his feet, and it threatened to throw him down. Gilbert stepped aside. Robin rammed the bar through the chain behind the lock. He imagined a whiff of horse sweat. He hoped the first lance blow found his heart: it would be an awful thing to have a lance thick as an arm plunge through your body yet miss something vital. You would hang on that bar like a sparrow on an arrow, feel the coarse wood grinding between your organs, listen to your blood splashing over your legs. The bar thumped against the bottom of the cage. Gilbert grabbed the tentpole high up. Robin saw a flash of silver out of the corner of his eye. He levered his feet against the cage and they heaved.

The chain parted and flew aside as noise engulfed them. A thousand pounds of golden fury brushed back the cage door and the two men. Like an eagle the beast took off into the air. The scream of the horses was drowned in the roar of the tiger. Robin and Gilbert staggered back just as lance points rattled onto the cage bars where they had stood. Iron hooves clipped them in the back, and they wrapped their hands around their heads. They crabbed across the sand to a haven behind the cage. What they saw was like a fresco from Hell.

The giant cat was fully six feet above the ground astride horses and men. Paws struck, claws dug, and teeth met through bone. God's engine of destruction swept away a man's face and part of this throat. Rear feet slid across a horse's withers to send blood free-wheeling into the air. The tiger leapt, clawed, and shouldered its way towards freedom, shearing through leather and horseflesh like cheese. Soldiers screamed and fell from their saddles to come under the hooves of the panicked horses. Lances flew, saddles burst asunder, scale armor split and showered like beads. At the last the tiger set its feet into a dying rider and sprang away. It hurled itself into yellow fire and black shadows and was gone.

Robin came to as a gust of cool air blew through the bars of the empty cage. Raiders afoot materialized from the dark. Their vendetta against the camp was forgotten as they raced to help their comrades. Some shielded their faces from the twisted mess the tiger had left. Gilbert crouched like a ship's figurehead and craned for a glimpse of the beast. It seemed now as mythical as a dragon.

"Gil, let's be off."

The Scotsman turned towards Robin, and for the first time he noticed Gilbert's eyes were the same color as the tiger's. The man nodded his tawny head.

Keeping low, the two knights scuttled like badgers until they were well clear of the camp. Then they rose and trotted away from the fire and noise, out onto the vast sand plain. It was quiet and cool out here. They kept half an eye out for a flash of molten gold, but all was black and silver under the light of a million million stars.

Dawn found them at the seashore. With the sun came heat. Gilbert reckoned they were twenty miles above Acre, with thousands of Moslems between them and their comrades. Their only chance to avoid recapture was to flag down a Christian ship, but the sea was bare. They poked along the shore in hopes of finding a stream that flowed out of the fields to the sea. There were none. They tried digging a hole in the sand just above the shoreline, to see if the water that collected was fresh on top. It wasn't. Robin looked out at the Mediterranean, peaceful and flat. Birds winged by, high up against the white-blue vault of sky.

"What do the gulls drink?" Robin croaked. "Flying must be thirsty work. God! I've never been so thirsty!"

"Hattin was worse," Gilbert commented. Since their adventure last night, the Scotsman talked more readily. Robin wondered if it would last.

He leaned against a rock to rest. "What was Hattin?"

"A campaign. A disaster," Gilbert replied. As they sat and rested, Robin pulled the story out of him little by little.

"It were four years ago. Guy of Luisgan was King of Jerusalem. The Saracens had taken Tiberias, on the Sea of Galilee, which is fresh. It was summer. There were some Christian women held hostage in Tiberias, and Guy's wife was one of them. Guy was content to leave them there. He reckoned they wouldn't come to no harm, and we couldn't help them anyway. The only water was the Galilee, and the Saracens would be five score deep around it. We'd have to cross the desert and fight a battle without water. We had a great army. We would have taken the entire Holy Land, including Tiberias, in a year. As long as we didn't do anything foolish. But the bairns started cryin', 'Save the ladies of Tiberias!' So off we went.

"It took us all day to get there, and we were out of water when we arrived. We were thirsty. We mounted this hill like a saddle called the Horns of Hattin. We could see the lake below. The Moslems were all around it. Now you know Saracens can't stand up to one of our charges, but instead of rushin' down there and taking the water, Guy and some others decided to camp atop the hill. Ah guess they reckoned the Saracens would disappear in the night.

"That night the Saracens came to the bottom of the hill
and fired the grass, and we had to breathe smoke all the
night long. We couldn't get past the fire. No one had had
water for a long time. We even stopped sweatin'. Come
the morning, after the fire had died down, the Moslems
attacked. We were so weak we could hardly stand, but we
stopped their first charges. One flank even broke through
and got away. We rallied around the king's banner, but
they had us. Men just fell from their saddles, and the
horses fell on top of them. Ah couldn't even close my
mouth, my tongue was that swollen. Ah was knocked
down and couldn't get up.

"That was the end of God's army. Saladin had sworn an
oath to behead all the Templars and the Hospitallers, and
he did. The Saracens drew lots for the honor of killing
Christians. Some of them had never held a sword before,
and they went at it mincing, taking little whacks at the
men's necks, so a real soldier had to dispatch them. Saladin
cut off Reynald of Chatillon's head in one stroke. He'd
made a vow to do it: Reynald had raised caravans during a
truce. They threw the rich knights into foul keeps for
ransoming, and sold the rest of us as slaves in Damascus.
There were thousands of us. There were so many slaves
we went for three dinars, which was the price of a pair of
sandals. There were more oxen and mules than anyone
could use, so they just turned them out into the desert.
And we'd lost the True Cross to the heathen.

"There wasn't a free Christian left in the Holy Land
after that. And all for a lack of water."

Robin Hood didn't feel quite so thirsty, although the sea
before him still looked cool and dark. They started walking
again. Their armor squeaked at every step. Robin noted
that the shells they crunched beneath their boots were the
same as those on the shores of England. Gulls keened
overhead as they rode the hot updrafts from the desert
along the shore. Robin asked, "Who bought you?"

Gilbert tossed his yellow hair. He looked young without
his forbidding helmet. "A leech. They know more about

medicine here, real medicine, that heals ye instead of killin' ye. Ah helped him in doctoring, and got so Ah could do it m'self. He never bothered me about becoming a Moslem, nayther. He had this hauberk made for me in Damascus, where they make the best armor, and a Milanese sword. Which Ah've lost."

"This was in a big city?"

"Oh, aye. A monstrous big city, bigger than London. They put up torches to light the streets at night. There are gardens everywhere. Cobbled roads and fountains. Good, clean, fresh water. The streets are full of women in their veils. Lots of Christian slaves. Good thing too, for we made all the liquor they pretended not to drink."

Robin smiled despite his discomfort. "How did you win your freedom?"

"Word came there was a large army beseigin' Acre. So one night Ah killed m' master, dressed m'self as a Moslem, and walked till Ah found the Christians."

Robin grunted. The bandage around his head burned with heat. Blood and fluid had dried his hair into a sticky, itchy mess. The beach before him shimmered with more than sun. "If it's all the same to you, I think we should surrender to the next group we come across. Better to be captured than die of thirst." Gilbert grunted and Robin took it for assent.

The shoreline turned to rocky beach backed by low cliffs. Miles down the shore they found a ship pulled up on the strand. It was an Arabian dhou. The vessel had sharp lines like a tern's body, and the sides and bottom were clean. The triangular sail drooped at such an acute slant it looked unstepped. The crew sat upon the shore in the shade of a cliff wall. The dozen men worked with something in their laps. With their hands away from their sides, Robin and Gilbert crunched across the shingle towards the Arabs.

The men made no move except to watch their captain. He was a small man, almost black, with a rose-colored turban, a white shirt, green felt pantaloons, and bare feet.

"Look, my friends," the captain called in Persian when the Christians were within earshot. "Look what Allah the bountiful has brought us— customers!"

The men laughed as Gilbert translated for Robin. The captain went on, "You look very thirsty, royal lords. Would you care for some grape juice?" He held up a skin and winked. "I must warn you though, due to my own negligence, this juice has fermented. We would pour it out, but it is all we have. Would I offend by offering it?"

Robin Hood laughed with cracked lips. The man was as bright and cheery as a monkey. His face was gold-toothed and lined like a mink's. The captain laughed again and the crew joined in. Even Gilbert smiled. The knights sat and accepted the skin. They didn't want to finish it, but the Arabs insisted and fetched more from the ship. The Christians soaked their throats until they brimmed over, then told their tale.

"Very interesting," said the Arabian when Robin had finished. "And the tiger swept right by you, between you even, and left you unharmed? Indeed, Allah, who sees all and knows all and despises waste, looks upon you with favor. You are both destined for great things. It is our pleasure to be here and provide you with our humble fare. Surely our children and our children's children will know of you and speak of this day."

Robin and Gilbert waved off the compliments. The Britons had by now drunk a wineskin each, and what felt like their weights in water from a barrel. Robin's belly sloshed when he moved. The crew broiled fish over a fire. They made tea. There was butter and goat's cheese to go with it. Robin settled back on his elbows in the sand and groaned with delight.

"If it weren't for the killing," he said, "I could hope this Crusade lasted twenty years."

When Gilbert translated that the crew had another great laugh. Their captain explained that he had to make one last stop before departing for Alexandria, and thence to Bagdhad. All the time they sat there, he and his men worked on tiaras, brooches, armbands, and other gaudy jewelry. They defaced them with knives, twisted them so the jewels popped out, pricked their fingers and smeared blood into cracks. Robin was about to burst when the captain explained why.

"My friends, we must uphold an image. Do not wise men say it is better to contract leprosy than an image? We are fearless sailors, my crew and I, and we sail farther than anyone else beyond the horizon in quest of fabulous riches. Upon our return, we cannot bring just any old thing—spices or mother-of-pearl, or silks and teakwood—but must have gleaming jewels and gold icons that were ripped from the hands of ogres and monsters. These bloodied items sell for more than unsoiled ones. Besides, in the process many jewels fall out, and these we keep."

"You should meet my cousin Will," Robin said. "You and he would get along. But I'm afraid we do you a dishonor, good sir," he said through Gilbert, "for my companion and I have no coin to repay you your kindness."

The captain waved a stiletto airily. "Do not discommode yourselves, my friends. Our lives will be long. You can repay me at some point in the future. If not in this life, then another. All this trouble, this warring," he pointed the blade towards Robin's armor, "it is passing. It lasts no longer than breaking wind. Wise men care not for the distinction of Moslem and Christian. I say, there are only customers you have, and customers you have not met yet, and I never argue with my customers. (Except over prices, of course.) Commerce is our saving. Your people and mine might fight for a year, or ten years, but they will trade for a century. By making peace and talking business here on this beach, we fulfill the deepest wishes of Allah." His white smile sparkled in his brown face.

Robin nodded. "Then I offer my thanks, and will remember you in my prayers." Gilbert grunted.

The captain stood up to look out at the ocean and the wind. "It's time to go. We sail to the south. Would you

care for passage? Antioch, perhaps? Jaffa? Memphis?" He
grinned wider. "Acre?"

Robin laughed again, and he and Gilbert helped the
crew make weigh. Soon they were off the shimmering
beach, seated in the prow of the ship, their faces awash
with the warm tangy breeze. They ate dates and watched
porpoises sport. The captain announced they would make
Acre after nightfall. "All good commerce takes place in the
dark," he added, and laughed.

He took a turn around the small ship, then sat beside
them. "To pass the time, we should have stories. I am
renowned for my story-telling. I spend far too much time
in hearing and telling them, but my wife says my stories
are a blessing from Allah, and I am to use them to bring
infidels to the light. Rest awhile, while I speak. You mentioned the tiger. It reminds me of one of the voyages of
our greatest hero, the merchant Sinbad. . . ."

Now I had not been home from the sea but one year
before the compulsion to travel again made its mark upon
me. So, leaving my home in the hands of my most capable
wife, I obtained passage on a merchant ship and brought
aboard my trade goods.

Our journey progressed well, with all aboard making
many propitious trades, until one day when we passed a
dark cliff cut with a deep bay. It was then low tide and the
full of the moon, and none of us realized the force with
which the tide moved up this cleft. Before we could adjust
our sails, our ship was overpowered and swept into the
defile. The vessel foundered on the rocks, smashed into a
thousand pieces. But Allah was merciful, as always, and
most of us gained the shore. Fortunate we were to have
our lives, and glad, but we were too spent to bestir ourselves and seek shelter from further peril. And so it was
that the natives of that land found us and carried us off.

These people lived in terror of a great beast who dwelt
in the forest adjacent. To allay the ravenous tendencies of
this fiend, the natives were forced to set out one of their

own members for the monster to feast on. Great was their rejoicing when there were deposited so many sacrifices at their feet. They secured our party in a large house built of stout logs, and every night dragged another member away. This unfortunate they bound and left on a rock outside the village walls before sunset. During the night the beast would come, and the victim's piteous screams filled our ears. With the rising of the sun there would be seen nothing but streaks of blood on the rock, and great footprints going back into the forest.

Finally there was only a man from Salabat named Rachid and myself in the log prison. Knowing that one of us was to die that night, yet wanting to resist the evil wills of our captors to the last, Rachid and I made a pact. Whomsoever was taken that night would call out as the beast attacked him, so that the other might learn something of the beast's nature and profit by the knowledge, such that he might even save his life.

Soon, as the sun lowered in its course, our captors arrived and carried Rachid away. The hours of the night were many, and each as long as a lifetime, until finally I heard the cries of my companion. "Allah preserve me!" he screamed. "The beast has hands that crush me like a wine press!" Then the screams stopped, and I knew that Rachid had joined the blessed ranks of Jamshy'd and Bahra'm.

Now there was only myself left, and I resolved to make as good a showing as I could. Using my teeth, I rent the sheepskins that lay on the floor of my prison, and padded my clothing with the pieces. Then I committed my soul to Allah, and prayed that the few good deeds I had accomplished in my life might weigh against my many sins, and that I might enter Paradise and see the magnificence of that beauteous garden.

Soon the natives came for me, and I was roughly bound and carried past the village walls. The natives left me on the rock just as the sun set and hurried into their village to bar their doors. The blackness of the night was complete, the heavy air stultifying, and I fell into a swoon. Then I awoke as the marauder approached. My prayers to Allah were torn from my lips as a great pair of hands, many times larger than my own, closed around my chest. They squeezed mightily, but the padding of sheepskin beneath my clothing protected me, and I did not expire, although I feigned death. The monster then carried me over the floor of the forest, and I was at length thrown into a cave, this all in the blackest of nights.

When the sun rose, to my amazement the beast stood revealed as an ape, taller than a man and many times stronger. I remembered then the tales of giant apes that live far up on the hillsides of Egypt, and I shuddered without shame. But the ape did me no harm, thinking me dead, and it left. I then inspected my surroundings, and found the cave to be littered with the garments and jewelry of many victims. Gold was to be seen in plenty, and rubies and emeralds, as well as jeweled daggers and brooches for turbans and sashes. With one of these daggers I released myself from bondage. I then crawled to the mouth of the cave to see where lay the monster and whence I might escape.

To my dismay I found that the cave was high up on the face of a cliff that looked out over thick forest and a jungle pool. The giant ape, spent by its nocturnal exertions, had drunk a great quantity of water from the pool and lain down to rest. It was sleeping directly below me, and I could not hope to escape without rousing it. But as ever, Allah is merciful, as He will always be for the faithful and obedient, and He sent forth a tiger, a great striped cat of unbelievable ferocity. It came from the forest to drink at the far side of the pool.

Quick to take advantage of this blessing, I slashed my arm with a dagger and smeared my blood onto the sheepskin. This morsel I then waved outside the cave mouth. The tawny beast, upon seeing the bloodied sheepskin, which no cat can resist, leapt at once into the pool and swam in my direction. The great ape was alerted from its slumber by the noise, and awoke to see the maddened cat advancing upon it. Immediately the ape arose and attacked the tiger, and the fury of their clash sent the birds of the forest aloft in terror.

I took that moment to fill my shirt with the spoils of the cave, taking only the finest diamonds and rubies and pearls, and, unwinding my turban and tying it securely to a bush, I descended to the trees which overhung the pool and slipped away into the forest.

In keeping with the wisdom of ancient travellers, I followed a stream until it met the sea, and there I encountered a shipload of my fellow countrymen filling water casks. So amazed were they at my story, and so cognizant that I was indeed blessed by Allah, that they did not ask of me any fare, but welcomed me aboard, feeling that my mere presence on their ship would bring good luck.

Thus did we sail back along my original route. On the way we made many fortuitous trades, trading rice for peppercorns, and the peppercorns for sugar cane, and the sugar cane for silk and damask. We saw many fabled creatures along the way, such as black birds who could not fly, but swam below the waves and caught fish in their beaks, and fish with ears like rabbits that they used to paddle on the waves.

Eventually we arrived at Basra, and thence to Bagdhad, where I sold my jewels and silks to make a handsome profit. I gave a tenth and a tenth again of my riches as alms, and then settled to enjoy the life of a prosperous merchant, with many prayers to offer to Allah, and many tales to tell.

Robin Hood looked around at his followers. Of the children, all but the oldest were asleep. Even some of the adults had nodded off. More than the quiet outside, that fact told Robin the unnatural storm was over.

"And that was it," he whispered to the last listeners. "The Arab and his crew dropped us ashore at Acre, at night, and we just walked into our camp. We tried to thank him, but he just waved and laughed some more.

You'd have thought he was potted all the time." Robin shook his head. "Oh, and he said one other thing. As he left us off, I realized I hadn't learned his name, and I needed that for my prayers. Do you know what he told me?"

The children around his feet shook their heads dumbly.

"He said, 'Oh, I am ashamed to tell it, for I was named after one of our great heroes, and have proved so unworthy. My father named me Sinbad.' Then he laughed again and sailed away."

Katie, first to doubt, asked, "Was he really Sinbad?"

But Tam interrupted her. "What happened to the tiger?"

Robin looked blank. "Tiger? Oh, from the Saracen camp! Last I saw, he just ran off into the night. He could have gone anywhere."

"*Anywhere?*"

"Aye," Robin whispered. "Anywhere."

Chapter 17

The passing of the unholy storm left the smell of spring strong. In Cedwyn's cottage, the smell triggered the nostrils of a cat.

Cedwyn had wanted a black cat. Witches needed a familiar that was strong and pure, stealthy and secret, fit for the night, and unafraid. But since black cats were destroyed at birth, Cedwyn had to be content with a gray striped one. Its name was Rhiannon.

Asleep by the extinguished hearth, Rhiannon visited hell on phantom mice and dream snakes. The cat was stretched on her side, as flat and limp as a jellyfish. But a cat's ears are never asleep, and hers swivelled now towards minute scratchings in the wall. The cat opened her eyes wide and brought her ears erect. Her tail flickered at the tip. Knowing the humans were gone, a mouse crept from its hole. Rhiannon licked at the ducts behind her fangs for the smell. It was an old male mouse whose last meal had been pine seeds. Rhiannon lifted her body. Ashes that trickled off her coat made more noise than she did. She crouched and froze. The mouse hopped away from the wall and looked around. As it turned the cat slunk forward. The myopic mouse looked her way and she froze again. The tiny beast waffled. It could smell cat, but not recent cat. It found no tell-tale heat spots on the dirt floor. The mouse hopped forward and reached a mandrake spike. It nibbled, looked around, sniffed, nibbled again, looked around, sniffed, nibbled. It tugged at the root to gauge its weight. It nibbled some more. At every twitch of the mouse's teeth Rhiannon edged forward. The mouse saw the room only as a blur, but it would detect a quick movement. Rhiannon moved fluidly so the stripes along her body melted against the background. She closed. The only sound she could not control was her heartbeat. The mouse stopped nibbling. The cat took one more step, and the mouse bolted. Rhiannon plunged, skipped to change direction, scrabbled her feet under her, pushed off with her hind legs to sail through the air. Her front paws collided with the wooden wall just as the mouse disappeared. Rhiannon bounced off the wall, yowped, landed on two feet and then two more, regained her stance, and looked around. No one had seen her miss.

She licked the mouse hair from between her claws. She went back to the fire and back to sleep.

Chapter 18

"Rob, the one-eyed villain is gone."

"Oh God, Gil, don't tell me that."

It was the morning after the storm. Men had exited the bolthole at the back of the mound, then chopped away the trees piled against the hall door. They were piled there more thickly than anywhere else, but that could have been because the hillock was simply the biggest feature around. No one commented either way. Gilbert had taken sword and shield to check on the prisoners. Now Robin Hood had his report. Leaving the others to hack away, he led Gilbert and Little John toward the lower meadow. They had to thread past the fallen branches that littered the common. In some places the butts had gouged up the earth in huge divots. Little John clucked his tongue. "Lot of free firewood."

They came to the tree where they had chained One-eye (they never had learned his name). The top of the birch had broken off at the first branch. There was no trace of the prisoner.

Gilbert pointed with his sword. "He climbed twelve feet, straight up, during a storm, dragging a chain."

"But he was sick," said Little John.

"He was mad," said Robin Hood.

They went to check on the man in red. They walked along the track and far up the slope and came to the tree where the renegade had been chained the day before.

"What, is he gone too?" burst out Little John. But when they got closer all three men crossed themselves. The manacles were there along with a tattered red leg bone. Beyond was a hand. Scraps of cloth no bigger than oak leaves were churned into the black soil, which gave off a graveyard smell.

"Wha?" asked Gilbert.

"The boar," croaked Robin. A picture welled up in his mind: chained helpless, blind in a howling windstorm, set upon by a monster big as an ox, with champing jaws . . .

"He needs a Christian burial." The others agreed. It would appease the man's soul and prevent his ghost from haunting Sherwood.

"I'll gather him together," offered Little John.

"Thank you, John. I'll send Tuck up here and keep the rest away."

Robin and Gilbert turned back for the hall.

Gilbert asked, "Whar d'ya s'pose that one-eyed bastard will gae?"

It took Robin a moment to translate Gilbert's Scottish accent. The outlaw chief shook his head. "If he's smart, he'll run and keep running till he's so far no one understands his tongue. Because if I find him again, I'll hang him from the first tree."

"He can tell where 'r camp is."

"Lots of folks know where we are."

"Not our enemies."

At the hall, Black Bart had brought out a long saw, and he and Ben Barrel clove the tree that leaned against the hall door. When the door was finally clear, they could all see the long gashes along the wood made by tusks, and the mark of cloven hooves wide as man's hand. The outlaws continued to clean up. It was a habit, and unnecessary. They had to leave Sherwood soon—within a week, as some counted. Although no one discussed it, Robin Hood suspected many would be glad to go. His foresters were afraid of the forest. They looked continually over their shoulders, and started at noises. Ben Barrel and Arthur

A'Bland went with their wives to fetch water from the pond, which was within sight. Even the heartiest people snapped at one another and cuffed their children. Red Tom and Polly emptied their cottage. Their roof had been thatch, but not a straw was to be seen. Clara and Mary righted a cauldron and scoured it with grass, then laid a fire to start soup from venison bones. Grace swept up the stained glass from the hall floor and asked what to do with it. There were only splinters left, and Robin told her to bury it somewhere, but to save the leading. The unmarried women's cottage was flat, its stone walls knocked to rubble by a massive branch. Grace, Jane, and Katie fished out their few belongings and pieced them together. The children worked mostly under Will Stutly, picking and stacking faggots into ready bonfire heaps. Others he made pull up handfuls of grass to strew in the cave for a sweet smell. Meanwhile people moved into the cave. They carried their beds—some being dismantled to fit through the tiny door—or their ticking, their cloaks and chamberpots. Robin instructed the siege panel be kept by the door. He made a mental note to run practice sessions on installing it before nightfall. The children should learn too. He ordered Red Tom and Polly to board over the windows, and do whatever else they could to fortify the hall further. Sheaves of arrows were hung on the walls. The bolthole tunnel was swept clean. People moved slowly and quietly, and talked in low voices, as if words could stir up another windstorm. Only the children carried on in excited whispers.

Robin Hood surveyed all this. There was little point in cleaning up, he thought bitterly, but hard work brought an untroubled mind. By the end of the day there would be no trace of the storm except for the white tips of branches above the glade. The unseen effects would last much longer. The Fox of Sherwood was most disturbed that they couldn't set up pickets. Without a screen of sentries they were helpless. Anyone could attack them at any time. Or had the storm rendered their enemies incapable of attacking? The itch to know—curiousity, Robin's biggest vice —set deep and would not dislodge. He hunted up Brian.

The new man patched turf on top of the hall. "Brian," Robin called, "have you ever been to Nottingham?"

"No, m'lord."

"Don't 'milord' me. I'll have no one call me lord. Come down here. Never been to Nottingham, eh? Then I'm sending you there in disguise."

"Yes, mi—, uh, Robin."

"Now don't be nervous. I just want you to walk around town and find out what you can."

"How?"

"Just act vaguely stupid and ask questions about everything you hear. When you're not hearing anything new, come home. Can you do that?"

"Uh think so."

Robin Hood looked at the sky. It was blue but somehow thick. "You'll need an escort . . . through the woods. I'll send Little John, Arthur, and someone else. They'll take you to the edge of the forest. Fifteen miles out, fifteen back: they should make it back by sundown if they don't dawdle. And you'll need new clothes. It's open season on Lincoln green these days. See Scarlett—no, dammit to hell, that's wrong." Robin blew out his cheeks. "Come with me."

They entered the hall to pass into the cave beyond. They could see Will Scarlett abed, a fat and lumpy ticking over him. Cedwyn spooned a thin broth into his lips. Old Bess had to hold the feverish head still. Tam sat in a corner near the head, not touching his father, gnawing his lip, and trying not to cry. Will was heavily strapped with rags, and his wounded leg was elevated on a board. Skin showed very white. The bandages were soaked in blood.

Robin led Brian into the cave to the chest of clothing. His follower carried a torch. He was obviously much affected by Will's condition, because he muttered vaguely that, "Someone should do something."

Robin Hood whipped around so suddenly Brian almost

dropped his torch. "Don't you think I'm doing all I *can*? What the hell else should I do? Will's my own cousin! Don't you think I *care* what happens to him?" Then he stopped. Brian held up his arms in anticipation of a blow. Robin cursed himself. "Oh lad, I'm sorry. It's been a terrible hard spring, and I'm worried sick over all of this. It's none of it your fault. It's mine. Can you forgive me?" Brian mumbled a reply. Robin decided to get on with the job at hand. He opened the chest and rummaged around, then drew out a tattered cloak. "This will do, I think. You'll look poor. Say you're a tiler out of work. You are, so that's no lie. St Mary's church might need some tiling. Too bad we didn't have more warning, we could have sent someone in and *made* tiling work. Try it on." He fished around and found some trousers and ratty hose, and a rag of a shirt. "Go barefoot. Or wear your boots to the edge of the woods and hide 'em. We'll rip the soles from the hose. Now, when you get there, just ask around about everything that's going on. People love to tell news, and the more the better. If you're fresh from out of town they'll love you. They'll talk your ear off. Act a little bit stupid, but not too much, so they'll explain in full but not give up. Practice this." Robin lowered his head, slackened his lips, and stared at Brian's wishbone. Brian tried to mimic the pose. "Not too stupid, mind. No one likes to talk to a dunce. That's better. Intent. Good. Ask at the edge of town first, then work inwards. Go to the marketplace last, because if people see you asking their neighbors the same questions they'll get suspicious. They might call the guard, and they'll lock you up because it's the easiest thing to do."

Brian had stripped his Lincoln green and donned the rags. He plucked at them to set them right, which was impossible. "What do Uh ask?"

"We'll need mud on your face. Ask about the storm, if it was as bad in town. Say you had to sleep in the woods under leaves. Ask if anyone was killed, and who. See if the guard was kept on the walls, or whether the sheriff let them inside. Ask who's been on the road, and whether they caught the rogues, or if anyone's seen them. Ask about the boar: has anyone seen it up close, or by day, or have they seen it do any magic. Does it poison water? Does it destroy crops and eat them, or just wreak havoc? Has it killed anyone? Is anyone trying to do anything about it? Are people getting their seed in? Ask after the king, and the sheriff. Ask about Sir Guy of Gisborne. And see if the one-eyed villain turns up, though I can't imagine how. Ask anything you think of that might bear on us. We can't play dice in the dark. Keep your ears open. Have you got all that, lad?"

Brian had nodded his head till he was dizzy. "Uh think so, Robin. Uh'll try."

Robin clapped him on the shoulder. "Stout lad. That's all we ask. Now get you gone. You should make Nottingham gate before it closes. Take this." Robin opened another chest and gave him a fat purse. "Buy anything you think we need. But ask Marian before you leave. Make *sure* you get what she says." Robin laughed, but sobered suddenly. "Get garlic, whatever it costs." The new orphan of the road shuffled out of the cave.

Robin Hood stopped at the sickbed on his way out. He bent and sniffed along the bandages.

Without turning her head Cedwyn reported, "No corruption yet. It's too early. But there will be. It's swelling fit to burst the bandages. In some places you can see bone. It really should come off." She addressed these comments not at the outlaw chief, but at Old Bess. Will's mother merely shook her head with her mouth clamped shut.

Will's moans subsided as the hot soup took effect. Robin studied Tam. He debated whether to send the boy to work or not, but decided to leave him here with his father. His father would be gone soon, like his mother before.

Marian came to the door and signalled her husband to step outside.

"We have a new problem," she said. "Shonet."

"Shonet?" Robin had forgotten all about her. "That's right. She was sick last night. Is she with child?"

"No. There are lines of pain around her eyes. I fear it's something inside."

The outlaw chief rubbed his forehead. "God of love, what's brought this on?"

Robin's pretty wife had her own set of lines around her eyes. "It's just plain sickness, Rob. Not black magic."

"Then why doesn't she . . ." Robin stopped. Why doesn't she send for Cedwyn? Because Shonet was very devout. She had been a prioress before coming to Sherwood. She must have dropped her vow somewhere along the way, but like many of the folk in Sherwood was not questioned about her past. Although she had never said as much, Robin Hood suspected Shonet disapproved of the witch Cedwyn and her old ways. He thought this through while Marian waited. "All right, why doesn't she see Gilbert, then? He knows more of medicine than any five leeches."

Again Marian shook her head. "Because he's a man. Shonet entered the priory as a girl. She was a novice before she could talk. I—I don't think she and David have even—"

Robin waved his hands to cut her off. How one woman knew this about another he couldn't guess. It made him wonder what all the women of Sherwood knew together. "What do you suggest?"

"Cedwyn must read her."

Robin nodded, glad Marian had made the decision. "All right, where are they?"

David and Shonet were in their cabin. David had carried her there first thing, but would have to carry her back into the cave for the night. They had moved into this cottage when they married, and David had slaved every day until after dark to make it presentable. The stone and wood exterior gleamed with a coat of milk white paint. David had walked across snow to Nottingham to get the powder for the paint. The door was freshly planed ash, white and fine as bone. Robin wondered why the fury of the storm had left this cottage untouched as he knocked. Marian and Cedwyn were behind him.

David answered. He was a handsome man with a bony face, who wore his black hair long because foresters had cut off his ears. When he saw the party at the door he said nothing, but let them in with a defeated air.

The interior of the cottage was dazzling. The plank ceiling and walls were white. A large gilt cross decorated one wall, and the bed had a sprawling red quilt. A hand-carved bedstead took up most of the room. Shonet was in bed. When she saw the party her eyes filled with tears. Marian immediately knelt down to take the woman's hand.

"No, Marian, no, it's not right," she pleaded. "It's not Christian."

Marian hushed her and stroked her hair. Shonet's one vanity was her red-gold hair which she brushed thrice daily. Cedwyn tried to look unobtrusive as she moved to the other side of the bed. Marian cooed and stroked while the witch started her diagnosis. David and Robin looked on helplessly.

Cedwyn looked into Shonet's eyes, at her tongue, at her palms. She fingered the sweat on the woman's forehead and tasted it. She passed her hand under the sheets. Shonet flinched. To Cedwyn's unspoken query, she pointed at her lower abdomen. Cedwyn rubbed her palms on her gown. Then she laid her chapped hands over Shonet's eyes, gently, and moved her hands downwards. Robin, Marian, and David watched as the witch slowly drew her hands down Shonet's neck, onto the breastbone, then slowly onto the stomach. As Cedwyn's hands continued, they began to tremble and arch, then twitch and shake uncontrollably while her face grew taut. She drew a sharp breath. Finally Cedwyn could take the pain no longer, and she jerked her hands away. She flexed her tiny hands again and again.

Shonet had been close to passing out, both from hyperventilation and worry. Now she opened her eyes to look at the witch. Cedwyn slowly shook her head. There were tears in her eyes. She let them fall as she squeezed out the door. Shonet burst into sobs and covered her face. Marian wrapped her arms around the woman and hugged her, murmuring as to a frightened child. David looked at everyone at once, then leaped out the door after Cedwyn. Robin Hood was close behind.

David caught up to the tiny witch, grabbed her roughly by the shoulder and spun her around. Robin Hood removed his hand, but the husband was oblivious.

"Will she get better? Can you cure her?" David demanded. The folk within earshot—a number of them had found jobs close by—paused in their tasks. "I want to know! What did you find in there?"

Cedwyn looked small and very frail. Robin had never seen tears on her cheeks before. She whispered, "She has the crab in her vitals." David came stock upright. "It is growing. There's nothing can be done."

David looked wildly at the two of them, then bolted back to his cabin. Cedwyn sniffled and then blubbered, and Robin took her in his arms. He patted her back absently and wondered what else would happen.

Later, Friar Tuck led them in a special Mass of Thanksgiving. It was long and tiresome. Stomachs without breakfast growled, but people attended silently and responded quickly.

Over their breakfast of venison soup, Elaine finally put the question. "Robin, when do we leave for London?"

The leader of Sherwood stopped eating, as did everyone else. He finally replied. "It's a ways off yet. It will take us a fortnight to walk there. So we've—"

"Six days," said Ben.

Robin sighed. That soon? "We've little enough to prepare. Let's put it off for now." They echoed his sighs, and everyone agreed that was best.

But that afternoon people left off the cleanup and made ready to move. Will Stutly searched for material to stitch into rucksacks. Red Tom packed his carpentry tools. Black Bart sorted iron. The children chattered about the trip and what life would be like in London. Little John, Arthur, and Grace returned to a changed camp.

Late that night, as the somnolent masses muttered and
hissed in their sleep, Robin Hood knelt by his bed on the
dirt floor of the cave and prayed. "Lord of us all, Father,
from Whom all wit and goodness falls, thank You for this
day and Your protection. I hope I have pleased You in
following Your teachings and precepts. I know in my heart
that I am set adversities to test me in my faith. I accept
Your judgement, and hope I never waver. I pray not for
my sake, but for the minds and souls of my followers, who
need Thy guidance, as do I. For myself, if it not be too
impertinent, I would ask only one boon. Whatever the
future may bring, might You hold off any more problems
until I solve these? My mind is awhirl now, and I fear I
might falter if assigned more. But I will abide by Your
judgement as always. I apologize for being such an unworthy vessel. I promise to try harder, tomorrow. Amen."

And Marian hugged him until he fell asleep.

Sir Guy of Gisborne forced his horse right up to the
tower, despite the animal's skidding on the rotted sandstone. His hounds would not follow. Guy threw the reins
to the ground, barked to his men to stay put, and jerked
open the black door.

Bats by the dozens spilled out into the fading light.
They whirled and spun around the man's head as he flailed
his arms. Then they were gone, like dirty snow carried
before the wind. Guy swore as he stomped up the slimy
stairs.

At the topmost chamber he threw aside a tapestry and
lunged inside. But again he threw up his arms when he
beheld a dry and dusty boar's head that stared at him from
the wall. He hadn't noticed it on his last visit. The heavy
odor of the room assaulted him like a phantom from child-
hood. Only his anger got him inside and opposite the
woman.

"You! You whore! What the hell have you done?"

Taragal looked older and more tired than when last he'd
seen her. Her neck was stringy under the gold circlet. But

her nostrils flared as she lifted her head high. "Be damned in your talk! What *have* I done?"

"You know well what you've done! This curse'd boar! The thing is killing my serfs' flocks and raining destruction! It's driven them indoors, and *whips* won't drive them out! It will cost me a harvest, you bitch! And why did you cause that storm? I lost two men from the walls!"

The sorceress reached to her table and gathered dust from a bowl in her palm. She replied evenly, "You asked for the boar. You have it. As to the storm, I didn't cause it. The boar did. It has its own mind, its own magic. It's alive with ancient evil that wants no one alive in Sherwood." She gestured as she talked, and in the half-light, Guy could not see brown powder spray from her hand.

The viscount clawed his hands in the air. "Are you—are you saying you *can't control it?*"

The sorceress shrugged, and her gown slipped from her shoulder artfully. "What do you think, you can pull a stone from a dam and then hold back the water? Play with magic, know not what you pursue, and it will wash you away as if you never existed."

Guy knuckled his temples. "If you can't control it, you stupid . . . How is the . . . the . . . boar to destroy Locksley?"

"I don't know."

Guy spat, but it sounded a sob. "You're *useless!* *Useless!* I'm *done* with you."

"No, you're not," she replied. She came closer and took his hand.

Chapter 19

At the man's entrance the bats took flight. Some had hung by one claw, dozing or defecating as they woke. Females flew with pink babies clutching their breasts. Others flitted about visiting or playing. But the sudden influx of moving air and human scent set them aflutter like leaves. They spun and swirled and twisted in the air, and beat their way out the door into the dusk.

They listened for hawks, for the sun was not quite down. Owls were a bigger concern, with their hooks carried on silent feathers. The wind pushed here at the top of the ridge, and the black string of the flock spiraled sideways and up like smoke. To men they were silent. To themselves they travelled in cacophony. The animals' large ears rang with the blare of each other's sonar, the click of beetle carapaces, the buzz of mosquitoes, the rumble of bees and the whine of gnats. They seemed almost to live on the air itself. They sparkled against the night sky like black stars. These creatures were little brown bats, called pipistrelles, with heads and tails like bears, and bones in their wings like a man's hand. They were softer than rabbits, cleaner than cats, smaller than mice. Some were twenty years old. Their movements were jerky. They flew like stones skipped over water, for they were more flying mice than birds, and they had to work very hard to stay aloft. These animals weighed no more than a stalk of grass. But at their appearance men threw up their hands and crossed themselves and jibbered prayers.

In their colonies they could be stoned. In trees they could be surprised and eaten. But on the highways of wind the bats were free and safe.

Chapter 20

"I know what to do. I'll find Puck. He should be able to tell me what's happening in these woods."

Marian stopped. "Has it come to that?"

Robin waved a hand. "Oh, Puck's all right. We're friends, he and I. He won't hurt me. But I have nothing to give him."

"And you'll have to walk through the forest alone."

Robin hadn't thought about going through the forest alone. Before thinking he said, "I can always get up a tree . . ." Will Scarlett had gotten up a tree.

Marian said, "I could go with you. He might not mind me."

Robin Hood shook his head. They discussed this in their cottage, away from everyone else. "I have to go alone. He won't come out for anyone else. He might not come out for me. Especially if I'm empty handed." Whenever Robin went to visit the fairy, he took milk or cheese, or raisins and apples, or honey. Venison would not do.

"Is it worth it? He might make things worse. The forest is so strange."

"We're in dire straits, Marian. He may be willing to help."

"Or he may pull the laces out of your boots. Or lead you into a swamp."

Robin rubbed his chin. "Ah well, you're probably right,

but I have to try. I'll pull something shiny out of the treasure chest." Marian reached on the wall for Robin's baldric and sword, but he only shook his head. "He don't like steel, either."

"Take something. Or someone. Take Much." Robin thought about that for a while, then agreed.

After Mass the outlaw and the idiot stalked up the slope towards the top. They carried their bows in their left hands with an arrow ready to nock. The hum of spring was loud in their ears, and the new grass slippery under their deerhide soles.

"Where are we . . . go-ing—Rob-in?" asked Much. Much the Miller's Son was a squat rock, a parody of a man squashed down by a giant. He had a head like a sheep's bladder with grizzled black hair. His eyes were small and piggish, his teeth large and snaggly. His bowlegged gait and partial hunch carried him sideways as much as forward. Sin-ugly he was, but his friendship was indispensable. He was fiercely loyal to Robin Hood and Marian. Once, while Robin had lain with a split scalp in the middle of a town, Much had held off five soldiers with a wagon tongue until Robin's foresters had arrived. It was only later they found Much had a crossbow quarrel in his stomach.

"We're off to see Puck, Much, and with much pluck we'll find him. I just hope he can tell us something about the boar."

They trudged onwards with the face of the slope before them. The trees they passed were oaks, ash, and blackthorn—druids' trees. Robin Hood noticed they flushed little game. There was a paucity of grouse, pheasant, and woodcock. There were no owl pellets or fox droppings. And Will Stutly had told him that, judging by the lack of cropped buds around, the deer had moved off. Had they temporarily gone to ground because of the storm? Or was this another sign the camp was marked?

"Puck. Puck," mumbled Much. "Who's—?" The idiot had only met the woodsprite three times.

"The little bugger. Looks like a stork with hair."

"Oh." He was silent for a while. "Why are we go-ing—"

"I told you. To talk about the boar. Puck should know all the magic there is around." The outlaw chief crossed his chest as he said it.

"No. Why are we go-ing to—Long-don?"

"Oh. Sorry Much, my mistake. We're going to London because the king has commanded it."

"Why?"

"That's what I keep wondering. He says he needs arch-ers to . . .," Robin waved a hand in the air, " . . .shoot arrows. Richard's after war in France. He wants us. And it's partially my fault for antagonizing him. So we must off to the city. Do you like that idea?"

"Dun-no." Much's low tireless body rolled up the slope like a boulder in reverse. His breathing was steady. "What's it like?"

Robin sighed. "Many, many people. Houses everywhere. Lots of smoke. Very few trees. Shit and flies. Miles of slimy docks swarming with rats."

"Uh don't like rats."

"Me neither. But there are other things. Pageants and parades. Festivals. Easter plays. Thousands of candles at Christmas time. Strange, interesting people in fancy clothes. Men with black skins, black as soot. And jugglers. You'll like them, Much."

"Uh want to stay here."

Robin sighed again. "So do I, old friend."

"Uh thought we was free and could do what we want."

Robin Hood laughed. "Who's the fool here? You sound like my cousin." Then he remembered Will Scarlett, a shade of a man on a deathbed. He looked up the slope. They were almost to the top. The outlaw had forgotten his fear of the forest in his conversation with an idiot. There was a lesson there, he reflected. "I don't know, Much. I don't know."

They breasted the top. It was a narrow space, not thirty feet wide before the slope tumbled down again. The wind at the top of the ridge was clean and cool, and it stroked Robin's face like a mother's hand. Behind him was his own valley, that flowed in a southeasterly direction towards Nottingham, then the Midlands, and finally to the sea. In front of him, at this most extreme end of the Pennines, was an equally broad valley that the outlaw had never entered, although this strange valley had always intrigued him. It was a magic place, the land of the fairies, or so they thought. Men who went there did not return. The trees in that valley had never heard an axe ring. The birds were unafraid of men. The streams ran clean. It was beautiful to look at, but cold somehow, lovely yet deadly, like the green-black cobras he'd seen in the Holy Land. Robin shuddered just to look at the valley. A man lost down there would never reach God. His shade would wander for all eternity between heaven and earth. And the things it would see . . . Robin Hood turned away.

"Let's rest a moment," he said, and they sat facing the familiar valley, their home. Much pulled a strip of jerky from his shirt and munched noisily. He offered some to Robin, who accepted. Robin's camp was invisible, hidden by a million million leaves. All of England, it seemed, lay just below their boot tips, and it was all green. He could see for miles, and there was no trace of men. They might not exist for all they had touched this corner of the world. He found no fear here, but how different was this valley from the one behind him? Every tree might harbor a dryad, every rock a devil. Did they? Or did they not?

Warmed by the sun and relaxed by the walk, Robin wondered again about the things men knew and the things they knew not. It was a common thing for him to ponder, and no one he had ever met could answer the questions that spun from his mind like sparks from a grinding wheel. There were so many stories, and so few facts. Was it right to live in the woods, so far from God's representatives? Could a man find God here? Hadn't Christ gone to a mount to lecture, to a desert to think? What need had He for a city? Yet Sherwood was different. It was a place where many things came together: a place of lines.

Men were wary of lines. Where one region ended and another began, so that at their junction was a space like neither, was the place to be careful. In such places Heaven and Hell met. If a man wandered there at the wrong time, he could be sucked into the pit without hope of redemption. These lines were everywhere. The sun came from God, so the space above earth was for mortals. The underworld had no sun and was ruled by Satan. Earth and the underworld met at a cave, a space suspended between them, so men should avoid caves. Whether carried off by fairies, or lost because of their own laxness, people disappeared down caves and were never seen again. Near the mouth of a cave one could hear a sobbing, the voices of Hell. (In the same way, a man's mouth was a cave that led to the bowels. The proof of this was a death rattle—the soul leaving the body—which mimicked the sob of a cave. And didn't the church teach it was a sin to meddle about inside a Christian body, because it disturbed the soul?) Weren't caves inhabited by bats, the eyes of the devil? And didn't bats exit a cave only at dusk? Dusk itself was a line. Day was for man, night was for monsters, and at twilight no one was safe. At night one bolted the line of threshhold and shutter, and strung it with lines of garlic and charms. There was the line around a village, the line between the familiar and the strange. A man should never venture too far from home, but stay near his hearth and chapel. If he stayed with what he knew, he would not mistake one of Satan's snares, which snapped up the curious like ducks. A stream was a dangerous place, for it split the land in a line. If a man had to cross, he made sure his right foot first touched Christian soil and not his left. (A man's body—God's last and greatest work—was also split in a line: the right half with the heart, and the left without. There was potential for evil in every man, and anyone who was dominated by his left hand or foot leant closer to Satan than Christ.) A bridge—over a stream, so doubly displaced and doubly dangerous—was a line in the air. But used properly a bridge could save one's soul, since witches and ghosts could not cross running water. For not all lines were bad. They could help a man prosper. Oft times they meant food. When hunting, a clever man followed the line where forest met field, for there game was richest and most varied. But there were things that hunted men, and crossing the fingers and whispering a prayer never hurt. The break between farm and forest, that divided man's work from nature's, was a clear marker too. It showed where men should stay. For everyone knew the forest was filled with witches and devils and madmen.

And outlaws. Every day Robin Hood reflected how far from God's master plan they deviated. They had no chapel, just one valiant friar. They had only temporary homes, and they lived oftimes in a cave. They sowed no seed, but reaped from others like vandals. They ate more meat in a week than others did in a year. They crouched like wolves around a great lime tree, a tree that must have seen druids burn their captives in wicker baskets, and savages danced in blue paint. And before men, what? Sherwood's fields were pebbled, marked by fairy rings and foxfire. Blackthorn and oak grew overhead. Nightshade and fennel curled around the trees. Bats stippled the night, snakes raced at their approach, hares loped at the edge of the forest. Looming over the outlaws' very heads, like a ship of doom from some forgotten sea, was this slope which hid a valley untouched by men. If magic flowed downhill like the land, then Robin's camp had magic you could stir with a stick.

What would be their final fate if they continued to live here? Would they grow old and fade away? Would their children build a town with a church, then a cathedral? Would they wake one night to the Apocalypse? Would devils stream down the hill and carry them straight to hell, to be pricked in the legs and driven through fire, to be encased in steaming stone to thirst forever for water, to be whipped until they were bones, to have their tongues ripped out with red-hot pincers? Robin Hood shuddered as he thought of his burden: the lives of two dozen people, and the care of their souls as well. How long would he burn in hell if he dragged these innocents with him?

A hand on his leg startled him. "Rob-in," Much drawled. "Look."

The idiot pointed to a patch of daffodils. As they watched, the green stalks moved as if from a rabbit. Then they parted to reveal a perfectly round head the size of a chamberpot. The head had pointed ears that stuck up past the skull, crazy hair, and great round eyes like a cat's. The body that came forth was no taller than a baby, and was thin as a stick. This was Puck, guardian of the forest, sergeant of Oberon or Hern (maybe). Robin Hood had mixed feelings about Puck. Several times he had saved Robin's life. Now he might answer all his questions. Or he might just warp their bows and run away. Succor and mischief were his trade. Puck and his friends—each more bizarre than the last—had danced men around trees until they were cross-eyed. They stole babies and replaced them with changelings. They sucked the milk from goats, leeched nourishment from wholesome food, and fired barns. Yet they might also lead a man to gold, or a lost child to its mother.

The outlaw chief got to his feet, put on a brave smile, and proferred a brass ring set with onyx. Fairies, kings, and prostitutes always welcomed gifts.

The funny half-man twisted his head to one side like a goose and squinted at the ring. He took it from Robin with a hand of three fingers. It was a large ring from a fat baron, and would have made a heavy armband for the fairy, but Puck set it atop his head and yanked it down. Somehow—Robin could not watch—he got it over his melon head and around his stringbean neck. Robin felt venison crowd his throat from below.

The fairy chieftain gabbled like a duck. He fingered the onyx below his chin, pleased. Strike while the iron is hot, thought Robin.

"Puck, you go everywhere. Do you know about the boar?"

The tiny fairy did not reply. He rarely did. Instead he waggled his head like a fish on a line, then crouched over on all fours and pretended to root at the ground.

Oh, God, thought Robin. Guessing games.

"The magical one. The cursed one. Do you know it?"

Puck put upright fingers to his mouth and pawed the ground.

"That's right," said Robin. At least he thought it was right. "What is it? Where does it come from?"

"Why is he so lit-tle?" asked Much.

"Hush."

Suddenly the fairy was gone, although Robin had only blinked. The outlaw shot upright and cast about. "Puck! Where are you?" Much got up and looked under his seat. "Puck!" There was a chittering like a squirrel's, and they saw Puck halfway up a tree, head down. The fairy scrabbled around the tree trunk and leapt to another farther away. Robin snatched up his bow. "Come on, Much!" He added, "God damn him to hell!" under his breath.

The chase was on. The two humans tore down the hillside after the fairy. Puck would hop to the ground, then leap up into a tree, run along the trunk, then descend swinging on the end of a branch. He would jump like a deer and scoot like a rabbit, always over the highest bracken or under the lowest brambles. He never ran in the clear for more than two seconds. The humans bulled and puffed and swore their way after him, and the miles stretched away. The men shredded their clothing and punctured their soft boots. Branches stripped the fletching from the arrows in their quivers. Robin lost his knife and Much his hat. The Fox of Sherwood remembered curses in Turkish, Arabic, and French he thought he'd forgotten.

Finally Puck stopped so short the men bowled right over him. Puck hopped up, ready for more. The ring Robin had given him was gone, either hidden or lost. Puck had no more use for things than a jackdaw.

"Puck," panted Robin Hood, down on one knee, "you stinking . . . black-hearted . . . motherless son of a . . . Moslem pig . . ." Then he noticed where they were.

A hummock overlooked a swamp. Tall yellow grass spanned a glint of water that led to a highland two bowcasts away. The water looked strangely flat, as if overlaid with grease. The distant highland—almost an island—had grey-skinned stunted trees and many vines. It was very quiet. The boy Robin had seen this place with his companions, but no amount of taunting had driven him any closer. As he and Much watched, Puck skipped to the edge of the water and scuttled onto it like a water beetle. Much looked dully at his leader. Robin Hood thought of Marian's imagined swamp. Finally he rose and muttered, "Come on. Might's well see this finished."

They trudged down into the grass, which hissed against their legs like serpents and seemed to push them back. The water hid green-grey mud that sucked at their feet and stank of corruption despite the chill. They floundered halfway to their thighs. Robin Hood hoped leeches were still dormant. Puck went ahead from grass stalk to grass stalk and barely got his toes wet.

Finally they reached the highland, and it was just as silent and oppressive as they had feared. The land was mud or treacherous roots, and they stumbled a dozen times to fall and cut their hands. Vines hung in their faces and trailed over their necks. But eventually the fairy brought them to his goal. At the sight Robin Hood mumbled prayers and had Much cross his fingers on both hands. Together the three odd fellows mounted the ancient barrow.

Robin had seen mounds like this all his life. England was rife with them. Some were seen along common roads. Others were forgotten in isolated hollows. Some were unrecognizable, buried under brush or trees. No one knew what was in them. People said they were fairy mounds, or giant-built, or gateways to Hell, or graves of ancient kings. No one Robin had ever talked to had tampered with one. Yet here someone had. The earth was turned around a hole like a new grave. There were no tracks, since they would have been washed away by the torrential rains of a few nights ago. Or were there sharp-cut hoof marks here, as if Satan had clawed out of the hole? Or had it been a boar? With his crucifix in his good right hand, firmly planted on his knees, Robin Hood peered into the sundered barrow at the fairy's behest.

He saw a hole. It was shallow, not six feet deep, with sloping sides. At the bottom was some splintered wood. That was all.

"Puck . . ." he began. But the imp hopped down into the barrow and dug at the earth. He uncovered a scrap of dingy white which he dragged forth and presented to the human. Robin shook off the gummy soil.

"What is it, Rob-in?" The idiot's voice was loud in the silence. A tawny owl piped and made them both jump.

"It's . . . I think it's a swaddling blanket, Much. But there's blood on it. Puck, what's it mean?"

Puck mimed someone carrying a baby in his or her arms. Then he flicked his hand across his scrawny throat with a cutting motion. Robin Hood grimaced. Puck mimed setting his burden atop the barrow, like putting flowers on a grave.

"And the boar came for the . . . child? And fell into the barrow?" Puck nodded vigorously. Robin shuddered. Flakes of mud crumbled from his clothing. "But who did this? What did he look like? Was it even a man?"

Puck hopped in the air and clapped his hands. He stretched his hands over his head. "Someone tall," said Robin. The fairy stretched his arms wide. "Broad shouldered." Puck aped shagginess around his head and chest and forearms. "Hair-y," said Much. Both sprite and man looked at the idiot, who looked back blankly. Puck feigned walking with his chest out, pumping his legs and taking great strides. "Powerful, strong," said Robin. Finally Puck leaped forward to touch the two men where they knelt at the rim of the hole. He stroked Robin's belt and boots. "Leather," said Robin. Puck nodded and passed his hands from the tip of his head to his bare stork's feet. "Leather all over," said Robin. The fairy nodded, then stopped as something in a tree caught his eye. Robin turned but could see nothing. Puck trotted away and began to climb some grape vines.

"But the only one who wears all leather," said Robin to the stillness, "is Hern." Robin Hood pictured the figure he had met in his family's ruined homestead: tall, broad-shouldered, powerful and kingly, shaggy like a deer in winter, wrapped in leather like a bible. It made no sense. Why would Hern talk to him of being favored by Sherwood—or whatever he'd said—then set loose a black-hearted boar to plague him and his followers? Were the Sherwooders at the whim of these ancient beings—gods, Cedwyn would say—in some sort of game or intrigue?

"God's fish and teeth," Robin breathed. "The answers are no better than the questions." He cast about for Puck, but there was no sign of the fairy, or anything else living. "Come, Much. Let's get away from here. Back to camp."

On the way out they learned the leeches were awake.

High over the town of Nottingham, Sir Guy of Gisborne sailed into the sheriff's chambers. He had been up all the night, and had no sooner arrived at his castle home than he found a messenger with a summons to the sheriff. A dawn ride down the long miles to Nottingham found him more gaunt and haggard than ever. Untroubled and unmoved behind him came the Kite. And here before him, in chains, was a man in filthy green with a head bandage.

"My men found him on the road," explained the sheriff. "He ranted about Robin Hood and demanded to see you. We can twist nothing else out of him."

Guy looked at the one-eyed scarecrow. The exposed side of his face was deathly pale, with bright purple veins under the skin: blood poisoning. The man's clothes were ragged, and his hands bloody and begrimed. But he held his head steady with a madman's strength.

"What have you?" demanded Guy.

"Sir," rasped the man. His voice was strained as if he had been screaming. Sir Guy of Gisborne could smell dried pus and rotten breath. "I know where lies Robin Hood's camp." The sheriff and his guards jerked up their heads. "I've been there, and escaped. I can show you the way, but you'll have to take me with you."

Guy glanced out at the morning sky, his brain ahum as with a thousand bees. Before this day was out he could have Marian in his bed, broken and tamed. But he needed details, hundreds of them. "Very well, tell me slowly. How were you captured? What happened to your face?"

"T'was that poxied whore, Marian. She put out me eye—"

In the blink of an eye Sir Guy leapt forward and kicked the man full in the stomach. The man fell on his side and retched.

"*Whore*? I'll give you *whore!*" Sir Guy hopped forward and kicked him again. And again. He aimed for the man's throat and the bad side of his face. The guards fell back lest they receive the same. Sir Guy shouted as he kicked. "You black bastard! How dare you use her name! I'll put out that other eye! *I'll kill you!*" He kicked again, but the sheriff caught Guy's arm and shook him.

"What the hell is going on? How do you know this man?" Guy tried to jerk free, but the sheriff held on and shook him again. "Answer me! Who is this man? What is he talking about?"

"You heard! He's been to Locksley's camp! He can tell us its strength and position. We can ride right in."

"I *asked, who* is he?"

Guy hesitated. He hadn't thought what to tell the sheriff. As he juggled lies in his head, Sir Rowland could see it all plain as day. The sheriff interrupted Guy's plotting. "He's working under your orders, isn't he?" Suddenly Rowland's mouth fell open. Thunderstruck, he forgot every curse he knew. Then he got out in a strangled voice, "This worm posed as Robin Hood, didn't he? That's why he's in green. Only the devil and Locksley wear green.

He's the one from the road, the one everyone's looking for, isn't he?" He shook Guy's arm until the man's head wobbled. The knight reached for his sword, but the sheriff let him go to level a finger. "This is the rogue responsible for killing those nuns! And *you* put him up to it!"

"He did none of that! T'was Locksley who did it. My man here was to pose as Robin and terrorize people, not kill them."

"But he did!" The sheriff tripped over his own words. He couldn't say them fast enough. "Him and some others! There were four of them. God knows Robin Hood doesn't *murder* people!"

"He does!"

"You're mad! He wouldn't do it! He never has! He kills *my* men! He robs *barons* and *bishops*! But kill peasants? And *nuns*?"

"It's no matter now! It's done! He can tell us where the camp is! We can smash Locksley!"

The sheriff rubbed his face with both hands. "Nuns! Guy, Christ on the mount, what have you done? You're mad!"

Guy backed up against a stone wall. The sheriff's guards put hands to their pommels. The lord screamed, "You're in it with me! You were party to this! You gave me leave to attack Locksley as I will!"

The sheriff thought for a long time. The room was so quiet pigeons flew onto the windowsill and walked inside the room. The Kite was there, looking out. Finally Rowland said, "No. Not I. I never talked to you. You're mad, and this is your fault."

"You were there! I have witnesses!"

The sheriff was calmer now. He wiped the sweat from his brow. "Nay. Not I. This is your problem. You've shit your bed, and I'll not climb in with you. You're stark mad to have done this, Guy."

"*Sir* Guy!"

"Or he is. And when a dog runs wild, the master makes amends. Now get out of my castle and out of my sight."

Guy was so outraged he stuttered. "You can't *mean* it! You'd side with *Locksley* against *me*? Who's mad?"

"That you cannot tell shows your state. Now get out."

Dismayed, Guy pulled at his sword, but the sheriff's men matched with long steel. The lord cried, "This is our chance to *kill Locksley*! We'll wipe him out like a nest of rats! He's off-balance, afraid of the night! He has to be! You don't know what he can *do*! Half of England would rise up and help him, or they would have if not for *me*! He'll pull his people together and go anywhere, overnight! He'll wreak havoc on us! He can call down *feys*! We have to strike NOW!"

"I don't want to hear any more! Get OUT!" The sheriff waved wildly to his guards. The two men stamped forward. Sir Guy might be a noble, but the sheriff paid his men from his own purse.

Guy started at this new assault, unbelieving. He could not form coherent words to argue. He wiped spittle from his lips and looked all around. Only the Kite returned a steady gaze. Guy stormed out of the room. The Kite came forward and grabbed One-eye under the arms and dragged him away.

The sheriff scowled at the back of the door. How was he to explain this to the royal justices? What story would they believe? Sir Rowland dismissed his guards. They closed the door behind them.

The sheriff flopped into a chair, poured himself some brandy, and stared out the window.

As Robin Hood and Much approached camp they heard screams. They were thin, plaintive wails that echoed over the woods almost like bird song. People in the camp shuffled around with their shoulders hunched as if it were raining. At the western edge of camp, Allan A'Dale was on watch with his daughter at his leg. Robin Hood asked, "Allan, what's that noise? Is it—"

The minstrel nodded. "Shonet."

The screams came only every so often, as if the woman

were fading. Every shriek made them jump. Robin Hood found Marian and Cedwyn and Friar Tuck around Will Scarlett. Tam was there, asleep. Robin's cousin was dull white and very still. He looked like a fish too long out of the water. The attendants sat and did nothing. Even Friar Tuck's giant dogs stayed on their bellies at Robin's approach.

Filthy from his travels, Robin stood back. He asked the assemblage, "Can ye do nothing? These screams—"

Marian shook her head. "She started this noon. Something's broken and the crab tears at her vitals. Every breath rips her like a knife. We've purged her twice. There's nothing else we can do."

"But they're so—grating. Cedwyn, can't you give her something, some concoction to ease the pain?"

The tiny witch put her hands to her face. "I already did." She hiked up her skirts and ran for her cottage.

The others watched her go. Robin said, "There's nothing for it? She's just to get worse until she dies?" No one answered. "Then why don't we do something else?"

Friar Tuck snapped, "Such as?"

Robin Hood waved his hands in the air. "I mean, if she's going to die, maybe we could . . . put her out of her misery?" As the cleric's brow clouded, he hastened, "We do it with animals. We don't let them suffer—" Another scream lifted to heaven and died.

Friar Tuck wore a dark brown robe and tonsure. He was the jolliest of men most times, except when plying his vocation. Robin Hood had sought Tuck out when Sherwood needed a cleric. In an age when Benedictine was a synonym for corruption, when priests kept wives, bishops dealt in money, and friars spent their time hawking and hunting, Robin Hood had found a man who believed in his vows, a sterling example of what a holy man should be. Friar Tuck worked for God and not himself, and as he grew older he grew more adamant, more dedicated, and more stubborn. He started now in the voice Robin knew well. "Animals have not souls we must consider. Men are not animals, and I'll trust you keep that before you at all times. To send an innocent to an early grave, before God has called for her, is the most grievous of sins. The man who would take that on himself would have naught but damnation before him for all eternity. No pardoner could sell him a license to Heaven. Neither gold nor prayers could save him. So I'll not have you nor anyone else bring up the suggestion again. He that does will face my wrath, and the wrath of God." The cleric too hiked his skirts and stumped out of the hall. His dogs trailed behind.

Robin looked a query at Marian. She replied, "When Cedwyn's potion failed, David sought Tuck out. He was frantic. They got into a fight. At first David was just railing against God and fate, but soon they got to the same issue. He asked if God would understand if a husband took his wife's life. You can guess the rest. David's with Shonet now. He'll be mad with grief soon."

Robin Hood took his wife's hand. She was so pretty, so young, yet so beset with worry lines. "My Marian. We could sit down with Job, I think. What's next?"

"Supper." Marian patted his hand and led him from the sickroom.

The crowd at the long table was quiet. There was no screaming—Shonet had collapsed for the moment. Everyone's nerves were raw, and rather than chance any altercation they remained silent. The silence bore on, broken only by slurpings from Much and gnawing from dogs. Robin's ears ached for the sound of Sherwood's joking and laughter, the songs and the stories. It was a relief when Allan A'Dale went for his harp.

Allan A'Dale had not learned to be a minstrel, he had been born to it. He could create songs of fifty stanzas on the spot: happy songs or sad songs. He could sing one hundred hymns without repetition. He was always most sensitive to the moods and half-expressed ideas of the group. Often when he sang, he was the one most surprised at what came out. But at the first chord Robin had a premonition of disaster.

"There were three ravens sat on a tree,
Downe a downe, hey down, hey downe,
There were three ravens sat on a tree,
With a downe.
There were three ravens sat on a tree,
And they were blacke as they might be,
With a downe, derrie, derrie, derrie,
downe—downe.

"The one of them said to his mate,
Downe a downe, hey down, hey downe,
'What shall we for our breakfast take?'
With a downe.
The one of them said to his mate,
'What shall we for our breakfast take?'
With a downe, derrie, derrie, derrie,
downe—downe.

"Downe in yonder green-e field,
Downe a downe, hey down, hey downe,
There lies a knight slain under his shield,
With a downe.
Downe in yonder—"

Gilbert's bark made the entire table jump. "Tha's the *last* song we need right now! Dead man, dead deer, and losin' a battle! What do *yu* know of fightin' anywa'?" Everyone stopped, stunned. Elaine's baby squawled. The Crusader went on. "Our steel and our right arms keep us here, and you're good for nobbut strumming th't harp! Where do you get off—"

Robin called, "Gil, that's enough!"

"—singin' a song about *fightin'*! We're *surrounded* by enemies, no *end* of them, and *now's* the time when *every one of us* must pick up a sword—"

"GILBERT, THAT'S ENOUGH!"

The Crusader stopped in mid-word. Confused, he put his bowl down on the table.

Robin was red to his ears. "I'll not have you or anyone else address a follower of mine in that tone, or on that subject! If Allan chooses not to fight, that's his concern, not yours! We need to fight *and* we need to sing, and there was a time we did more of one then the other! God made each of us what we are, and none of us Gilbert of Northumbria! Allan has been a member—" Robin pointed, but the minstrel had gathered his family and walked away.

"See you that?" continued the outlaw chief. "Allan doesn't fight even in words. And if you'll recall, that was what Our Lord God, Jesus Himself, admonished us to do time and time again! Would that more of us could refuse the blade and the bow and work His wisdom. By God! Gil, you yourself test my patience to the limit. There are more ways to win than by gutting your foe! At a time like this, I could use a lot less fighters and more . . . people who don't fight," Robin finished lamely. He was out of words. He grunted, threw his hat upon the ground, and went back to eating. Everyone else attended their bowl.

Gilbert stomped away.

Cedwyn was crying, and hating herself for it, when Gilbert arrived. Their cottage was by itself at the bottom of the lower meadow, where the woods met the sunshine. Cedwyn could not live near others. As the Crusader came in she dove into his arms.

"Oh, Gilbert, my love. I tried and tried. I made the best physic I could. It did nothing. She's too strong. I'm supposed to help people, Gil. What will the others think?" Gilbert remained as silent as the trees outside. The witch wiped her red eyes with the heel of her hands. "Gil? Didn't you come here to talk to me?"

"No."

"No?"

"No. Rob sent me from the table."

"Oh."

She sat down at the work table in the middle of the single room.

"Why?"

"Ah dinna ken. He's angry."

Cedwyn fiddled with a marble pestle and picked crumbs of herb from a dish. "Angry. Gil, when Robin leaves to serve the king in London, will you really go with him?"

Gil answered without pause. "I'd have to. He's the king."

Cedwyn threw her arms in the air. She knew argument was futile, but she couldn't stop herself. "That doesn't matter! You already did your duty! You went on a Crusade, for Gilmesh's sake! Richard doesn't need any more of your service. From what Robin says, he doesn't deserve it."

Gil shrugged again. "It's naw for me to say."

"So you'd go? Leave Sherwood and me?"

Gil said nothing.

Cedwyn wanted to cry again, but denied herself. "I *hate* the way you just *stand* there like a dead tree. Nothing to say? When the time comes to leave you'll just pick up your sword and walk out? So you can fight people you don't even know? Is that all you're good for, *fighting?*"

Gilbert already wore his sword and helmet. Without a word he took his shield down from the wall and walked out.

"Don't come back!" the girl yelled. Then she cried till she was dry.

A little later, footsteps outside made her pause in her sobbing. She got busy grinding flakes in her mortar. But it was only Robin Hood.

"What do you want?" she demanded.

The outlaw chief pretended not to notice the swollen eyes and damp hair on her cheeks. "I see Gil has, uh, stepped out."

Cedwyn snorted through her tiny nose. "That man! I *hate* him sometimes! He drives me crazy!"

Robin hemmed. "Umm, yes. Marian says the same about me on occasion."

Cedwyn went on in Robin's direction. "A brute with a sword and no soul! Going off . . . off. And he won't tell me why. He never talks to me. Why did he never tell me that story about the Crusade? I never knew he was captured! I never know anything about him!" Robin Hood thought it was probably because they couldn't understand each other. Her Welsh accent was as impossible as Gilbert's Scottish. Robin Hood wondered how the two managed to communicate, until he remembered that Gil hardly talked.

Cedwyn pounded leaves into dust. "And he *never* told me about that tiger."

"That's strange, considering how taken he was with it. But that's Gil." Robin searched for some way to change the conversation. "Umm, Cedwyn, maybe I should have come to you earlier. But I wasn't sure what we were up against. I've learned somewhat about the boar." He told her about the barrow, the baby blanket, and Puck's comments.

"That's not much."

Robin thought it was plenty. "But it's easy to see the boar is evil, and Hern is behind it."

"So? Any fool can see that."

Robin Hood bit his tongue. "I was hoping . . ."

Cedwyn held up a finger. "If I drive away the boar, or kill it, will we stay here in Sherwood?"

Robin spread his hands. "I don't know. One really has nothing to do with the other. We're going to serve Richard until he's done with us. But with kings you never know. Something may happen and we'll stay, God willing. But we cannot remain if the boar is out there. And if it's magic and we can't kill it . . ."

Cedwyn glanced at the door, and Robin knew she was looking after Gilbert. "I can kill it. The tiger. What was it like?"

Robin wasn't sure he liked the question, but he'd come to her for help. He took a seat and thought a moment. This cottage was usually a very pleasant place, with its window of sunbeams and the smells of herb and flower. Robin recognized bearberry leaves drying on a plank, starweed soaking in a bucket of water, slippery elm bark stacked in a corner, stalks of trumpet weed crushed in a stone bowl. He breathed deeply and said, "It was very large. Big as a cow, though not as tall. A head just like a cat's, only shaggier. Whiskers out to here. It was yellow, or orange really—you know what I mean by orange? —with black stripes running up and down, sharp as if you'd painted 'em with a brush. It paced back and forth like a soldier on guard, and it kept flicking its tail. It was never still. It had power, like a giant from the Bible, or, I don't know what. It was quiet as a normal cat, though. Silent. It was wonderful. God was in His prime when He made that one."

Cedwyn had moved to the fireplace and picked up her cat. She held it by the scruff of the neck so it hung immobile and confused. She studied it as Robin talked.

"All right. That's enough. You may go."

"What are you going to do?"

"Never mind. You'll find out." She put the cat on the table and cleared a space.

"Will this take long? It's getting on sundown."

"You may go."

Robin Hood went.

Chapter 21

That night a tiger walked the English forest.

The great beast pulsed through the brush like a moonbeam. She slipped through the brittle bracken without a sound. She padded over dead leaves silently.

There was blood down her sides, and occasionally she stopped to lick at it. She would have to find some deer scat to roll in, to mask the smell. Meanwhile she stalked. There was something she had to find.

There were sounds new to her ears: squirrels skittering over bark, bats slipping through the air, a mole chewing worms, the midnight drone of bees sleeping. There were smells that were new to her nostrils: jackdaws, cool snakes, foxes, wolves very far away, hot deer, and men. Nowhere was there a smell like herself. Then came a breath of breeze, and she tensed. There was something miles off, something that should have been dead long ago. The carcass of a boar with blood rushing through it.

The vagrant wind filled her nostrils. The scent pointed with lines of fire. The new tiger threw her shoulders forward into a lope.

The tiger hunted the boar.

Chapter 22

Gilbert burst into the cave shouting as the other outlaws were stirring. People held their heads at the noise. The only words Robin caught of the barbarous Scottish were "Cedwyn" and "blood". The outlaw chief jerked on his boots and ran down to the tiny cottage.

Cedwyn's cabin was a wreck. The sturdy door was flattened in the leaves. The window was smashed. The plank work table was flat. The floor was strewn with herbs, grasses, liquids, shards of crockery, straw from the bed, and everything was spattered with blood, most of all Cedwyn's sundered gown.

As Robin Hood and Gilbert scanned the room, a voice called from outside. "Look here!"

Twelve feet from the door, pressed into the thin grass and last year's oak leaves were the bloodied tracks of a cat. Men crossed their chests. Black Bart put his grimy hand over a pawprint. It was as big as his spread fingers. The tracks pointed into the woods.

Robin Hood walked back to the cottage and stood with hand to chin. He looked down at the door. Long white scars marked its inner surface. He stood there so long all of Sherwood had time to hike down to this end of the meadow. Marian interrupted his thoughts only after she had inspected the cabin. She held up the bloody gown.

"Poor Cedwyn," she said, and tears rimmed her wide dark eyes.

"What is it, Rob?" Elaine asked. "What happened?"

Robin Hood sighed, as he had sighed often these last few days. "Yester eve I asked Cedwyn if she could do something to stop the boar. She asked me to describe the tiger, and I did. Then she started a spell with her cat."

"Rhiannon," said Gilbert.

"I don't understand," said Elaine.

Robin explained. "This door was sundered from within, because the scratches are on the inside. And a bird couldn't fit through that window. So it wasn't that some beast from the woods that did it. It came from in there."

"But what was it?"

"It was *magic*. Cedwyn must have conjured her cat into a—"

"Tiger?"

"There's a tiger in Sherwood?"

"*Another* fell beastie?"

"Aw, by Saint Columba!"

"It's killed her and dragged her off!"

"Cedwyn's dead?"

"Lord preserve us!"

"That poor lass."

Friar Tuck stated, "That comes of dabbling with the dead. She's trafficked with Satan."

"Tuck!" chirped Marian.

"That's nae true!" Gilbert shouted. "You shut your mouth, and all the rest of you!" The knight put his hand to his pommel. He turned to his leader and said, "Rob, we have to go after it. We have to get her back."

Robin Hood spread his hands. "Gil, just wait." He rubbed his forehead. "It's not possible. We can't go traipsing all through the woods. It's not safe, for one thing. And we have to prepare for London. Besides . . ." Robin balanced his words. "I did ask her to help—one more mark against my soul, I suppose." He watched Gilbert's face, but the Scotsman held no animosity against his leader. Too thick, Robin reflected. "This is Cedwyn's magic, and we shouldn't interfere. This beast *might* go after the boar and end it. It may pay back Cedwyn's . . . death." At that moment, from the upper common, they heard Shonet scream. Robin let his hands drop. "Let's to breakfast. We'll need it."

Gilbert might not have heard a word Robin had said. "I'm going after the beastie."

Robin arrested another sigh. His best fighter, off chasing a monster through the woods alone. "Very well, Gil."

As they walked to breakfast, a sad and confused lot, Ben Barrel shuffled up to Robin Hood. Ben Barrel's real name was Barley, but most people had forgotten it. He was built like a barrel of salt pork, and smelled almost as high. On the day that Robin Hood had first met the man and his family, it had been Ben who suggested he join Robin's band. Robin had thought then he had much to hide, and hide from. If Ben had never given his heart and soul to outlawry, at least he had been obedient. Now the large man removed his soft hat to deliver a speech.

"Master, if it's all the same to you, we'll not be going to London. Clara don't care much for the idea of a city. We don't want the little ones near its perdition. I've cousins near The Wash, I'm told, and what with my numbers and Clara's sewing we should get by out there. Have we your permission to leave?"

"Ben, haven't I told you and all the rest a hundred times, I am no man's master? We are all equal here, Ben, all God's children. We give of ourselves freely. I have no power to hold you, nor do you owe me any debt." To the questions in the man's eyes, Robin added. "Go, with my blessing."

Ben sighed with relief and smiled, and clumsily accepted Robin's hand. Then he ambled away to tell his family the news.

"God with you, Ben," prayed Robin after him. "May the tax collectors never find you."

During breakfast Robin quietly discussed their plans for the move to London. He talked about how they might acquire horses or mules, how they could rig drags to get to the road and then buy carts, how they would keep watch, where they would stay in towns, how they might celebrate Easter on the road, where they would be housed in London. He had no hard knowledge to go on, just assessments from when he himself had passed through London on his way to the Crusades and other travelling he had done. But they listened raptly. Many of his followers had never seen a city, or ridden a horse, or ventured more than twenty miles from home. They had a slew of questions, and many of them talked as if they had to descend to the gates of Hell. But no one else spoke of abandoning him, for which he breathed thanks.

The quiet meal was quieter because of absences. Friar Tuck was with Shonet in her cottage. She screamed off and on. Arthur's wife Mary attended her. David, up all night with his wife, now slept in the cave. Will Scarlett's laughter had almost faded from their minds. Tam was a memory. Tiny Cedwyn's place at the bench loomed large. Ben Barrel and his family packed in their cottage. Even Black Bart and Gilbert were missing: the light of Bart's forge shone from under the trees.

After the meal Robin Hood picked across the dammed stream to the smithy. Cold steel thudded on hot. A short search by Bart and Gilbert had failed to turn up Cedwyn's body. Now Robin wondered what Gilbert, who used only a sword that he sharpened himself, could need from a blacksmith.

The steady flat smack of the hammer masked the leader's approach. The shack was unwindowed, and grimy Bart was all but invisible in the blackness of the shack. Only his curses had color. He whanged away while Gilbert held onto a bar with long tongs. Bart would command the thing to be reinserted into the fire, and grouse about how it was done each time. Robin watched, with them unknowing, until finally Bart moved and he saw what they created. It

was a blade a cubit long, triangular in cross-section, with a
hefty cross bar at the throat where it would join a shaft. It
was a spontoon, a boar spear, designed so a man could face
a charging pig and survive. As the animal raced for him, a
man would set himself halfway back on the shaft. The
spear would impale the beast and the crossbar arrest the
spear against its hide. All the hunter then had to do was
hang on until companions dispatched the game. As he
watched, Gilbert pulled the bar from the forge with the
tongs. The intense yellow flare was reflected along his
glistening armor and golden hair. His face was grim.

What did Gilbert plan, Robin wondered. Would he
track the boar, and wait for the tiger to approach it? Or
was the spear only to kill the tiger? The Saracens had
mentioned tiger spears, from the description much the
same as boar spears. But hunting either animal alone was
unthinkable. Robin Hood wanted to say something, but
nothing came to mind. He walked away.

Towards the middle of the day Friar Tuck's dogs howled.
Shouting arose from Shonet's cottage. This long day had
seen the worst. Marian and Cedwyn had had to wrap cloth
around Shonet's limbs and tie her, for she would rouse
and scream, call on God and all the saints, beg to die, claw
at her stomach, pray and swear. The sounds had set everyone's hackles aprick. All of Sherwood felt the pain, and it
began to show. No one talked more than necessary. Children were cuffed. Arthur and Red Tom got into a fistfight.
Now it stopped, and the shouting began. Robin Hood
came at a run.

David of Doncaster drove at Friar Tuck like a demon.
The old friar held his brawny arms before him to ward off
David's blows, but did nothing else to defend. Little John
ran up, pinned David in a bear hug, and lifted him into
the air.

"He's killed her! The filthy hypocrite has killed her! He
smothered her or something, and killed her! I'll destroy
him!" Confined, David's rage burned hotter. He became

incoherent as he struggled in Little John's arms. Robin Hood took Friar Tuck by the sleeve and dragged him into the sickhouse. He closed the door behind them.

Shonet was still. The ravages of cancer were carved into the sunken eyes, the gaunt cheekbones, and the skeletal lips. She had drawn her bonds down into unworkable knots and chaffed the skin from her wrists. But the tumble of fair hair framed a face at peace. Robin Hood touched her forehead, then her neck. She was still warm, but there was no pulse.

Friar Tuck was sunk onto a low chest. He held his face in his great chapped hands and tears leaked from his fingers. Marian came in, looked at the bed for only a second, then knelt alongside the cleric. She put her arms around his shoulders and hugged him like a child.

"It's all right, Tuck. It's all right. She's with God now, and better for it. It's all right . . ." Robin Hood cut the bonds and arranged the wasted limbs, then drew the blankets over the fair head. He opened the door to let Shonet's spirit out, and as he did so, he prayed for Shonet and everyone else in his care.

Outside, they found David leaning against the cottage wall. His voice tolled like a bell. "She asked to be buried at her priory. Although—although she left there in shame, she said, that was where she—she wished to lie. I must see that she does."

Robin Hood nodded. He had been expecting something like this. God did not write messages in fire across the sky. He sent them in a thousand tiny whispers. "Very well, David. Shall I send anyone with you? Myself even?" The man of Doncaster shook his head. Robin set a hand on his shoulder. "David, don't fault Tuck—" But the widower shook off the hand and stumbled away.

Marian said, "Would that we could tell him. Any of us would have done the same, but we weren't strong enough."

It was later that day that Friar Tuck approached.

"Robin, I must go."

"You too, Tuck? Not forever, please God."

The old man shook his head. His unshaven jowls trembled. "I needs see my abbot. I have a wealth to confess."

Robin's mind hummed for a reply. His words these days had as little effect on his followers as they did on the weather. "Tuck," (how had Marian put it?) "what you did, any of us would have done, sin or not—"

The old man startled Robin by grabbing his hand. "Nay. I'd not have that on any man's conscience. Or any woman's. Nay." He seemed to forget what he'd said. "I have a wealth to confess," he finished.

"Stay with us until Easter, maybe. It's a joyous time. It has to be."

"No."

Robin Hood sighed. "Very well. Would you have anyone go with you?"

"Nay, Rob. Only my dogs. They and I are fit company. I'll be back, anon." He went to gather his things.

It was quiet that night in the cave, and everyone went to sleep early.

The next morning Sherwood waited on departures.

Gilbert, it turned out, had left before dawn. No one had seen him go. He'd taken no supplies, no arms save his own, no clothing, no advice. He might have never existed except in their minds.

David left next. He had a drag of two thin poles fastened to a harness. On the drag was a white-wrapped body that looked too thin to be a human being's. A rosary surrounded the winding sheet, and it held down a posy of wildflowers. The wives had prepared the sheet, the men the harness. The children had gathered the flowers without being asked. There had been no ceremony, no eulogy, for Friar Tuck was not to be seen. People kissed David's cheek or patted his shoulder, but he was in a hurry to be off, and left without saying much. The sharp ends of the poles scored the sweet grass as he lurched away.

Not long after Friar Tuck emerged from the Bear's Den.

He whistled to his dogs and tried to slip away, but before he knew what he was about, he was surrounded, nor could he take another step until he had had his hand shaken by every man, and a kiss planted by every women. The rough old cleric's face was wet with his own and others' tears before he trudged off into the woods with his hounds. He followed a different route than David.

Robin Hood reflected it was a strange crowd indeed that gave the same treatment to murderer and murdered. But everything was topsy-turvy now. Two days before he'd had a score of fighting yeomen. Today his force was half that. He'd striven to keep his people close and protected, and they were blown before the wind like leaves. He deserved it, he guessed. He'd been presumptuous before God. His plans should fall apart.

Then Brian returned. He came laden with several satchels, half a dozen chickens, and two knights following behind on balky mounts.

"Brian! Well met," said Robin tiredly. "It's a sadder camp to which you return, but more the welcome because of it. I reckoned you'd wait along the road for one of us to come fetch you."

Brian shrugged off chickens and the children's questing hands. He sat at the table and accepted a cold draft of water. "I had much to tell you, master"—he stopped at Robin's upraised finger—"Robin. I thought I'd chance the forest. And on the road I found these two asking the way to Robin Hood's camp." The dismounted knights wore the livery of King Richard, and stern faces that must mean bad news. Robin Hood recognized them from the feast: they had neither been quick to anger nor slow to Richard's orders. By unspoken consent all of Sherwood ignored them. If Robin's people could share a common opinion, it was that knighthood counted for little under the greenwood. One of the knights made to hand reins to Black Bart, who just stared back.

"What did you learn in Nottingham?" Robin asked Brian, but he was interrupted.

"Here now, you base knave!" shouted the more red-dened knight. He marched forward and jerked off his gloves. "What mean you this with such treatment? By the living God I've never seen such impudence! We bear news from Richard Lionheart himself!" He drew back his gloves as if to strike, at which everyone present shuffled their feet and set hand to belt. Only Robin Hood stood still. The knight looked around and stopped. "Well?" he roared more loudly. "Are you listening for Richard's command?"

"Sirs," said Robin Hood slowly, "we've had more calamity in past days than other communities suffer in fifty years. I think I'll hear good news first. Wait your turn. Go on, Brian."

Brian coughed and drew on his water. "Uhhh . . . As you asked, I went straight to Nottingham and asked on the skirts first about the boar, the guards, the storm, and such like." And he narrated his conversations with admirable accuracy. Robin Hood was amazed that Brian had remembered all he'd been told, and he asked God to forgive him in doubting the man. Brian went on and on. Heard from an outside source, the news was refreshing but not new. The storm, boar, sheriff, and all were much as the outlaws had guessed it would be. Saladin had died the year before, but otherwise the new year brought few surprises. Robin Hood was pleased: at least he was no more in the dark than anyone else.

"And what did you buy?" asked Marian when Brian paused.

"Oh, heaps. And not too dear, I hope. I've still some of the money you gave me." He handed Robin a purse that seemed scarce diminished. "It's a hard spring all around, but I got the chickens for a good price. I bought all the garlic they would sell me." He tapped a bag that announced itself. "I got the other things. And a Jew from Canterbury was selling these." He unwrapped a piece of old pigskin to reveal four crumbly white cones.

"Salt, by God!" Robin cried. The whole assemblage echoed the word. "Brian, that's wonderful!"

"Venison will be a whole new food with salt on it!" said Little John.

"Stew with salt!" said people. "Or just plain to suck from our fingers!" "On bread!"

Robin Hood clapped the newcomer on the head and ruffled his hair. "Brian, why did you not join our band earlier? We *need* a man who knows what's important!"

Brian flushed and went on with a stammer. "The Jew had something else like salt, called sugar. He said it was sweet, like honey, but a summoner in the crowd said it was a temptation from the devil and we were not to partake. The Jew had to put it away."

"I've had sugar," said Robin. "And if any food can be a temptation from Satan, it's that. Never mind. This salt is priceless!"

For the first time Black Bart spoke from the edge of the crowd. "What d' they say about us?"

Brian stirred in his seat, spent some time replacing his cap. "A lot, none of it very good. They spoke of the Robin Hood murders." He looked up as if not to continue, but folks were hungry for any news, especially about themselves. "There was loose talk about 'Robin Hood wears green, and only the devil wears green.' Or, 'He has twelve followers, and that's a coven.' They think we really did kill those people, those nuns."

"Damn it to hell!" Robin barked. "We're outlaws, not robbers! Robbers live off the people, but outlaws are sufficient unto themselves. What of all those we help? Where are all the ballads about us now? Who'll stand and not deny us?"

"No one, looks like," said Bart.

Brian said, "I'm sorry, mas—uhh."

Robin clapped him on the shoulder. "Never mind. It's not your fault for telling the truth, lad. There're few enough in this world can do that. You did well. Extremely well."

"If you're all done with peasants' stories," growled a lord's voice. "We'll deliver our news of Richard and leave this pisshole of a robbers' roost." Away from the Sherwooders stood Richard's forgotten knights. Their shields were up, their hands on their pommels.

Robin Hood walked out between them and his people. He had only his knife at his belt. "You'll leave this pisshole soon enough, although your horses might not like you hanging under their bellies. Speak your piece and be gone. Our ears are weary of venom."

"We come to tell you you are commanded into Richard's presence before the castle L'Argent. 'Tis on the banks of the Trent in Staffordshire, near Stoke-on-Trent. You'll get there immediately without delay."

"We were commanded to London for May Day."

"Richard commanded you there, and now he commands you to L'Argent. I was present for both commands, so you may take it from me for veracity."

"How far is this castle?" asked Little John.

"Near seventy mile by the roads," said the knight who had not yet spoken. Sherwood hummed like the wind in the treetops. Seventy miles! So far! Was that to the sea? Or the mountains? Robin said, "Roads are fine, but if it's Stoke-on-Trent we want, quicker to walk the Trent."

"Please yourself."

"What does the king do at L'Argent?"

"Who are you to ask?"

Robin replied evenly, "A soldier called at his bidding, who can serve best when he understands best. Is he taking the castle? Is he returning to London and needs escort? Am I to bring my entire band, or just yeomen? How long—"

"You're to *bring* yeomen, you're to come *right* away, and you're to keep your damned *insolent* questions to yourself." The knight—was he Berwick?—actually smiled. "Those were Richard's *exact* words."

Robin Hood nodded. "Richard still maintains a personal interest in the men under his command, I see." He pondered momentarily what this could mean, but had no knowledge to draw on. There seemed little to do but accept. An irate king such as Richard might return with fire and sword and no mercy at all. "We accept," Robin told the men, which statement seemed to insult them the most. With a mischievous grin he asked, "Would you stay and sup with us? You can rest easy about decorum. The salt will sit nowhere on our table."

"Neither shall we." The two mounted and only then looked at the sky for the time. It was late, but they turned anyway and rode off. "I suggest you start walking, and soon," called Berwick, "or the king will have your ballocks for breakfast!" He ducked his head as the horse entered the trail, and their hoofbeats faded away.

Robin Hood turned to his followers. Every face was rivetted on his. "My friends, know you again that the Lord moves in mysterious ways. We are not for London after all, but for the far reaches of the Trent. Blessed are the ways of the Lord. Come, let's bank the fire and get a good supper in us of salt and cock. Would we had some ale to go with it."

"How about brandy?" asked Brian, and held up a crock.

Robin shook his head and smiled. "Brian, you're a wonder."

By the next day's afternoon the fighters were ready to depart. Black Bart had edged knives and arrowheads. Such spare food as there was was wrapped. People had new soles to their boots, nearly-new cloaks against the weather, and new bowstrings. Leather rucksacks bulged and quivers were jammed tight. The yeomen milled around and around the great table, eager to be off, loath to leave.

Robin Hood himself was edgy. He disliked working in the dark, but he could not formulate plans without information. He had prepared the camp and his followers as best he could. He would have to rely on God and his people from here on. Marian would remain behind. Someone had to wait for David and Friar Tuck and Gilbert to

return, and for Will Scarlett to die. With her would stay
Allan A'Dale by his own request, Elaine, the children, the
older girls Polly and Rachel and a fuming Katie, Old Bess
and Tam, Arthur's wife Mary (lost without her other half,
Ben's wife Clara), and Young Mary. Robin thought it a
shame to take Polly's only parent away, but he needed
Red Tom's sword.

The Fox of Sherwood had with him Little John and
Much, Arthur A'Bland, Black Bart and Red Tom, Brian,
old Will Stutly, and the two maids, Bold Jane Downey and
Grace. Half of them were untested in combat. Much and
Will Stutly were good company but little else. And there
were gaps in his ranks no amount of wishing could fill. He
was without Gilbert, Will Scarlett, Friar Tuck, Ben Barrel, David of Doncaster, and Shonet.

Robin Hood's farewell to Will Scarlett had been short
and painful. Scarlett's lips were drawn back like an old
woman's. Black lines of blood poisoning reached to his
crotch and beyond. He picked at the sheets.

"Hi, Rob," he wheezed. "You know, maybe I should
have let you take off this leg."

Robin Hood shook his head. "No, Will, you were right.
If I can't have you whole to drive me mad, I don't want
you around." Will laughed, but the motion pained him.
Robin said, "You get some sleep, Coz."

Will grabbed Robin's hand. "Rob, take care of Tam, will
ye? See he grows up honest and smart."

"You're not going to die, Will!"

"Promise."

"I promise."

"Bury me . . . bury me alongside a road, so's I can see
what's going on. But don't mark the grave. Just grass."

Robin Hood wished Tuck were there. He was so good at
comforting rituals. "Get some sleep, Will."

The dying man closed his eyes. "Just remember Will
Scarlett, is all." Robin's tears fell on his cousin's face as he
kissed him goodbye.

Now with a hoarse voice Robin blathered final orders,

recommendations, warnings, and last minute thoughts for the defense of Sherwood until he ran out of ideas. Marian attended with the patient, unlistening nods of wifedom. Normally any expedition exited amidst cheers and jests, but this time was different. The forest glade was so quiet people could hear the swallows fidgetting with their nest in the eaves of the great hall. Robin looked at his party, lost in thought. Ten followers at a king's command. It were sad times for England when she needed a handful of rag-tag outlaws. The departure waited on his word, but he held it back. Something—the events of this wild spring, the strange scents on the air, the electric charge all around—*something* was not right. He would not be easy in his mind until he discovered what it was. Some dread beyond what he could see stalked him.

A sound made him look up. Out of Ben Barrel's cottage came Ben himself, struggling to get his fat arms and bow through the straps of a satchel and quiver. Clara and Tub helped him as Glenyth lugged Bridget Ann along.

"Ben, what's up?"

The fat man took his place in line and fiddled with his accoutrements. "We, uh, talked, and the wife, here, decided we should stay. Or that I should go, rather, and they, uh, stay."

Robin was out of laughter, but he could still chuckle. "We're glad you're with us, Ben." He looked at the sky, which presaged rain later. Would it be warm? "Let's up, lads and lasses. The quicker we're away, the quicker we're back." He kissed his wife, who pulled him close.

"See?" she whispered, "we're not yet to leave the forest. God watches and He helps. We'll be all right, and so will you."

Robin Hood smiled and kissed her again. Others did the same. Then the yeomen straightened up and the wives and children stepped back. The gap between them was very wide.

"Let's go," said their green leader.

The party stepped away. Their feet were quiet across

the forest floor. They could hear honking as it filtered through the treetops.

Much pointed. "Look, Rob-in. Geese."

Robin craned his neck. A ragged V split the sky, high up against the clouds. "Aye, Much. The first of the year. Lucky creatures to go where they will, at no one's command. Now lift your feet, you lot! We've no wings, but we can travel."

Chapter 23

The geese pulled themselves through the sky with great reaches of their long wings. They curled their pinions together and shoved down on the air, then snapped their wings upwards with feathers parted. Then they did it again, and again. To stop for even a second was to drop towards the earth.

They had been flying since before dawn, five miles up, covering fifty miles in an hour. Cold air passed into their lungs and became power. The muscles of their breasts burned with a heat that would kill a man. Yet all along they honked to one another—a brash *gahng gahng* that carried for miles. They called to their mates to say hello. They queried the leader about stopping. They commented on the shape of the ground below them. They asked one another about the cloud formations and rain. They teased and cajoled and whined and berated and joked. No one goose was ever silent for long.

At the sight of a certain rock spire they swerved onto another tack. The rock was only confirmation. Each goose carried in his or her head the lines of the world, the shape of the magnetic field, the smell of the wind high up, the rotation of the earth, the whirl of the stars and the moon. A blind gosling stolen from a nest could find it again by night if dragged to the other side of the world. There came a call, the signal for a night's rest, and the entire flock

stopped beating as one. Wings outspread, their stream-
lined bodies dropped like thistle seeds in a glide.

The water was good. In the heart of this island, just
north of a broad forest, was a calm lake. Marsh grass lined
its edges. The geese could see a long way. Men and
wolves and foxes would have difficulty getting to the center. The water had the color of living things. There were
hummocks where they might dry their feet. And memory
showed that millions of birds had landed here year after
year, molested only by water rats and turtles. It was a
good place.

Still in formation, but farther apart, the plump oily
bodies kissed the water and settled in. The giant V of the
sky split into a hundred tiny Vs on the water. The wind
touched them again, for they had felt no breeze while part
of the sky. Greedily the geese poked at the marsh line and
ducked their heads for food. It was there. Wild rice,
tadpoles, green grass shoots, crawfish, duckweed, egg sacs,
flies. They circled around and tossed their heads and
waggled their wings and shredded grass and strained mud
and pecked one another and chatted and chuckled and
grunted constantly.

These were greylag geese, wild and common the world
over, with plump grey bodies and pink-tinged bills. Inter-
mediate between swans and ducks, the males had bodies
twenty inches long with a wingspan of five feet. Their legs
were set forward on their bodies so they could walk and
graze easily. Their necks were long and straight, their eyes
big and black. They were perfect machines, sleek and
powerful, oiled against the water, downed against the
cold, engineered for flying the length of the world. They
were intelligent, brave, clever, loyal, long-lived, and fun-
loving. They worked hard and rested little. They had
covered five hundred miles since they last touched ground.
They were ready for a rest.

A squawk of terror, quite un-gooselike, rang across the
marsh. A mate ran to the terrified gander and quickly
added her cries. At the same time a furious beating
drummed on the pond. The flock had spread out. Un-

gainly splashings sounded all around the compass. Goose rumps were pointed skyward, with the owner's, heads caught below. The birds lathered the water as they drowned. Mates circled in helpless terror, shedding bright green droppings like feather dust. Then from the marsh arose the hated two-legged shapes of men as they lurched forward after their prizes. They had planted nets laced with fishhooks in the choicest grass. Other nets were pegged underwater with bait below to trap a bird's head. The men had grass tied to their clothes, and they wore wide wicker baskets on their feet. Now they thrashed stout sticks against the grass as they advanced upon the milling geese. Boys pushed off in coracles toward the drowning birds.

Some geese took off immediately. Some advanced hissing with wings out, but they were at a disadvantage on the water. The men could not club them very well, but neither could the birds attack with their beaks and wings. And there was little point. The birds impaled on fishhooks had either wrenched free or spilled all their blood on the matting. The entangled birds, full of water, had sunk or ripped loose. The men shouted as they came, and three birds were stunned by the sticks. The leader started the chorus of *GAHNG-GAHGN GAHNG-GAHGN GAHNG-GAHGN* and the others took it up. In a peal like thunder and surf, the flock sped for the open spots, flailed the water with wide thrusts, leapt aloft, and pulled for the sky. Some unconsolable mates, male and female betrothed at birth, were left behind to fall victim to the hunters.

The birds pulled for altitude. There were no men up here. Farther on, a few hours flying, was a secluded place where men had never come. They marked the marsh as An Evil Place. They flew on and left it behind.

Chapter 24

The first words that Robin Hood heard at the king's encampment were not encouraging.

The outlaws had left the wooded trail and dropped into a valley. In two long days, the outlaws had walked across the tailbone of the backbone of England, the Pennine Chain. They had picked their way over hill and marsh with the shrinking Trent at the left. It was a lovely and relaxing walk. The river was slow and wide, the swans plentiful and equally slow. Robin tried to enjoy the trip for its own self, tried to avoid thought of the troubles ahead and behind. Eventually they came to Stoke-on-Trent in the Cheshire plain. The river and their journey had ended.

Richard was camped to the south of town, in the middle of what had been someone's field of winter rye. Will Stutly clucked his tongue at the waste. Nearby on a swell was a motte and bailey castle. This was the standard Norman retreat of England, fast becoming outdated by the newer all-stone keeps. A motte was a mound of earth, a bailey an encircling wall of wood. There were actually two connected mounds: a lower one with no buildings for livestock, and a higher one with a log fort at the summit. The outlaws looked at the distant conglomeration of tents, horses, knights and attendants. The camp had the look of a mudflat astir with geese.

"Why build in the bottom of the valley?" asked Red

Tom as they legged along. "I thought the Normans liked to be high up, close to God."

"Must be cozy in the winter though, sheltered from the wind and all," commented Little John.

"But these bugs must chew your ears off nine months of twelve," replied Robin Hood. The black clouds had greeted them upon entering the marshy valley. The air here was dense and cool under a grey sky. Everyone was swatting and shrugging from the onslaught of flies, mosquitoes, and midges. Only Little John seemed capable of ignoring them.

"If Cedwyn were here, she'd have a potion to keep them off," said Grace.

"Cedwyn is dead," replied Jane Downey.

"Oh, yes. I'd forgotten."

By the riverbank before Richard's camp were two soldiers in plain livery. They wore knee-length byrnies—leather coats with studs—and conical helmets. This far west, they were more Saxon than their eastern cousins. They both had full mustaches, hefty axes with four foot handles, and round strapped shields. They carried no bows. They wore cloth swaddled to the eyes against insects.

"What ho, good brother Saxons!" called Robin when he was within range. "Is this the castle L'Argent where Richard resides?" This question was superfluous, for they could see Richard's scarlet banner easily.

"Who are you to ask, with your devil's green and your Norman bows?" growled a man through his cloth protection.

Robin Hood frowned at the surly tone. He brushed insects from his eyelids. "As I might have known," he said. "True soldiers. It makes me homesick for the Crusades. I am Robin Hood, with my Merry Men, here at the behest of the king himself. Have you no civil tongue for an ally and Christian such as yourself?"

"Christian, better you'd stayed at the Crusades. But glad we are to see you, for the Lionheart can leave off chewing on us and make a meal of you. You've been the talk of his party, and you're in trouble such as only the devil knows."

Robin replied, "And wherefore has the king a grievance against us? Or should I more properly ask, has the king some *new* grievance incurred since we had him to sup at the last moon?"

The man shook his head until his helmet wobbled. "*I* am but a simple soldier without the king's ear, and glad for it. We were told to keep an eye out, and here you are. Now get you along. The king awaits. Nor think you to hie back to the woods. Our horsemen would run you down like a covey of quail and consider it good sport."

Robin looked again at the camp ahead. His followers were uneasy, as was he, and he strove not to show it. "Let's move anon, noble lads and lasses. We'll beard the lion in his den." Without a word to the soldiers, they strode off with their long-legged glide. The soldiers turned to watch them go.

"What's it mean, Rob?" asked Little John, and the others held their breath to hear Robin's answer.

"I don't know. Richard has been bad-mouthing us to his men, and lately it seems. I would think a king had too much to do to mull over old wounds, but they're as human as the rest of us." Robin thought for a while as the tents enlarged in their sight. Dogs ran out to bark at them. "Most likely he's received news of our 'marauding' from Nottingham. He holds us to blame for the atrocities committed by the blackguard impostors, and wants some accounting, I guess. We'll know soon enough, and damned be all soldiers everywhere, kings and all."

The camp looked to have been erected in the rain, for tents were staked higgledy-piggledy. The smoke of the fires was everywhere, but it kept the insects down. Horses were pegged around or let loose in a rope corral held up by stakes. The best horses, some saddled for messengers, were near the largest tent, which was upwind of the camp. This was obviously the king's: a travelling throne room. Everyone in camp—soldiers and servants, a few women— was gathered in front of this large tent. When the outlaws got closer they noticed two men in smallclothes with their hands bound behind them. The insects that plagued everyone seemed doubly cruel to these frightened men, who writhed in their bonds and swiped their faces at their shoulders to alleviate the itching.

Robin and his band approached the largest table near the largest firepit and stopped. People ignored them. The table was set with covered bowls and pots. They had stood in the smoke for a time, sniffing beef on the fire, when a tall man in a foxtail coat approached.

"You are Robin O' the Hood?"

"I am."

"Wait here." The man entered the king's tent.

"Friendly lot," growled Black Bart.

"Shush!"

The man came out after a time, but did not speak to the outlaws again. The idlers watched and whispered. His face burning with chagrin, Robin stood for a time while his followers waited. Then the Fox of Sherwood announced loudly, "Lads, since there seems to be nobbut animals prowling this camp, they'll raise no fuss at our feasting. Let's wrap ourselves around what we find and pay our hosts when they arrive." With that, he rested his bow against the table bench, grabbed a trencher of stale bread, and fished the cover off a pot. Little John, Will Stutly, Black Bart, then the rest followed suit. There was plenty of food on the table, and the twelve outlaws devoured every scrap down to the last dregs of honey in a pot. There was never a word from the sullen lot on the outskirts.

"Sweeter food I've not tasted in a long time," remarked Red Tom. "What think you of king's fare, Brian?"

Brian's eyes widened. He looked at the bread in his hand. "It—it tastes like any other," he stammered.

Red Tom rapped his crust on the table. "Better. Look. No weevils."

Much asked, "Why don't they eat, Rob-in?"

"Who, Much?" asked their leader innocently.

"Them," said the idiot.

Robin pretended to peer around him. There were maybe

two hundred fighting men all told, some of Richard's and some from the motte in colors of yellow. "I see no men, Much, only ghosts and phantasms. Still, I must remark, 'tis amazing a man men call FOOL remembers his MANNERS no matter the time or tide. Eat up, Much, and God bless you."

Red Tom commented, "I'll say Rob, you may drag us to hell and back, and we never know what's going to happen next, but you feed us well."

Robin Hood mopped gravy with a crust. "Not only that, but a SONG with a meal does WONDERS for the digestion. Let's have a round of—"

He stopped as the flap of the large tent was thrown aside. There in the morning light was Richard, King of England and France. Taller than most men, crowned with both flowing blonde hair and a circlet of gold, he stood against the drab surroundings like a young god. The crouching gold lion blazed on his broad chest, painted red as a sea of blood. In his hand he carried the famous Danish axe like a scepter. The crowd froze at the sight, until the flight of a raven overhead was loud. Richard walked into the brittle silence and surveyed the scruffy outlaws at his table. His face went taut then smug at the sight. He did not address them.

He marched to where the prisoners swayed on their feet. The regal voice broke the stillness. "L'Argent, Dumont, as sovereign ruler of England and France, we find you guilty of treason against your king. The sentence is immediate death. Father, administer the last rites."

The men wailed and would have fallen sideways if not caught by the guards. Quickly the guards trotted the condemned to a large stump at the woodpile. A priest followed every step of the way, reciting a prayer with his hands clasped together. The crowd fell back while jockeying for a view. The guards folded L'Argent over the stump with his neck exposed. The priest finished his Latin, touched the struggling head of L'Argent with oil and stepped back. A burly sergeant raised an axe.

Grace turned her head but the others watched as the axe came down. A single *thump* severed the neck, and a gout of blood sprayed onto the grass for only a short time. The body was pulled aside. Dumont was squashed to his knees, but he had fainted. He never felt the kiss of the axe, though it took two blows.

"Fare *and* entertainment," remarked Red Tom.

Brian whispered, "What do you suppose they did?"

"Backtalked the king, belike," rumbled Little John.

Through it all Richard stood immobile, with his thick mailed arms across his bright breast, the wind caressing his hair. As the headless carcasses were dragged away feet first, he turned to the Sherwooders.

"Robin Hood of Sherwood," the king declaimed, "get inside the tent." He pointed with his axe like an executioner himself. Meekly the outlaw chieftain got up and went. His followers, not told otherwise, followed. They crept into the tent and let the flap fall. Made in sections, the tent was big enough to accommodate thrice their number. The inside smelt of mustiness and mud. A pole rested on the rich rug to hold the roof high. There were chests around the walls and a small backless chair in the rear. It was quiet outside, as if the tent were erected in some desert and not amidst two hundred men.

"What do you think he'll do to us, Rob?" asked Ben Barrel.

"Ah," growled Black Bart, "who cares what the bastard does?"

"He could chop our heads off," said Brian.

" 'E can try," snarled Bart.

"Maybe it were a mistake to come," said Will Stutly.

Robin Hood fingered his bowstring. "Live and learn, Will. Or, learn and die. I doubt he'll kill us. I never heard of a king summoning someone just to be decapitated. Probably he wants us to explain that Nottingham nonsense."

"Well, see if you can't keep a hold of your temper this time, Rob," said Little John, and everyone turned to look at him.

"Keep my temper?"

"Yes," replied the giant. His long face was unnaturally sober. "Remember at the feast, when you and he got into that shouting match? It was . . ." He hunted for a word. "Unseemly."

Robin tossed a hand in the air. "Unseemly? My arguing with the king? What's wrong with arguing? Everyone argues with *me!*"

Little John shook a finger like a cucumber. "Now tha's not true, Rob, and you know it. We do what you tell us. But it's not right to correct the king. You argued with him in the Holy Land, you argued with him in Sherwood, and from the look on your face you'll argue with him here. He don't like it, and it isn't right anyway. He's our *king.*"

"Is that so? Well then, John, for your sakes if nothing else, as I live and breath I swear to say nothing to antagonize him. There is little point in contradicting him, anyway." Robin Hood stuck his thumbs in his belt. "God himself couldn't get a king to admit he's wrong."

"I'll tell you a story," said Allan a'Dale. "I'll tell you one of Jesus, Our Lord, who could have been the king of all lands, but chose not to be."

The children scrunched and shoved on the floor of the main hall. The women settled with chores in their hands. It was after supper, and a story was just what they needed to drive off the quiet and loneliness. Allan, a tall, bony man, father to three, settled himself more purposefully in his seat. "It goes like this . . .

One day in his travels Jesus came upon a mighty army. The army was as thick as locusts, ready to enter and sack a mighty city. A scholar had been sent out of the city to negotiate with the king of the army. But the king would hear nothing from the scholar, and pressed for war.

Seeing Jesus, and recognizing Him as the famous man of peace, the scholar approached. "Lord," he pleaded, "can you not intercede on the city's behalf? If they attack, scores both within and without will suffer." Jesus approached the invading king.

"Why do you make war upon this city?" asked He.

The king replied, "The warlord of this city has captured my son and holds him to a ransom of one hundred talents. On my honor, I will not pay the ransom, so I must war to get back my son."

Jesus said, "Your sword will rust in its scabbard, for I shall obtain your son's release. Then shall you know who here is king."

To this the king replied, "I have heard about you, Jesus of Nazareth. They say you are the son of God and that you perform miracles. I don't believe it. You may try to release my son, but if you fail, I will have you torn apart by wild horses."

Jesus nodded and entered the city with the scholar. "Take me to the warlord," He said. The scholar did so. In a palace rich with rugs and incense, Jesus addressed the warlord and asked if the ransom was still one hundred talents. The warlord laughed. "It is. Anyone may have the boy for one hundred talents, but it shall not be you, Nazarene, for you have not a single florin."

Jesus replied, "You shall have your money before the sun sets, but it shall cost you more than one hundred talents." And He left the throne room. As they passed out of the palace, Jesus saw a woman weeping in a garden. He stopped and asked her what was the matter.

It was the warlord's wife. "I am unhappy because my husband sports with a prostitute and ignores me."

Jesus said, "Go and wash your face, for your husband shall know you tonight." And He left her. Jesus told the scholar, "Take me to the richest man in this town."

The richest man was a Jew usurer. The moneylender had a fine house, but people crossed the street as they approached it. Jesus spoke to the moneylender and asked him what he wanted most.

The moneylender said, "What do I want most? I want more gold. Enough gold to fill a house to the roof!"

Jesus said, "No, you don't. You want to be respected, so people will greet you by name and not spit on you when you pass."

The usurer was much surprised, and said, "That is true. More than anything I would love a house and farm, that I might be treated as an equal by my neighbors."

Jesus asked, "Would you give a hundred talents to have it so?"

"Gladly," replied the moneylender.

Jesus said, "I will return." To the scholar He said, "Take me to the best farmer in the land." The scholar led Him to a large vineyard where the grape arbors were laden to breaking. Jesus said to the vintner, "What is it you most want in the world?"

The vintner said, "What do I most want? I want it to rain regularly, so my grapes will grow that I might harvest them and press barrels of wine."

And Jesus said, "That is not so. You wish to be free of this farm, where you were born and have lived all your life."

The vintner was amazed, and he said, "That is true. I would like to roam the hills and mountains by myself, taking my time and going where I wish."

"Would you give up your farm to be able to do so?" asked Jesus.

"Verily, I would," replied the vintner, "if it were left in capable hands."

Jesus said, "I will return." To the scholar He said, "Take me to the most adventurous man in the city." The scholar led Him to a strong man who was the chief hunter for the Roman soldiers. Jesus said to the hunter, "What is it you most want in the world?"

The hunter looked to the hills. "What do I most want? To be able to walk with my dog through the mountains, to find good water and kill the deer far from home."

Jesus said, "That is not true. Most of all you want to sail the sea."

The hunter looked surprised, but he said, "That is true.

But I am not a free man. I am obligated to the centurion as long as I live, for he once saved my life."

Jesus said, "I will return." To the scholar He said, "Take me to the centurion."

But the scholar became cross, and he demanded of Our Lord, "How can all this talk bring home the boy? We walk all over town and accomplish nothing!"

To which Jesus replied, "A man fails when he stops trying. If trapped in a dark cave, do you sit down and moan and wail, or do you look for an escape? My Father would have us try all avenues before we despair, for it is man's lot to persevere."

The scholar then led Him to the Roman barracks, where they found the centurion. Jesus asked the man, "What is it that you want most in the world?"

The centurion laughed. "What is it I want most? To fight, to serve, to drink, to whore. That is all a soldier needs."

Jesus said, "That is not true. What you want is a wife to keep a home for you and give you children."

The centurion was angry at this reply. "What you say may be. But I have seen countless women and they are all unfaithful. There is not one who would be true to me."

Jesus asked, "If I could find you a chaste wife, would you release the service of your chief hunter?"

The centurion was perplexed. "I might. But I doubt there's a faithful woman in the city, or in all the world of men."

Jesus said, "I will return." To the scholar He said, "Take me to see the prostitute who consorts with the warlord." The scholar brought Him to the prostitute. She dressed gaily, but wore much paint to hide her shame. Jesus asked the prostitute, "What would you like most in the world?"

The harlot laughed, "What would I like? Fine clothes, good food and wine, and lots of men to keep me happy."

Jesus shook His head. "That is not true. What you want is to be a good woman, respected and admired."

The harlot's eyes flashed, but she said, "What you say is

true. I would be decent and not a whore, but no one can change the past."

Jesus asked, "If you could attain a position of privilege, would you become the wife of a good man and remain faithful to him?"

The harlot frowned. "Yes, but I must first be respected before I could marry."

Jesus took her by the hand, and with His touch the prostitute was made pure. And Jesus said, "Come with me." Jesus, the scholar, and the prostitute went to the palace. There they met the warlord's wife in the garden. The lady asked what Jesus wanted. "Your husband has been sporting with a prostitute, who was this woman." The wife made to strike the harlot, but Jesus stayed her hand. He said, "Hire you this woman as your foremost handmaiden. She will gain respect as the consort of the queen. She can then marry a decent man and remain chaste to him. Thereafter, she will always be with you by day and her husband by night. Your husband can no longer consort with her." The lady weighed the words of Jesus, and agreed.

Jesus said, "Come with me." Jesus, the scholar, the prostitute, and the wife went to the barracks. Jesus said to the centurion, "Take you this woman to wife. She has been with too many men who love her not. Love her well and she will remain faithful."

But the centurion objected. "I cannot marry a whore."

Jesus replied, 'She is no longer a whore, but has been made pure. She will be a chaste woman who attends the warlord's wife by day and you by night."

The centurion believed what Jesus said and consented. Jesus said, "Come with me." Jesus, the scholar, the prostitute, the wife, and the centurion went to the hut of the hunter. Jesus said to him, "The centurion will release you from your obligation, that you might go to sea." The centurion did so, wishing him well in his travels.

Jesus said, "Come with me." Jesus, the scholar, the prostitute, the wife, the centurion, and the hunter went to the vineyard. Jesus said to the vintner, "This man has led an adventurous life as a hunter. Now that he goes to sea, the centurion needs another. You may become a hunter as you wish and roam the hills." The vintner liked the idea, and consented to give up his land.

Jesus said, "Come with me." Jesus, the scholar, the prostitute, the wife, the centurion, the hunter, and the vintner all went to the house of the moneylender. Jesus said, "This vintner will give you his lands. Work hard on the vines that you might become a good neighbor and be loved by all." The moneylender said he would.

Then Jesus said, "Give me one hundred talents." The moneylender did, praising His wisdom. Our Lord and the scholar went to the warlord's palace. Once there, Jesus handed the warlord the talents and said, "Give me the king's child." The child was brought forward and given over to Him. The warlord was amazed that a penniless stranger had earned one hundred talents in less than a day, and he demanded to hear the whole story. In tones of worship the scholar related the proceedings.

When it was finished, the warlord said, "You talk a good scheme, Nazarene. Everyone in it gave up what they had to get what they wanted. But not I. I have received one hundred talents without giving up anything."

Jesus said, "That is not true. The prostitute you consorted with is a decent woman now, handmaiden to your wife and wife to a Roman centurion. Your whore has been taken from you by your own greed." And Jesus and the scholar left the city with the child.

As Jesus walked from the walled city with the child on his hand, there was a great tumult among the king's army. The soldiers raised their swords as the Lord passed. Jesus gave the son to the father, saying, "Here is your child. Now sheathe your sword and go in peace."

The king was most pleased to have his son back alive, but perplexed as to how Jesus had accomplished it with no money and no army. The scholar explained, "Verily, sire, it was like a string of miracles. Without raising a hand He has caused, willingly, a moneylender to hand over his gold, a vintner to give up his farm, a hunter to leave the hills, a centurion to dismiss an obligation, a prostitute to stop whoring, and a warlord to give up his captive!"

The king hugged his son. "Then I was mistaken about you, Lord Jesus. You have my thanks."

The scholar raised his hands to Heaven. "And there is the greatest miracle of all! He hath caused a king to admit he was wrong!"

And Jesus smiled.

"We've seen them!" called Roger and Delancey as their horses pounded into the courtyard of Sir Guy's castle. "They're leaving the forest! They bear west along the Trent!"

Everyone gathered in the courtyard: Guy's men, servants, the silent Kite, and the one-eyed villain crawled from his pallet. The scouts held their story as Guy made the trek from his high tower. The crowd parted to give their master wide berth.

"Are you sure it's them?" demanded Guy. "Are they afoot? And how many?"

"It must be they, for they wear green. They walk. We saw them this morning. We almost missed them, for there are only twelve and they keep low. But they did not see us, nor will the peasants alert them. We made sure of that."

Guy rubbed his hands. Robin Hood and eleven followers. That left only six or so unaccounted for, tallied with what he had learned just recently.

"Women. Were there women with them?"

"Women?"

"Yes, women, you stupid lout! Were there women in the party?"

The first knight stammered. "I—I don't know. I never . . ." He turned to the other knight, "Delancey, did you see? . . ."

Delancey shook his head. "I know how a woman walks,

if Roger doesn't." This brought snickers. "They're all sizes—you can see Little John and the idiot Much and a great fat one—but there are no women."

Guy nodded. "No, I didn't believe it either." He thought for a moment more. He glanced at the sky. It was too late to ride today. But tomorrow . . . He racked his brain, but there was nothing else to consider. His stomach tightened and his loins quivered at the thought of his prize. He could hardly get his words out.

"Fetch lances! Sharpen your swords! Tomorrow we ride to Sherwood!"

Chapter 25

The hares frolicked in their strange parliment. The males fought and ripped fur from one another. Bucks and does played *pas de deux*, where a hare would leap straight up while another ran underneath. They found a nest of baby mice and tossed them around before eating them. They leapt and fought and danced and boxed until a rumble made them freeze. They stood on hind legs and bulged their eyes. They swivelled translucent ears. Underfoot they felt the heavy tread and the lighter. Long hind feet thumped danger. Then they broke in all directions across the meadow.

Into the meadow thundered horses and riders. The men shot their heels and lashed with quirts. Their mounts were covered in lather and the beasts' eyes showed white all around. One had a cut across an eye, another had a stone wedged under a shoe, and bits tore at their mouths. All wheezed, but the pace was never slackened. Behind them trailed dogs. When the panting hounds entered the meadow and spotted the hares, pandemonium descended.

The hares sought to outrun their enemies, and the dogs were blind to everything but cotton tails. The hounds spurted ahead of the horses. Sounding *how-oo!* they twisted like squirrels to track the speckled blurs and laid-back ears. They sped under hoof and foot. Horses balked and stumbled. Men cursed and swung quirts. Hares banged into one another as the dogs did the same. A hoof stove in a hound's ribs. A hare went end over end to have its back broken in one bite. A rider left his saddle to fracture his wrist on the turf. Hare and horse and man alike screamed. With a shudder like a hailstorm the charge ground to a halt. Men leapt from the saddle and cursed their dogs and kicked them. They lashed their horses across the face. They cut the throat of the wounded dog and bound the man's wrist. They looked for hares to kill, but the animals had vanished.

Finally the men remounted, the dogs skulked behind, and the party set out again. They were up to speed when they reentered the woods on the far side of the meadow.

When the wave of chaos had receded like a storm, the hares came out to play.

Chapter 26

Three elemental beings flashed through the forest on parallel courses. A great shaggy boar plowed over brush and bracken. A powerful stag leapt like a cloud over hedge and heath. And burning its own trail across sun and shadow bounded a great cat of orange and black. Each moved on a line with Robin Hood's camp.

"Holy Mother of God! Look at that!"

Allan, the women, and the children of Sherwood dropped their tasks and looked at the top of the mound. A great hart, the largest they had ever seen, loomed over them like a lost god.

Marian blurted, "Quick! Gather the children! Be ready to run!" She reached for her bow, but the women were frozen. Before anyone could find the legs the stag leapt from his perch and landed on the common without a sound. He tossed his great head and slowly stalked towards them, close enough that they could smell musk. The beast was larger than any two stags: he stood taller than a man at the shoulder, and his head was in the trees. His skull was big as a barrel. The stag's coat was a dark brown, with shaggy hair long as a man's fingers. The humans crossed their chests repeatedly and mumbled ineffectual prayers. These people knew this was no normal stag. It was too big. And at a time when other deer had only buds in velvet, this monster had a full rack of lined and crosshatched horns with wicked points, some twenty in all. And its eyes were a deep fiery green.

This was Hern, Marian thought. The one who had haunted Robin's dreams. The one who sought to drive them from the woods. But also the one who had told him, "Sherwood shall be with you."

"What—what do you want?" she asked. She was trapped against the common table. She made to edge away, but the beast stuck his powerful neck out, gesturing with his horns, pointing her to the left. In reply Marian edged that way. The beast followed. The eyes tracked her face like a witch's lantern. She turned to the others, and reached for the children who clutched her knees. "It wants us to get inside. There must be trouble coming. We needs bolt the door and mount the panel. Katie, break out the weapons. Clara, Mary, get moving."

The stag watched them move with grass green eyes, then he turned and drummed off into the woods. The tracks he left were large and cloven, like Satan's.

Marian called to the crowd. "Move! Get the children inside. Never mind the food! Tam, TAM! Check the bolthole, you know best how!"

Please God, she thought, *how long did they have before the trouble arrived?*

Guy pressed on headlong. Guy had thirty-two men all told, each with crossbow and double-stuffed quiver, lance, broadsword, and mace. Besides their arms they carried siege tools: spades, axes, bars and torches. Several hounds trailed or led or got underfoot. The Kite was on point, his face grim but his eyes alight. The last man was only partly there, crouched on the saddle, hanging on with all his might. It was the false Robin, now a fragment of a man, steeled with hatred and insanity. He had given up the directions to the camp as well as its layout. Guy had no use for him, but if he could cling to a saddle he could accompany them.

The forest they traversed was mostly open, with pebbly

meadows and sun-spotted glades. Climax trees shaded some places to gloom while other areas were as bright as the center of Nottingham. Occasionally the Kite would lead them through brush to cut off some of the trail. At one such point, as they kneed their horses to breast a break and dragged their lances by the tips, the bracken split. A brown blur sailed overhead.

"God, what's that?" "Whose horse?" "No! LOOK!"

The largest stag they had ever seen stood spraddle-legged in their path. The beast loomed above the bushes, more like a bear than a deer, and glared at them with human green eyes. The horses shied and pranced backwards. The stag charged. Guy screamed as his horse smashed sideways into the brush, scrabbling in any direction away from those wicked tines. The lord tumbled from the saddle onto his head and shoulders while his men shouted on the trail. Riders dove off their horses to get out of the way. A soldier howled as a tine caught his sleeve and arm. The hart cleared the path. Then a man afoot levelled his crossbow and shot. Another string sounded, and the bolt glanced off the stag's withers. Having reached the end of the party, the deer flashed over a hedge and was gone. By the time Guy was upright on the trail his men were laughing with relief as they picked themselves up and remounted.

"Did you see? We drove it off!"

"Two bolts, with only one hitting!"

"Two hit!"

"Nay, Roger, yours missed!"

"But it was so BIG!"

"Shut up, you—"

The stag shattered the bracken and plowed into the tightest group of knights. A soldier screamed as his thigh was pierced by a tine. Then the stag was upright, chopping with its hooves. A man fell from the saddle, senseless or fainted. Horses bumped into one another. A crossbolt left the string to strike the shoulder of the next man. A scream was cut short as twin hooves crushed a soldier's chest. Sir Guy jerked at his mount's head and swore uselessly. His party would be scattered to the four winds in a moment.

Then a crossbow went *whonk* and the hart pitched backwards onto its rump. Blood cascaded from its neck across the white breast. The Kite had hit it with his weapon, the strongest in the crowd. Guy barked a laugh. The Kite used steel barbed arrowheads smeared with rotted offal. The poison ensured that even if an animal got away, it would die of slow infection. He and the Kite cheered as the stag dropped back from the attack. With a rattle of antlers on wood it bolted into the forest. The ground it left was wet with blood.

"A killing shot for sure!" gloated the Kite. "You lot!" he added.

Sir Guy roared, "Get ahorse, you apes! We've work to do!"

"Beaudieu is dead!"

"Leave him! Bring his horse! Kick that one awake! We've wasted enough time!" Within minutes the party resumed its breakneck pace along the forest byways. They stayed to the clear wherever possible. They did not see the stag again.

Far from camp, the boar ran with its queer but quick gallop. It crossed an open glade and ducked between two tall rocks at the far side. As it did so, a lightning bolt struck.

Whatever it was streaked in from the side, low and round and very fast. The strike was like a thunderclap, the weight like a rock that clung. The thing was perched on the boar's back. The assailant was nothing the boar had ever met before, but it smelled like a cat. There came a scream like a crow's, only immeasurably louder. Saber teeth got the boar by the back of the neck. Razor talons skidded down its throat and legs. The boar reared and screamed, but the talons and teeth found new purchase. Black blood sprayed. The tiger pressed her height advantage. She laid one paw across the boar's neck and tried to force it down so she could sever the spinal column with her teeth, or else break it. The boar tossed and shambled about, unable to dislodge its assassin. Then the monster of evil did the only thing it knew how. It charged.

Blind, the boar surged forward, faster and faster. It snapped off saplings, plunged across holes, barked off trees. Leaves stuck to the blood. With her teeth sunk to their full length, the tiger, lighter by hundreds of pounds, could only hold on. Then the two collided full with an oak tree as wide as a house. The tiger, foremost on the depressed head, took the force of the blow. She lost her grip and fell. The boar backed off, lowered its head, and rammed the cat against the tree trunk. It slashed the belly with its tusks, back and forth, and charged again and again until the cat was still.

The frenzy ended. Leaving blood and food behind, the boar raced for the camp of Robin Hood.

Sir Guy of Gisborne and his men thundered into the camp at Sherwood like the Apocalypse. They separated and circled and shouted and roared out challenges, but there was no one about: no man, no woman, child, or dog. The small huts were cold and empty. Only the large hall sent up plumes of smoke. Guy shouted his men to him. They pointed their horses at the hall like siege weapons.

As they did so, the door popped open and a forest of levelled arrows appeared. "Loose!" came a high-pitched cry.

With one sound the wicked shafts struck the party. Horses screamed, men swore, blood erupted. Three knights were bowled from the saddle. Two horses dropped. There came the cry again, a woman's voice in command, "Loose!" A third volley followed, and a fourth, almost at five second intervals. Sir Guy scrambled to the rear of the party. He shouted curses without commands. It was the Kite who called, "Get your bows up, you lice! That's naught but children in there!" The men risked a look from behind their mounts. The bows were clutched in pudgy or bony hands, some arrow tips only thirty inches above the ground. One arrow struck a tree, tilted, and fell loose. Sir Guy's army recovered their courage. As Guy wasted many more words, his men slid their crossbows over the saddles. With a metallic *whang* a quarrel thunked into the doorframe. Then another. One bolt passed inside, high. Then the door slammed shut.

"Hurry!" called Guy. "Get up there, you motherless sots, before they bar it! You there, fire the huts! Burn everything!" Five men ran to the door and set to with axes. The door was fresh oak and green, and the first blow was like striking a mountain. Sir Guy ran up and hit his men in the back. "Harder! Faster! Get us inside! Strip off those boards!" Behind Guy, forgotten in the rush, crouched the one-eyed traitor. He flexed hands that itched for Marian's throat. Other men set torches alight and leaped to their horses. Savagely they ripped the beasts' heads around, whirled the torches to get them blazing, then bashed them through windows in the huts or stuffed them amid the soggy thatch.

The Kite hit men on their armored shoulders with his crossbow to get their attention. "You lot! Circle the woods and look for children escaping! GO!" He looked with disgust at the men sprawled around the camp. One dead, three hurt before they had even gotten here. Now two more wounded. Stupidity. Yet twenty-four should be enough, if Guy's information was correct. The Kite turned and spurred for the slope. If there was a bolthole, it was there.

Inside the main hall, Marian and Old Bess shooed the women and children into the cave. Marian spoke rapidly but clearly above the pounding at the door. "We must ready the children to leave out the back. They must take to the woods. Rachel—"

"But *why?*" asked Arthur's wife Mary.

"Mary. They'll *kill* us if they get in here!"

"Will they?" Mary tried to think about it. "Not the children, surely. Nor us. It's Robin they want. Your Robin."

Marian waved her hands the same way her husband did. "No, Mary, no. That's Guy of Gisborne out there. He's sworn to wipe us out. *All* of us. He won't leave a stick standing or a mouse alive. God willing, he'll spend himself trying to get through the door. If we get the children out, then ourselves, we should be all right."

"But—"

"STOP ARGUING AND GET MOVING!" Marian and Bess shoved the children into line. The women opened a chest and drew out tiny oilskin packets of food and tinder to tie to their clothing. They wiped the children's eyes and hugged them, and chattered advice at them all the while. Marian tried to calm her mind enough to think. "Rachel, you're the biggest, so you take Dale. Elaine, give him over, *now*. Katie, you take Bridget Ann."

"I don't want to handle a child! I want to fight!"

The slap across Katie's cheek was very loud. Tears started as the girl grabbed her jaw. Marian flared, "This is no time to argue! Do as you're told and take the child! Polly, you've sense, drag Glenyth with you. And keep her quiet, whatever it takes. (Stop sulking, Katie, or you'll get another.) Mary, you're a woman today with a woman's work. You guide Elaine. Good girl."

Tub asked, "What are we to do?" meaning the boys. He covered his cheeks lest he receive the same as Katie.

Marian spoke very calmly. "You, Tam, and Allan are to be unhindered. I want you free . . . so you can move if necessary." Her voice broke as she prayed inwardly for forgiveness at her reasoning: that the boys would be unable to resist running around, maybe giving chase. They would be targets. They had a good chance to get away, and it gave the laden girls a better chance. But would God forgive her endangering their lives? She brushed her eyes quickly. "Where's Tam?" she gulped.

"With his da."

Will Scarlett lay on his bed, as he had for a week. His face was grey and clay-like against his gay clothes. He could neither lift his head nor move his lower body. Sweat ran from his forehead as from a sponge. The stink of putrid flesh was strong. Beside the cot quivered his son.

"Tam," croaked the father, "go with the rest. Keep to the dark spots and get under the leaves." He cracked a ghost of the smile, a death's head grimace. "No trees, hear?"

The boy cried and pulled at his father's lace cuff. "Da, I don't want to go. I want to stay here with you and Grandmama." Will weakly pulled his hand away. When the boy clutched again, the hand cuffed at his tousled head.

"This is . . . no time to argue, Tam. I've taught you all I know. Now go. Rob'll be back soon, and it'll be all right." The boy cried more freely. Painfully Scarlett groped under the cot. He held out his slim knife and scabbard, the white blade he called Throatcutter. "Here, lad. It's all I have to give you. Now go."

The boy cried and hugged his father. But he took the knife and ran to join the others.

"Remember what we've taught you," Marian exhorted breathlessly. "Move in spurts, like a squirrel."

Bess said, "Keep your face and eyes down, don't look at the enemy."

Marian supplied, "Move into the shadows, stay there if it's safe. It'll be dark soon."

Bess said, "Don't squirm if you get a few bugs on you. No talking of any kind."

Marian had to finish before she broke down completely, "Get to a safe house and stay there until we collect you. May Our Lady bless and protect you all."

Allan A'Dale was in front of her. Allan, trained in no weapons, vowed to harm no one. Marian had forgotten about him. He wore a rag of stained green from the chest of clothes. "Marian, I'm going outside first."

"What will you do?" Marian asked. Elaine stood behind her husband, silently supporting his every word.

"I'll hide among the brush. I'll watch over the children, see that they get away safely."

Marian bit her lip. "All right." God, why wasn't Rob here? The next moment the bard had kissed his wife and children and run out the back.

Suddenly Mary blurted out, "Marian, are we to die?"

"Don't be foolish, Mary! We'll be all right! Rob must know of this! He must be on his way right now!" Her voice rose on the wave of lies. She had to stop talking. "All right, children, hunker down right here. I'm going to the end of the tunnel, and I'll call. Allan's gone ahead to signal if it's clear. This will be no harder than one of our training games. No talking from now on. Not a word until you're safe, understand? Listen!" She crept on all fours up the rough tunnel.

The invaders had ripped away the front door, pulled the boards and smashed away the remaining window of Christ in the temple, only to find the massive shutter behind. No simple bar held it closed. The women and children with Allan A'Dale had gotten into place the siege panel that had sheltered them from the storm. The thick oak, the brackets of black iron, the stone-lined sockets and heavy pins made this section stronger than the stone and log walls to each side. This panel was the only protection between the Sherwood folk and death, and with the fanaticism of men too busy to think about their task, the raiders concentrated their attack here. Axes rained on the panel again and again. The portal was soaked in oil which lessened the blows and made them slip. But as blow after blow crashed onto the door the splinters rose and the axes began to bite along the edges. The thick panel began to come apart.

Marian crawled along the tunnel. It was hand-hewn from the old watercourse and shored with timber. It narrowed as it rose. The end was screened with brush. She peered out. Although it was only noon, the light was failing. Clouds were stacked from treetop level right to Heaven. She could barely see Allan, crouched in a patch of brush forty feet away. Brushy birch and bracken grew thick here near the brook, and Robin had transplanted even more shrubbery around. The tunnel exit was parallel with the top of the mound. With the brush, trees, and rocky stream bed beyond, they were out of sight of the common. As long as escapees stayed low and quiet, they could leave the camp and never be seen.

The children rustled behind Marian like mice. She tugged at their sweaters and brought them forward. First was Polly with Glenyth. They would need the longest lead to get away, for Polly could not carry five-year-old Glenyth very far. Marian resisted giving more advice and settled for a prayer instead. Allan signalled all clear. Marian pointed the girls off to the left and patted their backs. As they had practiced many times, the two crept out and disappeared into a hole in a thicket. Only a mild rustling marked their route. Marian looked at the sky. The oppressive clouds were a godsend. The dark would hide the children. And a breeze was rising to mask their noise.

In twos and threes, at Allan's and Marian's signals, the other children melted into the protection of the forest. Rachel with baby Dale in a sling in front. Katie with baby Bridget Ann. Mary, ten, with Elaine, six, with who-leading-whom a hot contest. Then Young Allan waved to his father with scared bravado. Allan the Elder looked equally brave and scared.

Marian had tolled off Tam and Tub to go last. She popped up to look for danger, as did Allan. Was that drumming? Or wind? She looked again and patted their backs. Then suddenly, like a witch's brew exploding, a dozen things happened at once.

Tub and Tam raced through the brush as three knights at full gallop burst into sight. They had pounded up the track from the common. They spotted the children with a shout and levelled their wooden lances, heedless of the treacherous footing under the tangle. Tub slipped and fell and scurried back to the cave mouth. Tam stopped cold and covered his head. Allan A'Dale broke cover and lurched forward. And the boar broke behind him

Frozen, Marian watched it all happen. The boar appeared in the undergrowth as if vomited straight from

Hell. The evil thing, looking two weeks dead with its bloody fur and gaunt aspect and glowing tusks, charged everything in sight: runner, horses, and children. The second and third horsemen were almost pitched headfirst as their mounts locked their legs. Oblivious to any boar, the first rider, in coat with studs and leather helmet, shot straight ahead for the boy and man. Allan reached the child in quick strides of his long legs almost under the nose of the horse. He caught Tam by the armpits and hurled him high and away towards the far thicket. The knight's horse, mad with panic and goading and the stink of boar, put on an unholy burst of speed. The rider barely had time to aim, but his wooden lance caught Allan A'Dale full in the back. The rod ripped through his body so that the point smashed into the ground and broke. The great warhorse's charge continued on, and the minstrel's body was carried on the shattered lance. Ten feet, then twenty he was dragged on his face amidst the crackling brush. Iron-shod hooves clopped on his legs. The knight almost lost his seat as he ripped his lance free, then man and animal thundered away. Allan was left crumpled and unmoving.

The boar had slashed at the passing horse, then turned to snap at the other two. But those animals, deaf to commands from their masters, wheeled and pelted back down the slope. The boar made a beeline for the tunnel mouth.

Tam had disappeared into the thicket. Marian rammed Tub headfirst into the tunnel and scurried after him. The hole was a tight fit for a man. Maybe the boar could not negotiate it, but she tensed her rump and heels against those razor tusks. She was so harried she had yet to shed a tear over the brave minstrel. She staggered out the end of the tunnel into the cave. Here the tunnel was as tall as a man, shored with timbers for the first twenty feet. A hollow grunting echoed far back.

Clara had caught Tub as he stumbled out the hole. "Marian, what is it?"

Marian was scratched and dusty. Dirt fell from her hair.

"It's the boar. Huge and horrible. It's coming. We must collapse the tunnel."

Bess waved her hands. "But that's not part of any plan!"

"It's our only way out!" cried Clara.

"We've no way to follow the children!" echoed Mary.

Marian waved a shaky hand. "There's no other way! Grab tools, quickly!" She herself ran to a niche and snatched up a polearm, then ducked into the tunnel as far as the meager light extended. She could hear the boar snuffling and shoving its way clear. Every foot gave it more room. Marian stabbed the polearm behind the right shoring timber and pried at it. She wanted to cry. Where was Hern, or Puck, or Robin now? "Help me!" she called, and Tub bounded forward. Between the two they dragged the post away from the wall, so that it and the top beam fell. They held their breath as the dirt roof stood firm. Then it let go with a roar. Dirt poured down. Rocks bounced at their feet as they retreated. The shoring members behind them held. They pried at these until they fell, but not as much of the roof collapsed.

"Will that do it?" asked Tub, frightened.

"I don't know," Marian replied. "I don't know anything about any of this!" She reversed the polearm and sunk its ironshod end into the dirt. There was resistance. "Maybe. For now."

They returned to the light. As Marian's sight cleared, the first person she saw was Elaine. Tears started in both their eyes.

"Oh, Elaine, I'm sorry. Allan's dead. He saved Tam's life, but they killed him." Elaine only nodded, stiff-necked. Marian thought, *she knew as soon as it happened.*

Clara and Mary keened at the news. "Oh, God! What's to become of us?"

Bess shouted them down. "The children are safe, and that's all that matters!"

The pounding of axes was loud at the front door. The panel was splintering. A shaft of daylight appeared on the hall floor, and they could see bright steel flashing.

Marian said, "Bess, broach a cask of lard and smear the floor there. The rest of you, bring up your bows."

Clara yelled, "Marian, we can't fight them!"

"I know, I know! But we have to do something until Robin gets here!"

Chapter 27

Mice burrowed into their nests as brush broke. A badger drew backwards into its sett at the drumming of hooves. The chink of tack sent deer leaping over bar and break. The tang of horses and the meat-smell of men was everywhere.

But it was the scurrying of children that caused the greatest disturbance, for instead of passing over or through, these young beasts burrowed like the animals themselves, and drove them out and far afield. Sparrows took off from within their bush. A covey of quail burst from a copse. Snakes slithered from folds of deep grass. A crow on a branch cawed at the disturbance below him, and bats left the hollow of a tree. A red squirrel chittered and a fox yapped.

The hunters, with leather and wood in their hands, noted these markers and steadily closed in.

Chapter 28

Allan A'Dale crawled to the top of the slope through a red mist. Voices called to him from everywhere: Robin's, Tuck's, Elaine's. Gilbert's voice called him a coward and damned him to hell. Over the voices were singing and glorious music, music such as he had always wanted to make and never could. Maybe this was a good thing, maybe soon he'd make music like that. But not right now.

"I'm on my way," he said to the air, "but I've . . . somewhat to do."

It was so dark and so red atop this knoll. Was he blind? Where was the sun? Where were his sons? Were they safe? What about Elaine? Would she remember him? Why was he atop this knoll? Why couldn't he just lie down and rest?

His hand encountered something cold and metallic. A giant lizard on the road to Hell. No, a knife blade, or a sword. It had to be a blade, it was so cold. He saw a glint of gold like an angel's harp. He groped for the narrow end.

Allan A'Dale pressed his lips to the lip of the ancient horn. He sucked a great draught of air that burned inside him, and blew out his spirit in one long blast.

Sir Guy shouted and swore until his voice was hoarse. He berated the men who chopped at the panel, he surveyed the camp that was now his, he exulted in his victory. The cottages were burning. The panel was sundering. His men scoured the forest. And Robin Hood was miles away. He couldn't lose now. The day was his.

Suddenly he was rocked by the blast of a horn. The sound shook his brain right down to the pan. Men dropped their tools to grab their ears. What the hell was it? Gabriel sounding the Apocalypse could not be louder. So loud was the sound they couldn't tell when it stopped, for their ears rang with noise. A soldier pointed to the top of the mound.

"Get up there and cut him to pieces!" Guy screamed, though no one could hear him. He had to shove at men with his sword to get them started. Three of them circled the building to climb the sod.

Guy swore again and spat. The signal horn. So that was where it was. No matter. Robin Hood must be far away at Richard's camp by now, and he wasn't coming back from there. No one who mattered would hear the signal.

But his ears continued to ring.

Robin Hood and his people waited for a long time. "I wish he'd come in here and get it over with," said Grace.

Robin said, "Rest easy. We keep expecting ill, but it may not be so. He summoned us originally to help him in his campaigns (whether we wanted to help or not), and he still needs the help. A king always needs someone to do his dirty work." He levelled a finger. "And don't give me that sour look, John Naylor. I've told you again and again, a king is just a man. He gets up in the morning and pisses out the window like the rest of us."

In that moment the tent flap snapped aside and the king strode in. Robin realized the monarch must have been standing there listening for some time. He bit down hard on his traitorous tongue.

They could see there would be little arguing with this man. The ruler of England and France stalked to the rear of the tent, then turned and stood before his throne to face Robin Hood and his band. The filtered light in the canvas tent shone around Richard like a halo. His forehead was broad, his beard tightly curled and trimmed, and his golden hair fell about his shoulders like a lion's mane. As he passed by they could smell rich perfume. He stood silent for a long moment, and in the silence even Robin had to concede that there was more to being a king than wearing a crown. If God had created a better race of men on the Earth, then it had to be the royalty of Christendom.

More unsettling than the king were the six soldiers who entered with him. These men wore helmets and swords, and they carried halberds. Two stood behind the king and four by the entrance. Two lordly knights flanked the king. Robin recognized Montague of the badger and the portly knight John had knocked flying at the feast. The whole entourage had the set mouths of men ready for trouble.

Finally the king spoke, "Robert Locksley, Earl of Huntingdon, also Robin Hood of Sherwood Forest." A long pause followed. Robin thought this sounded suspiciously like the opening of a trial. His followers moved away from him a trifle. "By word that has come to us, you have been up to more than mere poaching and outlawry. Either crime by itself brings a penalty of death, but you have been grievous in God's sight by delving further into depravity. You have assaulted innocent people, taking their lives and their goods. You have committed towards women acts both carnal and unnatural. You have harbored a witch and trafficked with the devil such that a monstrous boar has been set loose on the countryside. You have practiced witchcraft in a coven of twelve such that the weather itself has been perverted. You have had intercourse with The Evil One and his agents the feys. No doubt there is more. In all these things, you stand accused as a traitor, heretic, adulterer, outlaw, poacher, and witch. What say you to these crimes?"

All the Sherwooders except Robin were aghast. The outlaw chief had turned bright red. But he kept his head for the sake of his fellows. He said quietly, "I've been called worse names, albeit not today. Who brought these charges?"

"Question you your king's pronouncement?"

"A defendant has a right to know his accuser. Your father saw to that." Little John covered his face in both hands. None of the other outlaws could watch.

At the mention of his hated father, Richard stiffened. "You stand accused by a landed nobleman, a knight of the realm, and a loyal subject. Unlike yourself, who has renounced all civility for the ways of peasants and wood-mad idiots!"

Robin Hood clutched at his chin, tried to keep a hold of his temper, and thought furiously. A landed man, a knight had spilled this rash of foolishness into the king's ear. Who could Richard have talked to recently? Not even in Nottingham had this much villainy been laid to his name. Who could have ridden into this camp? Or how had Richard come here? Robin thought till his brain seemed ready to burst. Berwick on summoning him had mentioned it was seventy miles by the roads. Had Richard come that way, he would have passed by—

Gisborne.

"It was Guy of Gisborne said this, didn't he? He made these accusations."

Richard jerked his head higher as his men shuffled their feet. "It was he, and other reputable men."

"Who?"

Richard stabbed out a hand, and Montague put into it a sheaf of parchment. The king read, "The Bishop of Hereford attested to your thieving."

"A fat leech wrapped in gold."

"A man of the Sheriff of Nottingham, one Valette, spoke of your assault on the sheriff's party."

"They should stay out of the woods."

"It is common talk of your assaults on the peasantry—"

"What care they for peasantry!"

"—such that your victim's bodies were never even found!"

"Get to Guy, the spider in the web!"

"Gisborne's knights have suffered at your hands—"

"Not this year they haven't, but they will!"

"—and his huntsman has seen you in the woods consorting with fairies!"

"Guy *has* no huntsman! No decent man will work for him!"

"He has! 'Tis a man called Kite, dressed all in leather—"

"Leather!"

Robin Hood's lips froze on the word. *A man in leather.* Where had he heard that? From whom? He pawed through his memory. Puck had mentioned . . . that a man in leather . . . had fetched the baby to the barrow and unleashed the boar. But Robin had taken him to mean Hern. And someone else—who? who? the impostor Will Scarlett! —had mentioned a man in leather who set them on the road, but Robin had missed asking about it. If it were the same man in leather . . . and he worked for Guy . . . Suddenly it was all clear. Guy's huntsman had set in motion the witchcraft that cursed the boar. The huntsman, at Guy's bidding, had also created the false Robin Hood. And now Guy had filled Richard's mind with poison against him. All the madness of this spring, all the suffering and confusion—it was all Guy's doing, to fabricate a conspiracy against Robin Hood, to besmirch his name, to unman him, to drive him from the forest. And here he was, miles from his home. And there was Guy, waiting. Or moving.

And as all this burned through his brain, Robin heard the horn.

Very slowly Robin Hood turned his head. Very slowly he put his hand behind his ear. He moved towards the tent opening, but the guards make it clear he could not pass. He rubbed at his ear. It was impossible, he told himself. Impossible. But panic started to bubble in his stomach.

The king waited with gloved hands on his belt and murder on his face. The lion on his chest seemed poised to leap. Robin's hair-splitting in the face of death, his mockery, his inattention and now his turned back enraged him until his neck went purple. "What are you about, you base outlaw?" he shouted. "I should have you flayed to bones!"

Gently, Robin Hood said, "I thought I heard the horn."

Black Bart asked, "What horn?"

"The big long one, the old one on top of our mound."

Bart growled, "That's near fifty miles, Robin."

"Didn't you hear it?"

People shook their heads. But Little John said, "If Robin said he heard the horn, he heard it." The giant shifted his staff in his hands.

Now Robin Hood agonized over what it meant. "I think I heard it," he said.

"It must be trouble," said Bold Jane Downey.

Robin nodded absently, "Aye. It must be Sir Guy. He's there. He's attacked the camp."

His people all spoke at once. "What?" "Guy of Gisborne?" "That's right, Guy hates us." "We have to go then!" "Now! Right now!"

Robin Hood faced the king. "Sire, I beg your leave—"

Richard made a sound like a lion in a trap. He jerked off one heavy glove. "You—common—*lout!*" and he struck Robin Hood across the face so hard he fell to his knees.

In an eyeblink Little John took one long step forward, raised a fist like a bucket of rocks, and punched the king of England square in the lion. The blow boomed like a tree hitting the ground, and the king flew backwards and crashed into his tiny throne. The guards stood stunned until Montague shouted orders, then they levelled their pikes and closed ranks for a rush. At that moment Bold Jane Downey kicked away the single tent pole.

An avalanche of warm canvas fell upon the crowd. People struggled to keep their feet and knocked each other down. Black Bart, the smith with the sharpest weapons, jerked loose his sword and slashed upwards. The canvas parted like straw and sunlight spilled across them. The Sherwooders tumbled through the rent like mice spilled from a grain sack, Robin in the arms of Little John even as he tried to gain his feet.

Outside men stared with open mouths at the mob that boiled from the stricken tent. Robin Hood was set down to face two dozen confused soldiers. Two hundred more ran from all parts of the camp. His people demanded orders. Soldiers demanded orders. The retainer in the foxtail coat and the leader of Sherwood looked at one another. Robin thought for a second he might talk his way clear, but just then Little John picked up the first soldier to emerge from the tent. The giant slammed him onto the next three, then grabbed the rent canvas and dragged it shut like a blanket. The retainer shouted the worst thing he could imagine. "Regicide! Regicide!" Someone else clarified, "They've killed the king!"

"That's done it," Robin said to the air. He looked for a way out of camp. The rope corral of saddled and unsaddled horses was the closest thing to hand. "Ahorse! A-hooooorse!"

Black Bart was already there. The grubby smith whipped his sword Devil's Tongue through reins and ropes alike. The nervous animals avoided the blade, retreated from the noise, banged into one another, and quickly became a maelstrom of rearing, milling brutes going in every direction. Robin pointed his followers to them as he desperately counted heads. The soldiers were only now closing in on them, but many had crossbows and polearms. Near the tent, Bold Jane Downey slashed toe-to-toe with a man three times her size. Red Tom and Arthur were shooting instead of running. Much fell down in the muck of the corral. The horses pressed to get free. Even if they caught some, Robin knew half his people had never even been on a horse. The next few minutes were going to be busy.

Somehow he still had his bow. The retainer before him pushed men into line. All the while he shouted, "Loose! Loose!"

Might as well steal a sheep as a lamb, the outlaw

thought. Robin Hood fit an arrow to his bow and sawed back the string. "Shut up!" he shouted, and the hundred-pound bow sang like a trumpet. The arrow crashed into the retainer's shoulder and kept going. The man was knocked around and down. Robin swept the live arrow-head along the line of crossbowmen, and to a man they dropped their weapons to dive flat. Whether Robin Hood was a regicide had yet to be determined, but it was known he was the greatest archer in England. Robin could still hear clanking behind him. "John," he called without turn-ing around, "get Jane on a horse!"

Little John was shepherding people towards the corral. Now he took three long steps and reached the knight pressing Bold Jane Downey. Little John flicked out his quarterstaff like a boy rapping a goose with a stick. The man's helmet dented and he slashed his own foot as he crumpled. Little John picked Jane up in his free hand. "Let me go, you beast!" she cried, but Robin's lieutenant followed orders. As a wild-eyed horse surged past the two, Little John dropped his staff. He caught the horse by the mane and it jerked to a halt with a piercing whinny. The giant set Jane atop bare-backed. "There you go, lass, now ride." Then he grunted sharply, twice, and Jane gave him a queer look.

Robin Hood threatened soldiers with a drawn bow and shot those who persisted. A charging swordsman got a red-fletched arrow through his lower body. A shaft pinned another man to his comrade behind. A nobleman resplen-dent in yellow left his horse as the animal went down with an arrow through its neck: the horseman flew ten feet to land on his face with an impact that must have killed him. More ranks formed farther away, and bolts whickered in Robin's direction. He crab-walked towards the corral as fast as possible. He bumped into Red Tom, still flinging arrows into the assemblage.

"Rob, we must get to camp." Red Tom was Polly's only parent.

"I know, and we're here killing the wrong people."

"Robin!" Jane called. "We're all ahorse."

If you could call it that, Robin thought. His people were on top of horses maybe, but hardly riding them. Butts and heads stuck up at weird angles. Little John was still running down a huge draft horse. Robin snagged a mare just before she trampled him. Several kicks got him pointed east with several dozen soldiers in the way. He looked to see who was in the lead. "Bart, go! Along the wall!"

Black Bart was astride a black horse with red trappings, and he had his wicked sword in the air. With a "Harrhhh!" he charged an assembling line of pikemen and crossbowmen. Bolts *fizzed* past his ears and steel barbs pierced his clothing, but he was swearing when his horse hit the line and bowled men over.

"After him!" called Robin, and the Sherwood folk pointed their beasts as best they could. Second in line was the new man Brian. He had never been on a horse before, and he could barely hold on, but he had seen Black Bart's feat and he saw the pikemen on his side. With a gleeful shout he booted his horse towards the phalanx. They set their poles and shoved upwards, and Brian toppled from his saddle with a half dozen holes in his body. He landed on his neck with a sickening crunch and the pikemen finished the job. At the edge of the crowd, Black Bart wheeled his mount to look back. "That daft bastard!" he cried. "What did he do that for?"

"Never mind!" shouted Robin above the tumult. "Keep going!" They were almost in the clear. The assemblage was too scattered or confused to stop them, or too reluctant. Most men just wanted to get out of the way. Robin, at home on a horse, wheeled his mount to do a quick head count. They were all with him, some doubled and some clinging, but they were there: Black Bart on a king's horse, Bold Jane Downey laughing, Grace on a grey going too fast, Red Tom like a scarecrow swiping at men with his bow, Ben Barrel already puffing, Will Stutly on a shaggy swayback, and even Much held in place behind Arthur A'Bland. Little John brought up the rear on a large and laboring steed. Robin Hood panicked momentarily: there were only nine people. Then he remembered Brian was dead. He hoped his new enemies gave him a decent burial. The outlaw chief reined in until everyone but Little John was before him, in case anyone fell off, then he set his head and rode.

He had to get to Sherwood. He *had* heard the horn—he knew it now. Gisborne was there, probably with the Sheriff of Nottingham and other toadies. Somehow the sound of terror had carried to him. Why he alone had heard it, he did not know. But it was up to him to get them home. He clamped his jaw until it ached as the party entered the forest at the far side of the valley.

The land alternated between forest and meadow, slope and plain. They rode flat out for two miles, and the party was already strung apart. Little John was far behind. Red Tom and Jane and Bart, used to horses, had the lead. Arthur and Much were barely galloping. They'd have to switch, mount the idiot behind someone else. But Robin was loathe to stop for even a second, all the while knowing they couldn't keep this pace. Horses could not gallop fifty miles. And their pursuers—and there would be plenty—could push their horses, because they did not have to ride the fifty. They had only to catch Robin Hood.

As if in answer to Robin's thoughts, Ben Barrel's horse stumbled and fell headlong, banging its jaw on the stony road. Ben landed on his outstretched arms. As a cry went up, the party shuddered to a stop in a low defile.

"What do we do, Rob?" sobbed Grace. She barely clung to her horse.

"We must get to Sherwood!" yelled Ben. He held his right hand in his left. It was either broken or sprained. He ignored it: he had his family on his mind.

Robin looked at their faces and set his jaw. "We'll have to split the party. We'll leave the ones who can't ride to catch up. I'm sorry, and don't argue. You lot will take to the woods, get off the road, because Richard's men are going to come fast and furious any minute."

"Is that our dust or theirs?" asked Jane. Everyone looked back down the road past Little John. There was some dust, more than they should have left.

Robin called, "Hoi, John, move!"

The giant moved sluggishly on the panting horse, and as he drew abreast, Robin saw why. Two crossbow bolts were lodged in his back. The big man sank his head onto his mount's neck. "I'm sorry, Rob."

"John! God alive!" cried Robin Hood. One quarrel had entered his right side above the hip. The other was square above the kidneys: a killing shot for any normal man, but John was like the giants of old. The bolts were stuck as if in a tree, with only a tiny ring of blood around them. No one touched them. Bold Jane Downey circled closest to see.

Two wounded men changed everything. Robin searched his memory as his mind roiled. "There's a road . . . about a mile ahead . . . that goes south, isn't there?" People nodded. "We'll have to send you to ground it. Get you to a farmhouse."

"I'll take him," piped Jane.

"I need you with me."

"I want to stay with Little John."

"All right, I don't have time to argue. Keep a lookout for a prosperous farm, back from the road, a neat place where they know what they're doing. Take this." From his tunic Robin drew out the small pouch of gold and gave it to the tiny woman. "Get a midwife. Offer them this. If they still won't help you, put a sword against the master till they do. Ben, you go with her."

"I can ride!"

"No, you can't. Jane, go. You too, Grace." Bold Jane nodded and took the reins to Little John's horse.

"More dust," said Will Stutly. They could hear thunder.

Arthur A'Bland suddenly hopped off his horse. He caught at Robin's saddle. "Give me your arrows."

"What? What now?"

Arthur waved a hand. The man had never been good at

expressing himself. "Give me your arrows. Some of them. And the rest of you, give me, uh, five. Each." Sherwooders pulled arrows over their shoulders and handed them to the ex-king's forester.

Robin asked, "Arthur, what—"

The grizzled man pointed to a stone outcropping forty feet up one side of the narrow road. "I'll climb up there and shoot. Ah've a clear shot down the trail. They can't get past me." Robin looked around. It was true. No horse could climb the wooded slopes, and the only exits were along the road.

"If they come after you," Robin added, "escape over the top of the ridge."

"Aye, aye. I never liked horses anyway. Save m' family if you can." Before Robin could thank him, the squat man had run off with a sheaf of multi-colored arrows in each hand.

Robin Hood called, too loudly, "All right, Arthur will slow them up. Jane, take Ben here—yes! I command it!—and John and protect them. Much, you help her. Tom, Bart, Will, swap onto those horses. They look stronger." Robin himself took a horse with a saddle. There was an edge to his voice as he fought panic. Mounting, Robin looked around. As always, they all waited on his word. He was so unworthy of that, he thought. He would have liked to kiss his friend Little John goodbye, he would have liked to tell them all how he loved them, but there was no time. He settled for, "You are all loyal, you are all wonderful. Never had a man better friends." His voice broke as he said, "God keep you all." He croaked, "Let's be off!" And they rode.

The splintered party pulled away and gained speed. Robin Hood was left with Red Tom, Black Bart, and old Will Stutly. Four people too late to rescue their families. Robin shook his head at the tears that formed in his eyes. Had he offended God this badly, with all his plans and all his vanity, that his doughty band of Merry Men was reduced to this? Where were Gilbert, Little John, David of

Doncaster, Shonet, Friar Tuck, Bold Jane Downey, Brian, Cedwyn? Dead or scattered to the wind. Marian was trapped in Sherwood with a crippled Will Scarlett, Allan and an old woman and the wives, and the children. He prayed Marian could handle whatever trouble there was, but she might as well be alone. He knew they'd never make it in time. It was all his fault. This never would have happened if he'd stayed in the woods where he belonged. Tears ran down his cheeks and were dried by the wind.

No one could save Sherwood.

Chapter 29

The god Hern, lord of the forest, ancient beyond even these trees, was dying.

His breast was no longer snowy but red. The wound was in his neck. Blood around the wound showed purple and black, and it hung in fat gobs like leeches. Every tick of his immortal heart sent another rivulet pulsing into the open air, because the barb lodged in the artery was steel, and iron and its brothers were anathema to the ancients. The steel carried by Romans had driven the flint-bearers back, and cold iron spread an aura where fairies could not go. This barb in Hern's neck was steel the length of a man's finger, and every move sank the barbs deeper.

The lord of the forest could see only white before his eyes. A roar thrummed in his ears, and his nose was full of the smell of his own blood. The cold finger jarred in his nerves. Stumbling, he leant against a tree. The stag thumped his hoof on the soil, over and over, in a strange and eerie pattern.

He missed the answering whicker. It was repeated more loudly. A grumbling, growling, breathing-through-fangs hissed near his feet. Hern clucked his tongue. Now came the ticklish part. Slowly, slowly, so as not to fall and drive the dart deeper, Hern lowered his front legs. He could neither see nor feel nor smell the ground below him. He moved by pure instinct. Then the quarrel's nock touched something.

The badger had nestled backwards deep in her sett at the sound of trouble. She kept her rump pressed against the back wall and waited. She smelled the blood and wanted it, for she had young ones within her. She could wait for the hart above to die. It would not take long from the quantities spilled. But there had come the thumping, a jarring rhythm echoing in her breastbone, tingling in her toes, that lifted her up on her flat sprawled feet. The rapping drew her against her will. It could have drawn her to her death and she could not have resisted. Up from her hole she climbed, into the pool of blood.

Out in the light she disliked it all. The stag was unlike any other. He smelled old, as if his meat would be tough. The arrow smelt of man, and near the top was long-corrupt bat flesh. The cloying in her mind told her to touch the polished wood, and she had to. It felt alien, smooth like a cow's horn, rich with man's oil and spit. The shaft slipped against her rough black paws, but finally she grasped it along the curled pheasant feathers. Then the stag jerked his head up, and the barb was loose in the badger's paws. She dropped it quickly.

The stag lurched upright, breathing hard and fast. The dripping stopped. The beast stood that way for some time, long enough for the sun to cross the blue star in the sky. Then he lurched off. The badger knew he went to find water to bring him back to life.

The badger chittered to herself. It was just as well. The meat would have been dusty and stringy. But the blood was sweet, and she lapped it from the leaves.

Chapter 30

"We've done it, milord," said the sergeant at the door. "The door's broken." The men held the pieces in the hole.

"Get in there, then!"

"Milord, might they still have some arrows left? They were right quick with 'em before."

Sir Guy levelled his sword at the man. "Pomfret, I'll feed your balls to my dogs unless you get in there *double quick*. But very well, you cowards, up shields and charge!" The eleven men lined up with their kite shields in two ranks. Guy threatened and cursed in the back. Forgotten, One-eye hovered behind the lord like a rabid wolf among the dogs. "Let's go! Get inside! And mind you, I'll kill anyone who harms a woman without my order!"

On a count from the sergeant the men shouted and kicked the panel apart. They rushed into the hall. As they had expected, a cluster of arrows hit them. But the shafts did not hit the shields, for they were aimed lower. Men howled and tumbled as steel smashed into their greaves or knees. Coming from the bright outside to the gloomy interior, it took them a moment to locate the source of the arrows. A black cave mouth gaped at the back. Only eight made it to Marian's makeshift bulwark of tables and benches across the mouth. And when they got to the tangle there was no one behind it. The men locked shields and paused. Sir Guy ordered them to stand fast and let him see.

Guy had heard the great hall concealed a cave behind. The cave mouth was narrow, and Marian had been clever to make her stand there. But her women were no match for armed knights. Guy peered past a shield into the dark. Torches in there had just been extinguished, for he could still smell them. The sconces in the hall were empty. With a curse he ordered two men to fetch burning brands. He ordered two more to drag out the howling wounded. While he waited he called to the dark."

"Marian Fitzooth! Come out!"

The voice that replied was so clear and liquid it set Guy's loins astir. It came from around a corner, probably to the right. "I'm Marian Locksley, you Norman bastard son, and we'll stay right here. Robin Hood will be back shortly with forty fit men, and he'll take care of you."

Guy laughed. "Robin Hood has not forty men. He has twelve fighters all told, few in number and far away. Now come out and I'll let your peasants go. It's you I want."

"You're a liar, Guy, and a bad one."

Guy got angry at this impudence in front of his men. He shouted, "I *order* you to come out!"

There was only silence, which he took as a worse insult.

A man had returned with a well-caught brand, and Guy cuffed him towards the dark. The party dragged aside the tables and benches and entered the cool cave with shields up. The second rank of four carried crossbows. There was sand underfoot and a hint of water. Guy's dogs barked. Wavering light revealed Marian's party huddled in a jagged corner. Sir Guy laughed in triumph when he beheld them. There was only an old woman, two good wives, a slender pale nun, and a fat boy. Each had a bow and arrow. Marian was as dirty and disheveled as if a wall had fallen on her. But she was radiant, and she stood in the forefront with a sword and Locksley's shield. Behind the party was a sickbed with a red-garbed man on it. He looked dead.

Marian glanced behind her. With crossbows trained on them, she dare not order her people shoot. Old Bess's

knees cracked as she dipped for her cleaver. Clara and
Mary were frozen. Elaine clutched Tub's hands on his bow
and string.

Guy's face was wooden. "You'll need more than that
sewing needle to keep out of my arms, Marian. You're to
be my wife."

Marian waggled her sword. Her voice shook as she said,
"You come here and I'll fix your husband's tool, you sorry
pig-fucker."

Sir Guy shook his head as if slapped. He barked, "Sweep
them from both sides and get them down. I'll attend
Marian. *Now!*"

At the command the men leapt forward with the flat of
their swords. Marian and the wives took a swipe, but it
was over in a second. The men repaid them the arrows in
their comrades with hobnailed boots. The women were
banged, cut, kicked, and knocked flat. Their weapons
were trod underfoot.

Sir Guy charged Marian. He wore fine chain mail to the
wrist and heavy horsehide gloves. He fended the woman
back with his sword, then lashed out with his fist and hit
her in the jaw. Her head whipped back and she fell onto
the women behind. He threw down his sword, caught her
by her black hair, yanked her forward and cuffed her
again.

"Marian Fitzooth," he breathed in her face. "It's over.
Your husband is led astray. Your home burns. The children in the woods are dead. And *you* are *mine!*" Marian
glared hatred at him in the wild torchlight as she felt
underneath her for a dagger. The lord slapped her again
heavily, then elicited a scream when he jerked her upright
by her hair. He gestured with his chin to the cowed
women and child and the sick man on the bed. "Kill
them."

"There! See?" Delancey shouted. The Kite had been
right. Children were abroad in the woods. Sir Roger and
Delancey of Nottingham had spotted two bright figures,

girls from the way they ran, fleeing like hares across an open stretch for a thick laurel stand. They would never make it. The black knights levelled their lances and centered their attention on the tiny backs.

A brown blur materialized to one side, and they saw the giant stag who had attacked them earlier. His breast was purple and black with congealed blood. There was no stain of fresh crimson. *He should be dead*, they both thought. The knights slowed their charge as the stag stamped his feet. From the virgin floor around the knights erupted a fence of briars that shot to the sky. The brambles filled the men's vision before they could move. Vines and nettles darkened the air. Roger felt the thorns wrap his horse to him, thorns like tiny lances that twined tight, then tighter. He reached to protect his eyes, but his arms were already ensnared. Somewhere far away Delancey and his horse combined a scream. The snag was so tight a sparrow could not have walked through. Roger felt his blood leaking through his mail as the briars grew thicker and taller. He shouted for help, but thorns were in his mouth.

Long after the men were dead, the briars slowed and stopped. Both man and mount were suspended six feet in the air. By then Mary and Elaine were far away, snuggled under the laurel, fast asleep.

Allan and Tam argued quietly but vehemently.

"Up the slope!"

"Along the slope, you ninny, so we stay off the skyline! And we're supposed to hide, not run!"

Tam clutched his father's knife like a Bible. "Maybe we can help! Maybe someone is in trouble!"

The younger Allan retorted, "We'll be the ones in trouble! Marian told us to hide. So did Robin! If we're out and around, Robin will kill us!"

"Shut up, you! We're not supposed to argue!"

"Who's arguing? *You're* arguing!"

"I *hate* you!"

"Well, I hate you too!"

Tam yelled, "If my da were here—" Then he stopped as

he thought of his father. And Allan's. "Never mind. We're not supposed to argue. We're supposed to hide. There is a cave in this slope somewhere, isn't there?"

"Yes, I think so." Allan was crying. "But it's all mucked up from the storm."

"Don't cry."

"I'm *not crying!*"

Unseen until it was upon them, the giant stag reared up like a mountain under the grey sky. He looked awful, bloody, and ready to kill. His rack was bigger than a king's bed. The boys covered their heads and whimpered at the feet of the great beast. They felt a puff of air. Lightly the deer sprang over them, turned and kicked his back legs against the slope. The grass (or the earth?) parted to reveal a niche barely wide enough for the two boys. When the deer fixed them with his green human eyes, they scampered into the niche and wove the grass together to conceal the opening.

When they peeked out again the stag was gone.

Polly, never one to fool around, had taken to the icy brook that ran down the slope and to the pool. She had with her Glenyth, who at five could ask a thousand worried questions. Red Tom's blonde daughter carried the child against her chest and told her to keep still. They had left quite a trail behind them in the damp leaves, so Polly picked her way upstream until her numb feet began to slip. Then they exited onto a rock shelf and skipped from boulder to boulder. The girl hoped the water drops would not be noticed. Soon they were far from camp, at least a mile. She thought they might be safe. Then she felt the drumming under her feet and heard the chink of bridles. She hunkered under a holly bush and begged Glenyth to be silent.

There were four men who sought them, all on horses. Polly could hear the animals' nostrils whistle as they labored for air. She prayed hard and fast.

"Here! It went under there," called a man.

"A heavy one."

"Lot of trouble for a few brats."

"Guy buys the bread."

"By Peter's *beard* I hate these woods! There must be a plaguey fairy in every tree."

"Shut your mouth and keep looking! We're all right as long as it's daylight."

"Hell of a thing, hunting children."

"All you two ever do is complain. Let's just *whoa!*"

Another man yelled, "What?" then he too took a spill off the back of his horse. Polly could not resist a peek, and she had to let Glenyth look when the baby threatened to talk. A thin knight whose leather hung like a sack had gone over backwards off his mount when a tree branch landed on its rump. The horse had kicked the man as he fell, and now flounced around nervously a long throw away. A second knight had moved towards him when another widow-maker fell on him. Polly knew that was no accident, but she feared to pray and dispel whatever magic was at work here. The last two knights jumped off their mounts before they were thrown off.

"Are you hurt?"

"What happened?"

"The fairies heard you talk!" This in a loud whisper.

"What's *that?*"

"Not the *hart!*"

A creak turned into a groan, and a perfectly healthy tree leaned towards the men. They shrieked as the forest giant toppled onto them and trapped them among its branches. The shrills that Polly and Glenyth made were lost amid crashing. When the girls looked up they were awash in soft green leaves, the tree's crown kissing them at every hand. As the crackle subsided, they realized it was quiet. The men had broken free and run down the slope after their swifter horses.

Unhampered by the baby, Katie was halfway up a tree when something caught her by the breeches. The powerful something pulled her from the trunk. Upsidedown, in the grip of its teeth, she was trotted away. She clutched the baby Bridget Ann all the while she swivelled to see who had her. As she suspected, there were cloven feet below her. It was the monster stag, larger than a horse. She did not know whether to be awestruck or terrified. The deer dumped her down a bank and she tumbled into a hollow. Leaves were kicked over her. She stuck her head up just in time to see her savior leave, then pulled her head back down. He was not the friendly deer of this morning. The beast had black blood all across his breast, and his green eyes shone like lanterns. Katie pulled the leaves further down and waited for sunset.

The Kite always hunted alone. He jerked at the bit in his horse's mouth. The stupid beast was uneasy and he could not see why. The stag was dead, and there was nothing in the area but children and small animals. He had read the signs. He jerked the reins again when he saw the tracks. From the length of the stride and shape of the foot he could see it was a largish girl. He saw she was encumbered because she brushed leaves aside instead of ducking down. Broken branch tips stood out white. The Kite sneered. One would think Robin Hood could train them in moving through the forest. The girl was away from the rest, making towards open space instead of hiding here in the cover. The Kite smiled as he thought of the girl. He could have a wench and drink her blood besides.

A sound carried to him, a cessation, a hush. He could not see in this thick brush and animals made it noisy. This piece of Sherwood was thick with animals, more than he had ever seen in one place, despite the fact that Robin Hood had his camp nearby. That was a sure sign of witchcraft or deviltry. He pulled the thonged peg from his crossbow. He could smell the corruption on the arrowhead, a smell of triumph. The Kite trotted his mount after the tracks. They pressed through bracken and he saw the trail on the other side. They crossed over a pile of disturbed leaves. He smelt the tang of leaf mold. Normally he would investigate, but the flight was plain before him. The girl had churned the leaves to hide, then changed her mind and moved on. It was all so obvious. They moved into the clear. Rachel and Dale were left behind under the leaves, the girl with the baby's mouth pressed shut.

As the Kite followed, the tracks changed somehow, although how he could not say. Had the girl thrown the baby to one side? Was panic making her take longer strides? Or was this the last burst before fatigue? Some vague unease pricked at his mind as the tracks entered another copse, but he ignored it and moved on. He could taste her blood and hear her bleats already.

He stopped at the brush. He glimpsed light brown within. He swung the crossbow behind his back. "Come out, my little poppet. I won't hurt you."

The horse screamed as the brush broke aside and a set of deer's antlers with twenty full points exploded into view. The Kite's last vision before Hell was that rack powered by a giant body, the wondrous stag to whom he'd delivered a killing blow. The tangle of sharp white bone struck him full in the chest, carried him from the saddle, and smashed his body into a tree. Pain froze him to his fingertips. He stared down at the brilliant green eyes, smelt his own blood, listened to the whistle of his lungs. As the perimeter of his vision went black, for the first time in his life the Kite thought about how an animal felt when it died. Then he thought no more.

The horse had run off. The stag had to plant both front hooves on the man's chest to tug its antlers loose. It left the body for the forest and bounded away. The tracks it left were now those of a stag, and not a largish encumbered girl.

Women screamed as swords lifted for the final blow, when there came a roar of black earth from the back of the cave. Timbers squealed and collapsed as the boar thundered into the hall.

It was hardly recognizable as a boar. The monster's face was so gaunt and lumpy it looked twisted. Dirt showered from its tufted shoulders. The limp in its back leg made its charge erratic and unnatural. Its tiny eyes were lost in the dark. In the weird half-light of the cave, the beast flashed white and black and red.

As the great boar tore free of what looked like a solid wall, men spun around and shouted and swore. They looked to their leader, and saw him clearing the door as if the boar were after him personally. "RUN!" screamed the sergeant. Torches flew to extinguish against the sand floor as Guy's men stampeded. And because they were moving, the boar charged them. The monster rammed full tilt into their backs. One man was trampled underfoot: his outthrust sword slashed the man in front of him. Another jabbed a blade onto the beast's back, but the steel skittered away. Long tusks ripped the man open from crotch to hip. The soldiers clawed one another aside as they scrambled, and the animal rammed them along. In the corner of the cave, dark and forgotten, Marian shushed the women and pressed them down with her arms. She prayed to Mother Mary, Saint Ann, Saint Brigid and every other womanly saint she could think of.

Sir Guy and his men was almost out the door when the stag appeared. He soared full length into the hall with antlers lowered. Twenty points met the invaders like the swords of Saracens. Guy himself was only saved when he covered his head and fell flat. Men were spitted like quail, ripped open and lifted from the ground, but the great deer barely slowed. Green eyes aflame, the spirit of Sherwood set his hooves on the backs of dying men, shook bodies loose like dead leaves, and leapt again, across the carcasses into the blood-ridden face of the boar.

The great beasts crashed in a thunderclap that shook the room. Squeals and bellows of rage rang to the roof. The animals locked heads and shoved and scrabbled for purchase in the sand. They were matched only in ferocity. The boar was lower and thicker, and it snapped its tusked jaws for the deer's slender legs, tossed its head to rip the flat belly. The deer was disadvantaged by the low ceiling and the low opponent. But he skipped aside as only a deer can, like a leaf on the wind, and chopped with his front legs. Whenever he could plant his feet he shot out with bloodied horns. As the two surged about the rooms like a hurricane they collided with walls, barrels, benches, and posts till the noise was deafening. Their hatred was so intense it was human. The battle went on and on—kick and slash, ram and dance, roar and hoot.

Marian rose now to pull women up. "Come on!" she called over the tumult, "we must get outside!"

"But the men are there!" said Mary.

"No, they'll flee the stag! Don't you see? It's helping us! And we can't stay here!" She glanced behind. They would have to leave Will Scarlett. He was unmoving, probably dead. The Sherwood women crawled for the door almost under the feet of the savage animals. Several of Guy's men lay dead or dying by the front door, amid guts and blood and brains. Guy himself was missing. Marian tossed off a prayer of thanks but added another for help. What would happen if the stag were killed, or Guy still felt like attacking? What if Guy's outriders returned? She crouched by the door and shooed the last of the women outside, hoping they'd find peace. All this horror had to end soon. Then something grabbed her from behind and pulled her down.

It was the false Robin Hood. He had lost his bandage. The enflamed hole Marian had made gaped large and black, and it was crusted with yellow as if the skull were showing. His face was no longer pale. It was bright red. The single eye blazed like a fire in the night.

"I'll have you, bitch!" His breath stank of infection. He tore at her throat to strangle her. His fingernails ripped the skin from her throat as his hands sank deep.

Marian felt a blaze of anger like she never had before. What had she done to this man that he hated her so? Her wind was stopped. She whispered, "I've had enough of *you!*" Savagely she brought her hand up from the floor and popped it into his remaining eye. The man shrieked, a sound lost in the din. He let go and clutched at his face. Marian cast about, took what she needed from a dead man's belt, and rolled after her assailant. She set the point of the dagger just below his rib cage and threw her weight on it. The sharp blade slid in and up, blood sprayed over her hands, and the body thrashed once. The Vixen of Sherwood pushed away and crawled outside into the open air.

Outside was paradise. A dim overcast lent a refreshing cool to the grove. The breath of spring stopped the sweat along her brow and dried the blood on her face. There was a scent of flowers borning. Marian could have stretched out in the tender grass and lain there forever.

Guy was there at the edge of the woods. He cursed and slapped at a skittering horse. He was oblivious to the pleas of the wounded and the three fit men beside him. All the evil Guy had conjured was snapping at his heels. While the women of Sherwood stood not thirty feet away, exhausted and unarmed, Sir Guy of Gisborne leapt to the saddle and fled. His dogs preceded him.

Marian was looking for a place to hide when a flash of brown went by like a monstrous eagle. The stag had leapt out the door. Marian, Mary, Clara, Elaine, Old Bess, and Tub were too weary to even shout as the boar came hard behind. The humans just crabbed out of the way.

The sprit of Sherwood turned to face the denizen of the dark. The boar was no longer underground or in the dark or under a canopy of rain. It was under a spring sky where a rent promised to break the cloud cover. As the humans watched, the color of the sun grew in intensity. Pale yellow increased to warmer amber, then to liquid gold, until the two animals were fixed in an aureate haze. Under the light the boar began to steam like a bed of ferns. It shrank away, lower to the ground, casting about for shade like a snake. It peered up awkwardly. The boar was suffering. The people could see it was blind on one side, riddled with holes, and scarred across its back. The stag was in worse shape. Strips of flesh hung from his belly. Blood obscured his vision. One leg was game from repeated gougings. The two animals panted and drooled and regarded one another. But they would still fight. The stag put out a hoof that turned under him. He stepped and faltered. When the boar charged again the stag would go down and stay down.

"Help it! Help it! We've got to help it!" shouted Marian.

"How?" asked everyone else.

"Attack the boar! Quickly!" Without waiting for the others, Marian stooped for a sword.

"It's charging!" screeched Tub.

Marian ran to the battle site. She shouted and the boar half turned. The stag wobbled again, then closed into the boar's blind side. Marian slashed at the demon's flanks. The blade cut deep into the fetid flesh, which parted more like pulpy wood then meat. She prayed to God a hundred times in a second as she slashed again, for if the boar turned on her she'd be disemboweled. An arrow whizzed past her. Clara had found a bow and shot. Then Tub sent a shaft that missed. Elaine brought a spear. Old Bess waved her arms and whooped. Marian hissed and swore. It would be a long day if this was the best they could do. Then the beast did turn its one good eye in their direction. Marian screamed and closed her eyes.

The stag leapt. The gold of the sun sparkled in his shaggy hide, sweat and blood flew away in mist as the spirit described a graceful and very short arc. The crouching boar was caught square in the side of the neck. Points splintered and broke along its spine. The rack slammed again to bracket the evil beast's throat. The deer's four feet plunged hock-deep into the soil. The boar bucked, but the bony points bore the monster to the earth. Stag and boar were jammed in place. Marian stepped up on wobbly legs and drove her steel thorn into the boar's side. Clara ran up, took the spear from Elaine, and plunged it into the beast's belly. The boar froze for a second, then kicked and kicked and kicked, and stopped. With a gasp it finally died. There was very little blood. The pig's body, gaunt and raw-boned before, seemed to shrink and collapse further onto itself until it was no bigger than a few spades of earth. Even its smell carried away in the clear air. As the people watched, it became just a pile of bones in a dried sack, like something dead a hundred years. Marian should have felt relief, but instead she felt some strange pity. This had not been the boar's fault. Something else had carried the animal past all normal behavior and existence. But what she could not guess.

The deer huffed with his nose buried in the soil. His nostrils blew dirt. He drew his shoulders tight and with another huff jerked his head loose. He tossed his stiff mane and blinked his eyes, more human than the disheveled women around him. The animal surveyed them all, and this time they did not cower. He fixed Marian with his eyes of green. In the depths she read gratitude, respect, promises, and much more she couldn't explain.

The hart was hurt very badly. He all but tripped over his own guts when he walked. He was so drained the black nose looked grey. But the beast turned slowly and stepped towards the mound. The outlaws watched as he picked up the slope and dipped his head towards the grass. The women below could not see what he nuzzled, but Elaine let out a tiny cry. The deer had touched Allan A'Dale's body. Hern turned for one last look at the crowd below, then limped off into the forest.

Chapter 31

Warmed by the sun, flesh flies found the bodies scattered throughout the forest. They came in thousands to feed and grow fat on the brackish blood.

Chapter 32

"They're back! They're back!" It was Polly who called, on guard with a bow. She ran to her father. Red Tom slid painfully from the saddle to hug her. Robin Hood and Black Bart dismounted and let the reins drop. The horses just stopped where they were.

They returned to the camp the afternoon of the day after the attack. Their first sight was horrific and yet heartening. All but two of the cottages had been burned. Katie and Tam pulled at Scarlett's for firewood. The front of the main hall was a shambles of splintered wood. They could see Clara's broad rump as she scrubbed at the threshold. The coarse smell of blood and mud steeped the glade along with clouds of flies. Armored bodies were heaped in the lower common away from the lime tree. They saw pink skin at the pool where Mary bathed children. Adults and children both dropped their tasks and ran shouting. Robin Hood hobbled towards the hall as people flocked around. Then Marian ran out of the hall and engulfed him in her arms.

"Oh, Rob, I'm so glad to see you!"

"Was it Guy and the sheriff?" he asked, and everyone answered.

"Just Guy!"

"And his men!"

"More than a score of them!"

"They chased us in the woods with lances, but the big stag saved us!"

"It killed one man flat out with his horns!"

"There was a big fight between the horrible boar and the stag—"

"But the stag killed it."

"And Marian put out that villain's other eye and then stabbed him!"

"Bess slit the throats on the rest!"

"Guy ran away, the coward!"

Robin Hood held his wife so tightly she could scarcely breathe. "Are you all right?"

She stayed close and spoke into his chest. "Yes, Rob."

Robin cast about at the milling crowd. He raised his voice. "Was anyone hurt?"

The babble stopped. Marian said, "Yes. Allan was killed. He was struck by a lance saving one of the children."

"Me," whispered Tam.

Robin saw now. Elaine stood to one side with her three children around her skirts. Their faces were the same face, all stamped with sorrow. He said, "I'm sorry, Elaine. He was the best of men. But he was the only one killed?"

Marian said, "Bumps and bruises, but we're alive. The children hid just as you taught them, and they came through. Clara and Mary and Bess and I—and Tub—fought Guy in the cave. The stag saved us. The boar did too, in a way." She absently pulled a child to her.

"What of Will Scarlett?"

Marian shook her head. "He's gone, Rob. Or almost. We can't rouse him." Tam and Old Bess had faces bleak and resigned.

"Ah, well."

Red Tom asked, "Who blew the horn?"

"You heard it?"

Robin said, "I did. Who blew it?"

Elaine answered. "It was Allan." She pointed to the top of the mound with a quivering finger.

Marian shook her husband's shoulders. "But Rob, what

of you? Where is everyone? John and the rest? What did the king want?"

Robin Hood waved a hand in dismissal. "I'm not altogether sure what Richard wanted, but we're off the hook for going to London. The next time he sees us he'll have our guts for garters. Little John knocked him clear across a tent. Brian was killed by pikemen."

"Brian? He never said two words to me, he was so shy."

Robin nodded. "And I feel badly, because we had to leave him. We were being shot at. Our party got stretched out, and people were hurt. Little John caught some bolts, so Jane is with him, and Much and Grace. And Ben. Arthur stayed to watch our back trail. And we had to leave Will Stutly behind on a horse, because he couldn't hold on any longer. We rode all night." He sighed. "We should have been here all along."

Marian ran a hand along his beard. "Never mind. You did what you thought was right. Let's continue with the cleaning. It'll be a cozy night." And suddenly she was sobbing uncontrollably as Robin held her tight in his arms.

A little later Black Bart called Robin to the top of the mound. Marian nodded he should go. At the top Robin Hood drew aside a blanket. Allan's body had been hacked to pieces by swordsmen, one of whom lay nearby. The killer lay on his back, a sword locked in his fist. His face was frozen in a grimace and his eyes clouded. The front of his tunic was scorched as if by fire. Black Bart said, "Look ye here." He pointed to the brass horn which lay between the bodies. There was a straight cut in the bell of the horn, just a tiny one.

Robin Hood grunted, "I don't understand," though he crossed himself.

Bart explained. "The one doing the hacking was careless. He nicked the horn. The horn didn't like it." The smith picked up the heavy instrument as Robin stepped back. "Still alive," Bart mumbled. He moved the instrument away from the minstrel.

Robin crouched over the body and sighed a prayer.

Allan's body was wreathed in tiny buttercups, the only ones in sight in the entire common. Robin plucked one and twirled it in his fingers. "Early for buttercups. What did Allan call them, 'Bits of sunlight brought to earth'?" He set the tiny gem on the dead man's breast.

"We can bury him tomorrow, Rob, here."

"Aye, Bart. Him and a lot besides."

The two descended the mound in silence.

That night in the cave was quiet. The smell of earth was strong from the sundered tunnel. People lay about like sheep in the field, exhausted from the day. Elaine sang to her children in the stillness.

> "Oh, fare thee well, I must be gone,
> And leave you for a while,
> But wherever I go I will return,
> Though I go ten thousand miles, my dear,
> Though I go ten thousand miles.

> "Ten thousand miles, it is so far,
> To leave me here alone,
> Whilst I may lie, lament and cry,
> And you'll not hear my moan, my dear,
> And you'll not hear my moan.

> "The crow that is so black, my dear,
> Shall change his color white,
> If ever I prove false to thee,
> Till all these things be done, my dear,
> The day shall turn to night, my dear,
> The day shall turn to night.

> "Oh, don't you see that milk-white dove,
> Sitting in yon tree,
> Lamenting for his own true love,
> As I lament for thee, my dear,
> As I lament for thee?

"The rivers never will run dry,
Nor the rocks melt with the sun,
I'll never prove false to the one I love,
Till all these things be done, my dear,
Till all these things be done."

Robin and Marian talked long after everyone else was asleep. They whispered like children in the dark.

"But Rob, why? Why leave Sherwood now?"

"Because we're not wanted here, Marian. That boar was evil incarnate, beyond man's doing."

"But Hern killed it."

"He didn't necessarily do it for our sakes. They might have been enemies since—who can say? I don't pretend to understand. But Guy knows where we are now, and so does Richard."

"But Rob, it was never any great question where we were. Anyone could have found us with a little looking, or forced one of our friends to tell. And Richard will probably be too busy to return here. That's not what's bothering you."

Robin Hood was silent. "It's just . . . things. The boar, the magic, the haunts. It's this forest, Sherwood. Ever since I was a boy I've travelled here, but there are places where I daren't go. Now a score of things have conspired against us. Puck could have done something to protect us. He could have changed the face of the forest if he chose. So could Hern."

"Maybe the magic was too powerful for them."

"See? We can't begin to comprehend the factions here. Men are to have dominion over the animals, but here they rule us. And they want us out. None would miss us. Sherwood is no place for people."

"But what would be better? A farm somewhere, where we're tied to the crops and saddled with more peoples' woes? A castle cold and drafty and fit only for bats? Or some rat-infested town? Rob, we belong here. The Green Man as much as told me with his eyes. He wants us to stay and he'll always help us. I saw a promise there. Hope."

Robin Hood shook his head in the dark. "I don't know, Marian. It'll never be the same again. Look around you, at our numbers. We've lost men and women left and right, and we have nothing to show for it except that some of us are still alive. Most of it was Guy's doing, true, but look at the rest. Shonet came down sick. David and Tuck left. Brian plucked out of the saddle. Will's dead. Cedwyn was killed by her *cat*! Who knows what will happen next?"

"We don't, Rob. No one does."

"We should go where life is certain."

"That's nowhere. But never mind now. If we're to leave, let's discuss it in the morning. Solomon himself couldn't make a sensible decision in the dark."

"Very well, Marian. You've more wisdom than any dead king."

Marian was exhausted but not at all sleepy. She was too glad to have her husband back, to be rid of the responsibility. She wanted to savor it. "Rob, tell me a story."

"A story?"

"It always makes me feel better when you tell me a story. Something you've done. I know. Tell me about how you met Cedwyn."

"That's not a jolly tale."

"I know. But she's been on my mind. Her death was strangest of all. There have always been parts to her story I never understood."

Robin sighed and rested his head on Marian's hip. "All right, darling. I can deny you nothing. Let's see if I can tell it the way she told it . . ."

My name is Cedwyn. I am a witch. I have lived in that fen for four years, and they have been happy and productive years, even though I have been alone. A man does not need companionship to be content, and a woman needs it even less.

I went to the fen after my mother died. People have use for a witch only so long as she pleases them. My mother fell sick and could not fulfill their petty needs, so she was condemned and driven out of the village. She died of brain fever. I wandered and came here. I studied alone, and I believe I am a greater witch than my mother ever was, for my heart is harder than hers.

You're wondering what happened to those men, how they got like that. I can only tell you about two of them, for I know not what happened to the third. Some power of the fen must have risen up and taken him because he was evil. Or some animal got him. He's dead just the same.

Those knights—false knights with no more honor than a jackdaw—were sent from the village. They must have been. No doubt someone told them a witch lived near by. Men think to sleep with a witch makes them immune to harm. That's horseshit. What could five minutes of passion bring but remorse? Whence would come the ferocious strength? And what would you gain from a witch's maidenhead—eternal life? Nay, that's not right, for folk believe a woman surrenders herself to Satan to become a witch. Folk believe anything said about a witch—anything at all. They think we can turn into *animals*, that we have *orgies* with Satan and kiss him on the *penis*, that we can turn *invisible* by sucking on a *cat bone*! It's all foolishness! A witch is simply a healer—that's what the word means in the old tongue—and nothing more. We have some tricks, but what of it? Anyone can learn them.

I was working on a spell. I wanted to see if I could turn tadpoles into frogs overnight, or more quickly than usual. You might ask why I would wish to do such a thing. The answer is: to see if it can be done. And it would aid in healing, or even growing new limbs. Imagine! I had taken a batch of fresh frogs' eggs from a clear pool. Clear water is important because it lessens the number of elements in a spell. But even clear water—even rainwater from a new barrel—may contain things we cannot see, things invisible to man's eyes, and I think that's what happened. I counted fresh eggs twenty-two, for that is a powerful number, and put them in a clay dish. Then I surrounded the bowl with many candles, and heated small rocks which I dropped

into the water. This made the water as warm as blood. I
fed tiny grasses and crushed insects into the water, and
began to say a chant taught to me by my mother. This
chant—I won't tell you how it goes—speeds healing in a
grievous wound. After each verse I breathed a fertility
prayer used to bring barren women to child. I was doing
this for a long time when I heard a marsh hen burst from
her nest. That could have been a swamp fox coming too
near, or a hawk, but something made me get up and look.
I heard the snort of a horse. Horses do not venture into
my fen, for they like not the soggy feel. Far off I saw three
knights in tarnished trappings coming to my home. Quickly
I gathered up some herbs and stuffed them into my apron.
I placed a spell of protection on the door and hid in the
swamp behind a batch of rushes. Mosquitoes and flies do
not bother me, because I smear catnip on my skin. And I
appease the animals of the swamp such that they are my
friends.

I watched as the knights dismounted. The first one—the
one you saw inside—was originally a coarse man, all covered with black hair like a beast, yet with none of the
nobility of a beast. The second man, the one who gib-
bered, you saw. The third was fat like a sow. And walk you
less nervously, please, and not so far from me. You dis-
comfit your horse.

The black man set his hand to his pommel, as did the
others. They murmured something disgusting, and laughed.
Then he reached for my door latch. How he hollered
when the spark hit him, and how he danced and swore!
Nor could he learn, for like a stupid ass he did it again,
and again when he tried to pry the door with his sword.
Then he banged on the door and swore and called, "Witch!
Come out! We are in need of spelling, for we have wounds
suffered in battle!" No doubt the only pain these ever
suffered was when they passed water. They swore and
banged on the door, and another tasted lightning. What
fools they!

No more fools than I though. I must have watched them

with my mind, for they all turned and looked square at the bullrushes where I squatted. The chase was on, and I the hare! Naturally I thought I could easily elude them, for I was unencumbered, while they had their heavy armor. So I moved away as they followed, bound for deeper recesses of the moor.

Two men followed me, but I lost them at a fork in what path there was. They separated. One man went back for his horse, and it was not a Hail Mary before he had run the ill-used animal into a bog. I knew that bog. There were no vines or anything else strong enough to support a man that he might pull himself back on the edge. I felt sure they had both drowned, beast and beast-man. I was safely ensconced in a shelter when another marsh hen exploded from behind me. And the slender man was there in a trice.

I heard him crashing towards me, and decided to try a spell. I took some chamomile and morning-glory in my hand and recited a spell of confusion, as is used to render folk unaware that you might tend their sickness or wound. The man came close enough, calling to his friends. "I found you, so I'll have you first," he laughed. I jumped up and blew the powder full in his face. You saw what happened to him.

But I blundered into the fat one. As is often the case with fat men, this one acted the fool. Yet fat men can have an evil streak caused by years of ridicule, and this festers in them so they turn as vicious as a mad dog when let off the leash. This man heard the slim one screaming, and he struck me full in the face. He was cruel, and I thought I might not survive this encounter without being disfigured or killed. As I lay there, a black veil settled over my eyes, and I thought it was the Mother Spirit clouding my vision so I might not see what was about to happen. I cried out like an animal and blacked out as the man struck me again.

But I did wake up. I was naked to the skin, and my clothes were in rags at my feet. I was awash in blood—it was even in my mouth and upon my breast. But there was

no stain of seed between my legs. The man was dead
beside me, rent in a thousand places. I knew the Mother
Spirit had heard my prayers and sent some animal, a great
wolf or a wildcat that had killed the man. But I was weak
and sore, and I vomited up great gouts of blood such that I
thought I had ruptured all my insides. After the purge,
with all the men dead, I wanted only to return to my
cottage. Leaving my ragged clothes—witches have no fear
of going mother-naked under the sun—I got home across
the fen. So weakened and confused was I that I forgot my
own spell, and burned my fingers in touching the latch.

Inside, I washed in clean water and donned my other
gown. I was wondering what to do next when the doorway
was darkened. It was the first knight, the coarse man. He
was covered with slime and stinking mud, and his face
waxed wrathful. "My horse is dead," said he. "Killed by
you and your stinking fen." He came towards me, slam-
ming his sword about, breaking my crocks and scattering
my herbs. He said, "I'll yet sleep with you, witch. And
when I am done with you, no man will ever bring himself to
do so again, so hideous will you be." He dropped his
sword in the dirt and drew a double-edged knife.

I had no place to go. There was but the one door. He
advanced until I was pressed against the wall, and I knew
not whether to watch the blade or his open hand. Evil
men who like to maim and kill have their preferred ways
of doing so. Some like to use a keen blade, and some their
hands. This man liked both, for he stabbed my shoulder
and knocked me down. Dried mud and filth fell in my
mouth as he mounted me and forced my knees apart. How
I hated him, and cursed him with every threat my mother
had known. He struck me in the mouth and knocked out a
eyetooth, here. He was fumbling at his breeches when I
had an idea.

Beside us was the table upon which sat my frog spell.
The table itself was wobbly, so I snatched at one of the
legs to strike my assailant. Little did I realize what I was
about, but it proved my salvation. For the whole mess of

candles, herbs, and bowl rained upon us. The jellied mess of eggs landed next to my hand. Even then it was a wriggly pile, for the eggs had sprouted tails just since that morning. The Spirit Mother guided my hand as I seized that mass and stuffed it into the bastard's open mouth.

The result was more than I could have hoped, and a fitting end to my test. For the man jerked into the air as if launched from a catapult. He thrashed and screamed and held his throat, and rolled as if from the Dancing Death. His agony destroyed what was left of my cabin, wrecking my bed and smearing muck over my only book. I ran outside, and I could hear him squeaking and shouting and sobbing for a long time. Then it was still. I walked out into the marsh to pray to My Lady and thank her . . .

"God, Marian, did I jump!" Robin whispered. "The thing in the cabin was the last straw. As I had approached the place, I'd seen a knight wandering in the marshes. He had lost his helmet, and it looked as if he would stumble into some hole, so I set out to rescue him. But it couldn't be done. He was crazed, gibbering about being lost, shambling forward as if blind. Nothing I could do would convince him help had arrived. He just pulled away and continued to nowhere, crying. He would have thought himself lost were you to take him to the center of London, though you'd have to tie him to a horse to get him there. I had to let him go. He'd drown in some pool before sunset, and maybe that was for the best. And then, going towards the cabin, I came across the body of another knight. This one's armor had been ripped aside, the leather burst, and something had eaten his guts. There was just a big hole from his ribs to his groin. You could see the spine at back. And blood everywhere, all around. So I was mighty nervous when I got near the cabin, and wanted only to get back to my horse and be away.

"But you know me, my curiousity wins out more times than my sense. I looked in the cabin. Glad I was the light was failing. That thing. I've never seen anything more horrible. It was like a man with frogs shot through him. There were tails and legs sticking out every which way, green skin merging to white." Robin Hood shuddered so hard he almost hit Marian with an errant hand.

"I came out of that cabin at a run, and three steps outside the door I heard this *screech*! 'WHAT ARE YOU DOING HERE?' Marian, dearest, I thought it was over. I was about to answer God for all my sins. I jumped straight in the air, and my heart jumped higher. Then I saw who had shouted. It was this little titch, this girl, shorter than a dog upright, paler than parchment and bruised besides. She weighed less than a suit of clothes. Her mouth was all lumpy so she couldn't talk straight. I stood there clutching my chest, and fully expected her mother—some vicious harridan with warts—to come around the corner. But she was alone. Then she struck this pose intended to frighten. It worked. I babbled out my story, that I had arrived at that inn and all the talk was of three knights who had ridden to rape the witch. Not that the township cared, may Mary forgive them their lassitude. Cedwyn seemed to believe this, but asked again what I wanted.

"I told her I had only come to help, and that seemed to enrage her further. I don't think she believed me. So I asked the only other thing I could think of, and that was whether she cared to join our band. I ask people that often enough. I thought she'd be content to run me off—and me content to go unscathed—but she looked around and said, "All right. I'll go." She stepped inside to gather some things. (I couldn't have gone in there for all the gold in Persia. And while she was there I thought about stealing away. The only reason I didn't is I was afraid she'd catch me.) She came out with a bag of herbs and implements, didn't even close the door, and walked off. Then she told me witches can't ride horses, so keep my horse on the off side. And Dobbin wasn't happy with her there either. At length . . ."

Marian gasped so sharply that Robin sat up. "Rob, don't you see? The man who was rent and eaten! It wasn't a great beast that killed him, it was Cedwyn in a *changed shape*! That's right! I know it! When the man went to attack her, she prayed to her spirit. Then she blacked out. When she awoke she was naked and had blood all over her, even in her mouth. She vomited blood and offal because it was *she* who . . . ate that man. She'd changed into a beast. It caused her clothes to rip off. She was weak and tired after, too!

"God's love, Robin! Think now! We thought Cedwyn had conjured a monster—the great cat—and it killed her and dragged her off. But we never found her body because it wasn't that she conjured a tiger, it was that she changed *into* one! It was right after you and Gilbert had told the story of the tiger! She started a spell and it went wrong. God, Robin, she's out there now, with the mind of an animal!"

Robin spoke out loud. "And Gilbert's tracking her."

The tiger had not died from the boar's attack. She was broken in many places, cut, and pierced, but she did not die. Painfully the great cat had dragged herself to cover to lick her wounds and sleep.

Now the knight with the withered hand pressed into the thicket. He had circled for days, reading the sign in the pressed grass and wet areas, following the tiger as it followed the boar. He'd found the site of their battle, read the cat's defeat. Now he had the track. There was blood at every step: the beast was dying. With his boar spear he could finish it and avenge Cedwyn.

He stopped. He could hear labored breathing. He smelt the ammonia of a big cat. Gilbert readied his silver-tipped spear and parted the speckled leaves to locate the chest. He saw stripes.

Wrong stripes.

The man parted the branches further.

This was no tiger.

It was a giant yellow house cat with black stripes. The stripes were painted vertically like prison bars. The cat's face turned towards him. It was marked like a badger's, and the ears were pointed, not round. The eyes were blue. Gilbert's mind ticked slowly. This was not a tiger. It was some fabricated beast, created by someone who had never seen a tiger, but had only heard about one. Robin had described the tiger to Cedwyn. She had started a spell to conjure one. And here it was, with blue eyes like Cedwyn's and an eyetooth lacking on the left side.

The mock tiger rolled its head and licked Gilbert's hand. Crushed ribs caused her to wheeze heavily. Deep gashes spanned her groin. Gilbert stroked her, and she purred under his hand. The knight wept. He laid down alongside the fearsome creature that burned in the setting sun. The cat reached up its tongue to lick his golden hair. Over and over he murmured, "Cedwyn, Cedwyn, Cedwyn." Happiness warred with panic, for he didn't know what to do. He looked at the sky overhead and the terrain around him. The sun was setting. It was miles to camp. He reckoned he could find it in the dark, once he got to familiar territory.

Gilbert shucked off his baldric and propped the sword and scabbard in a tree to keep the animals from chewing the salt in it. He pulled off his gypon and his coat of mail. The evening breeze was cold across his back. He put his sweater and tunic back on, and his horsehide gloves. He left his spear, sword, knife, armor, helmet, and shield. He didn't care if he met the boar.

He grunted as he hefted the cat across his shoulders. She was heavy, heavier than Cedwyn, heavier than a man. Her body was warm against his neck, the blood sticky.

Gilbert started for camp. He talked as best he could to Cedwyn and to himself. "Robin will know what to do. He'll know."

Chapter 33

The bee returned to the castle of wax. She bumped along the floor and rolled end over end into hundreds of other milling bees. Quickly she mounted the wall and began her dance. Up and around, back and forth, waggling all the while, she indicated a size, a kind, a direction, a distance. Other workers clustered close. As much as they could think, they were confused. That area had been barren yesterday, and here the gatherer reported full-blown flowers. Maybe she had gone bad. Maybe her mind was crooked. She smelled right, so she was from their hive. The scout stubbornly continued her dance. The message matched patterns of years and generations before. They forgot their doubt. The hive reached a consensus.

As dawn rose the bees left their home and streamed towards the glade.

Chapter 34

"Robin, Marian, everyone, come quick! Look! Look! Look!"

Robin Hood fought off the fog. That was Tam shouting. What was it, another attack? If so they were doomed. Then a rich and happy voice blared out, "You heard him, Coz! Stir your stumps! It's a new day!" Robin Hood sat bolt upright.

Will Scarlett stood in the doorway of the cave. He wore only his tattered white shirt and a codpiece. His skinny legs were hairy and pale. And whole.

"Look, everyone!" shouted Tam and Will together. The father and son danced in a circle. Still weak, Scarlett fell. But the two laughed like fools. "My leg's fine!" he croaked. "It got better in the night. I can walk!" His mother, Old Bess, pressed him to the floor, fussed and poked at the leg. Everyone gathered around. The ravaged limb was very thin, it was true, and the flesh under the skin was missing as if carved away with a knife. But there was no trace of poison. "I suspect I'll have a limp," Will laughed, "but I'll be dancing these women dizzy in a fortnight!"

"You're dizzy now," said his mother with tears in his eyes.

"And that's not all," called Tam from the doorway, "look at the common!" Leaving Will in a heap, people crowded to the door. Many stopped, fearful to step out. But Marian shoved through dragging her husband by the hand. They too stopped at what they saw.

The common and lower meadow was a sea of yellow. Where the day before there had been only charred houses, dead men, and trampled grass, there were now uncountable yellow flowers. They were buttercups, so thick they couldn't take a step without crushing a dozen. The drone of bees was loud.

"Allan's favorite," breathed Robin. Gingerly people stepped onto the golden field, each mumbling to his neighbor.

"It's magic," Marian said blearily.

"The magic of one good man," said Robin. Behind them Elaine clutched her three children to her and wept with joy.

"Hoy!"

Everyone turned. Gilbert walked out of the woods. A blushing Cedwyn was in his arms, her arms around his neck. She was wrapped in the Crusader's white gypon. Her naked feet dangled like a child's.

"And what of John and Jane and the rest?" Robin asked the morning air.

Marian answered. "They're all right. They must be." She looked up at her husband with laughing eyes. "And what of us? Shall we leave Sherwood for somewhere else?"

Robin Hood laughed and hugged her. "Leave? All this?" He turned to the crowd behind him.

"Hey, you lot! Let's get some breakfast on the table! We're work to do!"

Here is an excerpt from Mary Brown's new novel
The Unlikely Ones, *coming in November 1987 from
Baen Books Fantasy—SIGN OF THE DRAGON:*

MARY BROWN

THE UNLIKELY ONES

After breakfast the next morning—a helping of
what looked like gruel but tasted of butter and nuts
and honey and raspberries and milk—the magician led us outside into a morning sparkling with
raindrops and clean as river-washed linen, but
strangely the grass was dry when we seated ourselves in a semicircle in front of his throne. Hoowi,
the owl, was again perched on his shoulder, eyes
shut, and he took up Pisky's bowl into his lap.
Although the birds sang, their songs were courtesy-
muted, for the Ancient's voice was softer this morning as though he were tired, and indeed his first
words confirmed this.

'I have been awake most of the night, my friends,
pondering your problems. That is why I have con-
vened this meeting. We agreed yesterday that you
had all been called together for a special mission,
a quest to find the dragon. You need him, but he
also needs you.' He paused, and glanced at each
one of us in turn. 'But perhaps last night you
thought this would be easy. Find the Black Mountains, seek out the dragon's lair, return the jewels,
ask for a drop of blood and a blast of fire and Hey
Presto! your problems are all solved.

'But it is not as easy at that, my friends. Of your
actual meeting with the dragon, if indeed you reach

him, I will say nothing, for that is still in the realms of conjecture. What I can say is this: in order to reach the dragon you have a long and terrible journey ahead of you, one that will tax you all to the utmost, and may even find one or other of you tempted to give up, to leave the others and return; if that happens then you are all doomed, for I must impress upon you that as the seven you are now you have a chance, but even were there one less your chances of survival would be halved. There is no easy way to your dragon, understand that before you start. I can give you a map, signs to follow, but these will only be indications, at best. What perils and dangers you may meet upon the way I cannot tell you: all I know is that the success of your venture depends upon you staying together, and that you must all agree to go, or none.

'I can see by your expressions that you have no real idea of what I mean when I say "perils and dangers": believe me, your imaginations cannot encompass the terrors you might have to face—'

'But if we do stay together?' I interrupted.

'Then you have a better chance: that is all I can say. It is up to you.' He was serious, and for the first time I felt a qualm, a hesitation, and glancing at my friends I saw mirrored the same doubts.

'And if we don't go at all—if we decide to go back to—to wherever we came from?' I persisted.

'Then you will be crippled, all of you, in one way or another, for the rest of your lives.'

'Then there is no choice,' said Conn. 'And so the sooner we all set off the better,' and he half-rose to his feet.

'Wait!' thundered the magician, and Conn subsided, flushing. 'That's better, I have not finished.'

'Sit down, shurrup, be a good boy and listen to granpa,' muttered Corby sarcastically, but The Ancient affected not to hear.

'There is another thing,' said he. 'If you succeed

in your quest and find the dragon, and if he takes back the jewels, and if he yields a drop of blood and a blast of fire, if, I say . . . then what happens afterwards?'

The question was rhetorical, but Moglet did not understand this.

'I can catch mice again,' she said brightly, happily.

But he was gentle with her. 'Yes, kitten, you will be able to catch mice, and grow up properly to have kittens of your own—but at what cost? You may not realize it but your life, and the life of the others, has been in suspension while you have worn the jewels, but once you lose your diamond then time will catch up with you. You will be subject to your other eight lives and no longer immune, as you others have been also, to the diseases of mortality.

'Also, don't forget, your lives have been so closely woven together that you talk a language of your own making, you work together, live, eat, sleep, think together. Once the spell is broken you, cat, will want to catch birds, eat fish and kill toads; you, crow, will kill toads too, and try for kittens and fish; toad here will be frightened of you all, save the fish; and the fish will have none but enemies among you.

'And do not think that you either, Thing-as-they-call-you, will be immune from this; you may not have their killer instinct but, like them, you will forget how to talk their language and will gradually grow away from them, until even you cross your fingers when a toad crosses your path, shoo away crows and net fish for supper—'

'You are wrong!' I said, almost crying. 'I shall always want them, and never hurt them! We shall always be together!'

'But will they want you,' asked The Ancient quietly, 'once they have their freedom and identity returned to them? If not, why is it that only dog, horse, cattle, goat and sheep have been domesticated and even these revert to the wild, given the chance? Do you not think that there must be some reason why humans and wild animals dwell apart? Is it perhaps that they value their freedom, their individuality, more than man's circumscribed domesticity? Is it not that they prefer the hazards of the wild, and only live with man when they are caught, then tamed and chained by food and warmth?'

'I shall never desert Thing!' declared Moglet stoutly. 'I shan't care whether she has food and fire or not, my place is with her!'

'Of course . . . Indubitably . . . What would I do without her . . .' came from the others, and I turned to the magician.

'You see? They don't believe we shall change!'

'Not now,' said The Ancient heavily. 'Not now. But there will come a time . . . So, you are all determined to go?'

'Just a moment,' said Conn. 'You have told Thingmajig and her friends just what might be in store for them if we find the dragon: what of me and Snowy here? What unexpected changes in personality have you in store for us?' He was angry, sarcastic.

'You,' said the Ancient, 'you and my friend here, the White One, might just do the impossible: impossible, that is, for such a dedicated knight as yourself. . .'

'And what's that?'

'You might change your minds . . .'

'About what, pray?' And I saw Snow shake his head.'

'What Life is all about . . .'

432 pp. • 65361-X • \$3.95

To order any Baen Book by mail, send the cover price plus 75 cents for first-class postage and handling to: Baen Books, Dept. B, 260 Fifth Avenue, New York, N.Y. 10001